Crown of Stars

Saving Beauty

A Novel

Elizabeth D. Marie

CROWN OF STARS: SAVING BEAUTY

Editor: Linda Hickman
Cover Layout and Design: Elizabeth D. Marie

ISBN : 978-1-530-44066-5

Acknowledgements:

Thanks to the friends and family who helped me with editing, giving their feedback and suggestions. I could not have gotten through the process without you!

Thanks to my mom, for helping me sort out the difficult bits and the questions and for always supporting me in my writing endeavors. I love you!

Thanks to God—Elohim—for His Hand on this work, three years in the making. I give You the glory for every aspect of its development and completion. You have spoken to me through the characters and through every twist and turn of this story. This has been an adventure and I look forward to continuing this series and seeking Your truths through the stories yet to be revealed.

5th Division
2nd Division
The Reave
Torr Guard
1st Division
3rd Division
4th Division
6th Division
Freelands
The Four Islands
The Arid North
SeaTraders Cove
Highlands
High Mountain
ASTERIAE
Birchlands
THE PIT
GREAVANS
Mirklands
Torr Guard
The Reave
Shelt
Neice
Torguson
Freelands
Jol
= 200 songs (50 miles)

Chapter 1

Tall heads of sun-ripened grain met the morning's red-tinged skies. A hint of acrid smoke scented the winds crossing expansive fields to the cluster of thatch-roofed homes nestled between two fair slopes.

The rising sun crept across low-lying mists, highlighting the frames of tightly shut doors. A foreboding lay thick in the air, until a horse's scream split the uneasy stillness and a line of angry black clouds gathered over the western forest, just visible along the hill's ridge.

Five mounted horses crested its edge, appearing from the darkness—three dark and two grey. Unexpected thunder rippled through the air. The leader heeled his mount ahead of the others—a beast of black; a creature of war—and they picked up speed, descending on the village below, the thunder of hooves announcing their rapid approach.

The leader reined in his great beast at the outer rim of the village, the horse kicking up clods of moist black earth as it slid to a halt and lifted up its front legs in a short, protesting rear. Those with him formed a crescent moon behind him.

Wearing leather armor, they sat astride with the erect posture of soldiers, faces and hands stained with sweat and dirt and grime. Each held a torch, raised aloft. The torchlight flickered over grim and merciless faces. Sparks showered to the earth with a gust of cold rain-scented wind.

"In the Name of the King, show yourselves! Surrender to us your able-bodied children to fight!" bellowed the leader.

A dreadful silence met in answer. The clouds behind them grew thicker, turned darker and more ominous, while the light of sunrise lingered upon the village. The leader raised two fingers in a vague motion without looking behind.

Two soldiers rode forward without a word and lowered their torches toward the straw eaves of the two nearest buildings—one a stable and the other a home. The flames reached hungrily for the dry fuel just out of reach.

Face void of emotion, the leader's one stormy-colored eye fixated on the door of the center home, his other eye hidden behind a dark leather patch. A scar disfigured his face beneath the patch, stretching from his temple down his cheek, stopping at the corner of his mouth. Straight black hair glistened with sweat and dark scruff framed his mouth and jaw.

"Come out now, or this village and all within will burn. Obey the King's orders and you will live!"

Thunder growled overhead. Clouds erased the sun and turned the earth a dreary grey. The first drops of rain pelted the ground.

The door to the center house opened slowly, creaking with protest. The leader shifted, letting his hand rest lightly and comfortably against the hilt of his sword, belted at his hip. An old man stepped out while a girl stood behind him, holding back and hidden within the shadow of the doorway.

As the man walked forward, the rest of the village joined him with fear and hesitation. Only a few dozen in number.

Poor farmers. Old men and women wearied by the toils of life.

The leader mentally singled out the few children among them, ranging in ages somewhere between twelve and seventeen.

"Please," the old man before him implored. "We are only farmers, not soldiers. These are the only children we have left to keep our village alive. To harvest our crops. You have taken all the rest."

The leader took in his thin, slumped-shouldered figure with open disdain. "The King's Law commands all able-bodied men, women, and children over the age of twelve years may be drafted to fight, to preserve Asteriae and all her lands."

"The blood of our children cry out from the dust!" cried the man. "For over fifteen years we have sacrificed them to the King's Army and most never returned. How much longer would the King see us suffer?"

"Would you rather the For'bane come knocking on your doors? Do you think they would listen to your pathetic pleas for peace?" The leader drew his sword and pointed it at the speaker. "I have no time for you, old man. Is that your girl hiding in the shadows?" He motioned with the tip of the blade.

"I look after her. Her parents were killed in your War—," he began.

The leader's lip curled at the thinly-veiled insult. He twisted in the saddle to motion the soldiers toward the village. "Seize them," he commanded.

"No!" cried the old man. Others cried out as well and shrank away, trying to shield the children.

The leader bellowed: "Any resistance will meet with the blade!" He nudged his mount forward. The great beast snorted and stepped high. The villagers backed away from him, knowing the battle horse could kill them with a single well-aimed kick. Trained to break through the ranks of the enemy, these horses knew no fear.

Some of the women began to weep with helplessness. Three soldiers left their leader's side to round up the children, their horses separating them from the rest of the villagers like a wolf splits lambs away from the protection of the flock.

The leader stopped his horse abreast of the old man and stared down at him as the splatter of rain turned to a steady mist. "How old is this girl?"

His faded green eyes pleaded. "She is but fourteen, Sir. Only fourteen."

"Old enough to be wed, old enough to lift a blade in the service of our King."

Commotion drew the leader's attention. An older boy stumbled and fell. The leader reined in his beast and turned toward the soldier nearest the fallen boy, riding one of the greys. "What is the meaning of this?" he demanded.

"Sir, the boy is a useless cripple."

The leader stared hard at the boy's mud-splattered, flushed face as he struggled to lift himself from the ground. His deformed foot could not be mistaken, as he had no shoes to conceal the disfigurement.

The leader glanced to the skies. They would open up and pour down any minute. While the rain did not bother him, they needed to reach Torr Guard[1] by nightfall. It would take long enough with the recruits in tow.

He looked to the soldier again. "Take the girl. Move out!"

---

[1] Torr Guard : Torr, from Old English 'torr' from Latin 'turris' meaning 'tower, high structure, watchtower'

"No! You will not!" the old man cried out, his protest nearly lost in the leader's final shouted command, and as the grey moved toward the house and the girl, the old man lunged for the soldier's sheathed sword. Quickly, the leader intercepted with his great beast and in one swift, fluid motion pierced the old man through the chest with his sword amid startled screams of fear and terror.

The old man's mouth opened in a silent scream, his eyes wide with shock as the life drained from him and he stumbled backward. The leader yanked out the blade, crimson with blood, and watched with a fierce expression as the old man collapsed into the dirt.

The girl cried out, anguished—but also angry. She shoved at the grey, who protested with an angry neigh and backed up as the girl rushed forward to collapse on her knees beside the old man, whose blank, skyward stare proved him already gone from this world. Her long, straight blonde hair fell around her like a veil as she bent over her guardian, and her hands turned red with the blood she tried to staunch.

The leader looked down at her and used the point of his stained blade to push back the hair from the side of her face. "You going to cry?" he demanded.

She turned her head to look up at him. She had fair features, fairer than most—smooth, light skin and a good feminine form, with eyes the color of harvest-ready-wheat. She stared at him.

"Are you afraid of me?" His lips twisted in a smirk and he saw that though her gaze shone moist with tears, she did not cry. "You hate me," he said calmly, lifting his blade away to wipe it on a square of cloth he pulled from his saddle bag and then sheathed the sword. "That is good. Anger keeps you alive. You might live past tomorrow. That is longer than most."

The soldier on the grey drew up behind the girl, reached down, and grabbed her by the shoulder, yanking her to her feet.

"Do not touch me!" she shouted in surprise, struggling in vain.

The soldier hauled her up in front of him. She had no choice but to grasp the horse's mane or risk sliding off and under its powerful hooves as its rider immediately heeled the grey into a gallop.

The skies split open with a roar and flash of blinding lightning that would have terrified an untrained horse. A torrential rain soaked the group to the skin. Each rider carried a recruit, except for the leader. Two smaller boys rode on the other grey, one in front and one behind the soldier, making five children in all, with only the one girl.

She gripped the horse's thick grey-and-white mane as the rain washed away the evidence of her guardian's death from her fingers. She refused to look either left or right, whether planning her escape or silent in her own private grief.

Perhaps both.

Chapter 2

They rode for hours. If the rain did not let up soon, she would surely scream. With the rain came the comfortless, cold wind, biting into her chafing skin.

At last, they passed into a thickly wooded trail, offering some relief from the elements as the rain slowed to a drizzle. The horses snorted and plodded along, giving off a mixed stench of wet horseflesh and leather.

"Ho!" called the leader suddenly from the front. The procession came to a halt.

"What is happening? Where are we?" one of the boys, thirteen-year-old Carter, spoke bravely. He looked around at the dark, non-descriptive wood as if expecting to see an army or battlefield.

The leader appeared suddenly, guiding his black beast back through the midst of them, the other horses habitually withdrawing out of his way. He caught Carter's gaze with his one eye. "We rest the horses," he said shortly. "Dismount. There is a stream just ahead, but take care—the rain has made the earth soft."

The soldiers—already prepared for this—let their charges dismount ahead of them. Though not cruel, they did laugh and snicker when one of the younger boys fell flat on his bottom in the mud. The boys gathered into a huddle, shivering from cold and exhaustion, their bodies aching and sore.

The girl, however, refused to dismount and join her friends. A secret fear kept her on the horse, feeling safer there than on the ground.

The soldier dismounted, holding fast to the reins and cursed at her stubbornness. "Come on, little wench. I do not have all day." He grasped her ankle, his fingers slipping beneath the hem of her skirts, and tugged to get her out of the saddle. She kicked out at him.

The leader approached. "She is a soldier-in-training, not your mistress, Greer."

Greer backed off and the leader drew his horse abreast of the grey, quite close to the girl. She met his gaze and saw the mix of blue and grey in his eye and how the colors blended there, darkened with each emotion and turned now to a chilling steel. With an ominous calm, voice deathly quiet, he said, "Get off the horse."

Deep fear and dread fell upon her—more so than Greer's lecherous advances—and she stiffly obeyed. Her bruised leg muscles nearly failed her. She managed not to show too much of her pain and weakness, sure that her misery would make her a vulnerable target, and half leaned against the horse's side.

The grey turned its head and blew a soft, hot breath through its nostrils against her neck, as if inquiring in its animal way after her well being.

The non-judgmental kindness—and from such an unexpected source—nearly undid the turmoil of her carefully walled-in emotions. She had spent too much effort during the ride building that internal and mental wall to let it all go now. She knew the soldiers watched her, so she pushed the horse's nose away, feeling momentarily the velvet softness of its muzzle, and moved to join her friends.

She knew them well. She had grown up with them. Still so young; now forced into a War they had no desire to fight. She stood beside Carter. The two younger boys looked her way, both of twelve years and from separate families—birthdays only months apart and so alike they could have been twins. Bandon, sixteen and as cocky as a prince, seemed the least effected by the capture—as if he wanted to go to war.

Perhaps sensing Bandon's mindset, the younger boys looked to the girl for their support and guidance. Distance and necessity kept them from running, with no rope or chain to hinder them. They had never been away from their village, and knew nothing of the dangerous lands beyond or survival apart from their homes and families.

But they could learn.

Chapter 3

The leader moved toward the stream first. Having dismounted after his confrontation with Greer and the girl, he led his great beast with careful but sure steps through the muddy bog that surrounded the water's edge.

"Watch out for hidden mud holes," Logan, one of the soldiers leading a dark horse, informed the recruits as they watched the leader take point in finding a safe path across. "Get stuck in one of those and you may never get out again. They can snap a horse's leg if it pulls them down."

The leader ignored the recruits, completely focused on the ground he walked. His boots met the edge of the stream and he looked back. "Stay to the right of me. Here." He motioned to the area.

The soldiers spread out, leading their horses, and kept the recruits in their midst. It did not matter. None dared be foolish enough to attempt an escape. If they fell in the bog, they would be left there to die.

Bandon went first, shoulders thrown back in pride. The leader watched him from a short distance, measuring him with a calculating gaze, while he let his horse drink.

Only when all the recruits gathered safely at the water's edge and in his sight did the leader bend his knee and dip his hand beneath the flow. The icy water contrasted sharply with the damp, muggy steam of the bog around it. Rain water dripped from his hair and trickled down his face and neck.

The rain stopped. The sudden silence seemed louder than the rainfall from moments before. The soldiers looked up, noticing the change almost as soon as their leader.

The leader, still crouched, cast his eye across the surface of the stream. A faint rumble could be felt in the earth. His horse lifted its head slightly and snorted a warning. The leader placed a hand against its broad head and murmured Ancient Tongue[2] to its listening ear, keeping his gaze on the water. He stood slowly. The soft breath of his sword being drawn from its scabbard alerted the soldiers to his movement.

"What is it?" Greer spoke, nearest to him.

"The birds," the leader informed.

"I hear nothing," spoke up Bandon, the cocky recruit.

The leader glanced at him, sharp and cursory. "Exactly." Then, to the soldiers, "Something is coming."

The stream water rippled as it had not before. The trees trembled across the stream from them.

A large creature burst from the wood, sending trees snapping, uprooting one by its roots and sending it flying across the stream, end over end. Its greatest root struck one of the twins across the chest and head before he had a chance to react, throwing him flat on his back. He lay, unmoving.

The rest of the recruits cried out in panic and the soldiers drew their swords as the leader shouted orders. "Back up! Get to the tree line!"

---

[2] Ancient Tongue : the language tracing its origins to the beginning of the kingdom. Now used mostly in written form.

The creature stood two heads taller than the men who faced it, its skin tough and yellow-grey—the shade of aging parchment. It stood back on its short hind legs while using its long arms for balance. Its only covering was a grey loincloth and a leather harness around its neck and chest, under its arms.

The recruits scrambled back behind the line of sword-bearing soldiers, except for the young boy who lay unconscious not far from the creature.

"Thordan!" cried his friend Thane in fear and desperation.

The girl broke away and went straight for the creature, who stood now in the center of the stream as if momentarily disoriented, her intent clearly for the unconscious boy.

The leader grabbed her arm and yanked her back. "He is dead!" he thundered.

"He is *not* dead!" she contradicted angrily. "We have to get him out of there!"

The leader resolutely shoved her back with the soldiers. "Stay back or we all die!"

The creature let out a roar, exposing rows of squared teeth within a flat face—eyes large, round, and dark. It shook its head in confusion.

The leader turned and withdrew a finely crafted longcurve bow from his saddle pack and fitted it with an arrow from the same pack. As his fingers slid against the bowstring with an almost graceful familiarity, a soft sound emanated from it, like singing—beautiful and haunting.

Greer grabbed the girl by the wrist to keep her from charging forward again. The girl sank to her knees and watched with helpless desperation, eyes fastened on the boy's prone form.

The creature roared again and reared up on its hind legs, ready to charge again.

The leader drew back taut on the bowstring and let the arrow fly. It struck the creature in the jugular, ripping through the throat and remained imbedded there, spraying dark blood and yellow fluid down its chest. A distorted shriek tore from its mouth. It twisted its upper body in an angry, writhing motion and stumbled forward in a blind rage.

Swiftly, the leader loaded another arrow and let it fly, impaling its right eye. The creature stumbled and dropped at his feet, snuffed, and then grew still.

For a moment, everything seemed frozen in place. No one breathed.

Then the girl took lead, hurrying with the other recruits to their fallen friend—all except for Bandon, who went to inspect the creature with the soldiers, his face filled with fascination while theirs turned grim.

The leader replaced his bow in its pack and lay his palm briefly against the coal-black neck of his horse in a gesture of calm. He walked to the head of the creature, where it lay on its stomach, and probed it with the end of his sword. A dark word flew from his lips.

"A Rammer," remarked one soldier.

"But here, so far from the Divisions[3]?" said Greer, watching the leader for his reaction. "We are but halfway to Torr Guard...."

The leader kept his gaze on the Rammer, as if he did not hear the soldiers, but then he answered, "It is only an infant...confused. It may have slipped the Second Division ranks, to the north, and followed the stream—." He pointed to the broken trees with the end of his sword. He paused a moment, his gaze catching sight of the recruits huddled in a circle over the tiny broken body of Thordan in the mud,

---

3 Divisions : front lines, battle camps

several yards away. His one eye darkened and a muscle flexed in his jaw.

"What is this creature?" he heard Bandon say. "Have you fought it before?"

The leader plucked out the kill arrows, his silence allowing Greer to answer: "Rammers. The For'bane breed them like dogs for their size, strength, and speed. They are not very smart. This one is only an infant, newly grown." He nudged its arm with his boot. "An adult, fully grown and matured on the battlefield, is twice this size."

"Wait," interrupted Bandon, "did you say 'grown'?"

The leader stepped back, holding the arrows in one hand. "Not many survive that long," he said. "They are often like this one—unstable in their genesis. Their only purpose is to break our lines and create pathways for the For'bane to attack behind our ranks. Those who survive into adulthood are a formidable foe. Incredibly powerful—they trample anything in their path and are next to impossible to kill."

"Yet, you killed this one," Bandon said naively.

The soldiers exchanged a glance.

"Like Greer said," Logan spoke up, "this was only an infant."

The leader's gaze flickered again toward the circle of recruits. Without a word, he moved toward them.

Chapter 4

Having reached the place where Thordan lay, the girl did her best to mask her emotions for his sake. Thordan's eyes opened slightly in pain-filled half-consciousness. She knelt in the mud and slipped one hand carefully and gently beneath his head, trying to let her touch comfort him. "It is all right. We are here," she whispered to him, wiping a streak of mud off his cheek, one of the only places not bruised or bloodied.

One side of his head was crushed, the mud and sticky, dark blood matting his hair making it impossible to tell the full extent of his injuries. A trickle of blood smeared out of his nose and at the corner of his trembling lips, already a deathly grey pallor.

Inside, her entire being—every bone and muscle—screamed and ached at the horror and pain she witnessed, knowing death had come calling for this young soul.

Thordan slowly blinked, aware of her presence while fear haunted his eyes. The whisper of his fading voice choked on blood. "I am sorry."

The girl shook her head. "No, it is not your fault," she exclaimed quietly. "You did nothing wrong."

Thordan stared at her with full understanding in his eyes: He would not be returning home.

The other two boys gathered close. Carter looked stunned while Thane cried silent tears, holding tight to Thordan's hand. He looked from Thordan to the girl—looking to her for strength; for help that she could not give.

Now it came from her lips, whispered and apologetic, haltingly, as she looked at Thordan: "I am sorry. There is—there is nothing I can do."

Thordan stiffened, mouth open and trying to pull air into his crushed lungs. His face grew still.

Letting her hair shield her face, she closed her eyes tightly and pressed her lips together. She held still, hands still cradling Thordan's head, ignoring the blood that once more stained her fingers.

The step of a soldier's boot alerted her that they were no longer alone. "It is time to go." His cold words raked across her tattered nerves.

Crying and in a blind fury, Thane jumped to his feet and lashed out in a childish, open-handed swing. "You killed my best friend!"

Anticipating his move, the leader moved lightning fast and wrapped one hand around Thane's throat, effectively pushing him back.

The girl stood quickly, ready to defend the boy as her hands curled into fists. The leader caught her gaze with a dangerous warning.

"This will not be the last time you watch a friend die," he spoke harshly. He continued his words to Thane, but looked at the girl. "It is time to grow up. This is your duty now. Put away your tears." His gaze on Thane again, he released the boy abruptly. Thane stumbled and rubbed at his neck, gasping for air. "Tears are weakness on a battlefield.

This is war. You must never cry. Such childish bursts of emotion will only get you killed."

The girl barely restrained herself. When the leader glanced at her again, the hint of admiration there only made her anger grow; her silent hatred all the more determined.

"Get back to the horses." He stood there until they filed past him in an uneven line.

The girl knew that with the loss of their friend, their spirits had been broken, resigned to their fate as the King Law commanded. She moved closer to Thane and took the boy's hand, defying the leader with a look his way, daring him to interfere as she walked beside the boy, silently taking Thane into her charge and vowing to protect him at all cost.

The leader turned on his heel and strode back to his horse.

Chapter 5

Darkness fell as they approached Torr Guard, a training post sixteen longs[4] from the Divisions. Flickering torches guided their arrival amid large canvas tents and wooden-framed canopies for the forges and stables. An old stone tower rose at the north end of the camp.

Even at this late hour, soldiers milled about and some turned to observe the arriving soldiers and their recruits. There were a few women among them—their similar armor and attire making it difficult to distinguish their more feminine features. The horses snorted and lifted weary heads. Their ears pricked forward and they plodded ahead, anticipating fresh feed and grain.

The leader preceded his group wordlessly to the stables, generally ignoring passersby and watching everything with a slight turn of his head. He spoke an indistinguishable word to his horse, who stopped on command at the stable entrance.

---

[4] Longs : 1 long = 440 yards (.25 miles); 4 longs = 1 mile ---> see map

A boy with a missing arm hurried forward to take the headstall in hand and hold the horse while the leader dismounted. The boy barely looked him in the eye as he led the horse inside. The other soldiers also dismounted. Another boy, smaller than the last, took two of the horses while the one-armed boy hurried back to take the last two. His wide, haunted eyes took in the new recruits with curiosity and sympathy.

"Logan, take the new recruits to their bunks, then report back to me at the tower," the leader commanded. Without so much as a glance toward the huddle of recruits, he strode away into the night, disappearing from sight between tents and soldiers.

The tower had seen too much war and decay. From a distance, it looked tall, black and formidable. Up close, with crumbling walls and overgrown vines, it lacked that power. A gaping hole smashed in the side created the only entrance into an uneven stone-floored room. Torches mounted all around the circular wall lit the shadows within. A large, hastily-constructed wooden table in the center of the room was the only furnishing. Two messengers stood inside, opposite a third man who leaned over the table, studying the maps spread out across it.

The third shook his head at the two messengers and looked up at the leader's entrance. He straightened. "Captain Garren, thank the great Blue Star[5]," he exclaimed. "We feared your delayed return meant some harm or tragedy."

"Captain Mason. My troop and I caught up with some trouble," Garren explained calmly. He came forward and ignored the cautious looks of the two messengers as they took a step away from him. He knew their respect was based on fear, and after fifteen years, it really did not matter. He

---

[5] Blue Star : refers to the moon. Another way of saying "Thank Heavens"

ignored them. "What is happening? Why are there so many soldiers here? They should be at the Divisions."

"Captain, this may be a Division," Captain Mason informed him gravely. "Our men are being overrun. The enemy pushes through the ranks as we speak. Hundreds have died. If we cannot stop them at the First Division, our enemy will be at Torr Guard's doorstep by morning."

Alarmed, Garren shot a sharp glance toward the messengers. "When did this happen and how? What news from Commander[6] Bralin?" he demanded.

The two messengers glanced at each other before the braver spoke in reply: "Dead, Sir. He got shot through the leg by a bolt and bled to death trying to reach the Second Division to warn them…."

Garren's jaw tightened. A bolt. A shaft with sharpened alloy on one end, like an arrow, only three times bigger and its shaft imbedded with sharpened bone or stone, so when one tried to remove it, it caused extreme damage to the bone and muscle. A painful way to die.

Captain Mason nodded to the messengers. "You may go. Get some rest. I will send a footman[7] when I need you."

After the two messengers withdrew, Captain Mason spoke again for Garren's ears only: "Look, I am sorry. I know the Commander called you friend."

Ignoring the sympathy, Garren interrupted sharply: "We have been holding the line without incident for a year now. What changed? How could they break our lines without

---

[6] Commanders and Captains : Commanders are nobles who hold land and wealth. Captains are freemen of no former standing. On the battlefield, they are of equal rank and responsibility

[7] Footman : soldiers assigned to camp activity and security and especially to attend soldiers of rank

warning? The scouts have reported no movement—no reinforcements."

Captain Mason shook his head. "All I know is the First and Third Divisions are scrambling to regroup just behind the First Division line. If they cannot hold them there...." The rest did not need to be said.

Garren crossed to the map. "What of the Second Division?"

"They were overtaken. They did not have enough time." Captain Mason sighed and pressed two fingers against the bridge of his nose a moment. "I cannot confirm any survivors. They are too deep in For'bane territory now."

Garren studied the map a moment, seeing by the lines and markings their position and the enemy's. "I have brought in fresh recruits from the Freelands."

"You had best put a sword in their hands or get them out of here, because if we do not succeed in holding them off, this place will soon be crawling with For'bane."

Chapter 6

Logan led the recruits to a mid-sized tent located near the center of camp, south of the tower, guarded on each side by two footmen. Holding back the tent flap, he allowed Bandon, Carter, Thane, and the girl to enter first.

Dim torchlight filtered through the canvas from the outside and made shapes and shadows of several cots visible. Most of the cots had occupants. Seven sat empty toward one side.

"Get some sleep, you start training soon," Logan instructed. "Choose an empty cot, it will remain yours until you get transferred."

The girl looked away from the cots to the soldier. "And when will that be?"

"Captain Garren brought you here; he will decide that."

"And does he have the power to decide our fate as well?" she said. "Does he decide yours, too?"

"I am a soldier under command," Logan replied stiffly. "You will learn, soon enough, to obey." He turned and left the tent, letting the flap fall closed behind him.

The girl stood still for a moment. Bandon moved first and plopped down on the nearest empty cot with a contented sigh.

"Are you really glad to be here?" Carter inquired with surprise.

Bandon spread his arms. "What is not to like? Food, a place to sleep, and a job fighting the For'bane."

"We were taken against our will," the girl protested. "Our families need us—to survive the winter."

"Our families need us to fight in the Great War—so they can survive to plant crops again next season," Bandon shot back. "Besides, you do not have a family, so what are you worried about? That man—the Captain—killed your guardian when the old man tried to stop him from recruiting you."

The girl took a half step back, pain filling her gaze. Carter stepped forward at once, ready to defend her.

"So," interrupted a calm voice from the shadows. "You are the fresh meat brought in from the Freelands...." The figure moved forward from near the claimed cots to their side of the tent. A young woman, not much taller or older than the girl, came into the faint light. Black hair, cut chin length, framed her face. Her eyes and features were toughened and stern. She looked over the new arrivals with a measured glance. A young female soldier amid so many men, her hardened gaze and firm voice seemed more masculine than feminine.

"Who are you?" Thane asked curiously, his first words since leaving Thordan at the stream.

She smiled slightly at him, not exactly friendly, but not hostile either. "Call me Cala," she answered.

"You were taken as well?" the girl asked cautiously.

Cala laughed quiet and low. "No. I came of my own will. Not because I had anything to prove—," she glanced at

Bandon who folded his arms across his chest, "—but because I had nowhere else to go and no one to care if I am killed." She glanced behind her. "But not all of us. Most have the same stories as you."

As if her words gave permission, several others sat up from their cots or stepped closer. "Did I hear you say Captain Garren brought you in?" asked one.

"Yes," the girl answered, stiffening at mention of her cruel captor. "What about him?"

Cala shook her head, and lowered her voice. "Be careful of him. I am surprised the Captain would stoop to recruitment…considering…."

"Considering what?"

Cala stared intently at the girl. "The soldiers here are not so bad, once you get to know them. But the Captain? He is one of the most feared men in the Divisions. He is a trained killer. He will shoot you through the eye with one of his arrows without even blinking. Cold, ruthless, and incredibly powerful." She shrugged. "They say he became an archer fifteen years ago. He is the only one who survived of those recruited with him."

The girl looked around. "Why do you not run away from here?"

Their eyes widened. "And be branded a coward and a traitor?" said one in shocked fear. "Besides, any attempt would be foolish with the Singers around. You would never get past the edges of camp."

The girl hesitated. "I…I have heard stories of the Singers but…I did not think it could be true. Surely they would not kill us—just for trying to go home. They were like us once, taken from the territories."

From the seriousness on their faces, she dreaded the answer. Singers. The most feared warriors on the battlefield; trained as archers but more than that. They had skills more advanced than the average man. They could see farther, run faster, and hit any mark no matter how small.

A childhood horror story to those in the Freelands; some parents told their children if they did not behave a Singer would come for them—a monster who had become more legend and myth over the years since the start of the War.

"It has happened," Cala informed. "A sennight[8] ago, two young soldiers broke away from the battle—when there had been no call for retreat. They say you hear the Singer's song…just before you die. If you hear the song, a Singer is near."

The girl felt her hands grow cold. Singers' jobs not only included killing the For'bane, but killing anyone who tried to flee the Divisions. To do such a thing—they must have hearts of stone. She recalled the creature in the woods and the way the Captain shot it through the eye with the arrow; the way the bowstring sang when he touched it….

"Captain Garren…," she whispered, almost without realizing it.

Cala turned to the others. "All right, get some sleep, boys and girls. It may not come again, for tomorrow is war."

The girl lay on the cot she chose after the boys had settled. She stared at the canvas roof for a long time, too terrified to sleep, and just as tired from holding her emotions behind a wall for so long. Who would she go home to, if by some miracle she survived? She had no family. No guardian.

The Great War had gone on for over fifteen years. Would it ever end?

Could she at least do her best to keep Carter and Thane alive to see their families again? Could she protect them from the Singers, spoken about like monsters instead of men? She turned her head and tried not to see her guardian's

---

[8] Sennight : seven days

death at the hand of the Captain again in her mind's eye, as at last she surrendered to sleep.

Images of the day, twisted and dark and grotesque, haunted her dreams. When she awoke, she heard quiet crying and felt her own face for tears before realizing the sound came from Thane's cot nearby. She tried to shake the cobwebs of sleep from her weary mind. She could not have slept more than a couple hours. The torchlight seemed fainter and the darkness more intense.

She rolled off her cot and onto her bare feet, her worn and mud-covered cloth shoes abandoned at the end of her cot, and crept over to Thane's side. If the footmen heard him, would they cause trouble or just ignore him?

"Thane," she whispered near him.

He turned quickly as she touched his shoulder, startled, and stared at her with a pale, tear-stained face. "Oh, it is you!" he cried in a relieved, half-whisper.

"Shh," the girl urged softly, combing sweat-soaked hair back off his forehead.

"I am sorry," he said more softly, looking at her with intense shame and guilt. She knew he did not want to cry, that he took to heart the Captain's brutal words. *'Tears are weakness. You must never cry.'*

Holding his gaze, she replied steadily: "You are going to be fine. We are going to get through this. Together."

He nodded shakily and wiped his tears away with the backs of his hands.

The girl glanced toward the tent flap and could see the silhouettes of the two footmen standing guard outside. Even at this time of night, she could hear soldiers moving about and see their shifting shadows on the walls of the tent.

A commotion stirred further out; orders being shouted. Then, all at once, the tent flap was flung aside and a man strode in, resplendent in chain mail and steel plate armor—

glinting in the torchlight like silver dragon scales, those long-slain beasts of old—and wearing a deep blue sash around his waist. "Recruits, fall in!" he commanded firmly.

The others responded immediately, coming awake instantly, and gathered in rows, facing the man, while the new recruits pulled themselves from bed, groggy and confused, and mimicked the more experienced ones.

He looked them over with a steady gaze a moment before he spoke: "I am Commander Dillion, for those of you who are new. I will teach you how to fight, and perhaps—if you are lucky—how to survive. You will not get much sleep here on the field, so get used to it." Though firm, his manner and tone held kindness and he carried himself with a comfortable, manly grace.

"The enemy," he continued, "has breached our front lines. They have driven us back with the clear intention of overtaking Torr Guard, our last defense to the Freelands."

The recruits all looked at each other at this news.

"Now, we have just managed to hold them off about nine longs east of us, and we are sending everything we have to hold the Divisions."

He looked each one in the eye as he spoke. "I have been given two days. Learn everything you can and then it is your duty to defend our line with the rest of our brave soldiers."

"We are being sent to the front?" spoke one boy in surprise.

The girl spoke up. "How can we learn to fight so quickly?"

Commander Dillion gave her a stern look, eyes green as a fresh mossy wood. "I will teach you everything I know," he said firmly. "And if you will apply yourself, you will be as ready as any warrior." He raised his voice to be heard outside the tent. "Edwan!"

To those within, he said: "Cala, you and your group will join me on the practice grounds. The rest of you need proper clothing and shoes, and you will go with my footman here —," the man called Edwan entered to stand just inside the entrance, "—and will join me at the training grounds as soon as you are ready."

Chapter 7

Captain Garren observed a quiet camp, mostly empty except for healers and their patients, trainers and their recruits, and various assistants and footmen.

The sun began to rise, casting soft golden beams across the tops of tents and the broken tower. The training post had shrunk to a third of its original size overnight, bare spots between the widely spaced tents proof of their quick disappearance.

His attention drawn to the far training field, he made his way there to observe the new recruits. He had not slept since their arrival and still wore his full leather gear. Added to his usual sword strapped at his side, he also carried a quiver full of arrows between his shoulder blades and a longcurve Singers bow over his shoulder.

An open field met his eye, packed dirt with a stand for training weapons at one end and archery targets at the other. He saw the newest recruits at once, and for the first time dared to ask himself what their fates would be.

"Commander Dillion," he spoke firmly on approach as the Commander taught Thane beginner's hand-to-hand combat.

The Commander stepped back and turned. "Captain."

"I am here to select archers for the First Division," Garren informed him smoothly. "The new recruits will be included in selection."

Responding tension thickened in the air.

Commander Dillion glanced at the recruits, spread out in smaller groups behind him on the field. All had stopped practicing to listen and stare uncertainly. He tried to ease the tension by smiling slightly while responding in all seriousness, "I have hardly begun with either group, and archery has not been my highest priority."

Garren, unfazed, cast his gaze over the recruits. Most looked away from his penetrating blue-grey eye. "It is the priority now," he informed, looking again to the Commander. "Make your selections. I will return in two hours' time."

He left the Commander standing with excuses and protests frozen on his tongue. Though he did not fear Garren, duty compelled him to obey, even if he did not agree with the methods.

For the first time since arriving, Garren headed to his temporary quarters—a partitioned room in the officers' tent. A simple cot and a small square rug on the ground were the only furnishings, but at least it afforded him some privacy.

He made sure no one could see his discomfort while out and about his duties, but now beads of sweat along his brow and upper lip betrayed the pain he felt.

He wiped the sweat from his face with the back of his arm, then pulled a cord from around his neck to take hold of a small glass vial at the end, hidden beneath his uniform. He opened the vial and shook several flecks of white powder onto his tongue. He took a swig of water from his waterskin to wash it down and sank onto the edge of his cot, dropping his head in his hands. He waited for the powder to take effect. Slowly, his shoulders relaxed and he breathed more easily.

Chapter 8

The recruits watched Captain Garren walk away. Cala came to stand beside the girl, who spoke quietly, "What just happened?" She looked toward the archery targets at the other end of the field. "Is becoming an archer really that bad?"

Cala false-fiddled with the ties of her leather arm guards. All the recruits wore simple tunics and close-fit pants with leather jerkins. "Compared to being right in the middle of the battle, facing your foe with only a sword to protect you? You might think so…but there are rumors. The first Singers were recruited from archers. Back then, they volunteered. They say they have stopped the experiments—." She shrugged. "If you have the skills to be a good archer, you are just what they need."

The girl shook her head. "If they made me a Singer, I would never shoot my friends…no matter what the law says," she insisted quietly.

Cala stared at her. "Something changes when you become a Singer. They change you…."

"Change us? How?"

"I would not know exactly. I am not a Singer. But there is a reason they are used to give children nightmares."

The girl fought back a shiver of frightening awareness. She recognized the truth of Cala's words in the Captain's presence; the way his one eye seemed to look right through her—like he knew no emotion. She swallowed against the bile rising in her throat. That this could be the fate of one of her friends, or maybe her own.

Cala spoke the answer to the girl's next thought before she voiced it, including the rest of the recruits with her gaze. "Do your best. Whatever the rumors, archers are highly valued and well taken care of on the battlefield."

"How long have you been here, that you know so much?" Bandon challenged her haughtily.

Cala glared at him. "Typical training lasts a fortnight, except for now because the King's Army is being overrun. I have been here since Torr Guard was established. I no longer need training, so I am here to train you. I suggest you watch your tongue, or I might be tempted to do away with it." Her sharp, commanding retort silenced him, though his sneer remained stubbornly in place.

Commander Dillion approached, preventing further discussion. For a brief moment, his gaze hinted at apology, but he instructed the recruits with directness and command. He ordered them to assemble around him so he could first demonstrate proper handling of bow and arrow. "Our archers are trained to be familiar with the three kinds of bows," he began. "The longcurve bow is most favored, and Singers use them exclusively." He held one up. "It is strong and flexible and sends arrows further distances than either of the other two. It also supports the long arrow—used exclusively by Singers. The longcurve bow has several different styles and reinforcements to meet the specific needs or rank of each individual archer. The higher you rank, the better your equipment will be and the better your chances of survival."

He handed the longcurve bow to Cala and lifted a second bow, shaped much like the first but shorter and with a double string side-by-side. "This is the two-string, often called the Dragan[9]. You can fit and shoot two arrows at the same time, and it is meant to accommodate flaming arrows. The strength is similar to the longcurve bow, but the range is shorter, with a higher, tighter arc."

"What about accuracy?" asked one of the recruits.

"Accuracy depends on you. You control where your arrow flies," the Commander answered. "If you are looking for more dependable accuracy with less effort, the crossbow is what you want. It shoots straight at whatever you are aiming at, as long as you can aim. But where accuracy comes with less effort, loading each arrow is slower and takes more arm strength." He lifted the crossbow to demonstrate. "The arrow locks in so it will never stray left or right, and the power behind your shot lays solely in the mechanism of the bow."

Ten targets decorated the end of the field. The Commander instructed the recruits to line up side-by-side to shoot their targets, standing twenty paces out to start. Since there were fourteen trainees, ten went for the first round of shooting and only four went on the second round. After the initial rounds of practice using each type of bow, each trainee chose their own favored bow to hone their skills, with the Commander's and Cala's approval.

The girl looked over the selection before her. She glanced aside as a soft, smoke-scented breeze blew in from the east, and saw Carter choose a longcurve bow. His skills

---

[9] Dragan : from Old English 'to draw, protract' and also named after the mythical beast 'dragon' for the weapon's use of flaming arrows

showed promise. What if the Captain chose him? Would she ever see him again? How could she protect Thane and Carter if they got separated? Thane could never be picked. He was weak and fragile and though he tried, he could never shoot straight and only grazed the target at best.

The girl enjoyed the feel of the bow in her hands, but she could not leave Thane to fend for himself.

Back and forth, her heart struggled to know the paths before her. Until the Captain returned and the decision could no longer be delayed.

Chapter 9

Garren strode from the officers' tent and toward the stables. The skyline brightened to a familiar deep red-orange hue where he knew the Divisions had formed to hold back the invading enemy forces. Smoke lay stronger than ever on the breeze—warning of their impending doom; warning of the greater risks to Torr Guard and those that remained.

Everything in him demanded to be on that battlefield. He could feel their lives hanging in a precarious balance as if between two great cliffs. It tormented him.

He stopped at the stables for his horse. Open on one side, the structure faced away from the stronger winds while a stray breeze rustled across the straw strewn aisle. The odor of dust, grain, and horseflesh momentarily overwhelmed his heightened senses. In the shadows, one of the stable boys watched him, fearful of being noticed and called out. Garren ignored him as his beast's head appeared over the nearest stall door.

Garren approached his horse and cupped his scarred, calloused hands on each side of its muzzle and spoke an Ancient greeting in a murmur for the horse's ears only. The horse bobbed its head slightly in response and pawed at the dirt with one powerful, determined front hoof.

Garren unlatched the gate and stepped back. The great beast followed him into the open aisle and stopped, head lifted with ears pricked forward alertly.

Commander Dillion approached from behind, coming from the direction of the training fields. His quiet, sure strides slowed as he reached the stables, seeing Garren with his mount.

"Have you made your decision, Commander?" Garren spoke firmly without turning, one hand resting on the horse's forehead.

"Some show potential, though it would be against my better judgement if I did not protest. They have not had even a single day to train. If we send them into battle, they will be killed."

Garren looked at him a moment, gaze hardening. He called sharply to the stable boy, who scrambled forward, bringing a headstall with reins and struggling some under the weight of the saddle he also carried. He placed them in a pile beside the horse at Garren's indication, then slipped unobtrusively back into the shadows.

Garren lifted the headstall and his horse accepted it without hesitation. He answered the Commander coldly and with a hint of irritation: "This is war; people die. This is the world we live in, or have you forgotten that we all have to sacrifice something?"

"I left Cala in charge. They are selecting their weapons and receiving final instructions."

"Good. I need five ready to ride. We leave at once," Garren said. He hoisted the saddle onto his muscular shoulder to toss it up across his horse's tall back.

"I will inform them of their orders. They will be ready."

The Commander departed and Garren paused to watch him go, jaw flexing as an inner storm brewed in his gaze. He'd nearly lost his temper. Not many men would question him, nor show such honesty of thought. If Garren could be someone else—if he was not what he was—he might have considered the Commander capable of being his friend.

But friends did not exist, not for Garren.

And he did not like to be challenged.

He finished dressing[10] his horse and led it out into the red-tinged day to mount, then signaled it into a canter to the training fields.

Sensing his frustrations, his horse sidestepped as Garren drew up at the edge of the field to observe unseen for a moment as the recruits trained. He immediately saw those whom he had brought in the night before, standing mostly together. His eye fell on the girl with the long blonde hair—he heard the Commander call her Orabelle—as she took her stance opposite Thane. She attempted to teach the young boy something in the art of sword fighting, trying to help him better himself. He could see the makings of a leader in her countenance and had witnessed first-hand the determination in her golden gaze. She wanted to protect the boy, especially after the loss of Thordan.

Garren held back a moment more, remembering a time long ago when he had that same determination; that same desire to protect. The side of him trained against emotion rejected these thoughts almost instantly and he kicked in his heels.

His sudden forward motion brought him to their immediate attention. They stopped their various training and stared, fixed with apprehension as his great beast stopped in their midst with a fierce snort.

---

[10] Dressing : outfitting (a horse) in full gear

Commander Dillion stepped forward. "After observing your abilities and potentials," he addressed the recruits, "I have selected five of you to accompany Captain Garren to the Divisions as archers. You will learn quickly on the field—as we all must, to survive—and I urge you to be wise and accept any instruction others are willing and able to give. It will be your survival."

As the Commander spoke, Garren watched the recruits' faces, some filled with uncertainty; a few with curiosity.

Thane, face nearly ashen, looked too terrified of his new situation to feel much else. He would never survive, being the weakest of the lot. He would either die, lost on a battlefield without the wits to save himself, or turn and run in fear like a coward and die from a Singer's arrow.

The Commander began to call their names: Valara, a nineteen-year-old girl from Cala's group; Carter, from the new recruits; Stevan, a black-haired younger boy; Decklan, another from Cala's group. And last, Orabelle.

Garren watched her reaction closest of all. Having held careful control of her expression until now, she suddenly looked from Carter to Thane, torn. Something inside of her began to break. Garren could feel it. He wanted her to be as strong as he thought she could be. He did not know why. He kept his gaze on her, though she would not look at him. While the other recruits avoided his gaze out of fear, she avoided him out of hatred.

"Take up your weapons," Garren instructed, not giving them a chance to respond to their summons. "We leave at once for the First Division."

Thane turned quickly toward Orabelle, panicked, but she shook her head at him. She pulled him into her arms and her lips moved as she spoke some reassurance or encouragement into his ear that the others could not overhear.

Garren's jaw tightened and he turned his gaze away.

A pony-drawn cart and attending footman approached the edge of the training field, ready to transport the new archers to the Divisions.

The Commander made sure they equipped themselves properly. Each archer received a longcurve bow and quiver of arrows. Valara and Decklan were also given the crossbow, attaching it to a sling on their quiver, so the crossbow hung against their backs. Orabelle, Carter, and Stevan carried only longcurve bows.

They filed up into the waiting cart, with nothing more than the clothes and leather jerkins they wore and the weapons they were given. The cart lurched forward as the footman snapped the reins sharply across the pony's back.

Garren signaled his horse to match pace alongside the cart and spoke a final word to the archers. "Beneath your seat is a kit[11]. This is all you will have with you in battle, so never leave it unattended."

His beast broke into a canter and he rode on ahead of the cart; his broad back disappeared from their sights.

---

[11] Kit : leather satchel with provisions/personal effects.

Chapter 10

Ora and Carter sat shoulder-to-shoulder on one side of the cart, on one of the wooden benches running the length of both sides, with Valara seated on Carter's other side. Stevan and Decklan sat on the opposite bench, facing them.

Each one withdrew their kit from beneath their bench and took a look inside. Made of soft, water-repellant leather, the satchel had one shoulder strap and a long flap to cover the opening. Folding that back, Ora found some scant, meager supplies inside meant to help keep her alive and fighting: a roll of leather twine and bone needle, secured in a bundle by a short piece of twine meant to repair their leather armor, shoes, or even mend a weak or splintered bow shaft; a small pouch of emergency rations, including a dry yellow corn flour mix, and a smaller pouch of protein lard—a mix of animal fat with pine-nuts and almonds, ground to a paste. Typical Army food. Real meat, fresh or dried, became a rare and expensive commodity the longer the War lasted and especially was not to be wasted on the young and untrained who often died within days of being put into battle. Ora assumed those higher ranked and skilled ate better.

Ora and Carter, however, had not eaten since their capture, except for a crust of dried bread dipped in lard with the Captain and the soldiers before reaching Torr Guard last evening, and then a short bowl of rice and water while at the training field.

As poor farmers' children, they had grown up knowing hunger and poor food. Still, at least at home they could expect some fresh greens and hot stew. Here no greens could be found and they took the rice and water cold.

Also inside the satchel, Ora discovered a small leather waterskin, now empty; a folded brown wool blanket, only two feet wide and four feet long—barely adequate and cheaply made; a small dagger, and last her hand withdrew a small flat rectangle of thin metal, a hole punched in one end and strung on a strong, small-linked chain. She turned it over in her hands, wondering at its purpose.

The cart bumped over muddy ridges and ravines in the trail where many a cart, horse, and soldier traveled the night before. No one spoke on the ride. They all felt the weight of their circumstances and had no immediate desire to make friendships. Between the hills and occasional tree-lined valley, the closer they got to the Divisions the more intense the smoke and scent of blood and death became. Even the enemy's proximity seemed to have a rather distinct scent of decay and earthy odor, turning Ora's stomach the nearer they came to the Divisions. She breathed through her mouth at first, hoping the others would not notice.

An occasional rumble, like thunder, seemed to vibrate through the earth. They reached the edge of the First Division, a sprawling camp behind the front line, over the next rise. The mingling sounds of camp overwhelmed them —of forging weapons and armor; of the death screams from the Healers Quarter, overflowing with injured.

Garren turned his horse's head to walk back to them. His voice boomed to be heard over the noise. "The blacksmith will get you tagged, and the footman will show you to the

Archers Quarter. You fight for the King's Army now. Fight well, and you will live. If you turn and flee, mine will be the first arrow that kills you!" He kicked his horse into a gallop and beast and rider disappeared into the smoke and din.

The cart stopped at the nearest forge. Heat and flame billowed up and the sharp *CLANG!* of hammer against anvil rang out. Constant motion and commotion threatened to leave Ora's head spinning. She sucked in a deep breath, clutching her kit.

The footman dismounted from the driver's bench and walked toward the back. He slapped an open hand against the wooden side. "Out of the cart," he urged.

Quickly, they obeyed. Ora followed Decklan—the first out of the cart—and threw the strap of her kit over her head, cross-wise over one shoulder, so the satchel hung against one hip. She held her longcurve bow in one hand.

As they lined up beside the cart, a burly man stepped away from the forge and approached. Three other men remained at the forge and never paused in their work long enough to even glance their direction.

"New recruits?" the burly blacksmith demanded, covered in a day's worth of soot and sweat. He eyed the archers as he wiped his beefy hands vigorously and absentmindedly on a square of already soiled grey cloth.

"Just come from Torr Guard," the footman informed.

The blacksmith grunted. "Get out your tags and bring them to the forge."

Tags. *That's what those metal rectangles are called,* Ora realized and immediately pulled hers out from her kit. "Carter," she said quietly, when her friend looked confused a moment. The others saw and followed Ora's example as she led the way to the forge, following after the blacksmith.

The blacksmith heated the forge with a few pumps of the giant bellows, then lifted a hand to accept the tags. "The heat softens the metal," he informed them brusquely. "You will engrave your name, family, and territory. Whatever you want used to identify you. This way, if they find your corpse—if there is anything left of it—your families can be notified." Holding the chains in one fist, he lowered the tags into the red-hot heat from the coals until they glowed faintly. Then, he re-dispersed them. "Take them to the rail over there and use the nails. Do not burn your hands. When you finish, bring them back to me."

They took them to a horizontal hitching rail just beyond the forge where several armor nails were pegged into the wood. Ora pulled at one and it came out with little resistance. Carefully touching the metal tag, she felt the heat and did as the blacksmith instructed. She scratched her name firmly into the metal, though there would be no one to mourn her passing:

ORABELLE, DAU. OF NEICE, FREELANDS.

She glanced up to see the others nearly done. The metal still retained enough heat. She hesitated, then turned the tag over and scratched out these words:

STRENGTH FORGED BY FIRE.

Words of power, spoken long ago by her mother: *'Strength forged by fire makes even the weaker among us unbreakable.'* Her mother lived that truth daily, through nearly every trial imaginable…until the end.

The blacksmith paused his work long enough to drop the tags in a shallow pan of cold water and let them set a minute, saying briefly, "The water cools the metal and will harden it."

After they retrieved their tags and hung them around their necks, the footman led the five new archers through the maze of tents and soldiers toward a tall pole flying a narrow flag of blue and white, the top half blue and the lower white.

"This is the Archers Quarter. Commander Kane will give you your orders." He retreated, leaving them alone.

They looked at each other a moment, wondering silently what to do next. Garren's warning remained sharp in their minds. *'If you flee, mine will be the first arrow that kills you.'*

"This way," Decklan urged, nodding toward the middle-most tent by the flag pole. "I think I hear our new Commander," he added dryly.

As they approached the tent, they could hear an angry voice upbraiding whomever else stood inside.

Decklan drew back the tent flap and bravely stepped inside. Ora followed while the rest came in behind. A stocky, middle-aged man with a shaved head and face flushed with frustration paced back and forth on one side of a large wooden map table while two archers stood opposite him. A fourth man stood shadowed in a far corner, observing with careful silence.

The flushed man turned immediately when the new archers entered. "And who are you!" he barked with irritation, caught off guard.

Ora stepped forward. "We are the new archers, Sir. We are here for your orders."

His irritation cooled. "Ah, the Captain said he would be bringing recruits. And not a moment too soon, thank the Blue Star…." He eyed them. "Well, all right then. We need extra men—uh, women too—at the line. We are facing two Troopers today." He turned to one of the archers he'd been ranting at moments before. "Milo, make yourself useful and show them to their post!"

"Sir," Milo saluted and turned.

Ora watched the fourth man standing in the shadows, strangely unnerved by his presence as she felt his gaze. She tried to shake off the feeling and started to follow Milo, when all at once the stranger moved and stepped into the light of the lamps, his gaze directly on Ora.

"I will take them, Commander Kane," he said. "I was just on my way to assist." He smiled at the group. "I am Bron Tarak." He was tall with a pleasant enough face and smile, though one side of his face had strange, tiny criss-crossing disfigurements, like raised scars with the skin turned yellowish-grey. The marks disappeared beneath the neckline of his leather armor. The pigment of the eye on that side was the same yellowish-grey color while the other remained green.

"Very well," Commander Kane said gruffly.

Bron's gaze flickered to Ora with private amusement as if he knew she had been studying him. He moved through their midst with a smooth, confident stride, and they parted to follow after him.

Ora edged forward to walk beside him despite Carter's warning look. Standing on his good side, she could see he had a handsome profile. He carried a longcurve bow and quiver of arrows at his back. The arrows were long arrows. "Are you a Singer?" Ora said bluntly, quietly.

He looked at her and flashed an unaffected smile as he continued walking. "What gave me away?" he half-teased.

Ora looked away, surprised and slightly uneasy. Something about him.... She had felt it when he stood in the shadows, but now—he seemed much different than what she would expect from a Singer, and much different than the Captain.

She wanted to ask what happened to his face, but he had surely been asked that by everyone he met. So, she spoke her second thought: "You do not seem anything like the Captain."

Bron's jaw tightened ever so slightly. "Captain Garren? We are not all monsters, my lady," he spoke calmly; a shadow darkening his eyes.

So, he viewed the Captain as a monster. There, they could agree. Not daring to share these thoughts, Ora slowed her steps to rejoin her group without another word.

Carter touched her arm, coming to walk alongside her. He looked carefully ahead at Bron to be sure they were not being observed or overheard. "You should not be talking to him...."

"He is not like the Captain," Ora repeated.

"Is he not, though?" Carter insisted a bit sharply. "It is still his job to shoot us if we try to leave here!" Though he whispered, the words came out forcefully and Ora looked quickly to see if Bron had heard. He kept walking, giving no indication.

Ora thought a moment. She side-stepped a supply cart and looked Carter in the eye. The battle sounds and the thunder in the earth came closer now, as they neared the edge of the camp and the path that would lead them to the line. "The Captain brought us here. He killed my guardian. Anyone who stands against the Captain, I will consider an ally." She lowered her voice further still. "I am going to get us out of here...no matter what it takes."

Chapter 11

Garren fingered his tag, feeling the carvings from so long ago, worn but still legible:

GARREN, SON OF CORIN; JOL, FREELANDS.

He had fought for fifteen years and never once returned home. The last ten years he had served as a Singer, rising to the rank of Captain. He could have gone home. He could have gone to see who was left who might remember him as a boy. But, after what he had been turned into, they would either hate him or fear him.

He shifted position in the naturally-formed dugout and slid his fingers down the string of his Singers bow, letting the soft song it emitted distract him from unpleasant memories.

His gaze sharpened on the wooded landscape outside. If instinct served him well—it never failed him in the past—a For'bane weapons supply cart would pass through on its way to the line. He meant to plunder it before it reached its destination.

His eye caught movement and he slowly crouched forward, watching. Just as he suspected, this nearly invisible trail gave enough clearance for the supply cart pulled by two Walkers—creatures much like oxen. The cart was led by a

Sniffer-Skay and two other armed Skays appeared, following the cart several yards back. The Skays stood on two legs—their basic physique similar to humans—head and shoulders taller than Garren's six-foot-two-inch frame. They had tough and leathery, yellow-grey skin and flat faces with round yellow eyes and animal-like black pupils. They wore only loin cloths belted at the waist, revealing strong and wiry limbs and flat chests.

Three guards. They did not expect any trouble.

Garren moved slowly out of the dugout, keeping to the thickness of the wood on his side of the trail, timing his movement as the wagon came slowly, steadily closer.

He watched the Sniffer—distinguishable from the rear Skays by the wide-spaced nostrils. As scout, it would know of an intruder before the others.

Twenty-yards turned into ten…then five yards.

Garren selected a long arrow and drew taut on the bow, choosing his first victim carefully.

To the ears of the enemy, the soft warning song alerted them that some danger had found them. The Sniffer raised an arm and the wagon came to a creaking, protesting halt as the Sniffer and the Skays turned about, but could not locate Garren.

He needed only a moment. The arrow released and took down the first Walker, striking deep in the brain, just above the left eye. It stumbled heavily and dropped dead. The second Walker tried to bolt in a surprised panic, but the dead weight prevented the cart from moving, and rendered the second Walker immobile and bellowing in protest.

At once, Garren jumped from his hiding place next to the cart while smoothly and effortlessly fitting another arrow and holding it at the ready. Surprised screeches filled the air as the For'bane saw how Garren stood amongst them.

Garren smiled icily. "Only three of you? I am insulted," he goaded.

Closer to the cart and to Garren, the Sniffer overcame its bewilderment first and charged. Garren swung toward the attack and shot the Sniffer through the throat, then dove and rolled toward the cart, out of its path.

Coming to his feet immediately, Garren saw the Sniffer turn and fall as the two Skays came toward him from the rear of the cart, circling in on him. He stood between them and the cart and drew his sword, holding his bow in his left hand.

As the nearer Skay came at him with a pair of twin curved blades, Garren expertly twisted sideways to avoid the first blade and raised his sword arm high to block and deflect the other.

As steel struck steel, Garren lifted his bow and sliced the end down the side of the Skay's face. It shrieked in pain and anger and stumbled back a step as blood and fluid poured down its cheek. "It hurts, does it not!" Garren shouted.

Sharp pain seared down the side of his sword arm as the second Skay attacked. Garren's cry came more from anger and adrenaline than from actual pain. Cornered against the side of the cart, he turned and jumped up onto it and pierced the tip of his blade into the back of the wooden bench.

Switching the bow to his right hand, he backed to the far corner over the stacks of weapon crates covered with heavy canvas. He drew a third arrow and let it fly, striking the second Skay in the eye. A perfect shot. Only the largest foe remained, fluid still dripping like puss from its torn cheek.

Recovering from the blow to its face, the Skay shrieked with angry determination. Arm throbbing, Garren dropped the bow and reached for his sword, tugging it free and lifting it two-handed above his head as the Skay leapt into the air toward him. He jumped forward to meet the Skay's attack.

They collided in mid-air and Garren's sword plunged through the creature's shoulder.

The force of the attack pushed the Skay down to the ground, pinning it like a butterfly as the tip of the sword broke through the other side of its body and into the earth. It groped to free itself, reaching for a hidden blade kept strapped at its hip.

Garren righted himself and produced a bone blade with saw-tooth edges on both sides as he shoved a boot against the Skay's chest. "Looking for this?" he said calmly. Surprise flickered in the Skay's eyes. Garren leaned down and pressed the edge of the blade against its cheek. "Nice trick, eh? This is not the first time I have seen one of these —" nodding to the blade. "I know your strategies. It is a trick I learned from you."

His gaze turned to flint as he slid the blade down to its throat. "You want to know how your Sniffer did not detect me? How I managed to defeat you?"

The Skay stopped struggling. Its yellow gaze looked steadily into Garren's intense, one-eyed stare. Garren leaned in closer, lips curling in a snarl. "Because I *am* you!" He swiped the blade with violent force. Within seconds, the Skay drowned in its own blood.

Chapter 12

Never had Ora fought the desire to run so intensely. Never had she imagined being on this field of battle, fighting alongside others her own age—still so young—and a lone Singer; fighting just to survive the next hour; the next minute.

They stood, stationed on a rise just behind the front lines, their long-range arrows keeping anyone from breaking through and picking off enemy stragglers. They just kept coming, wave after wave, a constant thunder in the earth, with roars and shrieks.

In the midst of attacking For'bane stood a creature three times the height of the others. A Trooper. His slow, forward movement created the thunder that pulsed through the ground. Great chains wrapped around its arms and waist held two round iron balls, covered in spikes—flails—which he dragged slowly behind him. Once close enough, he would swing them at the soldiers like great iron maces, plowing through the line.

The sight turned Ora's stomach into terrified knots.

Amidst the chaos and overwhelming sounds of battle, Bron turned and shouted instructions, his focus on Ora who stood nearest him. “Aim for the head or throat. Focus on that Trooper. If he breaks the line we are all dead. But watch out for stragglers as well. Do not let anything get too close.”

“What about you?” Ora shouted to be heard as Bron began to back away. “Can you bring it down?”

He drew a long arrow and fitted it in his Singers bow. He backed away and flashed a grin. “That is what I am here for….” He turned and sprinted away, disappearing through the throngs of soldiers and other archers.

Ora’s breath felt sharp in her lungs as her hands grew raw from handling the bow and arrow without rest. Survival instinct kicked in after the initial shock of battle and the new archers focused on their targets, developing their skills on the go, trying to make each arrow count. Sweat stung her eyes and her body grew sore and weary. Smoke and haze from the campfires and forges tainted the sky and atmosphere thickly, blocking out most of the sunlight. Young footmen delivered fresh arrows for the archers ever-depleting quivers. Ora felt the tugs on her quiver as they jammed in more arrows, then rushed on to the next archer to do the same. She did not dare turn or break her focus from the battle.

“To the right! To the right!” shouted someone from the field.

Ora turned to see a Skay break through the ranks and head straight for them. It slashed through the soldiers with twin curved blades, grabbing one soldier with its long-nailed hands and ruthlessly throwing him aside.

Ora caught her breath, and fitted an arrow, arms already trembling with nerves and fatigue. What if she missed?

“Carter!” she shouted.

Carter turned, seeing the Skay. He held still, recognizing Ora’s own fear. If one arrow did not stop it, they needed another before it reached them. He drew an arrow against his bow from his depleting quiver. Ora would not have time to draw another arrow and shoot again, still inexperienced and slow.

"Shoot, Ora! Shoot!" Carter cried out.

It saw them now, its yellow gaze focused directly on them as individuals.

Ora froze. She could not move; could not think. In the chaos around her, what if she hit one of the soldiers? They were too close. Her aim and accuracy still needed work, especially at such short range. She could not keep doing this. Her body screamed for rest, wearied and exhausted.

Then, like emerging from underwater, everything sharpened into focus and her mind screamed at her: *Shoot! Shoot now!*

She gasped and let the arrow fly. It registered that her arrow struck, at the same time she also realized it had missed its intended target and buried instead in the Skay's thigh. Equally enraged and in pain, it let out a chilling shriek and only increased its stride, almost leaping for them.

In the next instant, the soft *WHOOSH!* of an arrow flew by her ear. A long arrow, come from behind her, implanted itself deep in the center of the Skay's skull. The force threw the great creature backward and to the ground.

Twenty feet away.

Ora turned quickly. Carter stood in shock with an arrow still held against his bow. Bron stood behind him, already drawing another arrow, his gaze filled with the storm of the battle as he caught and held hers for a brief instant.

She had not acted fast enough. It could have killed them.

"Get the arrows!" he shouted, before turning back to the fight again, not giving her the time to feel ashamed; not giving her the time to beat herself up for her mistake. The battlefield was not the place to dwell on or consider regrets.

Pulling out the blade from her kit, she hurried forward to dig out the arrows and return to the battle.

Chapter 13

Dusk fell over camp as Garren made his way to the Healers Quarter and into one of the main tents, past the moans of the wounded and dying. In partitioned rooms at the far end, the healers on duty tended to the day's injuries.

"Captain," greeted the healer as Garren entered one such room, respectful admiration in his tone. "I hear you took down a couple of Skays and a transport cart." Here on the field, men knew Singers more as strange and powerful allies than the stuff of children's nightmares.

Garren sat on the end of a tall cot in the center of the small room and held still as the healer and his attendant removed his stiff leather jerkin, leaving only his off-white tunic and close-fit pants. His glass vial hung visible around his neck, while his tag remained hidden beneath his tunic and against his skin.

The attendant withdrew while the healer examined the cut on Garren's upper arm and chose needle and thread.

"Make the stitches close together, I need to be able to use my arm and will not have time to come back in." He would remove the stitches himself when the time came.

"I am afraid it is deep enough it may scar," the healer informed him as he began stitching.

Garren's face remained stoic and he sat perfectly still, ignoring the prick and pull of the needle. "Scarring does not matter," he replied, keeping his gaze straight ahead.

The healer focused on his work without further discussion. The attendant returned with water and towels. As the healer made his last few stitches, a soft disturbance of someone entering the room caused Garren to lift his head.

The girl—Orabelle—stood uncertainly on the threshold. The healer turned. "Who are you? What do you need?" he spoke firmly, though not harshly.

"Commander Kane of the Archers Quarter sent me to get my hands wrapped," she answered, hesitating when she realized who was in the room.

"I am with a patient, you will need to wait in the main room with the others," the healer instructed and turned his back on her.

Garren studied her, while she studiously avoided his gaze. That she had survived the first day only meant she had just as much chance of dying the next, if not more. As an archer, she had a better chance of survival than most. Still....

He took note of the weariness in her countenance; the dark smudges under her eyes and the paleness of her skin. "How long have you been waiting?" he spoke before she could turn away, his address forcing her to acknowledge his presence as her golden gaze found his grey one.

Stiffening, she hesitated. "Two hours." She appeared to expect him to start a verbal fight with her. If she only knew what he used to be. Before. He might have liked her then—or she might have liked him. He noticed her hands. Raw and blistered.

"You are not holding the bow correctly," he said firmly without thinking. His jaw tightened and his gaze hardened as he realized his mistake. However, too weary to be angry, she looked almost hurt as she took a step back, nodded briefly, and turned to go.

Feeling an unexpected spark of compassion, Garren spoke firmly and quietly, gaze on Ora, while he directed his words to the healer. "Take care of her injuries next; you are done with me." He used the same tone he used when he ordered Ora to get down from the horse. A quiet tone, but one that would not be ignored.

The healer stepped away and motioned for his assistant to take over with the towel and wash basin. "Come and sit," the healer told Ora.

Ora took a chair just inside the partition doorway, still only a few feet from Garren, but as far away as she could get from him in the small space. The healer approached with a roll of white cloth bandaging.

"Use the ointment first," Garren commanded.

"But…Captain…," the healer protested in surprise, turning to stare at him.

"The girl is an archer," Garren said with a hint of anger. "She is useless without her hands. You will use the ointment." A warning brewed in his gaze.

Submitting, the healer lowered his gaze and turned to retrieve the ointment from a high, locked shelf. He produced the key from a leather cord around his neck, and his hand shook slightly as he fit the key into the lock.

Garren caught Ora's stare. He had surprised her. Ointment could only be used with ranked soldiers; the ones who proved worthy of the expense. The healers never wasted it on a new recruit fresh from civilian life. Such medicines had to be earned.

The healer returned to Ora and she turned her gaze pointedly away from the one man she must hate above all others.

"Open your hands," the healer instructed and proceeded to gently message the gel-like substance across the raw marks.

Garren watched a moment then turned his attention to his own injury, carefully moving his arm and flexing his hand in and out of a light fist.

"What happened to you?" Her unexpected question brought his head up.

He kept his tone casual. "A couple of Skays got in my way."

"Maybe you are not so invincible," she murmured, watching him for his reaction.

Garren stood and drew on his leather jerkin despite the protesting burn of his wound. He ignored her comment. If she wanted him to play the part of a monster, for once she would be disappointed. "You had best get some sleep while you can, Belle," he said smoothly. "You are going to need it."

Before she could respond, he moved past her and slipped out of the room.

Chapter 14

The healer finished wrapping Ora's hands and she left the tent some minutes after Garren. Torchlight, campfires, and forge fires lit her path between tents. Being around so many soldiers set her on edge, especially now, away from the heat and distractions of battle. She walked quickly, head down, too weary and stressed to handle her surroundings. She only wanted to fall into bed and forget the terrors of the day.

"Well, if it is not the little princess," sneered a voice from her left.

She stiffened instantly, a cold wash of fear and dread chilling her bones. She knew that voice.

Greer sauntered toward her, carrying a broadsword flat against one shoulder, leather covered in earth and blood. He smiled icily as he approached, glancing her over. "Chilly night, is it not?"

"Especially when you are around," Ora replied stiffly, surprising herself. She gripped her kit and tried not to let her intimidation of him show.

Greer's lips turned into an ugly sneer. "The Captain is not around to be your bodyguard this time, *wench*," he warned, a glint in his eyes. "So watch how you speak to a soldier. I might misunderstand."

"Is there a problem here?"

Greer's face instantly smoothed over as Bron stepped from around a tent and out of the shadows. For a second time, the man had silently appeared from the darkness, speaking casually in the presence of hostility.

"Only saying goodnight to my friend, here," Greer spoke with a cool pleasantness that turned Ora's stomach. His cold, warning glance threatened much pain if she discredited his words. Greer nodded to Bron, who leaned back against the pole of a tent awning as if he had all the time in the world to linger. He flashed an unaffected smile toward Greer as the soldier turned to depart. Ora caught Greer's private expression of annoyance.

She let out a soft breath of relief and hoped Bron would not ask anything about the confrontation. Bron pushed himself off the pole and came closer. "Looks like you got a little scraped up. You all right?"

Whether he meant her hands or her emotions, she decided to believe the first and leave it at that. She gave a non-committal shrug. "It is not that bad." She hesitated. "I saw the Captain in the Healers Quarter. He said I am not handling the bow…in the best way."

"Hmm," Bron said, considering. "Show me."

Hesitating a moment—feeling strangely shy of Bron watching her demonstration—Ora stepped to the side of the tent and slid the bow into her hands. She drew back with an arrow, holding her stance and ignoring the responding pain in her still-tender hands.

"Well, I am afraid I must agree with the Captain on this one," Bron spoke with quiet apology. "It is nothing too serious. The bow itself is part of the problem. You should be able to upgrade to a better one in due time."

Ora relaxed her stance. "Well," she admitted quietly, "time is not exactly on my side."

"You have as good a chance as anyone," Bron insisted. He flashed a smile. "You did well today."

Recalling the Skay, she answered, "I missed."

Bron's face grew serious again. "Yes, you missed, but you are learning. The For'bane are a formidable enemy—they are not easy to take down, even for someone who is skilled."

'A couple of Skays got in my way,' Garren's words came back to her. How had he survived with nothing more than a cut on his arm, if even a Singer admitted to them being 'formidable'?

She hesitated. "Could you defeat Skays on your own? I mean, in close combat?"

"You mean me, as a Singer?" Bron guessed her meaning.

She glanced up to meet his gaze.

He shrugged. "Our senses are more distinct, as are our skills. The For'bane can jump higher; run faster. But then, so can we. Facing a Skay in combat is no summer picnic—for anyone—but we Singers are better matched to win, if the need arises."

'They change you...,' Cala's warning came to mind.

Bron, as if sensing the tension in the air, smiled and stepped forward. "Let me show you something." He took the bow and one of her arrows and drew back. "Position your hand just a bit higher, here. You will have more control and you will not tire so easily. Is your shoulder sore? See, here. Straighten your arm. This should also reduce the rub burn on your hand, there. It will take getting used to."

Ora accepted the bow and arrow back, careful not to let their fingers touch. "Thank you," she managed before he bid her goodnight and stepped away, blending back into the shadows.

Once again, she headed to the Archers Quarter and the large tent she shared with many other archers. She slipped around the cots to her own, beside Carter's, and paused to look down on his sleeping face. She softly brushed a lock of his blond hair off his dirt-smudged forehead. He remained her only friend now, in this world of monsters and men.

Bron called Garren a monster for being a Singer, and yet he was also a Singer. The two men seemed complete opposites in character and personality. But Cala's warnings whispered in her mind. How did Singers change? And why did that change cause so much fear and mistrust?

Did she have the discernment to know the real monsters when faced with them?

She fell into her cot, weary with fear and confusion, and promptly passed out.

Chapter 15

In the First Division, the War Council talked endlessly of strategies to drive the For'bane back and reclaim the land they had lost. They managed to hold off the enemy advancement to protect Torr Guard and the Freelands. Joining the Council in an assembly as evening fell, Garren listened with half an ear to the discussions and theories and suggestions. To him, it sounded like a political debate—a sort of pathetic power struggle, ultimately all talk and no action.

Commander Dillion, just arrived with more recruits, seemed the only voice of reason in the group. At last, he spoke. "We have been fighting them for over fifteen years, gentlemen, and all our talk of strategies has gotten us nowhere. I have to ask the question: Do we or do we not want the War to end? We need to change our tactics. We need to start thinking actively offensive, not only defensive."

"And what would you suggest, Commander?" spoke Commander Strell pointedly, leaning forward in his chair at the head of the table.

Commander Dillion met the challenge readily: "The Singers. They know the enemy and have fought better than any of us. Maybe we should start learning from them."

All eyes turned to Garren, the only Singer present and the only Singer who carried a ranking title, allowing him to be present at the assembly. Not expecting this response, Garren remained in his relaxed position. He leaned back in his seat with one boot propped against the edge of the table. "We did not exactly appreciate the last time you tried to get information out of us," he replied with quiet cynicism.

Commander Strell stiffened. "We meant you no harm, Captain," he defended.

"Did you not?" Garren shot back.

Some of the men looked at each other in nervous apprehension.

"We are all on the same side here," Commander Dillion insisted. "I am only suggesting we work together, in that mutual goal of saving our lands and our futures. All of us. Captain, I know there is much you can teach us."

Garren dropped his foot and straightened in his chair. "We fight on our own terms because we are outcasts. You distrust what I am and yet you *made* me what I am." He looked around the table. "You want my suggestion?" he spoke low. "All right, I will tell you, even though I do not think you will like it or heed it. It means taking risks."

He let a long pause linger and could almost hear their unspoken questions in the heavy stillness. "We have to go to them. Take this fight to them. It is the only way to end this; the only chance we have."

"You mean their nests?" Commander Strell ran a hand through his short silver hair. "How? It sounds like suicide."

"It does, which is exactly why it will work. It is not a fighting method you would ever choose. You have always fought fair, at the front lines. But winning the War will take more than a fair fight," Garren answered calmly. He stood and pointed to the map spread out before them. "Our enemy focuses all their strength on the Divisions. They are following our front lines principle. They see humans as weak creatures of the earth, and will stop at nothing to drive us off the edge of the world. They are breeders. Their strength lies in their numbers and abilities to continually produce. Flush them out of their nests, destroy them, and give them nothing to fall back on. Then you will finally start to see an end to the War."

The clang of the hammer across hot steel brought Garren from his memories as he stood at the blacksmith forge in the newly-formed Second Division—since the old camp fell with the last attack. It was nearly dawn, three days since the Council meeting and Garren stood at the forges getting his blade sharpened. The morning promised rain by afternoon. He could smell the moisture in the air, mixed with the smoke of the forges and campfires.

"Here you are, Captain," the blacksmith on duty spoke and held out the sword, lifted crosswise in both hands. "Good as new—better than new even."

Garren took the sword and lifted it by the hilt to observe the play of firelight across the smooth blade.

"Captain."

Garren turned to see Commander Dillion approaching, his steel plate armor gleaming fresh in the morning light. His grim, serious expression caused Garren to tense as he slowly sheathed his sword, keeping his eye on the Commander. The uncomfortable power struggle at the last meeting could bring any sort of retaliation—new plans and strategies that usually ended up being worse than the last.

While the King's Law ruled the land, the officers ruled the battlefield, and everyone wanted to claim leadership.

That the War had gone on for so long with much bloodshed and very few results did not surprise Garren.

The blacksmith retreated back to work deeper in the structure as the Commander stopped before Garren, who wasted no time on a greeting. "What new scheme has brought you to me this time?"

He could respect Commander Dillion because, of all the Commanders—men born to wealth and privilege, Commander Dillion cared little for power. He cared only for the strength and survival of every soldier he trained. He held no false modesty or hidden agenda, and enough honesty to make dishonest men choke.

"Commander Strell is sending a troop of recruits to scout behind the lines. He is sending them to a nest," the Commander said in a low voice, standing opposite Garren.

"And this concerns me, why?" Garren replied cooly.

"It is suicide. They will die out there. They do not have a chance," the Commander insisted.

"I recall Commander Strell saying as much in Council." Garren began to walk and the Commander fell into step beside him. "You asked the question, Commander, and I think you know the answer: they do not want the War to end. Because as long as the fighting continues, they have power. They think they have control."

The Commander stopped walking. "That is not true," he urged. "Thousands of men, women, and children have died. No man could crave power so much to sacrifice so greatly —."

"And you are sure about that?" Garren turned to face him, staring hard.

The Commander wavered and his gaze shifted to the side in hesitation.

"You have far too much faith in people, Commander," Garren admonished, watching him a moment. "I have been fighting for fifteen years, and I have seen more than you can imagine. No one knows the truth better than I do."

"Look," the Commander insisted as Garren made a move to walk away. "Commander Strell has a problem, I can see that. He does not like that you spoke out and I know I am to blame for that. He wants your plan to fail, and he's using these recruits to prove it. To discredit you. These are recruits —barely trained—and they are going to pay for Commander Strell's pride."

"I cannot make the Commander do anything other that what he pleases, especially since I am the one who told him and the others it is the only plan that will succeed," Garren replied tightly.

"Go with them."

Garren turned to stare at him.

"He sends them alone on purpose, giving them no chance for success. But I know his plans. He is gathering them together now and sending them off in secret. If you went with them, and they survived—Commander Strell will have no excuse and you will prove the mission a success."

Garren sighed very quietly. Acting like a nursemaid for a bunch of recruits? He would rather face a full-grown Rammer.

"You know they will probably die anyway," he insisted.

"So, you will do it?"

"I will do what I can," Garren agreed through the bitter taste in his mouth. "Who does he send?"

"A couple of the new archers, Carter and Orabelle—."

He did not hear the rest. *Orabelle*. The one person he could not seem to forget; who had haunted his thoughts ever since that night in the Healers Quarter. He felt his heart give a strange, heavy thud and his jaw tightened with determination.

He had seen her only a handful of times since that night, and only at a distance. Though he would never admit it to anyone and hardly admitted it even to himself, he kept watch out for her. He wanted to see that she still lived.

"...Seven, just enough not to cause a noticeable stir with the other officers," Commander Dillion concluded.

"Where are they?" Garren forced his emotions down deep.

"He will take them through the Reave, is my bet. It is the only place not guarded by either side."

The Reave. The narrow ravine that divided two hills to the north of the First Division. It used to be a robbers' paradise where foolish travelers were taken, before the For'bane came and turned the lands into a bloody battleground. Garren nodded. "I need to get a few things," he informed the Commander.

"They will be leaving within the hour."

Chapter 16

Commander Strell strode ahead of the seven recruits. Carter and Ora took up the rear, as the only archers in the troop.

"Why do I get the feeling we are being sent on a suicide mission?" Carter spoke low to Ora.

Ora kept her gaze straight ahead, watching the Commander's broad back. "Shut up, Carter," she urged.

Carter grasped her arm. "Just whose orders are we supposed to be following? This man, Strell, is not our Commander and I have a suspicion Commander Kane does not know anything about this."

Ora pulled out of his grip and glanced at him. "Keep your voice down," she insisted. "I know. Whatever the reasons, I will get us out of this."

Carter lowered his tone to match hers. "We are being sent in without an escort. We are not soldiers, Ora, not really. They have to know that."

"Exactly," Ora answered. She watched the Commander's back again, not wanting him or the other recruits between them to be alerted of their conversation. "We can escape and no one will stop us, or even know. They will just assume we were killed."

Carter's eyes widened at the realization. He looked to the Commander, then back at Ora. "What about the Singers? They will shoot us as runners."

"If our own Commander does not know, I suspect the Singers do not know about this either. They will not be watching for us here. They would expect us to run for the Freelands, or elsewhere, not into enemy territory."

The troop slowed at the appearance of the two sharply rising hills close together and a rocky ravine that passed between them. As they drew nearer, a figure appeared on one of the high boulders at the Reave's entrance.

Commander Strell stopped and the others followed his lead.

Ora felt her skin grow cold. Her last spark of hope went out in a puff of smoke as she looked ahead to identify the figure. Captain Garren crouched on the boulder with the grace of a panther—a calm casual air, though his good eye glittered dangerously as he looked at the Commander. So much for the Singers not knowing. Did they have to be everywhere?

"Good, you are all here," Garren spoke smoothly. "Are these the best you have? You must be struggling more than you let on." He slid his longcurve Singers bow into one hand and absentmindedly slid two fingers down the string, creating a soft familiar hum.

Ora looked at the Commander. She could see the profile of his face and the way a light sweat suddenly beaded his forehead and upper lip. He had not expected to see Garren, though he tried to sound unconcerned. "Captain, I thought you would be out fighting some Skays or taking down a Trooper somewhere."

Garren stood. "You forget, Commander, I do not obey your orders."

Challenge lay thick in the air.

Garren replaced his bow abruptly and sprang down lightly and effortlessly from the boulder, a jump none of them would have made without injury. "Let us not waste time, then. Keep the lookouts posted. We will be back." His final tone left no room for argument, though Ora doubted the Commander would dare try.

The troop looked at each other in silent question, but followed Garren past the Commander, who stood by stiffly without another word.

Garren led them deeper into the Reave.

"So much for your plan," Carter whispered to Ora.

Once out of the Commander's sight, Garren stopped by the opening to an earthen cavern in the left side ridge. "If you want to survive," he began firmly, turning to face them, "you will do exactly as I say." He reached down and withdrew a large bundle and dropped it with a muffled clatter at their feet. "Starting with these."

The troop stared in fascination. Weapons. But not only ordinary stock weaponry. Nothing made by the blacksmiths in camp. Some made of fine-crafted steel, others of sharpened bone, and longcurve bows of wood reinforced in the middle with bone and steel.

"I had the pleasure of removing these from a few of our enemy—supplies headed for the line. If you survive this little mission, you may keep the weapon you choose."

"Is this a test?" spoke one of the older boys.

Garren smirked. "It is not exactly in my best interest to kill you right now, is it?"

The troop glanced at each other, wondering at the validity of the question. No one trusted a Singer.

Ora stepped forward first and bent to lift her selection from the lot. She straightened, keeping her gaze steadily on Garren. He looked at her for the first time.

"I accept your terms, Captain," she said simply, firmly.

His gaze moved to the bow she held in her hand. Something distant and unfamiliar churned in his gaze. His lips thinned, but then he nodded.

"Belle," he acknowledged her quietly—the second time he called her by that name.

She waited to feel hatred set in. It did not come. Perhaps, after days of fighting, she had grown weary of her constant anger. With so much at stake, surviving had become more important than anger. And something about his expression gave her pause. In that moment, he looked so human—so normal—she had to remind herself he was a monster. A beast.

Standing closer to him while the others still stood back, she spoke the question on her mind so only he heard her. "Why are you helping us?" She almost did not realize she had spoken aloud, so aware of her thoughts—so verbal in her mind—but she saw his expression change. A strange, uncharacteristic softness came to his eye, his lips parted—an expression so fleeting and so quickly concealed that she felt out of breath with the memory of it. Then his jaw tightened, his gaze hardened, and he turned to the others as if he had not heard her.

Unnerved and wishing she had not said anything, Ora picked up a new quiver of steel-tipped arrows and turned her attention to strapping it on. The others followed her lead and chose their own weapons.

"Leave your old weapons here," Garren instructed. "Move out." He motioned to the ridges on each side of them. "Keep an eye out. Archers behind, on each side, swordsmen in the middle. And keep quiet."

Chapter 17

The group made slow progress as Garren kept the lead. Relaxing his shoulder muscles, he trusted his senses to alert him if the For'bane came upon them. Those senses had kept him alive these many years.

By late morning, the air turned damp and warm. Clouds darkened the woods they traveled through on the other side of the Reave.

"Eyes to the trees," Garren spoke quietly as he circled back suddenly to the archers. He caught Ora in a brief glance, the first since they had begun. She looked at him strangely, as if she could not quite decide on his character.

He quickly squashed the thought that she might possibly come to understand him, though for a moment he let himself consider it. To have someone, even just *one* someone, see him as a man again and not a monster.

He turned aside from her and drew his Singers bow into his hands. He crouched and the others followed his lead, scanning the tree limbs high above their heads. Garren watched Carter and Ora draw their bowstrings taut, arrows steady and set to release. They showed strength and ability after only four days at the Divisions. Garren slid his fingers down the bow, letting the soft wind carry his faint song into the air. Tree leaves shivered. A quiet grunt reached their ears.

At once, in a move fast as lightning, Garren reached back over his shoulder for an arrow, set it, aimed high into a tree some fifteen yards ahead of them, and released. A dark form fell to the tree's base with a thud, its guttural cry cut short.

Other cries began to sound in response, high in the tree tops with some ahead and some behind—seeming all around them.

"Look up! They come from above, so guard your heads," Garren barked. "And stay together!"

Then they saw them. Some landed around them; some sprang like giant monkeys from tree to tree in order to get in position above the troop.

Garren counted nine, not including the one he had killed.

The six on the ground circled closer. Round faces with yellow-brown skin, shaped much like monkeys, with flat nostrils that seemed to sink into their skulls, and large round black eyes. They screeched and bared mouths full of narrow, sharp pointed teeth, drooling saliva as they screamed at the recruits. They crept closer, using short and awkward movements in a stealthy and almost shy manner, though their threatening demeanor said otherwise.

"Do we shoot?" Ora spoke above the shrieking. "What are they?"

Garren eyed their behavior. "Muels. Their teeth will tear the skin from your bones. Aim for the stomach. They are weakest now, we awoke them. Keep clear of their heads!"

The one nearest Ora took a bold step closer and shrieked. Ora let an arrow fly, piercing its five-foot body straight through.

Chaos erupted. Shrieks filled the air as the Muels on the ground charged. Garren quickly shot up at the closest tree

Muel. Its body landed at his feet and he kicked it away, creating a temporary obstacle against an approaching ground Muel.

Down to seven. Five on the ground and two still in the trees.

One of Ora's arrows took down another tree Muel. The oldest boy swung his sword, slicing through the midsection of the Muel coming at him.

Someone screamed and from the corner of his eye, Garren saw one of the boys go down, dragged away from the group. He shot the Muel quickly, already knowing it was too late for the boy.

"Carter!" Ora screamed and her voice shot through Garren like lightening, jerking him around. The last tree Muel launched itself from a lower branch and landed on the boy archer, throwing him onto his back in the dirt.

Carter used both arms, trying to fend off the creature's massive jaws as Ora shot it with an arrow. However, its toughened hide took the arrow in its side. The Muel barely registered the hit, intent on its victim.

Garren sprang across the distance toward the Muel standing over Carter, drawing the bone knife he had kept after his confrontation with the Skays. He slashed outward at the Muel's face, striking it across the side of its head.

The Muel staggered back, stunned and confused by the unexpected blow. It shook its head and raised a clawed hand to its face. Seeing blood on its hand, it shrieked in panic, and swerved to search out its attacker.

Garren went down on one knee and drew an arrow against his bow. He took aim as the Muel lurched toward him. Only feet away, he shot at once. The Muel dropped, instantly dead. Everything went silent and still. Garren heard his own breath, his pulse pounding fast with adrenaline.

He saw Ora, already at Carter's side, her hands pressed against the boy's bloodied and torn shoulder as Carter winced and gritted his teeth. So, the boy lived. But once infection set in, how long?

Ora caught his gaze, hers hinting at a mixture of fear and relief. Not anger. Not hatred. Perhaps gratefulness?

In the next moment, a flash of movement drew Garren's eye. He saw one of the boys making a hasty retreat for the deeper wood and instinctively drew an arrow.

"No!" he heard Ora's shout even as he let the arrow fly and it hit the boy in the back, between the shoulder blades. With a half-cry of death, the boy crumpled.

His gaze swept over the remaining recruits as they all froze, afraid to move lest Garren suspect them of trying to run as well.

Ora, Carter, and two other boys remained. Only four of the original seven. If they made it to the morrow, it would be a miracle.

Chapter 18

"He should not have run," Carter managed, his breath sharp with the pain of his injuries. "He should have waited…."

Ora pulled herself from her tangled thoughts of anger and heartache. For a moment she had felt relieved to have Garren with them—to have his fierce battle skills on their side.

Her mother's long-ago warning came to mind: *'Never trust a soldier. Never.'*

She focused on Carter, whose forehead had broken out in a sheen of sweat, and gently brushed his fan of blond hair back with one hand, the other still pressed against his shoulder. "Shh," she murmured, as Garren approached. She forced a tender smile at Carter, wanting to soothe his distress, even as her eyes stung with tears.

Garren's shadow fell over them.

Ora looked up at him at last. "I am not leaving him," she declared firmly. "You will have to kill me too."

Garren's jaw tightened. He hunkered down on one knee. "Get back and let me see," he ordered in his quiet, commanding voice.

Already, Carter's gaze grew dazed as the pain sent him into a semi-conscious state.

Garren's powerful body, so near to hers, forced Ora to shift away as Garren pressed his hands over and around the boy's shoulder.

Ora focused on his hands, not daring to meet the Captain's gaze again—too afraid of what he would say. He had strong hands. Capable and tanned, fingers slender like an scholar but calloused from life as a soldier. *He is all I have in this world,* she found herself silently confessing of Carter. Her gaze lifted to the profile of Garren's face. *You cannot let him die.*

Garren glanced at her and she felt the uncertain and uncomfortable sensation he knew her thoughts as if she had spoken them aloud. The blue-grey of his good eye deepened, and Ora felt trapped in his gaze—drawn in against her will. "I will not slow down for him," he warned, breaking the bond between them sharply. "Get him on his feet. Infection is setting in and we leave now before the other Muels sense it."

Dread filled Ora's heart. "What do you mean?"

Warning filled Garren's face. "His wound has been infected with their scent, from their saliva—it is a distinctive odor. It marks him as their prey. It will alert any nearby For'bane of our position. If the wound does not kill him, something worse will."

Garren glanced around the forest floor and dug through the leaves to produce a handful of moss and earth. He smeared and packed the mixture against Carter's shoulder. "This will stop the blood flow." He turned and called to the oldest recruit, Kee. "You. Get over here and help him up." He stood as Kee sheathed his sword and hastened over. "Belle, you take the rear. And do not forget your arrows."

He strode off to get his long arrow from the fallen boy's back.

Ora lightly slapped Carter's cheek. "Stay with me, Carter. You can do this. You have to get up. We will help you."

"You are not going to let me die?" Carter's quiet, sleepy voice held a hint of surprise.

"Of course not, Carter. I will never leave you," Ora insisted and helped pull him upright to lean against Kee, draping his arm across Kee's shoulders.

"I have him," Kee insisted. "Better not keep the Captain waiting or he is liable to shoot us all for tardiness." She heard the bitterness in his tone.

"I am sorry," she murmured, looking at him a moment in understanding.

But Kee shook his head slightly and looked away. "It is not your doing."

Ora retrieved her bow and arrows, wiping the steel star tips in the leaves and grass, and took her place behind Carter and Kee, with the other boy—Bev—between them and Garren. They moved quickly, as a roll of thunder warned of fast approaching rain.

Ora placed an arrow against her bow, though not drawn, as they traveled. If anything came after Carter, she would be ready to pierce its heart.

Chapter 19

The rain started, steady and heavy, turning the earth to sludge beneath their feet. Wearing boots, Garren managed without much trouble, but those with him struggled and stumbled to keep up in their simple leather shoes. Carter sagged between Kee and Bev now, nearly unconscious.

Satisfied that at least the rain washed away their trail and faded most of the kill scent left by the Muel on Carter, Garren slowed near a river. He eyed the expanse of it. The rain caused it to swell against the muddy banks and the water flowed quickly. On the other side, a clearing nestled against the side of a steep, rocky-ridged hill. He turned back to the group behind him, using his right arm to motion while the other held the hilt of his sheathed sword in a comfortable grip. "We rest there for the night," he spoke above the downpour. "Watch your step."

He moved out first, wading until the water reached his upper thighs, about halfway to the other side. He stopped and turned to let Kee and Bev pass, supporting Carter between them, and noted how deathly pale the boy archer had become. His head sagged in unconscious oblivion.

Garren's gaze switched to Ora, coming just behind, as her foot slipped on a hole beneath the water. Immediately, his hand shot out and caught her arm beneath the elbow, drawing her up so she would not fall beneath the surface.

Standing so, her face lifted toward his in surprise, he had a moment to study her. Rain poured down their faces, plastering their hair. Hers fell over one shoulder in an unraveling braid—shorter tendrils clinging to her cheeks. Her lips and cheeks flushed a rosy hue from the chill of the air and raindrops clung to her full dark eyelashes.

She looked away and pulled back from his grasp. He released her at once, hand sliding away from the softness of her skin. She moved on without a word, adjusting her quiver, upset from the stumble. Unobserved, Garren closed his hand into a fist, composing his features back to stone.

They made it to the far side moments later. Beneath a thick overhanging oak tree, Kee and Bev found a dry place to settle Carter.

Garren, seeing that Ora went at once to tend to her friend, moved away to scout the surroundings without a word. While the rain kept their scent clear of the For'bane, it also washed out the enemies' scents so Garren had a harder time knowing if anything came close.

He moved through the woods with the silence of a panther, looking for disturbances in the leaves or marks on the trees signaling another presence.

Muels kept watch over terrains and roadways and sometimes went ahead of the enemy to clear the way for new nests. Their calls would alert their troops in the area of any trespassers.

Finding nothing to cause alarm, he climbed to the ridge of the hill to decide on a place to rest where he could have the advantage of sight to the clearing below. Thick with trees, he found raised roots between two oaks that formed a perfect archer's post, still dry and protected from the now bitter wind and ceaseless rain. He sat back against one of the roots, facing the ridge and clearing below, and put his head in his hands, pressing away the tension at his temples.

Despite what others thought of him, every time he took an innocent's life, it sickened him. He remembered their faces. He held himself responsible. Why did they still insist on running when he warned them time and again what would happen if they tried?

He uncorked the vial of powder around his neck and shook out a few flecks onto his tongue, letting them dissolve and washing them down with a swig of water from his waterskin. He lifted his eyepatch to his forehead and leaned back, tracing a finger lightly down his jagged scar, waiting for the pain to fade—knowing a deeper, more internal pain that never would.

Chapter 20

Ora covered Carter with the blanket from her kit and then rolled up his to serve as a pillow for his head. With nothing dry enough for a fire, they all huddled side-by-side beneath the protection of the tree as the sky darkened and created haunting shadows of the wood.

"Where is the Captain?" muttered Kee, on Ora's other side as she snuggled against Carter, trying to warm him as he shivered. She had cleaned his wound the best she could, the rain having done a fair job already. He had become feverish, and she feared for him greatly.

Turning her mind back to Kee's question, she whispered back: "I do not know. But I am sure he is there. Even if we cannot see him, I am certain he can see us."

Kee responded with silence.

Ora lay on her back and stared at the tree limbs above, growing ever darker and nondescript as night fell. "Did you know them well? The soldiers who died today?"

The eighteen-year-old's answer came tersely, "No. Only the one the Captain shot." A long tense silence passed and Ora nearly held her breath, waiting. "He was my brother."

Anguish rushed through her and she wished she knew what to say. She had never lost a sibling, though she had grown up with Carter and could not bear the thought of losing him—so she assumed it was something of the same. 'I am sorry' did not do the loss justice, and Ora let the silence linger long enough that to say anything at all would feel awkward. Then she heard Kee shift away onto his side, signaling an end to any further conversation.

Ora sighed very faintly and slid her hand beneath the blanket covering Carter to find his hand. "Do not leave me, Carter," she whispered near his ear, squeezing his chilled fingers. "I do not think I could bear it." She lay her head gently on his chest and closed her eyes, hoping sleep would offer a respite from her misery.

Hours later, uncomfortable yet finally warm as the body heat on each side soaked into her, Ora awoke to movement beneath her head. She felt Carter's breathing increase and heard a low moan of pain and quickly righted herself to look down on him. "Carter," she whispered, seeing only the outline of him in the grey darkness.

"Ora," his soft voice answered back, tinged with pain. "What has happened? Where are we?"

Quietly, Ora filled him in from the time he had been hurt, to the boy being killed trying to escape, and to making camp for the night. The rain stopped at last and only the occasional drip-drop of condensation falling from the shivering leaves broke nature's stillness.

"Where is the Captain now?" Carter murmured, shivering from his fever.

Ora felt his brow, still warm but not as hot as before. There at least, she could feel some relief. "He sleeps in a tree, for all I know," she answered his question dryly.

"I think I see him. There, on the ridge," Carter said.

Ora looked up. The darkness turned to a softer grey, so she knew dawn could be only hours away. She could see an outline of a man near the base of a tree and the top of his bow propped up near him.

"Is he asleep? Can you tell?" Carter whispered.

"I do not know…maybe…." Ora watched Garren's form and saw no movement.

Carter gripped her hand, drawing her attention. "We have to get out of here, Ora. If we do not leave, we may never get another chance."

Ora shook her head negatively. "No, Carter. It will never work now with the Captain here. He will just hunt us down and shoot us in the back. Besides, you are in no condition to run anywhere."

Carter shook his head weakly in return. "I can make it. I am feeling better already," he lied. "You have to make sure he cannot chase after us…."

Ora grew very still, while inwardly her heart began to race. She could see her friend's face now in the grey light. "What are you saying, Carter?"

Carter's voice went nearly below a whisper this time, but she felt his urgency. "You have to kill him…."

Though she had anticipated those very words, hearing them spoken made her stomach twist in revulsion. "There—there has to be another way," she began, hesitant.

"We will die if we stay here. The Captain is just looking for an excuse. You saw what happened to that boy. What he did—."

"He saved your life," Ora felt inclined to remind him.

"Are you on his side now? I thought you hated him," Carter insisted.

"No!" Ora's whisper sounded louder than necessary. Quickly, she glanced up at the ridge. Did a Singer have enhanced hearing? She hoped not. She lowered her voice further still. "I mean, no, I am not on his side." Inwardly, she concluded, *I have just never killed another human being before.*

She could not show weakness in this. Carter spoke true. She had promised to take care of them; to protect them. No one said it would not get messy. But could she succeed? Barely trained and going up against the only ranked Singer in the King's Army?

Carter needed help now, not to be forced deeper into enemy territory, to fight and die for nothing.

Ora saw the pain and paleness in Carter's features. She steeled herself for what would come, and brushed a hand down his cheek. "Rest your eyes now."

Carter's face contorted with worry. "Be careful."

Ora reached for her bow and quiver above where her head had lain. She crouched, tugging an arrow free to place against the bow as she slipped a few feet away into the shadows beside the trunk of their sheltering tree.

Her fingers trembled as she drew back and aimed for Garren's place on the ridge. He was too far; too deeply bedded down within the roots of the trees and in the shadows. She glanced up along the hillside to the ridge, lowering the bow silently.

"Ora," she heard Carter whisper in question as she returned to his side.

"Be quiet," she hushed, laying a hand briefly on his shoulder. She reached for her kit that she had used as a pillow, keeping an eye on the others in case they caused a stir and interfered with her plans, as well as watching to see if the Captain gave any sign of wakefulness on the ridge.

She withdrew her knife from the satchel and slipped around the far side of the great oak tree to softly climb the slope to where Garren lay, leaving her bow and arrows behind. The trees and surroundings were too dense and shadowed for her to feel at all confident of piercing him with an arrow. This would have to be up close, swift, and sure. Her heart pounded, making her breath shorter, and the climb seem longer.

Killing Garren would not be easy, yet she wondered if she'd have the nerve to try it. If she failed, they were all dead. One minute she hated the Singer Captain and scorned him, but in the very next she felt confused by him—this man who killed but also rescued. The man who insisted she receive medicine she had not earned, while criticizing her lack of abilities with the bow.

She hated herself for having mixed emotions at all. He was a killer, and he had stolen them away from their homes, bringing them out here to die in an ugly War. Letting that bitterness surface made it easier to contemplate what had to be done.

She forced her breathing to slow as she came upon Garren, taking cautious steps forward. In the grey light, he lay on his back, left shoulder and head cushioned by the top of a root pushing up from the soil near a tree. She gripped the knife, knowing she would have to go for his throat. She would only have one chance.

She noticed he had removed his eyepatch. She had never seen a one-eyed man. What did he look like with one missing eye? She crept closer—the damp, soft earth making it easy to move without a sound.

She did not know what happened exactly. The next few moments all seemed to collide in a frightening blur of motion. She was several feet away from him, silent as a mouse, when all at once Garren jerked upward from a seemingly sound sleep and lurched forward. His arm shot out and he shoved her onto her back beneath him, the weight of his body pressed down on top of her, hand wrapped around her throat.

His eye blazed to life in the shadows. His *missing* eye. It was not missing at all, but glowed a bright yellow.

Ora opened her mouth to scream in fear and horror, but his choking hold on her throat prevented the sound. Pinned beneath him, she struggled in panic to pull air into her lungs, staring at his fierce gaze and wondering if this is how it all ended.

His other hand grasped her wrist, pinning her arm to the ground above her head and forcing her to release the dagger.

"Did you think I did not know?" Garren growled in a dangerously low tone. "That you wanted me dead?"

His face was so close to hers, his normal eye looked nearly black in the grey light. She fought for air in vain, choking.

"Your thoughts; your *fear*…they are like a toxin on your skin. I can smell it," Garren continued and Ora began to tremble in terror. "You want to see the monster? Well, take a good look."

A tear squeezed out the corner of her eye and rolled down the side of her face. The anger in Garren's gaze faded, as did the glow in his discolored eye, and he slowly loosened his grip from her throat. She felt the warm callouses against her skin as his fingers slid down her neck. With the release, she gasped for air, lungs burning as she coughed and choked and more tears stung her eyes.

She turned her head away, silently begging for him to move away from her. She had never known a man's body and his was entirely too close for comfort—igniting her imagination toward dangerous and frightening paths.

He answered her unspoken plea and abruptly rolled away from her, coming up in a sitting position, partly turned away.

Ora stared at his broad back when he did not move or speak. "You are a murderer," she managed, voice strained, getting her breath back.

"And killing me," Garren replied tersely, adjusting the patch back over his eye. He looked over his shoulder. "How would that make you any different?"

Hope failed her and she looked down, hand gently massaging her throat. The pressure of his hand would leave a bruise for sure. They could never escape now. She had failed. "Bron was right—you *are* a monster."

Garren sucked in a sharp breath and turned to face her. "Bron?" he spat the name. "I should have known." His gaze turned to flint. "He finds it far too easy to hide who he is—even when that means sacrificing all conviction."

Ora did not have the courage to challenge him. To ask what he meant. She had not meant to say those last words aloud. They just came out. She cleared her throat nervously. "So…what are you going to do to me?"

Garren stared at her. "How is your friend? His fever is breaking."

Ora's eyes widened. "How do you know that?" she murmured uncertainly.

Garren's lips pulled tight in a smirk. He crouched and stood, lifting his Singers bow. "I know a lot of things. Call it…advanced intuition." He stood over her and extended his free hand to her.

Ora looked at him in mistrust. Garren stood still, his features tensing, gaze like stone. Emotionally withdrawing.

Swallowing back her fear, she lifted her chin and reached up to touch his fingers. He pulled her to her feet and released her.

"Carter needs a healer," she said. "He might die otherwise. We need to turn back."

"Why should his life be more important than this mission?" Garren answered with disinterest. "Why should I care about *his* life?"

Ora spoke with a quick breath of insane bravery: "Because we all have a choice—to be monsters or men. It is not a matter of blood, but a condition of the heart. And I do not think you want to be a monster." She raised her chin with a look of challenge.

Garren's gaze narrowed slightly. He picked up her knife from where it lay in the dirt. "You are a little fool," he said coldly, but then a certain thoughtfulness changed the tone of his voice and softened the chill in his eyes. "A brave little fool, I will give you that." He held her gaze and she found she could not look away. He offered the hilt of the knife to her, holding the blade end flat against his hand.

She took it, surprised.

"To answer your question," he continued smoothly, evasively. "No, I will not kill you." He dropped his hand and took a step back, gaze growing cold once more. "Now, get out of my sight before I change my mind."

Chapter 21

Dawn came fast and Garren stayed awake to meet it. Sleep evaded him in the short time following his unusual conversation with Ora. Her words about monsters and men struck him deeply.

'I do not think you want to be a monster....'

His jaw tightened as he leaned back against the base of the tree, keeping an eye on the troop below for signs of movement. He watched Ora return to her place between Carter and Kee, and felt her grow quiet in rest, though he knew she did not sleep.

He had surprised her by recognizing Carter's condition from a distance, knowing his fever was breaking. Sensing a person's emotions did not come easily and he certainly could not read thoughts. It took concentration, and even his heightened senses could be only so reliable. But with Ora, he felt a connection to her and could sense her emotions more powerfully. He had felt her hate; her disappointment when she had learned he would come with them, and the pull of fear and anger as she had plotted his death. The anxiety of planning to kill another human being was different than any other emotion—especially from her.

She had a goodness about her. She wanted to protect people, not harm them—something he had not seen in a very long time, nor felt for himself. To her, fighting meant more than survival, it meant sacrifice for those she cared about. It meant saving them.

She stood up to him, trying to save Carter. Fear had not stopped her from trying. She had been terrified, especially after seeing his discolored eye—he had not meant for her to see that—and his reflex to choke her.

Curse him for admiring that. No matter how much he tried to dislike her—tried not to care—he felt like a moth drawn to flames. He could not refuse her request. Even if she persisted in hating him, he feared he would not be able to refuse her anything.

Morning light glinted like gold off rainwater still clinging to the high-limbed leaves, as Garren rose and descended the hill into the clearing. At his approach, the recruits began to stir and their movement startled a grey tree squirrel nearby.

Garren drew his bow and shot an arrow straight through its eye. Legs spread out in a reflexive run, the squirrel dropped dead at the feet of the group. The whoosh and strike of the arrow brought them upright in an instant.

Garren approached and pulled out his arrow, then sheathed his bow. "Breakfast," he informed stiffly, and walked away to the river without catching their gazes—not even Ora.

From the corner of his eye, he watched them rise. Carter moved more slowly. The others went to find dry underbrush and pull together the makings of a fire to cook the squirrel over. Carter prepared the squirrel, while keeping a wary and distrustful eye on Garren.

He disliked Carter for several reasons, but most recently for this last incident of sending Ora to kill him. The boy should have prevented that or done the deed himself, showing weakness on Carter's part. The only reason Garren saved the boy's life was because Ora's heartfelt cry had spurred him into action. What had Ora told Carter, anyway, of her failed assassination attempt?

Garren knelt by the water's edge to fill his waterskin, while his gaze swept the landscape back the way they'd come. When he returned to the campsite, the squirrel sizzled on a hastily constructed spit over low flames. Fat dripped and hissed as it splattered over red hot coals. He noticed Carter had given the skin to Ora. "We are going back," he stated gruffly, as the small group huddled around the meager flames and prepared to eat. They stared at him in surprise.

"Going back?" Kee repeated. "Why would you care to turn back now?" He glanced toward Carter.

"Because I cannot infiltrate a For'bane nest with you four stumbling behind me," Garren bit out cooly. "I need skilled fighters, not an overgrown farm boy whose best skill is talking back instead of wielding a sword."

Kee glowered, and Garren felt more than saw Ora's silent relief that he had not placed the blame on Carter's injury.

Brave little fool, he silently lectured her once more. Did she not know the only reason he did not bring Carter into it was for purely selfish reasons? That he did not want the others seeing it as weakness on his part? That Ora's persuasion had made him change his mind?

They quickly finished off the squirrel meat, packed their blankets, and took up their weapons. They followed after Garren, who meanwhile had waded out into the river.

He altered their route somewhat, trying to avoid another run-in with the Muels. They moved slowly as Carter grew tired easily. Sometimes Garren moved further ahead, then back-trailed to rejoin them. He did not speak to them and no one dared try to run while he was out of their sights, remembering the fate of the last boy who ran.

Garren's muscles ached from lack of proper rest, but he almost relished the pain. It gave him something to occupy his thoughts, a way to filter his rage and put aside his mixed emotions concerning Ora.

By noon, a heat wave hit—drawn from last night's rainfall—and the troop's steps grew weary and sluggish. Garren forced his own steps to slow, wary of the easy targets they made—another reason he preferred working alone.

Another hour passed. Garren, slightly ahead once more, crouched at the peak of a heavily treed hill. The way appeared clear. They were close to the Divisions. But a prickle of apprehension crawled up his spine. Just as he prepared to move on, a slight movement caught his ready eye.

At the edge of thick brush down in the valley, a Sniffer moved slowly, blending with the shadows and foliage, heading in their direction.

Garren silently drew an arrow, without his usual Singer's warning, aiming for the Sniffer's eye. He froze as more warnings triggered his senses, and he saw movement from several positions down the hill.

Skays. At least three that he could see, though he imagined it very likely there were more. Their behavior suggested a hunt, with his troop as the targets. How? Had one of the Muels gotten away and alerted the For'bane of their presence? Or, like wolves drawn by blood, had they been drawn to the human presence and Carter's injuries?

For the first time in a very long time, Garren's anger felt justified. And directed specifically at Commander Strell for wanting them to fail. He had wanted them to die, just to keep the War going on as it always had—with more lives lost every day.

Garren immediately retreated in perfect silence, holding the bow and arrow in one hand as he hurried back to his charges. They did not have much time. As he approached, they saw his tense features and halted. “This way. Now,” he said in a low, sharp tone, motioning with his bow. They quickly followed his long-legged stride off the path, into the thicker trees, and crouched low behind the brush.

Somehow, Ora ended up close by Garren’s shoulder. “What is it?” she barely whispered.

In a better position, he could see the path they had just traveled, to the place the enemy would surely appear. The others stayed flat to the ground behind him, unaware of the conversation, while Garren watched. He quietly answered Ora’s inquiry, “Skays.”

She was close enough for him to feel her breath—and the awareness of her heartbeat that haunted him every time she stood nearby. He sensed her shudder and glanced at her sharply. “You have faced one before, I take it,” he said dryly.

Her heart beat fast and loud in his ears. He needed her calm and rational. So, against his calloused nature, he softened his defenses against her. If he could hear her heartbeat, the Sniffer could too—if it got close enough.

“Belle,” he murmured to get her attention.

She met his gaze, wary.

“I am going to need your help.”

“I cannot fight a Skay, not up close. I…I already tried. I failed,” she stammered.

In a subtle, quick move, Garren reached over and gripped Ora’s hand. He felt the soft trembling there. She flinched and he chose to ignore it and the guilt it gave him.

“If that Sniffer gets too close, you are all dead,” he warned. “He will sense your fear as I sense it now.”

She stared at him for a moment. He hated reminding her that he was a beast. He hated it more than ever before. He had almost grown comfortable in this second skin; this other side of himself. The loner and the monster.

But now, in some powerful, mystical way, she had begun to chip away at the monster and remind him of the man of flesh that existed underneath.

"I need a second archer," he said firmly, drowning out his own thoughts. "And you are all I have."

Chapter 22

'You are all I have.' Strange words, coming from the lips of this man. His tone had not sounded like it was meant as an insult. His gaze held confidence as he looked at her. She felt no anger now. The past seemed, in the moment at least, to hold little importance. Nearly forgotten. If only one's past could be so easily forgiven and erased. For now, at least, it really did not matter. They were partners in a mutual need to survive.

Garren glanced behind him. He pulled his hand away about the same instant she realized he still held hers. "Stay put," he said to the others.

With the gravity of the situation, not even Kee issued an argument. Carter nodded slightly to acknowledge the order, looking weary enough to pass out at any moment. Ora gave her friend an encouraging half-smile, hoping it convinced him. She felt anything but hopeful, and far from encouraged.

Garren caught her gaze and inclined his head slightly in the direction they would go. She followed him in a stealthy crouch away from the rest of the group, all the while trying to steel her nerves.

She tried to think with the strength Garren possessed, to feel his confidence, with the realization that through his strength she might survive this. Because, right now, he no longer represented the nightmare—the Skays did—and Garren represented salvation.

"Where are they? What do you want me to do?"

"We have to lure them away from your friends, keep them occupied," Garren said.

Ora had an idea of what he meant. Once, when still a girl, she had watched a mother bird defend its nest of hatchlings from a passing cat. It feigned injury to its leg and cried piteously as it lured the cat away from the nest. Unfortunately, in that instance, all did not end well for the mother bird, who got killed by a second cat waiting nearby. So, while the mother bird saved its hatchlings from the cats, they later starved for lack of a mother.

"So, we are the bait?" Ora guessed.

Moving in a wide, half-circle back to the trail, while watching for the approaching Sniffer and Skays, Garren stopped a moment and turned to face her squarely, standing close as Ora stopped abruptly to keep from running into him. "No, you are," he corrected gravely. "They cannot sense me."

I am the bait, she thought with renewed fear. *I am the bird, luring the cats away from the nest.* Would this end the same way?

He stared at her hard. She could almost hear his cold, taunting voice once again: *'Are you going to cry?'*

She calmed herself and her features with a slow, silent breath and a subtle raise of her chin. "Then we should not waste any more time. They will be here soon."

He moved to the base of a tree, the closest branch a good seven feet up, and slung his bow over one shoulder. "I am going to give you a boost. Are you ready?"

Ora watched him crouch down on one knee and link his hands together in front of him. No time to hesitate. She braced one hand on his brawny, solid shoulder for balance and placed her soft leather-shoed foot in his hands.

He stood quickly, effortlessly, and leveraged her straight up toward the branch. She grabbed hold and pulled herself up on it.

Garren looked up at her from below. "Climb as high as you can. Skays can jump up to twenty feet."

"Can they climb?" she asked, still holding his gaze.

"Just aim for the head or throat."

Ora tensed. "And what will you do?"

"I will be nearby," Garren answered shortly and turned away.

Do not abandon us, she silently demanded at his retreating back before he disappeared from sight. How could she feel such mistrust toward him, while at the same time be so hopelessly reliant on him? When he looked at her as he had just done, with that strange expression in his eye, she almost believed a real man existed inside.

The sound of a Singers bow jarred her from her thoughts. Garren. And close by, just as he had said. She hastened to climb further up the tree, using hands and feet against tree knots and branches.

She could hear them coming now, a crackle of the underbrush; the disturbance of scattering leaves—drawn by Garren's song and catching Ora's scent.

Ora slipped on one of her footholds and nearly lost her grip, as the excited shrieks below signaled that the Sniffer and Skays had found her. She pulled herself onto a sturdy branch and leaned her shoulder against the trunk for balance. She reached for an arrow from her quiver and drew her bow. She hoped she had climbed high enough.

The Sniffer held back while the Skay nearest the base of the tree leapt upward, trying to reach Ora. Two Skays behind it followed suit, running into each other in a mad scramble to reach her. They reminded her of rabid dogs fighting over a hunk of meat, only much worse than a pack of dogs.

She aimed her first arrow carefully at the closest Skay, whose great jump reached very close to the branch she stood upon, clawing and grasping at the trunk in an attempt to get higher. Her heart slammed against her rib cage.

Do not miss, she silently commanded, took a breath and released the arrow. She could not tell exactly where it hit, but the Skay screamed and tumbled down, lost in the stampede for the tree as the others climbed over it.

She felt the tree creaking and groaning against their onslaught and managed to put another arrow in the second Skay, sending it to the ground where it writhed and grew still.

Two more came at the tree. They were gaining.

An arrow whizzed out of nowhere and struck one of the Skays straight through the eye as it attempted to climb the tree.

Garren appeared in a blur of motion in the midst of them, moving with the fierceness of a panther. He swung his drawn blade and sliced through the mid-section of the Sniffer, nearly severing it in half.

Ora flinched at his sudden and violent appearance, but could not look away—stunned. Within moments, Garren stood over a pile of dead For'bane, stained with streaks of blood, breathing hard, expression fierce.

Not sure she should move—or even if she could—Ora shifted her position cautiously, gripping a branch above her head tightly with one hand, her bow held in the other.

Garren looked up at the crack and rustle of leaves. "Come down, Belle," he spoke with quiet firmness.

Carefully shifting her feet, she secured her bow over her quiver at her back and began the tedious effort of climbing back down. Her arms and legs ached from tension and fear and from the climb up. She slipped off a lower branch so suddenly she did not have a chance to cry out.

She fell flat on her back onto the ground, her breath leaving her in a sharp rush. Stars and a flash of white light blinded her vision for an instant. Then suddenly, Garren knelt over her, his face close to hers. She stared into his fierce blue-grey eye. The splatters of blood made him all the more frightening. His hand went to the back of her head, cradling it.

"Belle," his voice sounded desperate. His gaze changed from the intensity of battle and rage to one of concern and fear—the blue of his eye offsetting the grey. "Belle, are you all right?"

Ora blinked, still in shock. As she realized Garren's closeness she told herself to jerk away but a wave of dizziness made her instinctively move closer to his strength. Her hands grasped his arms as he gently lifted her into a sitting position and her head dropped forward to brush against his shoulder.

For a strange, surreal moment, she hid her face against his shoulder in relief and he held her in wordless reassurance. She heard—could even feel—the thundering of his heartbeat, still racing with adrenaline.

Then, she remembered: Only hours ago she had tried to kill him—and he had come very close to killing her.

She straightened away from him. "All right," she said, meeting his gaze uncertainly. "I am all right." She wondered how well he read her tumultuous thoughts and emotions.

For a moment, everything seemed to grow still. Ora stared at Garren, amazed at the gentleness of his hold; the tender look in his eye. He had saved their lives. Again.

"Who are you, really?" she murmured out loud.

Garren touched the pad of his thumb against her lips, as if to shush her. His gaze darkened and he drew back, rising to his feet. He drew Ora to her feet as well and she saw the emotional wall rise over his expression. "You do not want to know," he said in a low, dark tone.

They hurried back to the group in silence, Ora trying to keep up with Garren's long, sure strides.

When they arrived, Garren immediately took note of the situation and demanded, "Where is Bev?"

Ora glanced between Carter and Kee and the empty place where the younger boy had been when they left.

Kee's chin raised in subtle defiance at Garren's sharp tone and he did not answer. Ora went to Carter and knelt at his side where her friend sat against the trunk of a narrow tree. She touched Carter's arm, but her gaze strayed to Garren.

"He took off," Carter volunteered with a weak, tired voice, "when we heard the Skays and the fighting.... Are you all right?"

Ora glanced at Carter to see his concern directed toward her. She squeezed his arm, trying to forget the memory of Garren's hands at her back, cradling her head, or his calloused fingers so lightly against her lips.

"I am fine, Carter," she assured him. Her gaze moved to Garren again as the Singer Captain drew his bow into one hand. "Please, do not go after him," she blurted with sudden, strong emotion. "There has been enough death."

Chapter 23

Surprised by Ora's bold words, Garren hesitated just a moment. He gripped his Singers bow and ignored her silent stare, as her lips compressed and her gaze turned demanding, '*Do not leave us.*'

"Stay put, little fool," he said curtly and turned swiftly to depart before she could react.

He had taken but twenty strides back through the underbrush and to the path when he heard it: a chilling and surprised scream, cut short and muffled. He turned back at once, feeling a sense of terrifying fear not his own come crashing against his chest. *Orabelle!*

Keeping his own fears in careful check, while his heart roared in his ears, he loaded an arrow and ducked to a crouch as he moved back into the underbrush.

He heard Kee's snarling tones first: "You should have just kept quiet. But do not think that is going to stop me—."

Hidden by the underbrush, he saw them and paused to assess the situation. He saw Carter first, lying face down, unconscious. A little further off stood his Belle with Kee behind her, his kit dagger held tight to her neck with a hand over her mouth.

Yes. *His* Belle.

White hot fury rose within Garren at the sight, and a bloodlust rushed through his veins. While normally he would jump forward and let his inner beast take over and cut his rival to pieces, Belle stood like an involuntary shield between them. If she got hurt.... Whatever humanity she had stirred to life in him would end if he lost her now.

He stepped forward, gaze dark, arrow drawn back at the ready. He stood with a calm, determined stance that belied the tension and rage building within.

Kee saw him at once. He paled and took a step back, gripping his hand more tightly across Ora's mouth. She reached up with one hand to feebly grasp Kee's sleeve. The eighteen-year-old swordsman flashed a smile around Ora's head at Garren. "And look! Here he is, come to save you like a noble hero of old...." His voice dripped with hatred and sarcasm and his gaze darkened with wicked intent.

Ora's eyes lifted in surprise but Garren dare not meet her gaze. His insides quivered with the weight of her emotions—emotions that screamed at him more intensely than anything he had felt in a very long time.

"What are you doing, Kee?" He said the name like saying the name of an acerdae[12], his lip curling into a sneer.

"I am leaving, that is what I am doing. And you—" he took his hand away from Ora's mouth, from lips Garren had traced with his thumb not so many minutes before, to point at Garren, "—You are not going to stop me, or come after me—" and his tone darkened, "—or shoot me in the back." He turned his head to look at Ora's profile. "Go ahead and scream now. Maybe a Skay or a Muel will hear you and eat your friend over there. Could make things more interesting...."

---

[12] Acerdae : those who deal in sorcery, witchcraft, and evil arts. Worshippers of the darkness.

Garren did not like the wild, insane look in Kee's eyes, a young man with nothing to live for but gratifying a twisted idea of revenge. And using Ora to get it.

"And why would I not?" Garren demanded.

Kee's attention switched to his nemesis again, for a moment lost in his gloating before remembering his earlier boast. "Why would you not come after me? Because I will kill her. Oh, I know what you are going to say," he hurried on, "but let me stop you, because I know better. You will not willingly harm a hair on her head. I heard her and her little weakling friend talking the other night. She was supposed to kill you, and would have died trying. But you did not kill her.... In fact, you seem almost determined to keep her alive. I wonder why?"

Ora stared at Garren as his gaze caught hers. He could read nothing in their depths except for her silent fear of Kee. Then, something in her expression changed and he witnessed anger and determination overrule her fear.

Calmly, Garren took a step forward and aimed the arrow against his bow straight at Kee's head.

Caught off guard and wary, Kee's confidence wavered. His upper lip glistened with perspiration. "Put down your weapon, Singer, or I will slice open her throat!"

Garren did not move. "Maybe I do not care."

Ora stomped the heel of her foot hard atop Kee's, hard enough to bruise the fine, unprotected bones beneath the soft, thin leather.

Kee loosened his hold and nearly dropped the knife. Ora ducked and Garren, already prepared for her actions, shot his arrow, forced to choose a non-lethal target in the shoulder to avoid striking Ora as the girl twisted away.

Kee's cry came with a mix of surprise, pain, and rage. He grabbed at the arrow protruding from his shoulder, stumbled back half a step, and fell onto his back.

Garren sprang to Ora's side as she stood in shock, one hand held across her neck. He grasped her arm to pull her hand away. "Did he harm you?" he growled with more menace than he intended.

Ora shook her head and pulled back; a shiver raced across her skin in response to his harshness. But, didn't she know his anger came from his need to protect her? Anger aimed not at her, but toward Kee? He had no experience or patience with the fairer sex, so he did not quite know what to do with this heightened awareness of her.

"Carter," she blurted in concern for her unconscious friend.

Kee rose up suddenly behind her with blade in hand, looking with hatred at Ora, who was standing far too close to him.

Garren did the only thing he knew to save her. He wrapped an arm around her, pulled her forward against him, and twisted aside so that as Kee drove the blade forward, Garren's body became Ora's shield.

He felt piercing pain flame across the left side of his back, though the force of Kee's assault was weakened by his injured shoulder, soaked in blood. Garren released Ora, reached back to dislodge the blade, and turned and drove the blade into the side of Kee's neck with a savage thrust. He tore it out again, watching as his victim fell, a splatter of blood hitting Garren's arm and chin.

He turned back to Ora slowly and saw her, with her hands over her mouth and a look of horror and revulsion in her eyes.

Chapter 24

Near sunset, they trudged wearily across the line into the First Division. Only three survivors of the original eight—unless Bev had survived somehow. After killing Kee, Garren did not leave them to go after the boy. He said nothing about it, intent on getting Carter and Ora safely back to the Divisions.

As they entered camp, Garren fell behind and out of Ora's sight and she moved to lead the way, Carter supported and conscious at her side. She kept one arm around him to steady him, her free hand holding her bow at her other side.

Though exhausted, she felt a confidence and a victory in having survived the nightmare. She kept her shoulders back and her head up, defying those who had sentenced her to this certain death, to this horrific War.

The soldiers roaming the camp grew still as they paused to watch the young survivors followed by the Singer Captain.

"We are nearly there, Carter," Ora encouraged her friend. Garren followed them to the Healers Quarter and stood in the shadows by the wall of the partition as the healer examined Carter. The healer peeled off Carter's tattered tunic. He was a slim boy, and his skin glowed pale and white in the yellow light of the tapered candles and lanterns.

"I will have to cut away the dead flesh," the healer spoke. "And he will need a draught to fight against infection." He looked at Garren as he remained bent toward Carter's shoulder. "This was a Muel, you say, Captain?"

"What can you do for him?" Garren said. His voice rumbled through Ora's senses, confusing her and causing a shiver to race over the skin of her back. She felt his gaze follow her, staying fixed on her, even though she kept her back turned toward him, as he spoke again: "He needs to be cleared for field duty and return to his post."

The healer called to his attendant. "Prepare a new mud mask to dress the wound. I will get him some draught. The boy's about to pass out." He looked at Ora. "I will take care of things from here. You may go."

Ora shook her head. "I am responsible for him. I will stay."

A soft brush of air touched her skin. Ora turned to see the Captain depart without another word, ducking out of the tent. She took a breath to call out to him. She should have thanked him. He had saved their lives, after all, and she had repaid him by trying to take his, and with disgust and mistrust.

Not wanting to consider the last couple of days any longer, Ora turned back to Carter and forced a smile of encouragement while the healer cleaned out his wounds.

Ora sat beside him on his good side as his eyes grew heavy from the draught. He leaned against her, head gently resting on her breast as she splayed her fingers through his wheat-colored hair, soothing him like a mother would her son.

The healer began to cut away the torn and mangled flesh he could not repair, and Carter soon passed out into a draught-induced coma, just before the attendant returned with a mud mask.

Chapter 25

After seeing his knife-wound properly tended, Garren strode immediately to the Council tent, where he knew Commander Strell would be awaiting a report—most assuredly, waiting for news of their failure, which only made Garren more livid than ever.

He had accompanied Carter and Ora at the infirmary because he wanted to be sure the healer would tend to them properly. He departed without a word or glance at Ora, intent on confronting the Commander before the end of the day.

His instincts demanded violence, but he had learned long ago when to deny those instincts. And as much as he loathed the Commander, killing him was not the answer.

Entering the tent, he immediately saw the object of his wrath leaning back comfortably, alone at the head of the table. Commander Strell started in surprise at Garren's abrupt, unannounced appearance. Garren took pleasure in placing one hand against the hilt of his sword and seeing fear in the other man's eyes. He approached, his glittering, dangerous eye pinning the Commander to the spot.

The Commander smiled coldly as he recovered himself. "Back so soon?"

"Let us not play games, Commander. You did not expect me back at all," Garren growled. He approached the table. The Commander stood, moving cautiously behind his chair.

"I followed your recommendation, Singer," he said dryly. "You are angry that it failed, but I told you it was a suicide mission."

Garren felt his skin heat up with the desire to strangle this man. "It is Captain. You will address me properly, Commander." He breathed deeply to stay focused as he came toward the Commander. His gaze sparked with fury. "You went behind my back and *made* it a suicide mission by sending in a single, small troop of young, untrained recruits!"

"They would die anyway. And now, *Captain*, it has been done at your hand," the Commander sneered. "We all know your plan has no hope for success."

Garren grabbed him by the front of his untarnished steel plate armor near his collar-bone, driving him backward. His fist landed hard against the Commander's face. The Commander grabbed at his face and staggered. Despite the blood trickling over his fingers, there was a hint of satisfaction in his eyes. Fear and pain from the attack was not without an equal blend of arrogance.

"Captain!" Commander Baire spoke, entering the tent flanked by two footmen. "What is this all about?" He stood on the threshold, observing the fury in Garren's countenance, as Commander Strell stood against the far wall.

"That…*thing*…is a monster, and it belongs in a cage!" Commander Strell shouted angrily, wiping at the blood gushing from his nose.

Commander Baire lifted his hand slightly in a staying motion to the footmen, who took a cautious step back and moved their hands away from their swords. No one wanted to take on the Singer, though if Garren attempted further harm to Commander Strell, they would be forced to intervene.

"You should thank me," Garren goaded darkly, ignoring the footmen. "I should have killed you…but, that would not be very diplomatic, now would it?" He moved to leave, then paused and turned back. He stared hard at Commander Strell. "If you ever go behind my back and try to pull a stunt like that again…I *will* kill you." He turned on his heel and strode out of the tent without looking back.

In the darkness of the cool night air, he took a deep breath and let his anger abate. He moved between the tents, staying to the shadows and away from the firelight so the soldiers would not recognize him. He found himself moving in the direction of the Archers Quarter.

Chapter 26

Ora left the infirmary where Carter remained sedated with a cleanly wrapped shoulder. She noticed Garren leaning back against a small tree near the outskirts of the Archers Quarter. His dark gaze found her before she could retreat. Firelight flickered across his features and his hard, sculpted jaw.

"Commander Strell will not be giving you orders again. You stay on the field," he informed her, his voice a low rumble.

"However did you convince him of that?" she spoke with mild surprise. She stood aloof and folded her arms across her chest as casually as she could.

He moved away from the tree to sit on a long bench outside the nearest tent. He held a wooden cup and, by the strong aroma rising with the steam just visible in the firelight, she guessed it to be kaff-bean[13] tea. The knuckles of one hand were chafed and somewhat bruised.

"Did you kill him?" She almost wished he had.

---

13 Kaff-bean : a bitter coffee bean, brewed in water just long enough for flavor—to a tea-strength consistency.

Garren looked at her strangely a moment, then smiled slightly, amused by her words. "Do you think I kill everyone I have a disagreement with?" His gaze drilled into hers, as he grew serious again. "The Commander had no right to send you out there on that mission. You were not ready."

"So, you beat him up…to prove a point?" Ora wanted to leave him sitting there. She felt compelled to stay. "I have already thanked you for saving my life," she began stiffly out loud. "I do not owe you any favors, and I am not going to forgive you for what you have done, either."

"I never asked, nor expected, any thanks from you," Garren returned.

Ora released a heavy, pent up sigh. She sat beside him, but not too close. "Let me see your hand," she said quietly as she shifted to face him.

Surprisingly, he obeyed without a word. She touched his hand before thinking what a shock it would be to her senses. His hands were strong and calloused, capable, and warm. She met his gaze for an instant, caught off guard, and his grey eye looked gently, softly into hers.

She turned her attention back to his injured hand, took her waterskin and poured a small stream over his torn knuckles, washing away the blood stains. Then, she reached into her kit and withdrew a strip of bandage cloth to wrap over the torn skin, to protect it from dirt.

Maybe she had lied. She did feel somewhat responsible, whether or not she should, and she did feel like she owed him a kindness—for protecting her and Carter, and standing up for them against Commander Strell.

"There. You really should be more careful about throwing punches." Ora let go of his hand and stood resolutely, intent that this be the end of any friendly association with him.

"Belle, wait."

Ora stood, her back to him. *Do not listen to him*, she urged herself. *Do not let him intimidate you.* She hated the veiled entreaty in his tone. She hated her compulsion to do just as he asked.

He was her commanding officer. And his words might as well be an order. She clenched her hands into fists at her sides. "Yes, Captain?" she said, cooly.

"I do not know what this is…." Garren's voice came behind her as he remained seated. "I took you from your home. I took the lives of your friends. I know you hate me for that. I do not expect any different. I know that war is ugly…but I will not deny it—I do not want you to get hurt. I do not want you in harm's way."

Could he feel the confusion in her emotions, like he had that night she had tried to kill him? What did he mean? Did he feel that same confusion?

She closed her eyes tightly, remembering Garren's cold, sharp warning: *'You must never cry.'* She had never felt so exhausted, so bruised, in all her young life. "I do not hate you…not like I thought…not so very much," she confessed.

After a moment of tense silence, Garren's voice came softly, "You are tired."

"I have not slept in days," Ora replied carefully. "Unlike you, I cannot go so long without rest and not feel its effects…."

She waited, expecting him to argue with her, to turn cruel and speak harshly. He surprised her by saying only, "You have been through a lot. Get some sleep."

Ora turned to look at him, trying to understand him. What a contradiction of character!

"Good night, Captain…Garren," she murmured.

"Good night," Garren answered.

Ora withdrew.

Chapter 27

Garren rode to Torr Guard after his visit with Ora, where Captain Mason remained, in charge of the training and the injured there. With the front lines so near, Torr Guard had changed suddenly to not only a training facility, but to a Healers Quarter, where the seriously injured were transported for long-term care.

Logan met him on his grey mount at the entrance to the camp. "Captain," he said gravely in greeting. "We have trouble."

Garren reined in his black beast. "What kind of trouble?"

"We have had reports of raids on the nearby villages…."

"Not my problem," Garren answered simply. "It is not my job to protect civilians." His horse snorted and bobbed its head, pulling lightly at the reins, sensing grain and hay not far away and as ready as its master to end the night.

"I realize that, Sir," Logan replied. "But they seem to be soldiers."

"Who?" Garren barked with sudden sharpness.

"There are only rumors," Logan began. "Suspicions have fallen on Beckett, Sholl…and Greer."

Garren muttered a thick curse under his breath, anger flaring in his good eye. “Does Captain Mason know of this?” he demanded.

“Yes, Sir,” Logan reported. “We just learned of this and he sent me out to meet you and inform you at once. He said you would want to prepare a troop to intercept them. We think they are riding toward Torguson, one of the southern hamlets.”

Garren looked across the camp and gave a decisive nod. “You were right to meet me. I need a fresh mount and five able soldiers, mounted and dressed for battle. We will not delay.”

Logan wheeled his grey around and the two men spurred their mounts into a gallop into camp. Logan rode to inform Captain Mason of their departure and organize the troop.

Garren waited for them at the southern entrance of the camp, mounted on a fresh horse, a light bay, that shifted nervously beneath him. He carried his sword and his bow over his shoulders, against his back, his quiver of arrows attached to his saddle and a long dagger strapped to his forearm. His hair glistened with a fine sweat. He had not had a chance to wash since accompanying the recruits on the scouting mission. He had not slept in nearly twice that long and his muscles and his mind protested the constant activity. Despite that, the shadow of a beard and the smudges of dirt and sweat only accentuated his intimidating appearance.

Logan and the other soldiers appeared from the darkness, riding toward Garren as he tightened the reins, bringing his mount to attention.

“It has been rumored we have rebel soldiers attacking the villages,” Garren informed the troop. “These are men you may know. You may have fought beside them in the War. But they are acting now as traitors and thieves. Do not forget that.”

He kicked in his heels, and the troop followed in a seamless organized motion toward Torguson. He leaned forward, adapting quickly to the motion of the new horse and using an expert hand to guide it. He wished for his own steady beast—a disciplined war horse used to the sudden noises and movement associated with battle. He did not know what they would face in Torguson. They may even now be too late to stop the attack. And were the rumors true? Could rebel soldiers, men he may have fought beside, really be ransacking and plaguing the Freelands?

The night turned cool. Garren let his senses take over, hearing the heavy breath of the horses, the soft thunder of their hooves racing across the earth; the quiet jingle of harness, and the shifting of leather against leather.

Soft, flickering torchlight far ahead—like pin-pricks moving in the darkness—alerted the men of Torguson's nearness, and of the presence of other riders.

Garren drew back his mount to a soft trot. The horse protested by tossing its head, pulling at the reins and giving a short, irritated snort. Garren twisted its head around, forcing it to turn in a tight, controlled circle, and joined the rest of his troop. "We go in fast and hard; take them by surprise. Do not force a battle unless absolutely necessary. Just show them who is in charge. We fight in the Name of the King against the For'bane, not his subjects. This stops now."

He kicked in his heels, letting his anxious mount have its head. His troop followed closely in response. They descended on the village just as one of the thatched roof homes went up in flames. Garren heard frightened screams and tasted a bloodlust of anger in his mouth—a piece of human emotion he had not let himself feel in years. He cared that these villagers would suffer unjustly at the hands of soldiers. Or maybe he knew Ora would care. He could well imagine her righteous anger. With her in his heart and mind, he had begun to feel more like a human than a monster. And yet, she still hated him. He could never redeem himself in her eyes—he knew that. His life, his thoughts, his deeds felt like a contradiction: Part-human and part-monster.

He reined in sharply, causing his mount to lift up its front hooves in a half rear just inside the village entrance. The troop fanned out behind him. "Halt in the Name of the King!" Garren issued the warning in a commanding shout.

The figures on horseback scattered in surprise before them. Garren drew his sword, urging his horse to pursue. Better to be clear of the village and cowering villagers, lest they get hurt in the skirmish. The troop leapt forward. Two rebels were struck down and yanked off their horses. One horse took off in fright, its unseated rider caught and trampled underneath while the other, struck in the temple with the hilt of a sword, tried to stagger to his feet, surrounded by the troop. "Sholl," Logan spat with disdain, still mounted as he used the tip of his blade to lift the rebel's chin and identify his face in the light of the flames.

Garren watched the third rebel, torch held high in hand, ride hard for the tree line and the deep darkness beyond. "Get those fires out," Garren ordered before riding off in pursuit. Gaining on the retreating rebel, Garren raised his sword with intent, keeping his other hand tightly controlled on the reins. All at once, the rebel twisted around and brought his mount to a sharp standstill as he dropped his torch behind him in the dry tangled weeds and grasses.

Garren's horse reared as flames shot up into the air and spread out across the grass in each direction, creating a wall of red-orange flame. Cut off, Garren brought his skittish mount under control and stared as the figure rode calmly several paces away and stopped at the tree line, looking back at Garren. Though not hindered by distance, the darkness of evening and the brightness of the flames' light in Garren's eye made it impossible to identify him.

The rebel turned and disappeared into the trees. Garren sensed the hint of arrogance and challenge—familiar to him as the same emotion he had sensed in Greer. But, because base emotions generally felt the same on a surface level between people, this in no way proved to Garren that the rebel was Greer.

Garren backed his mount away from the flames. His own beast would have jumped them before they grew too high, but this skittish horse never could have made it.

He shouted for his troop to bring shovels. If they did not put out this fire, it would spread and envelop the whole village.

Chapter 28

Late that night—after a restless few hours sleep on her cot—Ora returned to the Healers Quarter to sit at Carter's bedside. A healer's assistant came by and tapped her on the shoulder as she started to nod off. Ora jerked upright.

Wary of startling armed soldiers who may or may not react violently, the assistant pulled back quickly out of her reach. Ora stared at him but made no move to draw her dagger, tucked in her waist band.

"You should go now, archer," he said. "The boy will live and the War continues. Rest while it can be acquired, before you are called to the front line again."

Ora pressed a hand to her head a moment. "He will want to see me…when he awakens," she said with certainty, standing to look down at Carter.

"Of course," the assistant assured her with a nod of understanding. "If you have not returned by then, I will send a man to the Archers Quarter to report to you."

Ora looked at him and narrowed her eyes subtly, trying to determine if he was mocking her. She did not expect what she saw instead: respect. For her? But why? She forced a slight smile in response. "Of course." She left the tent, ignoring the moans of the injured and dying all around her, too tired to let their despair into her spirit, and knowing she could not help them anyway.

As she exited, she nearly ran in to the tall, brawny form of a soldier walking by. Startled, she jerked back and her hand moved to her dagger. "Bron!" she gasped as she recognized his features and relaxed.

As her hand left the hilt of the dagger, the Singer flashed a smile: "So, the Captain did not get you killed out there. I am glad to see it…." He glanced at the infirmary tent behind her.

Ora felt herself flush, though she did not know why. "My friend, Carter, was wounded," she explained.

Bron's smile melted away, replaced quickly with a look of concern. "What happened?"

Ora subconsciously placed a hand against her brow, feeling a wave of fatigue.

Bron took hold of her elbow. "Come and sit, here by the fire. The night is chilly." His deep voice soothed her anxieties. She found she wanted to lean on him as he led her to the nearest campfire. But a few other soldiers sat near the place, so she resisted. Not only that, Garren's face impressed itself on her mind strongly. She found she could not shake the remembrance of the Captain's arms around her when she had fallen from the tree, or the fierceness in his eye—a singular fierceness of protection toward her.

She sat where Bron directed her and waited while he stirred the coals and added more wood, as the nearby soldiers watched him with caution.

Ora thought about her last meeting with Garren, early that evening. She found that though she felt at ease around Bron, it was Garren's presence she wanted most. Two men, so very different, and yet her feelings for each were the opposite of what they should be!

She despised Garren for his coldness and cruelty, yet she trusted and respected his judgement at the same time. Had she really become a soldier then—that she had begun to understand and accept the ways of the War?

"Now, tell me," Bron encouraged, interrupting her thoughts. He sat near her on a long log rolled near the fire to serve as a bench. "How does it happen that you were sent alone behind enemy lines with the likes of Captain Garren?"

"Commander Strell instructed us," Ora admitted. "We were sent to scout through the Reave. The Captain waited for us there, at the Reave's entrance. I do not think the Commander expected him to be there."

"Indeed? The Commander meant to send you in alone?" Bron frowned. "Well, then I have to applaud the Captain for stepping in and bringing you home. That was poor judgement on the Commander's part.... I cannot begin to imagine what he was thinking."

Home? Ora mentally recoiled from the word. She did not have any wish to call this battleground her home. Perhaps she was not as much a soldier as she thought.

"And your friend? How was he injured?"

Ora held out her hands to the flames. "We were attacked by Muels...." She faded off as she stared into the flames, nearly forgetting Bron's presence. "The Captain agreed to turn back, even though we had not completed the mission. For Carter's sake."

"For Carter...or for you?" Bron's low voice brought her surprised gaze to his.

"What do you mean?" she dared to ask, not liking the shadow in his gaze.

Bron glanced aside, disturbed and lost in thought a moment. His jaw worked and then he shook his head. "Captain Mason sent us the rest of the recruits while you were away. I heard a rumor that one of the boys was asking for you."

Ora straightened in anticipation mixed with hope and dread. "Thane?" she blurted.

Bron raised a brow and smiled crookedly. "I do not know his name. Young boy. Small."

Ora stood so fast she nearly fell over as a wave of dizziness upset her balance. Bron jumped to his feet and grasped her arm to steady her. "Where can I find him? Where did they station him?" she spoke anxiously.

"I will take you to him," he said with a nod, seeing her desperation.

She followed him toward the outer rim of the First Division and into the Third Division, marked by a boundary of a wide road used by carts to bring supplies throughout and between the Divisions.

Fires lit the way, casting shadows off the walls of the tents. She kept Bron's shoulders in sight as he walked ahead in the darkness. He did not glance behind but once or twice to make sure she kept up with him. Ora refused to make eye contact with the many male soldiers walking by or standing near the tents or fires. She walked on with a straight back and chin lifted with confidence, belying the intense weariness she felt. She would not retire until she had seen her young friend. She must know if he was well. To see a familiar face—someone else from her own village in the Freelands—would be a healing balm to her bruised soul.

Bron stepped aside suddenly and Ora nearly ran into him before she checked herself, snapping from her thoughts back to her surroundings. "You would be just the boy I am looking for," he said to someone standing outside a tent. Ora could see the blue stripe sewn down the tent flap, marking it as a ranked officer's quarters.

Hearing Bron's words, she moved quickly from behind the Singer and her lips curved into a smile of relief and joy at seeing Thane. A quick glance showed he remained whole. "Thane," she burst as the boy looked her way surprised and broke into a grin as he recognized her.

She did not care what anyone would think, but stepped forward and threw her arms around the boy who hugged her tightly in return. "Ora, you are alive!"

Still holding on to him, she looked down. He seemed so frail. His arms quite thin. His face gaunt and eyes appearing too large, sunken in his face. His features pale, with just the smudge of color in his lips and cheeks from the chill of the night air.

But he lives, Ora calmed herself. *That is what matters.* And, judging by the clean, basic uniform he wore, he had not seen battle. Bron caught her eye and gave a fleeting salute with two fingers at his brow before turning and slipping away into the darkness. She would need to thank him later. She looked at Thane and stepped back, seeing the boy blush in the firelight and glance to see if anyone had seen the prolonged embrace. She cleared her throat: "So, you are a footman, then?" He nodded. "Who have they put you in service with, then?"

"A Commander Jeshura," Thane answered. "He is not here now. They have sent him to the Fifth Division to consult with the Commander there. But I am to remain stationed here and ready to serve when he returns."

Ora nodded thoughtfully, still watching him to see if she could determine exactly how he was doing—physically and emotionally—without being too obvious about it. His eyes still looked haunted. Lost. He missed Thordan. Seeing Thane again made her own heart ache at remembrance of the loss, and reminded her of her promise to look after him.

"Have you had dinner? Or does someone bring you a meal?"

Thane shook his head. "I ate this afternoon, before being stationed. The Commander is expected back at midnight. I will eat then, once I have been dismissed."

"Have you met the Commander?"

Thane shook his head again. "But do not worry," he insisted, brows drawn together. "I do not expect he is half as bad as Captain Garren."

Ora glanced aside. "No, I do not suppose there are many men as bad as he," she murmured and nearly choked on the words, feeling ashamed to even speak them. Why? Perhaps because she did not think him as terrible as she once did. Perhaps because she had spoken with him and come to understand him, if only a little.

"But here," she hastened and reached into her kit for a portion of bread. "I saved this. I am too weary to eat tonight and it will be hard and dried come morning. You will not be punished if you eat something as long as you continue to stand here and do not leave your post."

Thane hesitated just a moment, and she saw the hunger in his eyes and felt a sharp pang of regret. She had been fighting for two weeks and she should have been watching out for him. If only she could have found a way to stay at Torr Guard. But then, what would have become of Carter?

Thane took the bread, eating it quickly. He gave her a sheepish little grin of apology with just a touch of shyness. "I missed you, Ora," he confessed quietly.

"Well," Ora cleared her throat. "I am here now. I will take care of you. It is good that you are here. You will be safe."

"What is it like?" Thane hesitated. "Out there? What are the For'bane like?"

Ora remembered the Skay from the first day, how it jumped through the air at her, only to be pierced by Bron's arrow; the Trooper swinging his great ball-and-chain flails and crushing soldiers left and right like ants beneath a man's boot; the Muels dropping from trees and one landing on top of Carter, shredding his shoulder with its razor needle-like teeth. "There is not much to tell. It is war," she insisted, trying to sound casual. Sensitive Thane would never survive combat, she knew that now with absolute certainty. If the boy looked this bad now, behind the line....

"I am staying at the Archers Quarter in the First Division," she spoke, forcing back her disturbing thoughts. "I am expected to return there. Will you...be all right? Is there anything I can get you?" She glanced back the way she'd come, loathe to leave the boy so soon, but anxious for any word on Carter's condition, lest she miss it.

"The bread was just what I needed," Thane said. "Thank you, Ora. I am so glad you are here."

"Will you be here come morning? They may send me to the line again, but I will try to check in on you...."

"I do not know exactly, but I think I will be. Commander Jershua will probably sleep late."

Ora stepped forward and gave Thane one last departing hug and, with no curious eyes watching, Thane gripped Ora's sleeves and hid his face wearily against Ora's shoulder.

Do not cry, Ora silently commanded herself. *He will be fine. We will all be fine. I must stay strong...for their sakes.*

As she walked away in the direction of the First Division, she passed a hand over her eyes, pinching two fingers against her temple and against the pressure building there.

Then, all at once, someone seized her by the arm and spun her around. At the same time a sickeningly familiar voice taunted: "Well, if it is not the *belle* of the ball!"

Ora yanked away from Greer's grip around her wrist, but he held fast and sneered at her.

"Let me go, Greer, or so help me...," she ground out between clenched teeth, hoping he could not hear the startled and fearful thundering of her racing heart.

"What? What will you do if I do not?" He cocked his head and slid his gaze slowly, suggestively, down the column of her throat and to the line of her thin leather jerkin. He leered at her; his gaze darkened as his lids drooped to half-hood his eyes. She was terrified to discover an equal amount of hatred and lust there.

She pulled in a sharp breath and tried again to pull away from him, fisting both her hands. But Greer shoved her back against the support pole of an empty tent nearby, and she nearly fell as she struck the back of her head against the wood, sending a shower of sparks through her mind. Greer grasped her face in one hand, pinching her cheeks so her lips parted from the pressure against her jaw.

"That no-good Singer is not here to save you this time," Greer hissed. "Women are not soldiers. You cannot expect me not to take advantage of you. I am surrounded by blood and death, the stench of it fills my sleep and my dreams... but I will not be denied the right to taste of something beautiful. It is my right, as a man, to enjoy those things. And it is all you will ever be good for."

Ora felt bile rising in the back of her throat. Her twisting and writhing were in vain. His grip was like iron as he pressed against her roughly. She tried to scream, but her voice closed off in her terror and Greer's grip made it hard to breathe, let alone gather enough oxygen to shout for help. Would anyone come to her aid?

A haunting terror, taken root as a child, came upon her senses with a crushing, sickening force. Her limbs grew weak and she knew if she did not fight with everything she had, she would be lost. Her courage would fail her and Greer's strength and determination would overtake her.

His liquor-tainted breath fouled the air between them, and his face came closer with dangerous intent. Ora's hand crawled up the side of his leg, pressed against her thigh. He did not stop her, taking it as a sign of acceptance. But Ora had no intention of letting him touch her. As he tried to kiss her, she twisted her face to the side with a jerk. His mouth hit the side of her neck instead. She grasped the handle of her dagger in her belt and withdrew it. As his grip on her loosened, she jabbed outward in a forceful, blind defensive movement when he tried to take hold of her head again.

Greer grunted and let out a short, angry cry of surprise and pain. He struck Ora on the side of the head before she could retreat, sending her to the ground, where she scraped her cheek painfully in the dirt. He swore sharply at her, face and eyes wild and livid with pain and anger as he held one hand against his bleeding side. Already, a dark flow soaked through his leather armor. Her blade had pierced below the ribs on the right side. Unfortunately for her, the damage was minimal and Greer would no doubt survive to exact his vengeance on her.

"What is going on?"

"Who goes there?"

"Soldier! Are you all right?"

The words of the approaching men, drawn by the scuffle, came muffled and blended together with the shock of Ora's encounter and the disorienting sting of Greer's strike to the face. She could not get to her feet fast enough to escape before they arrived on the scene.

Then Greer pointed his finger at her. "I caught this one trying to escape. When I tried to apprehend her, she stabbed me with that knife. Arrest her!"

In the next instant, stunned by Greer's fast lie, she felt herself hauled to her feet between two of the soldiers. "No!" she shouted, trembling all over with fear and rage. She pulled against their hold, knowing it was pointless.

Chapter 29

Dawn colored the horizon at Torr Guard when Garren rose and went to the stables to dress his mount. He had rested nearly five hours. No headache bothered him today, as he had expected after so much activity—between battling the Skays and Muels, and riding out to save Torguson.

His great black beast stuck its head over the half-stall door at his approach and snorted a greeting. Garren gently grasped the horse's head between his palms and slid one hand across its cheekbone to the side of its neck and leaned his face against the broad forehead. He murmured Ancient Tongue to the horse gently and considered that there existed no other creature more noble, more pure, than these. His horse did not judge his character, and trusted in his every action. He led the horse out into the open aisle and dressed it himself, as usual, before starting out, pointing its nose in the direction of the First Division.

The sun rose and warmed his back as he rode. Relaxing his senses, Garren let his thoughts wander, trusting his horse to the direction and the path they traveled. He wondered if Carter had begun recovery and if Ora stayed at the sickbed. He could only imagine it was so. Ora was faithful and loyal.

He wished she was not, only because he felt a certain degree of jealousy toward both of them—that she would love Carter, because he knew she did. He had begun to wish himself in the boy's place, with someone to care; to see him as human again. Not that he needed looking after. He was independent and self-sufficient and he liked it that way. And yet, he could not deny the appeal of a woman's tenderness. He was not blind to Ora's growing maturity or to the subtle grace of her beauty in bloom. In this world of darkness, what hope did he have to anything beautiful?

He despised himself for giving in and speaking to her as he had the other night, admitting to her that he cared, and did not want her hurt. Could he be any more of a fool? Could their circumstances be any more impossible? An archer and a Singer both steeped in a war no one believed it would ever end in victory? How could he guarantee her safety within such a reality?

He put aside these thoughts with great effort and sharpened his senses to the surrounding lands he passed through, considering what business would occupy him when he arrived at the First Division. No doubt Commander Strell would try to get even for the last time they met. Garren's response of violence and threats only meant more distrust from everyone else. It did not matter whether what he did was right or wrong, being a Singer meant constant trial. It meant being an outcast.

He entered the outskirts of the First Division and frowned as a sense of unrest and unease swept over him. He slowed his horse to an easy walk and noticed several soldiers heading in the same direction toward the center of the camp, past the forges. "Is there trouble?" he urged firmly.

"There is an execution about to take place. One of the archers."

Garren kicked in his heels, urging his mount toward the center of camp. The only things that ever happened at the center of the camps were executions, punishments, rally calls —the delivery of crucial information, usually if they were being overrun. He hated the center of camp. Nothing good ever happened there.

Though the morning was bright and sunlight pierced the haze created by the smoke of the camp and battlefield, Garren saw the flames of several torches along the perimeter of the camp center, a small open field.

That is when it hit him, the source of his unease. Standing with hands tied behind a tall central post, Ora had her face lifted to the sky to avoid the stares of the soldiers gathering around to watch.

Garren took one look at the post, at his Belle—stripped of her outer wear and archer's gear, and wearing a simple off-white under-tunic that fell to her thighs, just above her knees—and at the piles of sticks and bramble built up around her feet. Two footmen approached on either side with torches held high. He nearly lost his temper. He almost let loose the monster clawing away at his insides as his anger grew like an internal furnace.

He rammed in his heels and sent his horse forward into the field. "Stand where you are!" he thundered to the footmen in warning. "Who is in charge of these proceedings?" he ordered as Ora looked at him with eyes wide in shock.

With a move of desperation, her gaze locked on to his, she yanked at the restraints binding her to the post. He saw the hope in her eyes, the pleading, but he did not dare keep his eyes on her.

He kept his expression closed, cold. A man stepped forward from the soldiers and drew Garren's harsh, expectant gaze to Greer. He hoped his surprise did not show.

He still suspected Greer as the rebel at the tree line, but when had he returned to camp? And how brazen, to stand now before Garren with the ghost of a smirk twisting his lips.

"She tried to escape. The punishment for a runner is death."

Garren felt like someone hit him in the stomach, but his tightened grip on the reins of his horse was his only outward reaction. He looked at Ora. "Is this true?" he demanded firmly. *Tell me it is not true*. He thought her smarter than that. Her bravery did not reflect a cowardly response such as what Greer accused of her.

He steeled himself against the desperate look in her eyes as she answered him: "I did no such thing. Your soldier attacked me and I defended myself."

By the expressions of those gathered around, he could only guess no one believed her story. Garren turned his gaze back to Greer, every muscle in his body tensing with rage."Were there witnesses?"

"I caught her in the Third Division, before the sun rose...."

"I went to visit a friend," Ora attempted in self-defense.

"You are fresh from recruitment. What friend could you —a First Division archer—have in another Division?" Greer insisted, before turning his attention back to Garren. "When I tried to apprehend her, she stabbed me with her knife. When the footmen came, she concocted the notion that *I* attacked *her*." Greer sneered. He raised his voice and let his gaze sweep over the onlookers. "She knew what would happen if she tried to escape."

Garren tried to catch Ora's gaze—to search beneath the layers of her emotions—but she had turned her head aside, trying to avoid the stares of the gathered crowd. Instead, Garren looked hard at Greer. "What time did you return to the First Division?" he commanded low, but not so quietly that the others could not hear.

Greer grinned. "I never left camp, Captain. You ordered me to remain and fight at the line. And here I will stay, until the Council commands me elsewhere." Garren recognized the taunt by the glint in the other man's eyes and knew he would not get a confession to confirm his suspicions. He could not convict Greer of any crime unless he had proof. Such a pattern could cause the King to revoke Garren's title and strip him of his honor and responsibilities.

Perhaps that was what Greer wanted.

But Garren would heed to caution. He would not give Greer the satisfaction.

His mount snorted and arched its neck, then shook its thick black mane as if with irritation.

He looked at Ora. *I cannot save her*, he realized, sickened at the knowledge.

He wondered with renewed hatred if Greer was using Ora to draw him out, to try and cause him to stumble in his duties as a Captain. He knew Greer disliked him—a Singer attaining a rank when Greer had not. He did not realize till now how far the man would stoop to usurp that title from him.

"You are not a ranking official. You cannot condemn to death, or carry out the sentence," Garren rebuked firmly.

"Is there some reason she should be spared the law?" Greer asked. "Just because a Singer did not shoot her first?"

"I did nothing wrong!" Ora cried.

"Silence!" Garren barked, and looked at Greer. *Focus*, he told himself. *There must be some way.* A muscle in his jaw flexed. "It is my jurisdiction to lay sentence."

"Then, by all means, pronounce it," Greer urged and took a step back.

For a moment, all was quiet, as if the air itself went still in wait of Garren's answer. Then, even as his heart ached within him, Garren raised his voice to announce: "Thirty lashes. The punishment for attacking another soldier without provocation is thirty lashes."

"And what about her attempted escape?" Greer demanded.

"As you stated, there were no witnesses to confirm her attempted escape. I will not sentence her under assumption." He stared down at Greer. "And as to your *injury*, you are not dead. The punishment for attacking another soldier is thirty lashes."

He twisted his horse's head around and kicked in his heels. It jumped forward and the soldiers parted to let them pass. He did not look back at Ora, but he felt her response just the same.

Her hope faded. Hurt. Betrayal. Those were the only emotions left.

Chapter 30

Numbness crept over Ora's heart as the two footmen who had prepared to lay the torches against the brush released her and took hold of her arms to drag her to the side of the field where two smaller posts stood.

She did not fight when they tied each wrist to a post, forcing her to stand between the posts with arms outstretched. Had she really thought Garren would save her? He had looked at her coldly and spoken harshly, and sentenced her to this fate without hesitation.

Before the footmen stepped clear, they cut and tore the back of her tunic to her waist, leaving it hanging from her shoulders. A burly soldier stepped forward, slowly coiling the ends of a long leather whip in his hand. He moved behind her, out of her sight, but not before she caught a glimpse of the torture device and the tightly knotted ends meant to inflict more pain. She closed her hands into fists and took short, deep breaths, trying to keep her panic and terror at bay, and keep from screaming as she imagined too vividly what thirty lashes would do to her.

There is no one to save me, she reminded herself. *I must endure it. I must be strong.*

"Thirty lashes," Greer sneered. "Begin."

Ora kept her eyes open, her gaze focused with determination on a place in the dirt where another's blood had stained the earth. Had they been wrongly accused and friendless as well?

She feared for Thane and Carter. Arrested and held in a holding tent till dawn, chained to an iron stake in the ground, she had heard no news on Carter's condition and no one answered her when she asked. And Thane.... Did he stand somewhere in the crowd, or was he still at his station in the Third Division? She hoped he was not there to witness this.

She tightened her hands even more at the thought. Thane needed her. Carter needed her. *I will not be disgraced by showing fear.*

The snap of the whip brought searing pain down her back, raking over her skin like hot coals. Blackness spotted her vision. She sucked in a sharp breath and it took everything in her not to cry out.

One. Two. Three. Four.

Her legs trembled and nearly buckled.

She heard a voice from the crowd but could not see who spoke: "This is madness! She cannot be subjected to a man's punishment! Thirty lashes will kill her!"

Recognition trickled through the overwhelming pain. *Bron?*

Seven. Eight. Nine.

Ora felt a whimper escape her and tasted blood in her mouth as she clenched her teeth. She sagged against the ropes holding her up.

Make it stop. Please. She did not know who she was asking. Perhaps it was a prayer. If no one else could hear her, perhaps Creator[14] would. *Please.*

The voices of the soldiers faded. Her vision blurred and grew dark.

Eleven. Twelve.

Her body jerked with each strike. She could no longer feel the source of her pain. It felt as if her entire body was on fire.

Thirteen. Fourteen.

She blacked out.

---

[14] Creator : the one, true God, creator of all things. Always referred to as 'Creator.'

Chapter 31

Garren paced the length of the waiting area with anxiety and a crushing sense of guilt. He had tried telling himself every kind of argument and excuse for his actions, but the feeling stubbornly remained. He ran a hand through the short layers of his dark hair, feeling the dampness of sweat and grime. His hand paused at the back of his neck to squeeze away some of the tension. It did not do any good. His stomach clenched and he turned as the healer pushed aside the partition to the room and stepped out into the waiting area. "Captain," the healer acknowledged with a nod.

Garren frowned. "Just tell me she will live," he said shortly, in no mood for small talk.

The healer cleared his throat. "She is still unconscious. The pain is too much, I think, for her mind to handle. She is frail and small. I have done all I can for her. It is best to let her sleep as much as possible and keep her still. I have tended the wounds, but they will scar."

Garren felt his strength nearly fail him. "I will see her," he said stiffly.

"Do not worry, Captain. She will not escape. She could not manage it now even if she wished it."

Garren moved past him with a stony expression. He slipped into the room, letting the partition close behind him, veiling him from the healer's sight. He stood still, looking in at the dimly lit space. Ora lay on her stomach on a padded examination table placed at the center of the small room, her face turned to the side. Still wearing her torn, blood-splattered tunic, her bare back was covered in criss-crossing lacerations where the leather thongs struck repeatedly in the same areas. Spotted bruising showed beneath the whip marks as well.

Though he was usually able to sense her emotions with little effort, he could sense nothing now. Her stillness frightened him. And nothing frightened him. Still, he opened his senses to her, searching for anything below the surface, but there came no response.

He moved closer, glancing back at the partition to be sure they remained alone. He came around to see Ora's face, eyes closed and a crease of pain marring her brow even in unconsciousness. Why could he not feel that? Hesitating, he reached out and brushed a finger down her cheek with the utmost gentleness, tucking a lock of her hair back from her face.

As soon as he touched her, he felt a burst of emotion through her stillness. Pain—overwhelming pain, not just physical, but coming from deep within. He pulled his hand back suddenly in surprise and leaned his hands on the edge of the table, the muscles in his arms straining as he leaned his weight on his hands and hung his head between his shoulders. His good eye gazed at her face as he saw a tear pool at the inside corner of her eye. He watched it move slowly, trail over the bridge of her nose and drop to melt into the table padding.

He groaned quietly, keeping his gaze on her face. "I am sorry, Belle. It is not enough, I know. But I am…." He glanced back at the partition again before turning back to Ora. “You must survive this.”

He pulled back suddenly, taking two steps back from the table. He winced and abruptly put a hand to his head as sharp pain pierced across his temples and sent his head throbbing. He pulled out the cord with the vial and tapped out a pinch of the contents onto his tongue.

He took a slow, deep breath. “I am sorry, Belle,” he spoke again and abruptly withdrew. He caught the healer’s gaze before leaving the waiting area. “Give her whatever she needs, and then see her removed to a holding tent. You will continue tending to her there. Use the best salve available to heal her wounds.”

“Yes, Captain,” the healer spoke before Garren strode away.

Chapter 32

As Ora slowly gained consciousness, the intense pain made her wish only to sink back into oblivion. She lay on her stomach. Her back felt like someone set fire to it, her skin prickled like a thousand needles, and her muscles ached. An involuntary whimper passed between her lips.

"Easy, now," came a quiet, unfamiliar voice.

Her eyes fluttered and opened just a slit. The blur of candlelight slowly sharpened to the edges of a wooden chair and the texture of canvas and cloth and a small portable side table.

A thin man's frame slowly came into focus. A healer.

Ora moaned. "How…long?" she barely whispered. She tried to lift her head and felt her senses swim. "Burns…."

"You need to hold still," the healer urged. "I have made a paste for your back, and your injuries need time to mend and scab over. I know it is painful, archer. You have been unconscious for two days."

"Where am I?"

"A holding tent in the First Division."

Ora let her eyes slide closed, too weary to keep them open. "Carter…," she whispered.

"Quiet now. No more talk. Do not waste your strength," the healer told her calmly. She felt the air move as he stepped closer and caught the aroma of chicken egg broth. Her stomach growled with hunger and she forced her eyes open again.

"Here, lift up your head."

"No," Ora murmured, brows pulling together. "I cannot pay for that."

"The Captain has seen to it. You must nourish yourself."

"The Captain?" Ora felt herself recoil. "Captain Garren?" She heard the bitterness in her tone, the anger, but at least no one had to be aware of the hurt she felt deep down at mention of his name. Why would he sentence her to harm and then treat her injuries? She turned her face away when the healer brought a spoon of the broth near her lips. "No," she said, voice cracking.

"Your stubbornness will be the death of you," the healer spoke coldly. He would do his duty toward her, but if she chose death he would feel no grief. "You make the decision. I will not be accountable."

Ora stared at him, seeing his face as he remained bent down, offering the broth.

"What is it to be?" he said. "I have other patients. The Captain's wishes will not deter me from their care."

Death. For a moment, she felt shame to even consider it. With the pain bordering on insanity, death seemed such a peaceful resolution. She missed her mother more now than ever. If she died, she may see her in the afterlife. Or maybe death was an eternity of sleep. She did not mind that idea either.

But then, what would happen to Carter and Thane? What would her life here mean, if she let it all end this way? And where would justice against Greer ever come from? She could not bear the idea of his living with the satisfaction of her death because she had refused his advances. Would he move on to harm another young woman the same way he had tried with her?

"I will take it," she murmured at last and with effort and pain, lifted her head to accept the broth. Despite a renewed sense of determination, she only managed a few swallows before the weariness became too much. She laid her head back down and passed out once more.

The next time she awoke, the burning had lessened along her back and she found she could move her shoulders with some effort and discomfort. She opened her eyes in search of the healer but he was gone. A candle burned low on the small side table, its light flickering off the walls of the tent. She turned her gaze, shifting her position on the cot to make out the shadow of a footman standing guard outside the holding tent.

So, I am a prisoner. Everyone believes I tried to escape. That I am a coward who tried to run away.

Ora felt a tear gather on her lower lashes and did not bother to wipe it away. She did not have to acknowledge its existence and there was no one around to witness her weakness.

She craved water. Her tongue felt like sandpaper and her throat raw. How long since the healer fed her broth? It seemed to be night then and night now. She licked her lips and opened her mouth to call for the footman, not sure if her voice would even carry enough to reach his ears, when suddenly the tent flap lifted and the healer entered.

His gaze met hers at once. He smiled. "You are awake. Good. I have brought you your evening meal."

"What day is it?" Ora found it easier to talk now. "How goes the battle? Have you heard anything from the Archers Quarter. How they are faring?" She realized as she spoke how anxious she felt to mend herself and rejoin them. To fight by their sides again. Among people she knew and understood.

"The fight continues as always," the healer said as he set the tray he carried on the side table. He turned to glance her over. "You have been here for four days now. You have woken a few times to eat. Do you remember?"

"Not…not really."

"Can you sit up?"

Ora felt sure she'd pass out again if she tried to move, yet determined to try. "Yes," she said. "I believe I can."

The healer placed a hand under her arm to support her as she turned carefully onto her side, careful not to let her back touch anything. She still wore the simple under-tunic, open at the back so no material touched the raw marks from the whip. She gritted her teeth and breathed deeply through her nose, as nausea prickled through her stomach and her head swam. Still, she managed to sit up somewhat on her side. The healer pressed pillows on each side of her to support her. He stepped back and brought her more broth as well as a cup of warm water that smelled sweetly of greens.

After several sips of water and the first spoonfuls of broth, she glanced up at the healer. "What will happen to me? When I am better?"

The healer filled the spoon again. "I suspect you will return to the field. A Singer may keep an eye on you more closely for awhile, to be sure you do not try to run again. Captain Garren has taken responsibility for you."

"What do you mean by 'responsibility'?"

The healer fed her another spoonful. "You are one of his recruits. That is why he could overrule your sentence. That, and he is a Captain, of course. But this also means that should you try again, he will kill you. It is his duty."

Ora turned her face away from the broth. "I am done now," she whispered.

Chapter 33

"Do you know what you have done?" Commander Dillion watched Garren as the Captain sat at the end of the council table. He shook his head. "It was one thing to announce a proper sentence, as much as I hate to see the girl suffer. Thirty lashes. Greer took it too far, trying to have her killed without official proof to his claim.... But to renounce your own sentence—."

"I did not sentence her to die. Had the sentence continued, she would have," he said coldly.

"Commander Strell is using that against you, to stir up trouble. He is trying to take your rank away from you, Captain."

"He and Greer both. I doubt they are the only ones." Garren leaned back in his chair and casually crossed his arms over his chest. "He does not have the authority. My actions have caused no injury to his precious War," he concluded darkly. "Therefore, he has nothing for any charge to take to the King."

"You are showing her special attention," the Commander continued calmly. "Do not deny it. I know you are paying for her care." He watched Garren steadily, and his next words came in a thoughtful murmur, "Is it possible?"

"Is what possible?" Garren threw back at him, irritated. He did not like feeling like this. Out of control. Restless. Agitated. So much so since Ora's sentence and injury that he could not even remain indifferent before the Commander.

Commander Dillion continued, unfazed: "Is it possible that a Singer can actually feel love, and let it overcome him? To feel emotion and care for someone despite all claims to the contrary?"

"You would mock me?" Garren warned, staring at him hard. "Remember, I can sense things that others are not aware of. Do not think I am not aware of your own… predicament."

The Commander's lips parted but he did not seem surprised. "I have seen enough of you to know you do not miss the truth of a man's secrets." He lowered his head somewhat. "I cannot marry until the War ends. Maybe I never will. As a Commander, I cannot show favoritism to anyone within my charge…but then, neither can you. I warn you as a friend. I know you do not believe in friendship, but I respect you and I have stood beside you in decisions past, so I hope you will respect my advice and see the wisdom in it."

Garren pushed back from the table after a moment and came forward. He offered his arm in a motion of friendship, holding the Commander's gaze. The Commander took it. "Thank you for your support. It is appreciated, despite the way it may appear." He drew back again. He blamed Ora for this. He had been a loner for so long, this attempt at socializing, even with the Commander, felt awkward.

He knew Commander Dillion meant well. Choosing to love Ora could lead nowhere. She despised him. To the world, he was only a monster at worst, and a soldier at best, fighting in a War that would never end, destined to die on the battlefield. There was no future for him beyond that.

Regardless, he was still determined to care for Ora the best he could. To protect her, as a soldier if nothing else.

A thunder of hooves from a single approaching horse broke the sudden silence between him and the Commander. "Captain!" someone called from outside.

A moment later, the tent flap lifted and Garren turned to see Edwan—Commander Dillion's footman—enter, gaze moving to Garren. "A messenger for you, from Torr Guard." He stepped to the side as Garren strode forward and threw back the tent flap to exit. His breath fogged the cool evening air, as a light breeze dried the perspiration from his brow.

With the flickering torchlight behind, the messenger's horse stood black against the night as its rider remained in the saddle, shoulders bowed from his long ride.

"What is it, soldier?" Garren commanded. He caught hold of the horse's headstall with a firm, calm hand when it snorted and pranced on its back legs with weary restlessness. Speckles of foam dotted its muzzle.

The messenger leaned down and held out a folded, leather letter packet. "From Captain Mason, Sir. The report of the interrogation of Sholl, the rebel captured in Torguson."

Garren took the packet and unhooked the leather eyelet to unfold it and read the letter within. His gaze scanned the writing in the torchlight, a muscle in his jaw flexed and his good eye darkened. "Where are they holding Sholl? I would speak with him," he demanded sharply.

The messenger stared at him. "Captain, he is dead," he said in surprise.

Garren looked at him sharply. "Dead? How?" he demanded fiercely.

"I do not know the details, Sir," the messenger replied. "I thought Captain Mason would give you the details in the letter."

Garren released the horse abruptly to step back as Commander Dillion exited the tent to stand behind him in question. "I need to find Greer," Garren said to the Commander darkly.

"What does the letter say?"

"Not much," Garren turned toward him, silently dismissing the messenger at his back. He met Commander Dillion's gaze with a shadowed look. "But enough." His mind raced through the events of the day. From the rider at the tree line in Torguson, to Ora's attempted escape and beating. Sholl's confession linked it all back to Greer.

"I need two footmen, *now*," he said, already starting off toward the far edge of camp. As he moved he caught the gazes of two footmen standing outside the Officers Quarter and made a short motion with his hand for them to follow.

Chapter 34

Ora jerked awake, lying on her side, not sure at first what caused her violent start of alarm from deep sleep. The healer gave her a strong tea to help her relax and sleep without much pain. She had never slept better, but when she pulled herself awake, she knew she could not have been asleep more than a few hours and sensed it was the darkest time of night. A lantern on the side table, having replaced the candle, cast soft orange light about the holding tent.

At once, she realized someone stood above her. She jerked her arm out, searching in vain for the dagger she knew she no longer possessed. The figure pounced on her, grabbing her arm and pinning it to her side, forcing her onto her back. Her breath left her in a rush of surprise and fear. One knee pressed against the side of her leg on the cot, and his free hand covered her mouth so tightly her lips pinched against her teeth as she tried to open her mouth to scream.

Terror ran through her like ice. Bile rose in the back of her throat when she heard his rough, deep voice. “Try and escape me this time, archer,” Greer sneered. “When I want something, nothing and no one will stop me. Try and scream again, and I will kill you.”

She felt his hand move to her shoulder and grip it tightly. She fought against him as he pulled at the shoulders of her tunic. She cried out as her wounds burned.

"You think that is painful? Wait till I am through with you…." He leaned closer and tried to kiss her and once again she twisted away from him; his lips bruised her cheek instead. Her hands shoved against his chest, her eyes burning with tears. A sob lodged in her throat. He shoved her head back and his lips seared the skin of her throat.

Suddenly, he was pulled back and his eyes widened in shock. Lips parted in a lost cry, Ora stared in frozen terror at Greer's face. At the dagger protruding from his gut and the hand of the man who held the hilt of the dagger, his other arm pressed tightly against Greer's throat, dragging him back off the cot.

Garren gripped the dagger, shoving it deeper into Greer's gut till the dying soldier arched backward, his mouth parted in silent surprise as the life drained from his eyes. "Now there *is* a witness," Garren said darkly. He twisted Greer away from Ora and let him fall to the floor, and stood over Ora with hands clenched, the muscles of his arms tense, and breathing deep with a violent anger in his steel grey eye.

Two footmen entered abruptly behind Garren moments after the Captain's arrival. Ora pushed herself up to a sitting position, lifting a shaking hand to push a lock of tangled hair back from her face. Her skin crawled with the memory of Greer's touch.

Garren stooped to retrieve his dagger—the strange one made out of sharpened bone—and ripped the edge of Greer's tunic to wipe the blood from the blade as he straightened. At his sharp command, the two footmen lifted Greer's body to carry it out of the tent.

Garren moved to follow them, but hesitated to glance over at Ora.

"Captain," she managed in a voice hardly more than a whisper. She looked away, feeling exposed as she wrapped her arms around her drawn up knees, unnerved by his searching gaze.

He turned to leave, breaking eye contact. As he turned his back, Ora bit her lower lip and trembled with increasing intensity as the full weight of what almost happened crashed over her.

Garren passed a hand over his dark hair, then abruptly turned toward her once more and came to the side of the cot.

Ora caught her breath. "So, now you believe me?" she blurted bitterly, wishing she could hide.

The anger and violence left his gaze—turning the steel grey to a softer, ocean blue—as his hand touched her knee.

Ora flinched and jerked away. Tears flooded her eyes, and though his gaze darkened and he frowned at her response, he sat on the edge of the cot and reached for her a second time.

"Belle, I am not going to hurt you," his voice rumbled quietly between them. His fingers brushed her cheek, his palm cupping her jaw lightly, and she felt stunned confusion at the gentleness he showed. There was nothing threatening in his touch, so unlike Greer's. But to let Garren comfort her seemed too cruel. It stung her pride. But, more than that, he had betrayed her.

She shook so badly now, she could hardly think straight, and did not have the mindset to try and hide it, torn between heartache and anger. Words tumbled out of their own accord. "You did this to me. After everything you said…everything you claimed. Why did you not let me die? You should have let me die…."

Garren pressed a hand firmly against the side of her head, bringing his face nearer to hers with intensity, commanding her attention. "No," he insisted huskily, roughly. "No. I will not let you die." A strange look came to his eye, and through her own scattered emotions she caught her breath, almost feeling the wrestling in his head as he fought some inner battle. "Greer will never hurt you again," he said in a low, even tone.

"He is not the only one."

Pain flickered in Garren's grey eye. "You can hold me in contempt. I know I am to blame. Curse me, Belle, for I am already cursed."

Her hands lifted to the front of her tunic, clutching at it, though it covered her. She shook her head, turning aside from his touch. "Mother warned me about you. Why should a battlefield be any different? Soldiers only ever have one thing on their minds, besides the War, and they only leave pain, death, and destruction in their wake." She hardly realized what she said, shoving her hands out against his chest just as she had with Greer, refusing his move to hold her, his desire to comfort her. The truth poured from her lips as she struggled to hold herself together. "I am nothing but a bastard, after all…and I could not save her. She is dead. I *hate* you. You are all monsters."

Garren pulled her against him, taking advantage of her moment of weakness when she could not fight him. She felt the firmness of his jaw against the side of her head, the light sweat of his dark hair against her temple. She felt the strength of his chest, the solid muscle pressed against her small, weakened frame. Horrified, a sob tore from her throat —strangled and cut off, desperate to control herself.

She felt Garren's hands inadvertently touch her bare back, his calloused fingers snagging against the abrasions there, wounds that would never fully disappear. Her breath caught back a cry of pain. Instead, she pressed her face into his shoulder and screamed, her voice muffled against him—

releasing pent up fear, agony, anger, and years of secret pain and heartache.

She felt her senses grow dizzy, her head grow light. Why could she not stop trembling? And in the arms of this man, of all people! This cold, calculating Singer who believed in no emotion, no tears. He would surely see her as weak now!

Her head fell back and Garren's hand came up to catch it and bring it to his shoulder, as her cry dissolved into another sob and she passed out in his arms.

Chapter 35

Keeping one arm around her back, Garren slid his other beneath her knees and lifted her into his arms, holding her protectively close. He moved to sit in the chair—the only other furniture in the space—with Ora cradled on his lap, as she remained unaware. He touched his lips to her brow, knowing this would be the only time. Once she awakened, she would despise him again and reject him. She had just begun to lower her defenses against him. She had believed him, when he said he did not want her hurt. And then this.... She would never believe in him again.

Her words haunted him. *'I am nothing but a bastard.'* His heart raged to know what she meant by her spiteful words. She had called him a monster again, but not just him. She had thrown out the insult toward the entire King's Army.

He leaned his head forward and rested his brow against hers. Her emotions twisted his gut. He had never felt so undone by anyone in his whole life, especially a woman. She was still young, he had to remind himself of that. He had destroyed her innocence and forced her to grow up too fast by making her a soldier; by bringing her here. It did not matter what the Law decreed. He could have taken the boys and left her, let her have another year at least.

He closed his eyes and lifted his head to lean against the back of the chair. Through the next several hours he remained this way, wakeful and watchful, dreading the parting he knew he must make. This time forever. He had let himself get distracted, and he'd spoken out of turn with her by letting his feelings show. It had not stopped her from getting hurt…by his own hand.

When the grey light of dawn brushed the edges of the tent and filled the shadowed space with soft light—the lantern flame having long ago burned out—Garren finally looked down into Ora's sleeping face and shifted to stand even as her lips parted and her eyelids fluttered with the first signs of wakefulness.

His heart slammed against his rib cage as he felt the soft touch of her emotions stirring to life, and the initial feeling of contentment and warmth that wrapped its way through his senses. He resisted the urge to continue holding her and never let go, and moved back to her cot to gently lay her down on her side, wanting to spare her the pain of her back.

Chapter 36

Ora felt warm and safe as she slowly gained consciousness. She lay on her side, and the pain in her back had faded. Nothing touched the raw skin. The thought caused her cheeks to grow warm and her heart to turn in confusion, with the memory of Garren's arms around her, his hands pressed over her back. The thoughts immediately following—of her spiteful words, the showing of her inner heartache and deeply buried hurts—caused her to draw in a sharply audible breath, coming fully wake. Her eyes opened, gritty and sore from the tears she refused to cry.

"Keep calm. You are safe."

Garren's deep, quietly spoken words had the opposite affect on Ora as her heart jumped to her throat and she sat up quickly, then faltered as a wave of dizziness and weakness washed over her. She leaned on one arm, legs pulled up beside her and let her head hang a moment, breathing deep.

She heard his step before she saw him. She felt his touch on her knee before she looked up to meet his gaze, and she could not quite decide what she felt about him. Hatred? Disappointment? Fear?

She felt too disoriented in those moments to decide, before she was forced to meet his gaze. He still wore the eyepatch. She had not seen his discolored eye since that accidental encounter behind enemy lines, but his one grey eye looked intently into hers.

He crouched before her, one hand remained lightly on her knee until she met his gaze. He kept his expression veiled. "What did you mean?"

She looked away. "About what?" she said stiffly, but her heart began to pound with anxiety.

Garren abruptly stood up and moved away from her, back to the chair he had been sitting in when she awoke. He sat, facing her, gaze steady on her face. "I think you know about what."

"It is not your concern—."

"Oh, I think it is," Garren interrupted firmly. He leaned forward with elbows on his knees, and threaded his fingers together in front of him. "You hate me. You might as well have blamed me for whatever pain you hide behind those golden eyes. I think I have the right to know just what you meant."

Ora swallowed hard and swung her legs over the edge of the cot to sit up straight, gripping the edge of the mattress on each side of her. She winced as the abrasions on her back pulled and prickled. "How long was I asleep?"

"Five hours. It is nearly dawn. Belle…stop avoiding the question."

She looked at him.

"I cannot make you tell me. The choice is yours."

Ora took a breath. He had shaken her emotionally, with his rescue. But more than that, with his steady calm. She felt defenseless. And yet, alone in this small space with him, she felt she could confide in him, that she owed him the truth.

Her angry speech the night before had been the start, and now she had to tell him the rest.

"My parents…were not killed in battle like my guardian inferred," she began a bit unsteadily. "Though it was the War that killed them both in the end." Her hands grew cold and she clenched them tighter until her fingers went numb. Her stomach clenched as the words spilled forth like bitter poison. "In fact, my father was not really my father at all…." Her voice choked off. She could no longer look at Garren, unsure of what she would see there once he knew. "My mother married a farmer she had known since they were children together. Shortly after their ceremony was completed, only weeks later, he left to join the War, when it first began, and he left my mother under the protection of his home and village. Soldiers came through the village on their way to the Divisions, and they ransacked the village—demanding food and accommodations and…pleasures." She stiffened. "My mother was…defiled. This happens to women all over the Freelands, even now. The men are taken into battle and there is no one to defend their wives and children. There is no one to stop the soldiers from doing whatever they please."

She took a breath and nervously tucked a strand of hair back behind her ear, feeling Garren's gaze. "My father sustained an injury in battle and was sent home to recover. He became ill and died shortly before I was born, and my mother claimed I was his child. No one questioned it. She only told me the truth, I think, to protect me and to warn me in hopes that it would not happen to me. Whenever soldiers came to the village, she would hide me. And she always took great pains to conceal her beauty. She was beautiful, my mother, and somehow her sorrows only made her more noticeable to men. She carried her heartache well, with grace."

"She moved us to Neice," she continued, "when I was four years old, and with an old family friend from my birth village—the man who became my guardian." She bit her lower lip and shut her eyes a moment, not sure she could speak of the ending.

A moment of silence passed. "What became of her?" Garren's voice rumbled gently. "You say the War killed your father and your mother.... You were alone, with your guardian, in Neice when I came. What became of your mother, Belle?"

Ora forced her gaze to lift and meet his, and held it. "Neice was no safer than any other Freeland village." A tear dripped onto her cheek, but she could not turn her gaze away this time, silently questioning the mix of blue that appeared in his grey eye—a stormy ocean suddenly tranquil and still. "More soldiers came, two years ago, and they took my mother. When they tired of using her, they...they tied her to one of their horses and dragged her to death." Now, her voice trembled despite all her attempts at strength. She could feel herself shaking. Nausea rose in her chest as she could still see the images sharply impressed on her mind.

"Where were you when this happened?" he questioned, his voice coming to her as if from a distance.

Ora blinked, seeing Garren's face before her again as the memories broke away. "My guardian hid me. But I saw... when they dragged my mother through the village street." Once again, her voice choked up. "I...I went to her. I could hardly recognize her. She just...looked at me.... Then, she was gone." She turned her face away and bit her lower lip. It was not the full truth, but it was all she could give. "Are you satisfied now that I have told you?" She tried to inflect anger toward him into her tone, ashamed to admit so much.

Chapter 37

Garren held still for several moments. Very still. "Why did you not tell me sooner?"

"Because you are a soldier, and not only that, you are a —."

"A monster?"

She glared at him. "What do you expect?"

Garren dipped his head and let go of a frustrated sigh. "I am sorry," he said, and realized he had never once apologized to her, not for anything he had said or done. He had always made the excuse that the monster in him carried the blame for his actions. There came a surprising release of pressure from his heart, saying those words. A relief. So, he said it again, seeing that Ora watched him, equally surprised by his words: "I am sorry I have been so hard on you. That I failed to notice, to even consider, your fears…fears justified by your circumstances. I have thought—hoped—at times, to be a comfort to you. And what I am has been the opposite. I have failed you, even more so than I originally believed."

Ora turned her face away, paining him. "You did not know, and I did not mean to tell you so much. It was by your order I was flogged, though I know you could have put me to death." Tears filled her voice, and she swallowed hard. He wondered if she would ever cry, and was that his fault too? For telling her she must not or she was weak? "But you did not believe me. I had begun...to see you differently. To think...better of you. To...believe in you."

Anguish filled Garren, but she shook her head slightly as if to clear it and continued before he could break in and speak, or worse, drag her passionately into his arms and hold her close and never let her go.

"I expected wrongdoing from Greer. As strange as it is to admit, I did not expect it from you."

Suddenly, Garren shifted and stood and moved to sit beside her. Ora refused to look at him, holding herself stiffly erect. His shoulder brushed hers and her voice faded: "I have never told anyone what I just told you. No one knows about my mother—or about me. Not...not even Carter." He sensed the frailness in her words. The vulnerability. The fear.

He reached forward to touch her cheek and the single tear that still glistened there, and felt deep distress when she flinched, as if instinctively expecting violence when he had meant to show only tenderness. She slowly relaxed and turned her face into his shoulder.

His hand moved to cradle her jaw as he settled her head into the hollow of his neck, careful not to touch her back. A few wayward tears soaked into the edge of his tunic near his collarbone, beneath the leather. She squeezed her eyes shut and his solid body absorbed her tremors. For some moments, she allowed him to comfort her.

He should have saved her. He knew that. Though he had done the best he could within the rules of war, without proof and only his own suspicions. But she did not see it that way. He could not say 'I am sorry' again, though the words nearly fell from his lips before he could pull them back.

"Never again can Greer impose on you or threaten you. He has paid with his life, so put it from your mind. Do not dwell on it. You carry no fault," he spoke against her hair. "What is done—what transpires—in war is ugliness. It is the imprinted, dark will of monsters. But not even that ugliness—not even the monsters—can destroy a heart that is pure, a heart that holds goodness."

Ora tugged away from him. She stared at him in thinly veiled confusion and their gazes held for a moment. Garren felt no desire to explain his words or the thoughts racing through his head. He did not want to tell her how much she affected him. How her soul seemed to connect with his. How her emotions crumbled his every defense. He stood and distanced himself.

"Where are you going?" she inquired softly.

"I received word from Captain Mason. I am expected in Torr Guard—to clean up a mess." He turned in the doorway and caught her gaze. "Belle…I meant to save you," he confessed quietly. "I am sorry I only ended up hurting you." He turned away again and slipped out of the tent, disappearing into the morning sunlight.

Chapter 38

Ora sat still for several minutes, staring at the place Garren had stood. How could so much have happened between them in so short a period of time? Only yesterday she had hated him. Now…her hate melted away. She did not know what she felt toward him anymore.

For a moment, she let herself believe he was someone else. Not a soldier. Not a monster. She had needed his comfort, even if just for a minute, before she could stand on her own again. So, she had pushed aside every uncertainty and the voices in her head reminding her she must hate him and never trust a Singer…and she had taken from him what she needed, whatever the consequences.

Now, she felt a twinge of guilt. Could she go on hating him, publicly or otherwise, after confessing her deepest secret to him, her deepest fears and pain, and hiding in his arms, accepting his comfort?

She swallowed hard and lifted her hand to her face where his fingers had touched her. As she straightened and stood, the skin on her back prickled and stung as the newly-formed scabs over her wounds pulled and cracked.

She slowly raised her arms and bit her lower lip to keep from crying out at the stiffness of her bruised muscles and traced her fingers over the torn skin near her shoulders. She was healing quickly now, thanks to the medicines, though she knew it would take time for the pain to fully leave, and for the wounds to mend into scars.

Soon, she would return to the battlefield, the only place she now belonged.

Chapter 39

Garren left the holding tent and did not look back. A shaft of sunlight nearly blinded him as he came out into the cold morning air. The sun peaked over the horizon between earth and hazy, smoke-filled skies, and fell across the walls of the tents behind him.

"Where is Commander Dillion?" he demanded a nearby footman, turning to him.

"Sir," the footman responded, swallowing nervously. Garren's eye glinted like stone, his features hardening to the familiar uncertainty in the other man's face. He found himself in a particularly sour mood. He clenched his jaw and listened to the footman's answer. "I believe he is at the Officers Quarter."

Garren started off, then paused to turn back. "Greer's body? Where is it?"

"Taken to be burned in the graveyard, as instructed, Sir."

Garren nodded shortly. "As you were."

As it happened, he did not need to go looking for Commander Dillion. The Commander was searching for him, and came upon him not twenty yards away, as Garren strode toward the Officers Quarter. “What is this I hear about Greer?”

Garren stopped. “I was just on my way to you.”

“What’s happened?” the Commander urged, brows lowered in concern.

Garren glanced about to be sure no one was close enough to overhear his words. “Greer trespassed on the archer, Orabelle,” he said quietly, “and I killed him.”

“And the girl?”

“Unharmed,” Garren insisted. “But Greer lied to us before, and I played right into his hands.” Inwardly, he upbraided himself. *I was more concerned with my reputation than her well being and I made an unforgivable mistake.*

“What will you tell the Council?” the Commander lowered his voice.

Garren glanced back the way he came. “That Greer was a rebel, and his charges against Orabelle—his claims—are false. He is to be burned in the graveyard without honors, and Ora will heal and return to her duties.” He looked the Commander firmly in the eye. “I need to return at once to Torr Guard and find out everything Captain Mason learned from Sholl. I must prove that Greer was in active aggression against our King and his duties as a soldier. He was the rebel I saw at the tree line in Torguson.”

“You are certain is was him?”

Garren’s lips thinned. “Sholl confessed to rebel dealings with Greer, and after all that has happened these last few days…I would stake my life on it.”

“You may have to,” the Commander warned quietly.

“Can I trust you, Commander?” Garren questioned seriously. “For Ora’s sake, I need to trust you. Look out for her.” He held out a hand, a motion unheard of for a Singer. The Commander’s gaze shone with understanding and respect, and he grasped the Captain's wrist in a return gesture of approval.

"You have my word, Captain, and my discretion."

Garren nodded shortly, mentally weighing the Commander's words and seeing truth and honesty in the other man's face. He departed from the Commander's company and made for the stables and his black beast.

"Take me to Torr Guard, **Emunah**[15]," he murmured, using one of the horse's Ancient names. He had named the horse **Ohev**[16] when he had first begun with it as a colt ten years ago. Through the years, the horse had proven itself a long-lasting and faithful companion, and so Garren sometimes called it **Emunah**.

The great beast responded to his light touch and turned its head toward Torr Guard.

---

[15] Emunah : Ancient Tongue meaning 'faithfulness'

[16] Ohev : Ancient Tongue meaning 'dear friend'

Chapter 40

Two days later, Ora stood in front of Commander Kane in the main tent of the Archers Quarter, dressed in her simple archer's uniform and soft-leather shoes with bow and quiver at her back. She stood straight, shoulders back, trying to ignore the prickling of the scabs on her back, still raw against the material of her tunic. A thin trail of perspiration trickled down between her shoulder blades, only making the discomfort worse.

Bron stood in the far corner of the room, an unobtrusive shadow once more—reminding her of the first day she had seen him—standing out of the way, watching and listening but not interfering.

The silence stretched until it strained her senses. She refused to shift or show her discomfort. Her punishment had been decided by one man, the Captain, but her future as an archer in the King's Army could only be determined by her Commander.

It was not enough that the Singers could neutralize her should she run. The Commander needed to be able to trust her to do her job and be accountable on the battle field.

She had finally accepted her fate and embraced her role as an archer, a fighter, working not for herself, but for the survival of her fellow soldiers and her friends. Because of Greer's lie, the Army questioned her loyalties.

It had been two days since she last saw Garren, and in those two days of recovery, she had tried to convince herself that she was better off not seeing him. How could she face him, after everything she had told him? The Singer Captain knew more about her than even her best friend. What did he think of her? More importantly, why did his opinion matter to her?

The Commander stood from the rickety chair behind his desk and set the quill he had been holding back in the inkwell. The sound came sharply against Ora's dissenting thoughts, pulling her back to the present and away from the memory of being captive in Garren's arms.

"You are becoming an exemplary archer," the Commander spoke in his forceful, gusty voice. He moved around his desk and crossed to stand in front of her. "You have survived the line and your mission into enemy territory, and that counts for something."

"Thank you, Sir," she answered with quiet firmness.

The Commander waved a hand toward the desk and the papers stacked and scattered across the surface. "I have confirmation here, from the Captain, of Greer's treachery in Torguson. In light of this evidence, all charges he brought against you have been dismissed. The word of a rebel cannot be trusted, and I need my archers on the field, where they belong."

Ora swallowed hard. "So I am…free to return to my duties?"

"Of course. You will report to the line at First Call in the morning." He glanced her over briefly. "You may return to your quarters with the other archers." He raised his voice to call his footman, and turned to Bron, who stepped forward from the shadows to join in quiet conversation.

She had been dismissed. Bron hardly glanced her way as she turned and withdrew.

Stepping into the sunlight brought a strong whiff of smoke-scented breeze and the first tangy bite of winter's chill. She waited while a group of soldiers passed by, and lifted her chin to slip in amongst the activity, shouldering her kit. She moved with purpose to the tent she shared with her friends, anxious to see Carter. She had not been allowed to see or talk to anyone during her recovery in the holding tent, and only learned enough to know Carter had been sent back to the line.

She did not expect to find him waiting for her outside their tent, and had not realized just how much she had missed his honest face until she saw him. It took all her self control not to break into a run and throw her arms around him. But her lips lifted in a smile of true joy as she looked him over. "You are here," she said, stopping in front of him. "You are all right."

He pulled her into his arms and her gasp and wince of pain made him immediately draw back again with remorse. "I am sorry, Ora," he insisted, brow furrowed. "I heard what happened. How could they sentence you to thirty lashes?"

"I did not try to run, Carter," Ora said. "You have to believe me. I would never have left without you."

"I never doubted you," Carter answered. "But why should Greer lie like that? Why should he want to see you punished?" The innocence in his questions was not lost to Ora, and she knew word had not spread about Greer's attack on her. Had Garren kept that quiet? To spare her?

"It does not matter," Ora insisted, but this time her smile came forced.

Carter tugged the kit off her shoulder to carry it as they turned to enter the tent. "When will you be sent to the front?"

"First Call."

Carter glanced at her in the shadows of the tent interior as they came to the cots. "So soon? Are you sure you can handle it?" The soft sensitive concern in his eyes warmed her heart. As they stood by her cot, he dropped her kit onto the thin mattress. She took his hand, threaded her fingers between his, and kissed his cheek.

"Thank you, Carter. You are a good friend," she whispered.

Carter glanced aside. "Is that all?" he said so softly she almost missed it. She felt as if her heart stopped in her chest, and she held very still, studying his averted gaze before it turned back to hers with question. "Just a friend," he concluded in an altered tone and offered her an apologetic, almost shy, smile.

Ora wanted to answer and say something, anything. But her lips stiffened in refusal against her.

Carter glanced away again, disappointment in his blue eyes. "Have you eaten?" he said before she could feel uncomfortable in the silence.

"No. Not yet today. The Commander sent orders for my presence first thing and I could not think about eating then," Ora admitted. "You will join me?"

"Come on," Carter obliged and led the way. As she fell into step beside him and left the tent behind, she felt herself begin to relax. But she knew that after the flogging and Greer's attack, not to mention her confession to Garren, nothing involving her past would ever be the same again—including her friendship with Carter.

Chapter 41

Inside the tower of Torr Guard, a nearly invisible stairway tucked against the wall curved down below the cracked stone-slabbed floor into pitch darkness. Captain Mason went first, holding out a burning torch, the light revealing only a few feet ahead of their descent. Garren stood back a moment, allowing the other Captain some room, before he followed. Their caution existed not from fear of the darkness, but wariness of the decaying state of the tower, and the treacherous, narrow steps.

A muscle in Garren's jaw flexed, and he trailed a hand against the wall to his left as a guide, his boots testing his footing on each descending step. As they moved deeper into the darkness, his grey eye searched in vain ahead of Captain Mason's light for what lay ahead. He refused to remove his eyepatch. "When did Sholl die?" His voice fell hollow and echoed softly against the cold stone walls, his gaze fixed on the shadows ahead.

Captain Mason did not turn when he answered solemnly. "Three days ago."

"And do you know what happened?"

"I have not examined the body. Commander Strell arrived and took over. I have not received any other report besides what I already told you in the letter," Captain Mason said. "The Commander's healer determined his death to be from an attack of the heart, caused by severe stress."

They reached the bottom of the stairs and Captain Mason used his torch to light second and third torches on the wall. The additional light revealed a large round room with outward sloping stone walls. One side of the room was sectioned off into iron holding cells. A long table sat in the open space before them, on which the prone form of a man's body lay. Captain Mason placed his torch in a holder attached to the side of the table, shedding light across the deceased man's face.

Garren approached to look down at the corpse, considering Captain Mason's last words. "Did you torture him?" He glanced sharply toward Captain Mason, calculating the other man's response through emotion even before the other Captain replied.

"He was treated as any prisoner of war, Captain," Captain Mason said with the slight shake of his head, features tense. "We kept him in his cell, fed him a daily ration, and questioned him at length."

Garren looked over the body without touching it. "Sounds like the Commander did not find your methods… satisfactory," he said.

"You think the Commander has something to do with Sholl's death?"

Garren lifted the dead man's hand, keeping his gaze on Captain Mason. "If his death was an attack of the heart, I would like to know how he managed to get hold of a poison-tipped needle."

Captain Mason stepped forward and peered at the man's hand as Garren's finger tapped against Sholl's middle finger.

Even in the ill light of flickering torches, Captain Mason could identify the round, bruised mark where a needle had pierced the skin just under a dirty, cracked fingernail.

"Somebody killed your prisoner, Captain," Garren informed him gravely. He dropped the dead man's arm and took a step back. He glanced to the stairs, then back at Captain Mason. "If he confessed about Greer being involved in the rebel attacks…what else did he know? Whoever did this eliminated him because he must have posed a threat to them."

Captain Mason hesitated.

Garren's eye narrowed. "What are you not telling me, Captain?"

"Before Commander Strell confiscated the body and took over the investigation," Captain Mason began slowly, quietly. "Sholl gave me something…just after he gave up Greer's name."

From inside his cloak, the Captain withdrew a small, hard object and held it between two fingers, offering it to Garren.

Garren took it and examined it in the torchlight, revealing a silver band, plain and burnished. Not a ceremonial marriage band, as only women wore those. It was large enough to fit over Garren's thumb. "This was his?"

"He gave it to me the night before he died. I thought it of small significance, until I saw the writing inside. A language much like I have seen on For'bane weaponry. But why would Sholl have worn such a thing?"

"This band is Freeland made…," Garren assessed.

"The man was terrified, despite all appearances. Maybe he knew he was going to die; that whether he gave us information or not, he'd just become a target because we captured him?"

"Has anyone else seen this? One of the footmen, perhaps? A trainer, or a recruit?"

"No one, that I am aware. I was alone with him for but a moment, when he gave it to me. I do not entirely trust Commander Strell, and have not felt any desire to hand this over to him." He watched Garren carefully. "When I saw the lettering inside, I knew I needed to show it to you."

"You are right to suspect For'bane. It is an ancient dialect from the time of our own Ancient Tongue. I studied it at length, before I…became a Singer. I have become adept at recognizing it, as they do indeed inscribe it on many of their weapons."

"And here I have always imagined the For'bane to be rather dull-witted creatures…," Captain Mason spoke dryly.

Garren kept his eye on the band and hardly reacted to the Captain's words. "They are intelligent, though not the same as us. Or maybe they were more intelligent before, but over time, their genesis process has corrupted them. They are violent creatures and their one instinct is to kill us, that is the law they live by."

"So, do you know what it says?"

Garren lowered the band. He stared hard at Captain Mason. "Then comes the age of beasts."

Chapter 42

Ora ate her dinner in silence, elbow-to-elbow with Carter after greeting several fellow archers. They did not ask her about her ordeal. They did not sympathize, but if they had, Ora would have hated it.

A bell signaled the end of their meal session and the beginning of the next. The archers hastened to clear what remnants clung to their bowls with fingers and crusts of bread, and relinquished their seats to the next group of soldiers, many appearing fresh from battle, weary and famished.

Ora looked across the tent and saw the slight frame of Thane near the entrance, limping behind a burly soldier in line ahead of him. She stopped so suddenly that Carter bumped against her shoulder.

"Ora?"

Ora kept her gaze fastened on Thane, afraid that if she looked away he would disappear forever. "You go ahead. I will be along in a bit."

"Do not try to get seconds," Carter reminded her. "They will cut off a finger for that."

Ora forced a slight smile. "I would not risk it. Do not worry."

Without waiting to see if he followed the other archers, Ora left Carter's side and wove her way between soldiers, benches, and tables to slip into line beside Thane. "I did not know when I would see you again," she spoke softly. "I thought you were stationed in the Third Division?"

Thane looked up, startled, and then his eyes lit up and he smiled weakly. "Commander Jeshura returned yesterday and removed me to serve him at the temporary Officers Quarter here. It is all very strange, Ora," he continued with an anxious crease in his brow. "Something to do with the alchemists—the work they are doing in the Healers Quarter here. A Commander has to be present to approve whatever work they are doing."

Ora glanced forward at the food line. "They are trying to end the War, same as the rest of us, I suppose," she said distractedly.

"They are strange men. I saw one talking to a Commander today, just before I was released to come eat. They wear long white tunics, but they never seem to have trouble keeping them clean in this place." Thane shrugged one shoulder. "How have you been? I am so glad to see you. It is such a large camp, I was not sure where you would be...."

Big enough that he must not have heard about her flogging.

"My master keeps me busy," she said wryly out of the side of her mouth, glancing at those around her to see if anyone listened in on their conversation. The soldiers were too interested in their meals to pay her any mind.

"Do you like being an archer?"

Ora looked again at Thane to see him curiously taking in the bow and quiver of arrows at her back. "It is better than being a soldier on the front line." She nodded toward his leg. "What happened?" she tried not to sound overly worried.

Thane shrugged again. "Twisted my ankle."

He did not look any better than the last time she'd seen him. In fact, he looked worse. It was not just the ankle, he looked seriously ill.

She knew this would be tough on him. He was not used to this environment any more than the rest of them, but he could not adapt like the others. He needed to go home, where a soft green carpet of grass blanketed the hills instead of mud, rock, and blood. Where the sky still looked blue and the breeze tasted of mountain flowers, pine, and clean wood smoke from village cooking fires—not soot, iron, and grit from forge fires. Where the stench of death and decay did not surround them day and night.

If she thought about that, she might go mad.

They neared the cooking tables. She noticed a footman eyeing her from the end of the first table, one hand on his sword in warning.

"Here," she said, reaching into her kit and withdrawing squirrel fur mittens she had fashioned while in recovery. She tucked them into Thane's satchel, which mirrored hers across his own shoulder, resting against his thin hip. "I made you these."

Thane's fingers sunk into the thin, smooth fur. "You… you remembered…," he whispered, almost as a question.

Ora held his gaze a moment as her heart squeezed within her like a vice had been clamped around it. "We would have given gifts at home to celebrate the day. This is the best I could do in these circumstances. So…in honor of the start of your thirteenth year." She inclined her head. "A couple days late."

She stepped out of line just as they reached the cooking stand, giving the footman a cursory glance to show him she had no intention of trying to sneak seconds.

She wanted to tell Thane to hold on. She wanted to tell him they would go home soon. But she could not lie. His only hope for survival was to forget. Just as she must forget.

"I will try to see you again," she said and forced her feet to turn and walk away as the boy's narrow shoulders disappeared behind the sea of soldiers.

When she returned to the tent at the Archers Quarter, Carter's cot was not only empty, but stripped of its meager bedding. She stopped on the threshold and looked around. "Where is Carter?" she demanded in surprise and wariness. He would not have been called to the front—not before her.

The others turned as she entered, some with uncertainty on their faces. They stopped what they were doing and watched her.

Then, Decklan stepped forward. "We thought they had sent you back to the front," he said gently.

"No," Ora insisted. "I stopped to talk with a friend." She looked at the archer firmly. "Did they send Carter back to the front by himself?"

Decklan crossed over to his cot, proceeding to loosen the ties of his leather jerkin as he prepared to rest. His calm movements only agitated Ora's nerves, which still bothered her since her flogging injuries and her time in the holding tent. "A couple of footmen came to take him to the Healers Quarter. I do not know why," Decklan informed her. He shrugged slightly. "I figured his shoulder was still bothering him. But then they stripped his bed and removed his belongings."

Valara, the oldest girl recruit from Torr Guard, appeared suddenly on Ora's right. "They are going to change him," she warned in a low tone, but loud enough for everyone to hear as she looked at the other archers. "That is how it happens. They pick us out from the archers, take us away, and no one ever returns—at least, not the same."

Ice-cold fear surrounded Ora's heart, making it hard to breathe. Hard to focus as her brain began to buzz. It seemed so long ago that they had talked about the Singers that first night in Torr Guard. How could she have forgotten the danger of being an archer? That the War was not just about the For'bane. It was the Singers, too. It was the will of Command to do whatever they wished with their soldiers, including experimenting on them.

Bile rose in the back of her throat.

"They cannot take him," burst from her lips as she shook her head, thinking desperately. It did not make sense. Would they not look for some outstanding skill for a potential Singer? While Carter did his job well, his skills were not exceptional and his physique was hardly noteworthy for a Singer—thinking of Garren's tall frame and bold strength. She could point out others in the room that she would have expected to be taken before Carter!

"Those are just rumors," one of the boy archers spoke up, addressing Valara. "They have not recruited Singers for three years at least. Too many…failures…."

"What does he mean?" Ora turned to Valara.

Valara lowered her voice, a warrior's attempt to be gentle. "He means 'deaths.' I have only heard stories, like most people. Not everyone who receives the mixing reacts… favorably. Something in the blood. There are different side-effects, and they vary in intensity by subject."

"*Subject*? You mean *person*!"

"We are all subjects of the King," Decklan insisted, trying to calm her.

Ora shook her head. "And so the King employs his officers to turn us into monsters?"

"We do not even know for sure if that is what is happening here," Decklan began again.

Ora ignored him and ran out of the tent. She moved quickly between soldiers, horses, and carts, navigating the pathways created by the maze of tents with familiar ease.

But her mind could only think of Carter, not her surroundings or even the call of several soldiers who had fought alongside her acknowledging her passing.

She made for the Healers Quarter, stationed not far away. The familiar sights and smells of medicine and sickness and death tasted like metal against her teeth and tongue and she pressed her lips together, passing down the rows of sickbeds without sight of her friend.

She burst through the far end of the second recovery tent out into the open air, into an area at the center of the Healers Quarter. She stopped abruptly, trying to get her bearings, and unfamiliar with the sights before her.

At the far side of a narrow clearing, surrounded by other tents, sat a cream-colored tent—very close to white—with a roped off section in front of the entrance. A small group of soldiers stood in a line, waiting to go in, behind the roped off section.

As Ora stood there, watching, a tall, thin man in a white, ankle-length tunic pushed aside the tent flap to step out and confer with one of two footmen standing guard outside. Surprised, Ora realized this must be one of the alchemists Thane mentioned.

She started forward, a knot forming in her gut as she searched the faces of the soldiers for Carter. Her breath felt labored with each step, as fear raced like ice through her veins.

Hands grabbed her arms on each side, staying her. Two footmen blocked her way, keeping her from going any closer. Where had they come from? Ora fisted her hands, trying to pull from their grasp. "No, please!"

Commander Strell appeared suddenly, coming from inside the tent. He caught sight of Ora and a frown marred his face. He glanced at the alchemist and handed the man the clipboard he held in his hands. "What is she doing here?" he demanded of no one in particular. "She is not on the list." He pointed a finger at the footman on Ora's left and ordered him, "Get her out of here."

Bron stepped from the midst of the group of waiting soldiers and Ora blinked at him in surprise.

She took the moment of stillness to finish searching the faces of those gathered. She did not see Carter. Where was he?! The footmen started to push her back toward the tent she had come out from. "Carter!" she called. Was he inside? He had to hear her! "Wait! Please, stop! What are you doing?" She shoved a fisted hand against the shoulder of the footman to her right, trying to see between the two men to the alchemist and Commander Strell. "Let me see him!"

The alchemist marked something on the clipboard and ignored her completely as he pointed out two of the waiting soldiers, motioning them to approach the tent.

"Whoa, hold on there!" Bron sprang to Ora's side as one of the footmen lifted a hand to cuff her. At his voice, they loosened their hold and stepped apart.

The alchemist drew back the tent flap to allow the two soldiers to proceed him into the tent. For a brief moment, Ora could see within—a large, uncomfortable-looking, reclining wooden chair, complete with wide leather restraints, and Carter, his arms and legs bound by the restraints. Two other alchemists and another man in uniform —a Commander—stood around him.

Ora jerked forward suddenly, nearly pulling free from the startled footmen. "Carter!" she cried.

Commander Strell strode forward as the tent flap fell closed again, obscuring her view of Carter before she could tell if he'd heard her. Was he unconscious? Bron stepped forward quickly and placed a restraining hand against the front of Ora's shoulder.

"You will leave this Quarter at once, archer, and return to your post," Commander Strell ordered with warning.

Fear for her friend kept her firmly planted. "What are you doing to him?!"

Commander Strell's eyes flashed. "Carter," he said tersely, "is a soldier of the King's Army. And take care how you speak to a Commanding officer, or was one flogging not enough for you?"

Ora felt the sting of his words, but kept her shoulders straight and her chin lifted.

Commander Strell continued to eye her with thinly veiled disdain. "Your friend has been recruited. He will advance the cause of the War as every Singer before him. It is a delicate process and my alchemists do not have time for troublemakers like yourself…."

Ora lurched forward. "No!" she cried. Bron stopped her, standing in front of her to block her way. He pressed her back as the Commander turned to return to the tent and the footmen advanced with warning against her. She ducked beneath Bron's arm—stretched out in warning before her—terror and rage clouding her judgement. "Carter!"

The footman on the left intervened and swung a closed fist at her. The blow glanced off the side of her face. She fell into the snow, pain flaming across her face as she raised a hand toward her lips, stunned.

Bron moved quickly to stand between Ora and the footmen. He reached down quickly and pulled her to her feet, hand slipping around her hip and supporting her at the waist. Blood trickled down Ora's split lip and a bruise darkened the area at the corner of her mouth. "She is going!" Bron thundered with a glare at the footman who had struck her.

Trembling, Ora broke Bron's grasp and dashed blindly back the way she had come, through the recovery tents, staggering and stumbling, bruising her thigh against the corner of a tall, side table near a wounded man's cot. She refused to look back even when Bron called after her.

Gasping in lungfuls of air, she pushed through the tent flap and stumbled to the outer perimeter of the Healers Quarter. She pressed her hands against the sides of her head, fighting back a dizzying wave of panic. Her split lip felt numb. *Think, think. There must be something I can do!*

Her hands moved to scrub her face angrily, wincing at the pain from the bruise near her mouth. No time for tears—she could not fall apart. She was Carter's only chance. She wiped away the smear of blood near her chin.

Her gaze swept the maze of tents before her. It barely registered that Bron did not follow her outside the Healers Quarter. He was not going to rescue Carter, or he would have done so at the alchemist's tent.

A horse neighed, drawing Ora's attention. Several yards to her right, a messenger grabbed the reins of his horse—distinguishable by the light-blue stripe of material stitched across the corner of the saddle blanket—and prepared to mount. A mail satchel slung across his shoulder rested against his hip. A footman stood at the horse's head.

A Captain approached from beneath the nearest tent awning, barking orders: "Captain Mason's hands only, without delay. I need you back here to take the same report to Commander Baire in the Fifth Division, got it?" The Captain muttered something cursory under his breath about another messenger suffering from exhaustion. "You will rest tomorrow," he concluded gruffly to the messenger, who only nodded. It took two clumsy attempts to pull himself up into the saddle, and he drooped wearily.

Ora's feet carried her in their direction even as the thoughts of her actions formed in her head. "Captain, Sir," she called on approach, gaining the Captain's immediate attention. "Is your message for Torr Guard?" Her heart lodged in her throat as she spoke with a desperate hope. This may be her only chance and she could not delay.

Garren mentioned Torr Guard the last time she saw him. That Captain Mason expected him to help with something. Might he still be there? Garren had influence. He was not only a Singer, but a Captain. If she could only plead with him, he might interfere on Carter's behalf. He knew firsthand what the experiments did to a person and she knew he hated it. He could not possibly allow such a thing to befall her friend.

The messenger looked down at her with exhaustion etched in every line on his face. How long had he been carrying messages back and forth between the Divisions without rest?

"I can carry the message for you."

"You are an archer?" the Captain inquired, taking in her attire and weapons.

"Yes. I am under the command of Captain Garren," she claimed boldly. It was not a lie, since she knew Garren took responsibility for her after her flogging. "He needs me at Torr Guard. He meets there with Captain Mason." She prayed her words rang true. After so many days, Garren could be anywhere by now. "I can deliver the message for you, so your messenger can deliver the report to the other Divisions." She held her breath, facing the Captain and waiting for his response, while trying not to let the urgency she felt show on her face.

She needed approval to leave her post, or risk the Singers' wrath upon her. No one would question or hinder a messenger. They moved freely between the Divisions and Torr Guard at all hours of the day and night.

"Get me that horse," the Captain barked suddenly, motioning to a footman walking by with a riderless messenger horse. "My messenger cannot be two places at once and I need these reports delivered before the night's end. Take this—," and he took a leather letter-packet from the mounted messenger and thrust it into Ora's kit. "How fast can you ride, archer?" His sharp gaze pinned her to the spot, warning her against folly.

"Like the wind, Sir," she replied at once, and she meant it. No need to confess the only time she had ridden a horse was the day she was recruited from Neice. The messenger horse was her only way into Torr Guard. So, without giving herself a chance to let uncertainty or old fears surface and paralyze her, Ora pulled herself up into the saddle.

"Captain Mason," the Captain reminded. "It is to be delivered directly into his hands."

"Yes, Sir." Ora clung to the horse, biting back a startled cry as the horse bolted forward of its own accord, knowing its path better than she did. Heart in her throat, she clung near the horse's neck. She would risk all fear and peril of the fast approaching night so long as she found Captain Garren at the end of it.

She would reach him, and he would save Carter.

Chapter 43

Garren stood, reviewing a spread of maps marked with the current lay of front lines and troops. His good eye had begun to tire with the strain of late night flickering torchlight. But, with others present he refused the desire to remove the eye patch and use the night sight of his abnormal eye.

Also with him on the main floor of the tower were Captain Mason—his footman stationed at the large hole in the side of the tower room serving as the entrance—and Commander Dillion, having joined them just after dusk with his footman Edwan and another Singer, a young man whom Garren had met before and knew as Skor.

Skor stood tall and slim like a reed with sandy hair that looked nearly silver. Garren knew the strength that lay beneath his deceitfully thin appearance—the strength of the For'bane that ran through the veins of every Singer.

Skor pushed himself off the stone wall and moved toward the table as Garren stepped back. He ran his long, slender fingers against the edge of the map closest to him on the table. "I have spent most of my days and nights these past months near the Birchlands border, near the Fifth

Division. I can slip in and out of For'bane territory and the Birchlands with hardly a Muel or Sniffer catching a glimpse of me."

Commander Dillion spoke up: "So you think we should organize our forces to move across the Birchlands border... and leave Torr Guard wide open?" His tone, low and calm, belied the tension caused by his words and the firmness of his gaze.

Even the footmen shifted slightly with discomfort. Captain Mason's footman stole a quick glance at the Captain before dutifully turning his gaze back to the camp outside.

Skor smiled. "You asked for my advice. I gave it. I have nothing to gain and nothing to lose."

Garren stepped forward again. "If we reassign the bulk of our troops to the Fifth Division...," he began, "we could flank the enemy."

Captain Mason shook his head, entering the conversation for the first time in nearly thirty minutes. "Commander Strell will not approve."

Garren suddenly turned toward the entrance and stared out into the darkness. A disturbance touched the edges of his consciousness—of someone's presence, growing with familiarity—just before a distant shout alerted them of an incoming rider.

Commander Dillion swung his gaze to Edwan, still standing at the entrance. "See who it is," he ordered.

Edwan obeyed and had only just stepped outside when a horse materialized from the darkness. The footman jumped back as the horse reared in frightened surprise.

Garren sprang outside and to the horse's side. He grabbed the bridle, drawing the horse back down to all fours and firmly restraining it. His expression turned grim, his lips tight as recognition swept over his senses even before he saw her face in the torchlight. "Whoa!" he commanded the horse.

"What is the meaning of this?" Captain Mason demanded, stepping outside of the tower.

Garren grabbed the rider as she tumbled wearily from the back of the horse. He kept one hand on the reins, and his other hand clasped her arm to steady her as she stood near him. "What are you doing here?" he demanded tensely. "What has happened?" Though he felt anger, he sensed her fear, the same disturbance he had felt as soon as she rode into camp.

Ora looked at Garren. "They have taken Carter," she burst out.

Garren looked toward Captain Mason in surprise as Commander Dillion came forward. "Take a breath and tell us exactly what you mean," the Commander urged.

Ora swallowed hard. She pulled the letter-packet from her kit and held it out to Captain Mason. "I brought your report from the First Division." Captain Mason took it as Ora turned her attention back to Garren, "They have recruited Carter to become a Singer.... You have to stop them. Do not let them change him...please!"

"I thought they were not recruiting anymore," Commander Dillion spoke up. "Not after all the... complications...."

Garren felt a deep and righteous anger brewing in his gut. He answered darkly, "They do whatever they wish. Even if it is not public knowledge, or publicly approved."

"I am sorry, archer," Commander Dillion said. "There is nothing we can do to stop this. I do not condone the actions and liberties the Command takes, but neither can I stop it."

Ora gripped Garren's arm, keeping his attention as she held his gaze. Her voice shook with the height of her emotion. "Do not let them take Carter. If you meant what you said the last time we spoke, then help me now!" she implored with desperation.

For a moment in Garren's mind, everything grew still. He could feel Ora's emotion—her pain and helplessness pressed tightly against his heart, impossible to ignore. Carter meant more to her than she would admit.

He knew Carter would no longer be the boy Ora knew if they turned him into a Singer. He would not wish that fate on anyone. Carter would not be human anymore.

"Get on the horse," he said quietly.

He did not wait for invitation or consent, but as soon as she pulled herself back on the messenger horse, he mounted behind her, supporting her with his arms. He felt her exhaustion, and her fear of horses was not veiled from his senses either.

"Commander," he said simply, firmly, looking at the Commander for his response.

Commander Dillion motioned to Edwan. "Get my horse at once. We have an archer to save."

Chapter 44

Ora felt small and fragile on the messenger horse. The ride to Torr Guard was frightening enough, tearing at her nerves. She was grateful Garren's swift reflexes caught her as she had fallen from the horse at the tower. She had felt his strength run into her when he had continued to hold her arm, keeping her steady as she had pled for his help.

She felt that strength again now—the iron breadth of his chest at her back and his arms on each side of her—keeping her contained. Garren handled the horse expertly, and never shifted his hold. Yet his physical strength did nothing to alleviate the fears that pressed around her heart.

She listened to the rhythm of the horse's hooves striking the ground, the breath pumping from its lungs and blowing from its nostrils. Her head ached; her own breath short and shallow.

It felt like an eternity passed before they reached the lights of the First Division. Garren led the way as Commander Dillion and Edwan followed to the Healers Quarter. Ora straightened away from Garren at the commotion outside the first healers' tent. A large troop of footmen holding torches gathered at the entrance as Commander Strell barked orders.

Garren drew the horse up sharply and Ora grasped his arm with one hand as her heart jumped to her throat. Garren held the reins in one hand and slid his other arm around her waist in support, a move so deft and subtle that she was not sure he even realized it.

"Commander!" Garren called firmly. "What's going on here?"

Commander Strell broke away from the group and approached. His glance took in Ora with surprise—then irritation. "This is none of your concern, Captain," he answered as Commander Dillion reined in his horse beside Garren's, with Edwan stopping behind him.

Bron stood beneath the tent awning, nearly lost in shadow. "One of the procedures did not go so well," he said lowly, in a rare moment of seriousness.

"Are you working with the alchemists?" Garren demanded, continuing to watch Commander Strell. He kept tight rein on the messenger horse as it shifted beneath him and Ora with nervous energy. "I thought after the last time the Council agreed to suspend the experiments."

Last time? What happened last time? Ora bit her lower lip even as a quiet sound of agony escaped her, coming from the pit of her stomach, pressed against Garren's arm. "Where is Carter?" she blurted out, unable to contain herself.

"Only temporarily, yes. We cannot abandon so much work for a few failed products," Commander Strell continued, ignoring Ora. "The alchemists have been experimenting with an improved genesis formula, working day and night for its success. Under the approval and supervision of myself and a few other officers, it has been agreed to continue with a new group of test subjects."

"It appears they have failed you yet again, Commander," Bron concluded, folding his arms across his chest with a casual arrogance.

Commander Strell spoke sharply, "You are dismissed, Singer Tarak!"

Ora flinched at the volume of the command, but Bron did not seem concerned. He only gave a short, cold laugh, and sauntered away into the night without another word.

"Where is the boy archer, Carter?" Garren voiced.

The Commander's gaze flickered over Ora again, and realization of her worst fears coming true struck her just before he spoke the words in confirmation, "Singer Carter has disappeared."

Singer.

The word hit Ora like a punch in the gut that left her gasping for breath as her mind swam. "No," she issued forth in a breathless whimper.

The messenger horse shifted sideways, away from Commander Strell, and Ora pulled away from Garren to dismount on her own. Garren grasped her arm to assist her down, while he kept his seat on the horse. Ora turned away from him as Garren addressed Commander Strell again. "Has he killed anyone?"

Bile rose in Ora's throat, burning through her chest, and she fought to swallow it back. To even suggest Carter would hurt anyone made her sick. There was not a violent bone in his body. *'They change you,'* the warning echoed again in her mind.

"He overpowered the footmen standing guard, and ran off. The alchemist with him is bruised from being attacked, but otherwise I dare say he will recover just fine." Commander Strell looked at Ora and his gaze glittered suddenly in the torchlight, making Ora's skin crawl with uncertainty. "What were you doing off your post?"

Ora stiffened. "I was sent to deliver a message," she hastened.

"I see. And you just happened to ride back with two officers to fetch your friend, is that it?" Two footmen stepped forward toward her. "I do not recall your transfer from an archer to a messenger." One footman grabbed Ora's arm and pulled her away from Garren and the messenger horse.

"I had a letter-packet to deliver to Captain Mason," Ora insisted, not daring to resist the footman after her last incident. "The Commander of the Messengers Quarter sent me to Torr Guard, he will confirm my words!" She had gone out of her way to avoid being taken as a runner. Her back prickled with the memory of the flogging, the skin flaming anew. She could not endure any more of that punishment.

Suddenly, Garren stood behind the footman, the edge of his long, bone dagger resting dangerously close to the side of the footman's neck. "Touch her again, and I will kill you," he spoke with deadly calm. The footman released Ora quickly and backed away as Garren replaced his dagger in his arm sheath and took Ora's arm firmly to keep her at his side. He faced Commander Strell. "She is my responsibility. Dismiss your men to search for the boy, we are wasting time here."

Commander Strell waved one arm in a silent motion. The troop obeyed at once, dispersing to begin the search.

"I will join the search shortly," Garren continued. "See if you can have a few other Singers track him. Your men might need their help to capture him if he proves to be…difficult."

Commander Strell strode away and Commander Dillion dismounted to grab the reins of the messenger horse before it wandered off on its own. He handed the reins over to a stable boy who approached.

Garren loosened his hold on Ora. She gasped, feeling her breath return suddenly. "Let me go with you," she pleaded.

Garren glanced at Commander Strell's retreating back and the troop moving away and pressed Ora several feet away, speaking in a low voice for her ears alone. "I think you have been through enough for one night."

Ora shook her head, her wide-eyed gaze meeting his. "I have to find him. What if he is frightened? He will want to see someone he trusts!"

Garren gripped her arm more firmly to stop her words. "That is enough. Let me handle this. I know more about this situation than you do."

Her lips parted to argue, and a flinty look caused the blue in his eye to vanish into a warning, steel grey. "That is an *order*, archer. Go to the Archers Quarter and be on your post before you get yourself in trouble."

Ora weakened in defeat, feeling sickened by what was happening. Tears stung her eyes as she searched his gaze. "Carter is not a killer—he is not a monster," she insisted.

Garren released her to lightly trace the bruise on her face, with a brief look of tenderness. She heard his quiet, resigned sigh. "I know, Belle."

He turned away, and she turned in the opposite direction toward the Archers Quarter, obeying his order through a veil of tears.

Chapter 45

Garren joined one of the troops, as they had divided into smaller groups to search late into the night. He kept silent and distant from the others, letting his senses guide him.

One reason Singers did not socialize with each other was because a certain wolf-like scent surrounded them, undetectable by humans. It stood out like a warning sign, an alpha-male signature that often made it challenging for Singers to get along well with each other.

Carter carried this unusual scent, which should make it possible for Garren to track him. Only, something had gone wrong with the boy archer and the new genesis potion. Like a rabid dog, the boy's movements and behavior were vague and unpredictable, making it more difficult for Garren to distinguish.

They made several sweeps from the Divisions up to the front lines, until Garren paused abruptly in the hazy light of dawn. He turned to look toward the Third Division behind them. "Stop," he spoke firmly.

The footmen nearest him obeyed and looked to him in question. The others followed suit.

"We are assuming the archer came toward battle," Garren said, his eyes narrowed. "Why?"

"Because…he is, ah, he is a Singer," one of the footmen blurted.

"You are operating under the assumption that he wishes to fight. But the archer does not want to fight…."

The formula failed to balance Carter's human blood with the For'bane—so he did not act rationally one way or the other. There was no telling what the boy was thinking, but if anything of his mind remained—if he had a moment of clear thought—he would surely default to his last human instinct.

Carter is a coward, Garren thought. *He only wants to go home. The last thing he wants to do is fight. He is a fool who nearly got Belle killed.*

He kept his gaze on the horizon, a low, thin orange line turning to grey as the rising sun melted into the smoky haze of the campfires.

"We are looking in the wrong place. We cannot track him beyond the front lines because he has turned back. He is trying to flee to the Freelands. To the last human element that is familiar to him."

Chapter 46

Ora waited in agony all through the night. She tried to sleep, but tossed about in agitation. Her fellow archers watched her with concern. She knew most of them accepted Carter's loss as any other in battle. Distressed, Ora rose before dawn, before the change in shifts, and slipped outside, taking her bow and quiver of arrows.

The distant clang of a blacksmith at his anvil rang through the cold morning air. Torches lit the pre-dawn and colored the smokey, cloud covered skies with hints of orange and red.

She skirted the center of the Archers Quarter and made her way to the small, rarely used practice field. The ground rose crusty and hardened in frozen furls and clumps from the early morning frost. Few archers had time to tread this path, and spent too much time and energy on the front lines, where their skills were constantly honed and tried.

Ora knelt on one knee at one end of the range. She could just make out the rimmed shadow of the targets at the far end. Faint torchlight surrounding the range gave her just enough vision to aim.

'Belle ... Let me handle this.'

Ora fitted her first arrow and, still kneeling, took a steadying breath and drew back. A soft, familiar *whoosh!* of air signaled the release of the arrow, and she strained to see the shadow of the shaft imbedded deep near the center of the target.

He is not my friend, she reminded herself stubbornly.

She rose to her feet and fitted another arrow. She closed her eyes a moment, remembering for an instant her home in the Freelands as a child, laughing and playing with Carter as they waded ankle-deep into the middle of the brook near the village, trying to catch small fish with their bare hands.

The ache inside of her intensified. So much had changed in so short a time. *I am not a child*, she urged. *No longer and never again.*

She drew back on the bow. *But Carter will be saved. Fates*[17] *would not be so cruel.*

Whoosh! This time, the arrow lodged near the edge of the target. Ora gritted her teeth and drew another arrow.

She kept at it until her quiver was emptied. By this time, the grey light of dawn colored the sky and she no longer relied on torchlight to see. Still, not one of her arrows hit the center of the target. Frustration filled her and the drive to gain the perfect score. She had to be the best. She couldn't fail.

She moved across the range to retrieve her arrows and refill her quiver to begin again. Sunlight glinted off the shafts, peaking through the clouds.

"Archer," came the command behind her.

She turned to see two footmen holding torches at the end of the range. She plucked the remaining arrow from the target, returned it to her quiver, and started across the field toward them.

---

[17] Fates : the unexplained workings of the world rather than a deity.

"Archer, you are ordered to Commander Kane at once," the first footman spoke again.

Chapter 47

Returned from his mission to find Carter, Garren reported to Commander Kane of the Archers Quarter. He stood across from the Commander in his tent, catching the man's surface emotions. The Commander took the news with complete acceptance and little regret—the same way Garren would, except how it concerned his Belle.

"Commander," Garren concluded. "Would you send for your archer, Orabelle? I would like to give her the report I gave to you."

He kept his tone and expression stiff and unyielding. The Commander eyed him a moment and then stood. "I will send my footman to fetch her. I must return to the field." He buckled on his scabbard, sheathing his sword. Garren stepped aside to let him pass.

Garren continued to stare at the spot where the Commander had been standing, yet, his thoughts were far removed from his surroundings. His jaw tightened, and a muscle flexed near his cheek.

He knew no matter how he said it, his report would break whatever fragile trust Ora had begun to place in him. Carter was the reason she fought as hard as she did. The boy had always been the reason for her strength. What would be her reason now?

Minutes passed. When she approached the tent he sensed her trepidation. When she entered, flanked by two footmen, her trepidation changed to surprise. "Captain Garren," she said.

After a moment of hesitation, Garren turned to face her. He nodded to the footmen, his features like stone, dismissing them without a word.

Ora remained just inside the entrance even after the footmen left them alone. "I—I was out practicing. I could not sleep," she blurted, staring at him. "I guess I am not a very good archer because I have not hit the center mark once."

Garren slowly approached.

Ora glanced behind him to the empty tent. "I thought Commander Kane summoned me."

"I summoned you," Garren corrected quietly, steadily.

Ora's hands trembled and she clenched them into fists at her sides, as she felt instinctively the foreboding news. "Have they found Carter?" Her voice came in a raw whisper and she swallowed hard, searching his gaze with sudden, increasing fear. "Oh Creator. What is it?"

Chapter 48

"It is about Carter," Garren confirmed gravely, gently.

Ora stepped back from him. She shook her head as he opened his lips to speak again. She spoke vehemently, anger sparking in her eyes, though heartache and pain wrapped their way around her heart. "Do not dare," she accused. "Do not dare to speak it."

Her warning fell on deaf ears, because Garren ignored her angry plea. "They found him this morning—."

"Stop!" Ora practically screamed at him. She struggled against his hold, fisting her hands as he grasped her wrists.

"Ora, he is dead," Garren insisted firmly, almost sharply.

Ora stopped struggling, as if his words and the truth took all the fight out of her, leaving her broken and lost. Her lips parted, with an ache rising from her heart and growing so much she did not know if she could bear it—did not want to; did not care.

"I loved him," her confession burst forth in a whisper as she stared at Garren. "I *loved* him."

Her pain expressed itself in an audible wailing cry as she gave in to the grief. For the first time since her capture, she could no longer hold back the tears, not even in front of

Garren. Her strength failed her. Her knees buckled, too weak to stay upright, but Garren pulled her against him abruptly. He wrapped her in his arms and held her up, gently pressing her head against his chest to muffle her sobs, keeping her grief to the space between them.

Neither spoke for some time. After a moment more, with a desperate need for strength, her hands opened and she slid them beneath his arms around to his shoulders, and gripped his leather armor, holding on to him in return.

He did not scold her for her tears. He did not push her away. This unexpected goodness in him—a war-hardened, tough Singer—only pushed the hurt deeper, only made her tears flow more strongly, as he stood with her, sharing in her private moment of grief without protest or complaint.

His lips moved near the soft skin at her temple as he spoke quietly, with regret. "I am sorry, Belle. Hold on; have courage."

She hardly heard him, and in her brokenness she hardly understood his meaning. Hold on? To what? *For* what? At last, her tears abated, but the empty ache remained and her heart lay steeped in lonely misery. Still, for a moment longer, she let herself cling to him, let him comfort her and be her strength.

What seemed an eternity later, she grew quiet, leaning heavily in Garren's arms and focusing on pulling air into lungs so tight each breath felt like a sharp dagger. Slowly, her hands—pressed against his armor and the breadth of his chest—curled into determined fists.

She stiffened her spine and calmly pushed against him. She pulled away, reminding herself that she was alone now and Garren was partly to blame for her loss. He was a Singer. His blood killed her best friend, the boy she had loved. They had tried to turn him into a monster, and they had destroyed him. And now, when she needed him to be cold and demanding, to push her, Garren offered comfort and kindness instead.

He obeyed her silent command and slowly released her, cautiously sliding his hands away from her back to be sure she could stand alone. He did not move away from her. Instead, his intuitive blue-grey eye skimmed the length of her body. "Sit down," he commanded in a low rumble, gently pressing her back toward the left side of the tent, where a narrow side table and chairs sat. He cupped a hand lightly beneath her elbow to steady her until she sat, the chair angled away from the table.

Ora looked away from him as she sank into the chair, her strength and emotion spent. Her legs trembled. her lip felt tender, and her bruised thigh throbbed, reminders of yesterday's events that all lead up to this tragic moment. Garren knelt in front of her and lay his hand lightly against the bruise on her thigh. His touch added comfort and concern —as if he knew of her pain there. He caught her gaze and held it and Ora felt another unknown barrier between them fall and crumble to dust at her feet.

Ora hung her head. With her long blonde hair concealing her face, she spoke in a voice barely above a whisper and heavy with guilt, "This is all my fault."

The space between them grew still and silent. Ora held her breath, wishing she had not spoken. She pressed her thumbs beneath her lower eyelids to wipe away any remaining moisture.

Garren caught her chin gently with thumb and forefinger, to draw her gaze. "You must keep breathing, Belle. The War is not over."

"And what if I do not have anything left to fight for?" Ora whispered. "They are all…dead. I failed them all!"

"No, no you did not," Garren said firmly. "Everyone dies, Belle. It is a part of life. Sometimes they go sooner than they should, but it happens just the same. You have been stronger than anyone; than all of them put together."

"When did you stop caring? Do you disregard death so easily? When did strength become so much more important than love; compassion?" she spoke almost bitterly.

Garren withdrew his hand and his response came stiffly: "When I realized you keep breathing and the sun rises and sets…whether you want it to or not; and the enemy cares not about your losses."

She could not deny the painful truth in his words.

When had she begun to speak with the Singer Captain so openly and honestly? When had she begun to view him as an ally instead of an enemy? Why had she gone to him, never once doubting that he would help her?

She thought she had found an ally in Bron. Yet, now she felt she had been wrong about him.

She searched the shades of blue and grey in Garren's normal eye, trying not to picture the way his other glowed yellow beneath the patch. She could almost hear his words again about Bron: *'He finds it far too easy to hide who he is —even when that means sacrificing all conviction.'*

And you do not hide who you are? she asked him silently, holding his gaze.

Garren leaned back slightly and glanced aside. She could not read his suddenly closed expression. Had he read the question in her eyes as clearly as if she had spoken it aloud? He rose slowly and stepped back.

Ora took a steadying breath and stood also, placing her hand against the edge of the table for support. Then she straightened bravely. "Thank you, Captain," she said softly.

Garren looked at her in question.

"Thank you for coming back with me. For…for trying to save him."

He did not answer, still watching her. A muscle flexed in his jaw and then relaxed. "My name is James," he said quietly.

She stared at him. He had given her his name. Why would he do that? No one had that privilege, especially a soldier with no command, of unequal and lowly rank. On the battlefield, an officer was known only by his rank and his surname. He had not told her by mistake, or by some strange impulse. His words came steady and with purpose.

She held her breath a moment in wonder, almost afraid to accept it. She could not give him anything in return. He knew her every fear and shame, but she felt he offered some strength and comfort—some pledge of hope—by telling her his secret name.

"James," she whispered, tasting the sound of it against her lips. She held his gaze, for once wishing she could read past the impenetrable wall behind his blue-grey eye; see beyond the mask of his face.

She closed her eyes against a new flood of tears. This was not the end of her mourning, but she had let Garren share enough of her grief. When she cried herself to sleep that night, he would not be there to comfort her.

"You will survive this pain, Belle," he murmured with confidence and determination.

He gave her a short, strengthening nod and turned abruptly to depart—shoulders straight and stiff with purpose and command. To the world, once again Captain Garren, the Singer.

To her? She was no longer certain.

Chapter 49

For seven days, Garren kept himself busy and far away from Ora and any associations with the First Division. A change in the air brought the first truly cold burst of winter. Mornings greeted him with frozen earth and the snap of breaking branches in the wind.

Garren listened to the sound, as he crouched at the base of a tree high on a ledge overlooking the forest, his dark form blending with the fallen branches and briar bushes around him. He raised his eyepatch to allow his gaze equal, unhindered vision, as he surveyed the land beneath him, holding completely still.

In the greying light of day, his discolored eye enhanced the landscape to varying shades of blues, greens, yellows, oranges, and reds. Anything with enough heat to be alive—be it beast or man—he would see as the warm colors.

The snapping of tree limbs sounded like a song to him, and he let it lull him into a wakeful doze. He slid his fingers lightly, thoughtfully, against the bowstring and picked up on the song, joining in with airy chords that lifted to blend with the wind.

A chill rushed over his back, seeping through the wool cloak draped across his shoulders. Garren lifted his face, his attention to the skies as flakes of snow floated down, melting against his cheeks and brow. High above, the clouds thickened, pregnant with a storm.

Garren breathed deep, letting his lungs fill with the cold and exhaled. He replaced his patch and hooked his bow over his back. The hair on the back of his neck prickled in high alert. Surprised by the sudden proximity to danger, Garren ducked his head and spun on his heel.

Something slammed into him with brute force, enough to knock him over, cracking his shoulder sharply on the rock where he had perched. The breath left him in a rush and for a strange moment he felt disorientated. Unprepared.

He twisted onto his back, reaching for the long dagger in his arm-sheath with one hand while fighting to push off his attacker. A Skay. It squealed in rage, as it tried to rip at Garren's chest with its long nails. It had no weapons and Garren could only guess that it was mad.

He yanked the blade free and jammed it into the side of the Skay's neck. He ground it deep until he felt the edge strike bone. With a move swift as lightning, his muscles hardened with rage, he wrenched upward, snapping his attacker's neck.

He shoved the limp body away from him and lay on his back, breathing hard and doing his best to ignore the hot pain searing through his shoulder. He gritted his teeth and released a growl of anger.

One thought assailed him: Ora had done something to him. She had changed something inside of him. And every time he stood in her presence, spoke to her, witnessed her thought and emotion, he felt it. She had tamed the monster. She had weakened him.

He could not get distracted again.

Chapter 50

Ora passed by the center of the Archers Quarter and glanced up as the wind whipped the flag bearing the color and insignia of the archers. The pole rose high above the tents, a beacon directing soldiers where they needed to go.

She shivered in the chill of a winter-bound wind, and brushed a chunk of blond hair back from her cheek as it came lose from her braid.

Her gaze caught movement. Even in the grey light of early evening, she recognized the brooding demeanor of the form moving between two tents. Garren. He passed the Archers Quarter and disappeared between the tents, following a trail on the far side of the First Division camp to the shelter of a rocky hillside, lit with few campfires.

Hesitating only a moment—remembering their last encounter—Ora silently followed him, peering into the shadows to see where he went. She had not seen him for days, yet she found her thoughts constantly drifting to him.

Through her sorrow of losing Carter, she had pressed his parting words close to her heart in a way she had not expected. She had not thought they would make such an impact on her. '*You will survive this pain, Belle*....'

She returned to the battlefield every day because she had no other choice. At night, she left the archers' tent and made her way to the practice field. She worked at her skill endlessly, till her fingers hurt and her arms ached.

She thought she would be happy once she hit the center of the target. Yet, it did not stop there. She grew more restless, more agitated. Sleep eluded her. Fear gnawed at her insides and she wondered if she was slowly losing her mind. Then, she remembered Garren. The way he stood with purpose and strength before her. '*The enemy cares not about your losses.*'

But he cared. Why had he taken the trouble to tell her himself; to let her weep in his arms?

When had he ceased to be her enemy?

"You can stop lurking in the shadows, Belle," his soft voice jarred her back to the present. He had come to a stop at the outer rim of the Archers Quarter, his back to her, his shadow outlined against the rocky hillside by the small campfire ahead of him.

Ora held still in the shadow of the last tent, a few yards distant from him. They were alone and the campfire remained deserted.

"I can feel your emotions, remember?" his voice remained steady and quiet. He turned to face her, gaze guarded as he looked at her, expression grim.

Ora swallowed hard and stepped forward. "Is it not an invasion of privacy to read a person's emotions as you have done with mine?" Ora watched him. "Do you do this with everyone?"

Garren glanced aside. "I cannot help it. I have grown accustomed to ignoring it, but with you—." He looked at her again, serious, as quiet steel entered his voice, "With you I cannot."

He moved to the campfire and sat. His movement drew her attention to his arm that he kept close to his body, confined in a sling to keep his shoulder immobile.

"What happened?"

A sigh came from Garren's lips, so faint she almost missed it. He looked at her steadily. "I am not going to hurt you, Belle," he encouraged. A moment of stillness descended between them. Garren stared into the fire.

Ora studied him thoughtfully. She believed him. She could see the tension in him, the buried anger, the restrained violence—strength meant to intimidate. But she knew he would not hurt her. As if he read her thoughts, Garren looked up to meet her gaze. Ora found she could not speak. She felt she had found an anchor here, in his presence. For the first time since hearing of Carter's death, the pain around her heart lessened and she felt she could breathe again.

"Can you not sleep?" he urged.

"Not since...," she let her voice trail away. He knew what she meant. Hesitantly, she sat across the fire from him, letting the heat draw the chill from her bones. She took a breath. "I have never imagined life without Carter. That is to say...we grew up together, we have been friends since we were very young. I never considered...losing him."

Garren watched her a moment, gaze unreadable. Dirt smudged her face, a day-old gash on her chin crusted over with blood, and her eyes felt gritty from long days and sleepless nights. Her fingers ached, calloused and tired from hours of shooting arrows into the For'bane lines. Self-conciously, she looked away and tugged a chunk of dried mud from the midst of her tangled braid.

She found she could not bear the silence. "Have you ever had a nightmare?" she questioned quietly, looking at him.

Garren held still a moment. Then, he ran a finger along his lightly bristled chin and spoke just as quietly, "Singers do not dream."

Her curiosity piqued, Ora leaned forward slightly. "Truly?"

Garren shrugged his good shoulder. "Whatever place dreams come from seems to be blocked. We sleep far less than…normal humans. Where is the use in dreams?"

"Do you never feel…tired?"

"We rest, some of us better than others." Garren tossed a couple pieces of wood on the fire. "Our minds continually process what we see and experience."

Ora swallowed hard, wondering what that process had done to Carter. If he had survived, who would he be? Could she have borne his living as an altered version of himself better than his death?

"Well, I have nightmares…all the time. Ever since I came here…and saw…this," Ora spoke, gazing off into the darkness beyond Garren's shoulder. "Most of them I could sleep through, but not the ones I have had lately. I cannot sleep through those. I cannot close my eyes without thinking about them, or seeing them again in my mind's eye."

"Belle," Garren's voice sounded far away, and gentle. Ora frowned, sure she had imagined it, and looked at Garren. He pressed his lips together and glanced away. "They say dreams are either memories or fears. Which are yours?"

"I think…perhaps…," Ora hesitated. She looked away. The heaviness in her soul left her weak and tired, with a strong sense of hopelessness. *I cannot turn to him! What was I thinking?* she silently upbraided herself. *There is no one but myself to rely on now.*

"My guardian lied," she blurted out. "I am not fourteen, I am nearly sixteen. I think it does not matter for you to know now…now that he is dead. He was only trying to protect me. If I were younger, he thought you would not take me. I knew better, of course, but he insisted."

"Why does your age bother you?"

"I am sixteen. Should I not be stronger than I am?"

Though he continued to look at her, something changed in his countenance. A softness returned to his gaze. A hard-fought wall he'd built between them seemed to come down. He seemed almost relieved, as the harsh line of his shoulders slowly relaxed. His voice held a tenderness, like a human being holds toward another in offer of comfort. "You are only as strong as your circumstances and experiences allow you to be."

"How old were you, when you were taken?" She held her breath, waiting to see if he would answer her. She felt a sudden desperation, a powerful need to relate to him in some small way, to see the human in him. She needed to know her struggles were not just her own, that maybe—once upon a time—it had not been so easy for him either.

Garren studied her without speaking. She was sure he would not answer, but finally his lips parted and slowly, he began: "I joined the King's Army when I was seventeen, a year after the War began. I alone survived—out of those in my village who went with me, I am the only one."

His features tightened like stone as he spoke the words, but she saw the deeply buried pain, like a faded imprint of the boy he used to be, of the emotion that used to be his. She wondered if he even knew it showed. She felt her heart go out to him.

But he continued, resolutely: "The War had just begun then, and the Armies were more heavily outnumbered. I became a Singer to survive. It was not a choice, but a necessity. We were being slaughtered. Like children, we did not know how to fight back. So, the officers found a way to create a power equal to the enemy, only they did not know the costs." A muscle in his jaw flexed. "My circumstances made me who I am. Sometimes strength is not what you hoped it would be. Sometimes it is the opposite."

"So you volunteered?" Ora whispered.

"I had nothing to lose, then," Garren said steadily.

Then? Compared to now? Ora bit her lip. "Carter would never have chosen to become a Singer."

"This is not the same Army it used to be," Garren returned. He leaned forward, holding her gaze. "I did not say it was right. The longer the War lasts, the more desperate mankind becomes to possess all the power, even at risk to others."

"What do you mean?"

"The need for power and control can turn men into monsters." He spoke with veiled gentleness.

Ora held very still, while her mind raced to comprehend his meaning. Her gaze locked with his as he refused to let her look away. He was trying to make her understand something.

"But you will not hurt me," Ora hesitated, recalling his earlier words.

"Everyone hurts someone," Garren corrected. "Even if they do not mean to."

But Captain Garren was different. Different than the soldiers who abused and destroyed in the villages, like the ones who had killed her mother. He was different from the officers who did not care how many people died under their orders, or who they sent to their deaths.

It was all about power to them.

"Why do *you* fight?" she urged.

His voice came resolute: "I fight against the monster inside. I fight to be free." He ran a hand over his short dark hair. "You should get some rest," he encouraged, signaling an end to their conversation. He rose abruptly, before she could take her leave. He hesitated, then walked away into the night without looking back.

She stared unseeing into the campfire flames. "Yes, Sir," she murmured. She rose wearily and returned to her tent, her sleep as fitful and troubled as ever.

Her conversation with Garren stayed with her, haunted her, through the next few days. She did not see Garren again in that time, as he seemed once more to withdraw from her both physically and emotionally.

The fourth morning after their conversation, someone shook her shoulder roughly, pinching the skin on her arm, pulling her from the first sound sleep she had found in a long while. How long had she slept? A few hours? She forced her eyes open and pulled away from the source of the shaking. The tent interior looked ashen grey with the light of pre-dawn.

She groaned her annoyance.

"Get up." It sounded like Decklan speaking, his voice sharp and commanding, urgent. "All archers are needed at the lines, immediately!"

At once, the words brought Ora fully awake. She rolled to her feet and fumbled for her leather armor, blinking the sleep from her eyes. She grabbed her kit and her bow and quiver of arrows.

Decklan disappeared from her side, hurrying through the tent amidst the commotion of the other archers. Ora caught up with him at the tent entrance as he held the flap open for them to file out. Cold winter air stung her cheeks.

"What has happened?" she spoke loudly, over the sudden din of a horn blowing outside, calling men to arms. Decklan looked like he had not slept at all in the few hours since they had been at the line. Smudges of sweat and dirt streaked his face and arms. A line of dried blood ran along his shoulder.

Did she look as bad as he did? There was no time nor place for a decent bath around here. Ora did what she could with a damp cloth, and a chip of soap she shared with a couple other archers.

Decklan glanced at her, his focus more on the skies outside the tent than on her. She saw snow, thick flurries of it, coming down to cover a frozen, bare earth. "We broke through the enemy ranks. The officers need everyone to help push them back. Snow is getting thicker, and a storm is coming in. We need to establish a new line before it hits."

They followed the flow of soldiers leaving camp for the front lines. Soon, Ora found herself in the thick of battle. She joined the other archers and followed the shouted orders of Commander Kane. The roar of fighting—the clash of swords and shouts of soldiers; cries of death and bloodshed—rose around her. And yet, they pressed their way forward, driving the For'bane back in retreat even as the snow began to fall more thickly.

Suddenly, a shout came from the left flank, carried from soldier to soldier until it reached the archers' line and Ora's ears. "Breach!"

Aiming for a target far out on the field, she slacked up on the string but kept the arrow firmly against the shaft of the bow as she turned to see who carried the warning cry.

At first, all she saw was the trickle of movement as several soldiers shoved into each other to escape the path of the enemy. Like the leak of a water reserve, however, the trickle turned to a bursting flood. For'bane appeared on the rise like a plague—mostly Skays, led by a Rammer running at full speed for them. The enemy spread out quickly as they forced their way toward the back lines. The Rammer quickly trampled anyone in its path, and the Skays quickly slaughtered any soldiers in their way. Some tried to retreat, while other brave souls fought to hold the enemy back but failed.

For a split second, Ora glanced at those around her and saw in their eyes the horrible fear and realization of impending death, and the driving instinct to run. She drew back on her arrow, turning quickly in the direction of the onslaught. “Hold the line!” she shouted above the roar, taking several paces toward the oncoming enemy.

She ignored the tide of soldiers moving about her and let her arrow fly true. A leading Skay fell to the ground as the arrow lodged in the side of its skull. A few For’bane around it hesitated before moving around the body. Ora drew another arrow. She had not survived this constant nightmare to let it all end here, watching the enemy destroy the only home she had left and kill the injured soldiers lying helplessly in the Healers Quarter.

She joined those still trying to turn the tide and close the breach. The Rammer stumbled to a rain of arrows in its face, just fifty yards to Ora’s right. It cried out in rage and pain. One Singer’s song was joined by another, the sound rising above the commotion suddenly and offering hope to the soldiers who heard it. There were Singers among them, joining the fight. As Commanders and Captains shouted and screamed orders, the King’s Army formed into a line—a last defense—and faced the enemy with determination.

A heavy tremble through the earth signaled the fall of the Rammer. But it had done its job of creating a path for the For’bane to advance, and the enemy kept coming.

“They will not pass!” the Commander nearest her yelled. “We fight for the Freelands! For those you have left behind—we are their last defense!”

Ora drew back on another arrow. She knew what the others were feeling and she could not blame them for their fear. Without fear, there could be no courage. She respected their courage. For indeed, everything in her screamed for her to turn and run.

She realized, from the day she first faced the battlefield, that for most of these soldiers and archers, it was not fear of the Singers that kept them here. It was an understanding that if they ran and escaped, someday they would still have to face the For'bane at their homes, in the Freelands, Birchlands, Highlands, and Mirklands. If they did not stop the enemy here on the battlefield, the For'bane would take it all.

And, if that happened, they would not just be facing the loss of their own lives, but also the lives of each and every one of their loved ones, too.

Her friends and fellow archers took positions on each side of her. She saw Decklan several yards away, and caught one final glimpse of him before the enemy was upon them.

Chapter 51

Garren jumped from his mount while still in motion upon arriving at the First Division amidst chaos and confusion. A tide of soldiers swarmed and flowed around him, streaming in from the front lines. Wounded were carried on the backs of other soldiers or on hastily constructed stretchers. The stench of death, blood, and fear permeated the air around his senses.

His great beast side-stepped, then trotted dutifully for the stables on his own while Garren fought his way through the tide of humanity toward the front lines.

A mix of snow and icy sleet pelted the frozen earth as the clouds thickened ominously above camp. He grabbed a passing soldier by the arm. "What is happening, soldier?" he demanded sharply.

The soldier looked wild-eyed as Garren released him. "The enemy. We pressed them back. They were retreating, when suddenly they turned on us. Our ranks have been divided. We are trying to regroup—."

Garren did not wait to hear more. The archers' line would be the last to retreat, as their arrows sought to hold back the enemy and give the soldiers a chance to escape. If everyone had been called to fight, Orabelle was out there in the thick of it.

He pressed his way against the tide and honed in on Bron, whom he saw leading a small band of bloodied, wearied archers. Ora was not among them.

He stood in Bron's path. "Where is Belle and her archer troop?"

Bron tried to side-step him, to no avail. "Where is *who*? We hardly made it out of that mess."

"You know who! Where is she?" he growled.

"The For'bane took her. You and I both know that no one who is captured ever comes back! You know what they do to them out there!"

"So you *left* her?" Garren grasped Bron by the collar of his leather jerkin and drove him back, rage filling his face as his muscles tensed and bulged with barely contained violence. "You son of a—."

Bron yanked back, knocking Garren's arm aside and breaking his hold. "We were overrun! How was I supposed to know it was a trap?" Bron's face turned red with resentment.

"You should have looked out for her," Garren shot back. "Instead you left her behind. You *ran*. I should shoot you through the heart…."

Anger sparked in the other Singer's gaze. His lips curled into a snarl. "What is so special about this one that you cannot let her go? That you would defend and champion her at every turn? Accept that she is dead now, and move on!"

With an angry roar, Garren turned and threw his fist into Bron's jaw with a crack. Bron stumbled, fell to one knee and fought to right himself. Garren stood over him, gaze dark and intense as Bron rubbed his tender jaw, already beginning to bruise.

Garren stared at him. "I always knew you were a coward." He turned to the nearest footman and bellowed orders for a horse. He mounted and turned the horse's head tightly back the way he had come, urging it into a dead run to Torr Guard.

As soon as the horse reached the place, Garren dismounted and strode into the tower, straight over to Commander Dillion. "The alchemist, Gan. He is staying in Torr Guard? I need to speak with him at once!"

The Commander turned from the war table and approached. "What is it, Captain?"

"The For'bane broke through the line. They have captured my archer and I am going after them before it is too late," Garren wasted no time with small talk. His commanding tone left no room for question.

The Commander glanced to his footman, Edwan. "Go find the alchemist," he instructed calmly. Edwan hurried to do his bidding, glad to leave the room and the angry Singer.

"You plan to go into a nest alone?" The Commander watched Garren, his voice filled with doubt.

Garren's gaze narrowed at the Commander's expression. His distress over Ora's capture overwhelmed him, showing physically in a brooding and violent exterior. He approached and leaned his arms on the table across from Commander Dillion. "They will leave a trail. It will lead me to them. If I can get close enough, I can hit them where it hurts. I can destroy them from the inside, as should have been our strategy all along."

The Commander sighed faintly. "They have captured soldiers before—only Creator knows why or for what purpose. Captain, do not make this a suicide mission. Do you truly think she is even alive now?"

In a fit of rage, Garren swept his arm across the table, knocking brass candlesticks to the floor where they were extinguished as they clattered on the stones. The table became shadowed in the lesser light of the torches mounted on the walls around the room.

The Commander took a wise step back away from the table, but he didn't even flinch at Garren's violent outburst. He kept his gaze on Garren, who turned abruptly to pace across the room away from him, taking deep, calming breaths.

Garren stopped near the entrance, looking across the field. His hands clenched and unclenched at his sides. His restless gaze caught sight of Cala, as the dark-haired, female trainer worked with a recruit on the field. "You cannot tell me if it was her, that you would not do the same. No excuses. No doubt." Garren spoke with forced calm.

Commander Dillion also looked out to the field from behind Garren. He stepped forward, still standing several feet behind Garren. "You are right," he agreed quietly. "Just as you know I am right to say there is no future between us, not as long as there is War." He sighed. "Cala is a superior soldier. She trains the recruits well, and takes no nonsense from anyone. That is who she is: a soldier. And so is your archer."

Garren's jaw tightened. Having his feelings for Ora exposed, even to the Commander, felt like ripping open a wound in the middle of a battle.

"I cannot stop you from risking your life to search for Orabelle," the Commander continued. "You are your own master. I know the other officers will not admit to it, but we all know how important—vital—you are to this fight."

Garren turned to meet his steady gaze. "I will never accept defeat," he insisted firmly. "This is not what I wanted, Commander. But…she is as much a part of me now, as the War has ever been. It's not just about me anymore."

The Commander came closer and lightly clasped Garren's shoulder in a soldier's salute. "Then, for both your sakes, I pray you find her safe."

Garren hesitated, then returned the gesture.

Edwan returned with a man in a clean white, ankle-length tunic.

"Gan?" Garren turned to address him at once. "The formula you were working on. You approached the Council about it some months ago. You called it exploding powder. Tell me, do you have some? I must know how it works and how to use it effectively. I have a For'bane nest to infiltrate."

Chapter 52

A sharp stench, like rotting onion, jarred Ora awake. A wave of motion sickness came over her. She rolled onto her side and struck her arm against something hard and wet. She sat up, groaning as she remembered what happened to her. She grasped the side of her aching head with one hand, blinking to clear her distorted vision. The icy sting of snow pelting her face and exposed arms and feet made her shiver, but also brought her to a more heightened awareness of her surroundings.

She sat in a square cage, thick wooden slabs serving as the floor beneath her, and rough-hewn oak branches serving as the barred walls. There was no roof, nothing to protect her from the elements. Thick, dark woods surrounded her on each side and the silhouettes of the enemy rose all around her, flanking the cart before and behind.

Too weak and stiff to stand on her feet, she leaned her bruised shoulder against the bars. They had taken her leather jerkin and she wore only her tunic and close-fit pants. Even her shoes were gone. The tips of her fingers and toes were turning blue from the cold. She curled her legs close to her body and despite the dirt under her nails, she closed her mouth around the tips of her fingers to try and warm them.

There was nothing she could do about her feet. She longed for a fire to warm her frozen joints.

The For'bane caravan wove along a narrow, steeply trenched pathway of mud and rock. Two Skays carried the cage by giant poles, one Skay in front and one behind, resulting in an uneven sway and jarring motion.

The caravan stopped suddenly, only minutes after Ora achieved consciousness. She held as still as she could. Her heart throbbed within her. Had they sensed her waking?

The stench that woke her wafted also from the dark cave-like entrance ahead. She craned her neck to see and as she looked, a tall, broad-shouldered form stepped out to meet them. Clenching her jaw to keep her teeth from chattering, Ora strained to see the creature's features in the grey light of day.

A Skay, but not like the others. This one seemed to have more intelligence, more command. And its face—something about it turned Ora's stomach with a strange ill-at-ease feeling. "Hurry it up." Its voice caused the knot in Ora's stomach to tighten further still. A *human* voice. The Skay was human!

She stared at him as the caravan and her cage drew closer. She knew she should look away before he saw her, but could not seem to manage it.

He looked every bit a Skay, tall with yellow-grey, leathery-looking skin. But his eyes were not the typical narrow, cat-like pupils with yellow animal irises. Instead, they were a pale blue—bright, intense, and filled with cold intelligence.

The For'bane in the caravan picked up the pace, obeying his command dutifully, like animals anxious to be home and to fill their bellies with whatever gruel they lived on.

Ora winced when her cage shifted abruptly as the rear Skay nearly slipped over a muddy patch, grunting in frustration.

They passed the blue-eyed Skay. Ora managed to lower her gaze and held her breath, praying he would not pay any attention to her.

Darkness fell all around her, thick, inky, and stale, as they entered the cave and began a sharp, steep descent into the belly of the earth.

A few minutes passed with only the movement and sway of her cage to orient her. Then, faint torchlight mixed with thin shafts of grey light streaming through rain-eroded holes in the ceiling revealed carved stone and earth tunnels branching off deeper into the earth. The stale air warmed only slightly from the fires. At least it was better than sleet, snow, and cold wind, though the stench remained.

Deeper and deeper they went. Ora began to shiver uncontrollably. She curled up on her side, back pressed against the bars, and shut her eyes tightly as her head began to throb. The fabric at the side of her ribcage pulled and stung and she remembered she had been struck. Too sore to move and unable to see it in the darkness, she hoped the wound was not too deep. The blood around it seemed dry.

At last the cage stopped in a shadowed corridor. Ora's eyes opened quickly, panic setting her heart racing. Is this the end? Would she be tortured and executed? What terrible things did these creatures do to their captives? She heard sometimes soldiers in For'bane territory were captured instead of killed and taken away—and none had ever escaped to tell of their experience. What could the enemy gain from taking captives?

The cage entered a tall, narrow cell with a single hole high in the earthen ceiling letting in a ribbon of grey light in the center of the blackness. No torches lit this section of tunnels that appeared to be made up of several rooms.

A Skay appeared before her and opened the hatch on the front of the cage, pulling her out roughly and letting her fall in a heap on the cold dirt floor. It looked at her and grunted.

Ora struggled to her feet, still shivering. "Where are my shoes?" she demanded boldly, staring at the Skay's yellow eyes. Even her kit had been taken.

The Skay grunted again and turned away, motioning to the two carrying the cage to follow.

"If you are not going to kill me—if you do not want me dead—you cannot just let me freeze to death!" she shouted after them.

They disappeared into the darkness. Ora's gaze searched in the faint grey light and dark shadows for the perimeter of her prison. There were walls on three sides and the tunnel across from her where she'd been brought through, which appeared to divide out into other tunnels, probably leading to other holding cells like hers. There was no door to keep her there, but she knew her legs would not carry her far enough to escape. Not yet.

Feeling weaker by the moment, Ora sank to the floor with her back against the furthest wall. Too terrified to willingly close her eyes, she watched the blackness and listened for any sounds alerting her of the For'banes' return.

Chapter 53

Knowing his human scent would be masked by the blood of the For'bane coursing through his veins, Garren moved from shadow to shadow among the trees outside the entrance of the For'bane nest. Still, he could not pass unseen through the entrance; too well guarded with For'bane constantly passing in and out.

His muscles bunched, anxious to enter battle and kill. He would not think twice about causing bloodshed, no matter how many enemy he came upon, except his survival also meant Ora's survival. She needed him, and he could not risk it. So, he waited in silence and watched. He crouched down among the rocky and earthen crags above the cave's entrance. In the deep night, he found a crevice opening up into a hallway below, narrow and freshly unearthed from the last rains.

He slipped between the rocks and tree roots, using the stronger roots as leverage, dropping feet first and landing in a silent crouch in the darkness. Having removed his eyepatch, he let his increased vision be his guide in the shadowed tunnels, moving with the stealth of a panther deep into the enemy's nest.

As he made his descent through the tunnels, he opened his senses, hoping for some trace of Ora's emotion to reach him; to tell him she lived and guide him to her.

He headed for the prison section, knowing it would be the darkest part of the caverns, without need for torchlight. The stench of death led him there.

His eye searched for the heat of her body. Deeper and deeper, he traveled through twisted tunnels and uneven mazes of rooms where the stench of rot and death grew stronger.

He stopped abruptly at the end of one tunnel that split off into two rooms. There were no doors to keep the prisoners confined. There were only twisted tunnels to confuse any would-be escapee and the For'bane constantly on the prowl. More than once, Garren had to slip into the shadows out of sight to avoid detection, knowing they could not sense his human blood through the mask of their blood in his veins.

He turned into the largest of the two rooms. There—the warm glow of a body in the corner. He felt the rapid beat of her heart. She lived. He took a slow, deep breath, feeling the flutter of her emotion—faint and weary and…altered.

He frowned. What did they do to her? Fury twisted in his gut. It had taken him hours to reach the nest since speaking with Gan at Torr Guard and leaving to travel into the For'bane territory—precious, wasted hours; time enough for his fears and imagination to run wild.

He stepped forward, then stopped when she moved. She half-stumbled to her feet and leaned back weakly against the far wall. Her emotions swam with confusion.

"Belle," burst softly from his lips.

She gasped as she stared at his shape, "James?"

He stood stiffly before her, wondering if she would reject him—that he had been the one to come for her—yet, not really knowing how she would react to his presence. It did not matter if she did not want to see him, because he would save her ten thousand times and endure the same pain each time if necessary.

Instead, after only a moment's hesitation, she lifted her arms toward him. At once, he moved to catch her, and held her as she clung to him. He felt the weight of her emotions and relief spill over his senses like a soothing balm, but she did not cry. He wished he could tell her it was all right to shed her tears, but he needed her to be strong. He desperately needed her to survive.

She trembled in his arms, nonetheless. For a moment, he held on to her as she refused to let him go. He felt he could not speak—that her actions, the feel of her trustingly in his arms, was almost more than his heart could bear.

She broke the silence before he could. She drew back at last, hesitantly—uncertain of him—surprised by her own actions, as he was surprised by them. "You came for me. I hardly hoped…." Her voice choked off. "I thought I would die here."

She shivered. Her skin felt cold. "Here." Garren removed his cloak and wrapped her in it. He refused to satisfy his hunger to have her back in his arms. "Did they hurt you?" he demanded quietly.

Ora pulled the cloak close. "I would have tried to escape, but soon after they left me here, they gave me something. I thought it was water, but it tasted bitter…. I have little strength, I fear." As she spoke, she listed slightly to the side, still pale. Garren caught her by the arms. Steadied, she leaned back against the wall.

"The effects will fade, so long as they do not return with more to give you," Garren surmised. "It is a long journey out of here. I will help you find your strength."

"How?" she whispered, holding his gaze.

"Here." Garren withdrew his waterskin from over his shoulder. "Drink slowly. As much as you can handle."

Ora obeyed without question. Her hands trembled with fatigue as she lifted the skin to her lips for each purposeful swallow.

Garren moved away to survey the walls of the room, to see how the other cells attached to it, and the maze of tunnels sprouting off of them. He stayed within Ora's sight and felt her gaze follow him, as if afraid he'd disappear. A moment later he stood before her again, and took the waterskin from her as she offered it back to him.

"Can you really get me out of here?" she spoke.

"I have no intention of doing anything less."

Why did you come for me? He felt her unspoken question, and her gaze searched the shadows on his face. "I know we have our differences, but I am your best hope," he urged gruffly, not wanting to answer her silent inquiry.

"I never thought I would hear such words from you. I never thought I would be looking to you to save me… And yet, you always come when I need you."

His brow furrowed and he frowned. "Most days I am the monster. This day, I am safe where you are concerned." He started to turn away.

"That is just it, you are *not* safe," Ora corrected, weakly grasping his arm with one hand to stay him. He looked at her, jaw tight, but she was not finished. "You are like this War you are a part of—intense and dangerous and determined, and that is all right; that is what I can rely on. You did not have to come…but you did."

He caught her face in the palm of his hand with an intense and tender passion as he looked at her. "Then rely on these words: I will get you out of this alive."

Chapter 54

Ora's eyes filled with the sting of tears. She closed her eyes to keep them from falling and gave a somewhat unsteady, yet brave, nod of her head. Her fingers curled around the sleeves of his leather armor as he faced her, and she held on to him tightly for a moment. In the stillness, the soft familiar chill of the bleak cavernous spaces returned to her skin, except for her fingers as Garren's warmth chased away the cold.

She had forgiven him—for everything the Command had created him to be, for all the misinterpretations and judgements, for the blood of her guardian, and every action he had been forced to make. For her, the thought was a revelation and an awakening of feelings she had never imagined were possible. It was why she had said what she did. Something inside of her was changing toward him, more than simple tolerance; more than understanding. She had thought that would be enough. Instead, the feelings had not stopped there. The butterflies returned to her chest. Yet, this time, they came warm and inviting instead of covered in icy fears. Could Garren sense that and the confusion it brought?

Her confusion grew, and when he opened his arms to receive her, she fell into them gratefully. She did not feel like a woman right then, despite the depth of her emotions toward him. She felt like a child, begging only to hide from all the pain and chaos around her. She wished for a different —a kinder—reality. She desperately needed someone who could show her comfort and tenderness, without ulterior motives or dark intentions. She had witnessed too much of the cruel side of men throughout her life.

Garren cradled her, held her, just as he had done before, demanding nothing from her in return. He pressed his lips near her ear to speak, voice husky and quiet: "I must leave you now. They are coming. If they find me here, they will kill you," he said. "Do not let them give you any more bitter drink. I will stop them if they try, but I would rather not let them know I am here just yet."

Regretfully, she loosened her hold on him, taking a deep breath of his warm, masculine scent—clear like an autumn wind. "And you will be nearby," she finished for him and looked up at him as he stepped back.

He became one with the deep darkness as he moved away, but she saw the glitter of his discolored eye and felt his soft breath fan across her face. "Always." The cold moved in with a rush to surround her, as if held at bay by Garren's presence and now set free to torment and taunt her.

She stood still for a moment and was almost convinced his presence had been just a dream, a desperate fantasy in her tortured, yearning mind—almost.

The shuffle of creatures approached outside the tunnel to her cell. Her breath caught in renewed terror. *Breathe*, she commanded herself. She moved back against the far wall and sank to a huddle, pressing her back against the wall and pulling her knees to her chest.

She kept her gaze fixated on the darkened tunnel. More shuffling, a grunt, and the thud of a body hitting the floor in front of her startled her. The glow of a Skay's eyes appeared first, before the shafts of grey light distinguished its yellow-grey skin and horrific features.

It stared at her, hatred and the thirst for murder pouring from its gaze and the snarl on its lips. It grunted again, snuffed, and backed out. Ora held still in surprise as the Skay disappeared back the way it came, and only began to relax when everything became still and silent once more.

"Belle," Garren's voice came very softly, and she almost missed it. She gasped and rose unsteadily as he materialized from the darkness into the shadowed light. She grasped him and he lifted her face. "I am still here," he reassured in a whisper. "But they brought someone with them." He nodded in the faint grey light toward the entryway, tone grave.

Ora moved away from him, glancing back to reassure herself that he would not disappear again. She moved cautiously toward the bundled figure on the stone slab that served as the threshold of her holding cell. She knelt beside the form and gently shifted the body to stare in shock at the face within the folds of torn clothing. She gasped and Garren knelt beside her. "Garren, it is…it is that boy," she hardly whispered, barely managing the words.

The boy—Bev—who ran away in the woods during the scouting mission so long ago, looked nearly dead. His flesh was stretched tight against thin muscle and fragile bone, from lack of sunlight and nourishment. They had forced him to take so much of the bitter drink and whatever it contained that his half-open gaze looked disoriented and glassy. Unaware of reality.

Ora looked up at Garren to see his reaction to the sight. His features were grim. He did not seem surprised.

A sickening and horrific realization dawned on Ora, as she watched his face. "You knew this would happen…." She fought a tremble and caught her breath sharply. "That is why…why you killed the other boy, for running. He could have escaped; I knew he could have. But…this is where he would have ended up."

Ora could no longer look at Garren, filled with sudden shame. She hated the kill method the Singers used, though now she began to understand it better. She bit her lip and returned her attention to Bev. She feared to touch Bev's face as he slipped into unconsciousness, that even that contact might cause him undue pain. She leaned away and pressed a trembling hand to her face as a rush of weakness coming over her again. "I cannot understand it. Why are they doing this?"

Garren laid a hand on her shoulder, his touch steadying her. "You do not want to know," he said gravely. He looked at her a moment in silence and nodded his head toward the back wall. "Go rest. I will see to the boy."

Ora obeyed without another word. Beyond her fear and anxiety of being in this dreadful place, her heart grew fonder of the Singer Captain as she watched him lift and carry the boy with careful gentleness to a straw pallet in the corner where she would have slept. He remained a moment, crouched at the boy's side. Then, he joined her in the shadows.

"Is there really nothing we can do for him?"

"Orabelle." Garren surprised her by using her full name. She knew what he had to say was going to hurt her. "He will not live. What they have done to him—." He stopped and began again: "No, there is nothing we can do for him now."

Ora took a slow, deep breath. "What—what *have* they done to him?" she whispered.

Garren held his silence on the subject.

Anger sparked through Ora, holy and righteous. "I think I am beginning to understand your rage," she confessed with a hint of that anger rising in her voice. "I would kill every last one of them, if I had your strength."

Garren did not answer immediately. They shared a moment of silent understanding. He replied quietly: "You do not want to be like me, Belle. I would give up this anger if I could. Before it, I was human. I do not even remember what that feels like...."

Ora gave no response. She knew his words held wisdom, but she also knew that reality was war. And she was so afraid of it breaking her, she could only hope the one thing to sustain her was her anger.

Chapter 55

Bev died a short time later. Garren knew it before Ora. He sensed the change, the soft odor of death; the unnatural stillness in the air around the boy's body. When Ora stirred in half-wakefulness at his side, he wished he could keep the truth from her, but sensed she became aware of it as well. He felt her mind was sharper now. The potion was wearing off —aided by the fresh water she drank from his waterskin. The For'bane would return soon to give her more, or do something worse.

Ora lifted her head from where it had drooped to rest on his shoulder when she fell asleep. He kept his arm curved around her and felt the flood of fear and sorrow enter into her being. He immediately tightened his arm around her, preventing her from moving away from him.

"I—I need to be with him. I need to let him know he is not alone," she sounded desperate in the darkness, though her voice remained a whisper.

Still, he would not let her move when she tried pulling away. "He is already gone, Belle," he murmured, not wanting to hurt her with his words but knowing he could not help it. Death did not affect him like he knew it would affect her. He was used to it; numb to it. Everyone he had known growing up was dead. What hurt him was the knowledge that Ora came from similar circumstances. He did not want her to be alone. He did not want her to feel that heartache. It had hardened him, and if that happened to her…he honestly wondered if it would kill him.

So, perhaps his motives were selfish. But he did not care. His death did not matter. But to live—to even contemplate breathing—without her goodness adding light to his shadow, would be unthinkable.

"You do not know that. He cannot be…not—not yet," Ora pleaded. "He…should not have been alone. And cold. And…."

Garren pulled her into his arms almost roughly and cut off her words. "Stop," he commanded softly. "He is gone."

He felt her slowly yield to his embrace, tired, weary, and emotionally exhausted. Her silent tears wet his tunic until it felt uncomfortable against his skin, but he would not move away from her. He would not leave her to mourn on her own—not this time.

"I am taking you out of here tonight," he said.

She lifted her head. "How?" she whispered in surprise. "I tire quickly. We are so deep in the caverns, and I am still too weak."

Garren slipped one hand to the back of her head, gently tangling his fingers in her hair. "You cannot stay here. We cannot wait much longer. Not after…." He let the sentence trail away, then started again. "They will remove him, and then they will come for you." He caught her gaze. "I will help you."

He glanced into the darkness where Bev's body lay. He would have prayed to Creator to spare his Belle from the truth—from seeing what the For'bane were capable of. Their bloodlust, their hatred, their drive to kill, maim, and destroy was too barbaric to explain to her. He could only hope—if Creator would bend His ear to a mortal's plea—that she be spared further revelation. *Keep what innocence you still have,* he silently urged, looking down at her, nestled in his arms. *Do not let this darkness overcome you.*

He heard the distant sounds of clanging in the forges deep in the tunnels. The For'bane were creatures of darkness and night. He knew their weakness. He and Ora would make their escape just before dawn. When they emerged into daylight, the fragile light of dawn would aid their escape by confusing the enemy.

He spoke quietly near Ora's ear. "If you stay close to me, I can help shield you from their senses. Just do exactly what I tell you. Are you strong enough to stand on your own?"

Ora nodded slightly.

He kept one ear tuned to the sounds of the forges. Most of the enemy would be working below, building up their weapons and growing new stock to fight. They did not know of his presence, so it was highly unlikely they would be watching for Ora's escape. Without the water cleansing the potion from her system more quickly, she would have still been weakened against attempting escape alone.

She was not alone now.

Chapter 56

The next twenty minutes passed tensely as Ora waited with Garren. She did not know why he waited and she did not ask him, knowing that silence was necessary. She trusted him to get them out safely. After all, he risked everything coming after her.

He came for her. She still could not believe it; she could not imagine why he should. After everything he professed about no emotion and survival of the fittest being his way of life, and yet he came to save her.

She sat very still against him, pondering, reveling, and soaking in his warmth while she could in these last precious minutes that stretched into an eternity. Would she be strong enough to make this escape?

At last, Garren shifted, cueing her into action. She drew away from him as he stood, moving silently toward the entrance. She could see his outline in the shadows as he paused, and then momentarily disappeared from sight around the corner.

She crouched, gathering her wits and what strength she had, waiting for some signal from Garren. He appeared again, silent and stealthy; she approached until she stood at his shoulder.

"There is a store room two tunnels down from here. There should be armor and weapons inside." She felt more than saw his questioning gaze.

"Just get me a bow and arrows," she replied firmly. "I can shoot if the need arises."

"We will hope it does not come to that," Garren said. "We do not want to be noticed. You are in no condition to do battle, especially against an entire nest of For'bane." He moved back against the wall, around the corner of the first corridor and paused with Ora behind him. He reached back and tapped her arm with two fingers. When she looked up at him he made a motion with the same hand to a shadowed doorway across from him, down a slight slope in the tunnel.

Crouching down, Ora moved cautiously away from the wall toward the doorway, staying in the deepest shadows. Her gaze swept the corridor for any signs of movement. She did not take a breath until she was safely inside the doorway.

A few moments later Garren joined her. He kept close to her, she knew, in an effort to conceal her scent from the For'bane. He retrieved her kit from the corner of the room. "Yours? Here." He raised the strap over her head and settled it on her shoulder. He knelt in front of her. "Hold on to me."

"What?" she said in surprise.

His calloused fingers brushed the cold skin of her ankle. "You need shoes."

She hesitated a moment. She had not touched him so purposefully since the drugs had altered and confused her mind. She braced one hand on his broad shoulder, feeling solid muscle beneath.

Garren tugged soft leather shoes over her cold feet with swift precision and stood, catching Ora's arm to steady her.

"I am fine," she murmured.

In the faint torchlight in the tunnel, she caught the doubt in his expression. He studied her a moment. "Let us go." He slipped out of the room.

Ora hesitated, then grabbed her bow and quiver from where her kit had been, before following. She nearly ran into Garren when he stopped abruptly at the corner of another tunnel leading up toward the entrance.

Garren growled low in his throat with frustration. Shuffling came from the hallway, moving toward them. He silently drew his sword and hefted it with comfortable ease in front of him, holding the blade straight up and down in front of his face.

It took Ora a split second as he stood there to realize he was using the blade's reflection like a mirror in the torchlight to see the enemy's approach.

Hesitantly, she touched his forearm with one hand. Holding the sword in the opposite hand near the wall, he reacted to her touch by moving his arm in front of her to keep her behind him. She felt the tension rising in him as a wave of weakness stole over her, the potion still affecting her.

Garren spun away from the wall and drove his sword into the body of a Skay who came around the corner. With a shriek of surprise and pain cut short, it fell, giving Garren just enough time to face the Skay behind it.

Ora, her shoulder against the wall to support her, took her bow in hand and drew an arrow tight against the string, prepared to help Garren fight.

Garren cut down two more Skays effortlessly before they had the chance to offer much of a fight. Everything was still and silent again so suddenly that Ora slowly felt herself relaxing. The other For'bane must not be close enough to have heard the scuffle.

Garren, standing several feet ahead in the tunnel, had his back to Ora when a new voice sliced through the darkness: "When will you stop this foolish fighting? We are your brothers. Your blood calls to us and we answer."

Garren stilled. Ora held her breath at the familiar voice. The half-Skay stepped into the torchlight from a second tunnel intersecting the place Garren stood. The creature with human eyes, who spoke with a man's distorted voice, watched Garren and did not seem to notice Ora.

Then, Ora realized Garren's proximity was masking her from the half-Skay's senses. Garren stood in front of her and did not move because he was guarding her.

Chapter 57

"You are not my brothers. My brothers died long ago, fighting to destroy you. As I will do, until my last breath," Garren said stiffly, watching the half-Skay. The half-Skay's pale blue eyes startled him. All the For'bane had yellow eyes. "What are you?" Hatred and disgust burned in his gut, for the enemy standing in front of him, and for the same enemy that warred in his own veins.

The half-Skay grinned and laughed low in his throat. "I am the For'bane!" he declared proudly. "We are the same—you and I…."

"We are *not* the same," Garren interrupted sharply.

"You belong to us," the half-Skay spoke, moving in a half-circle around him, keeping just out of the reach of Garren's sword. Garren saw two other Skays creep closer from the side tunnel, and watched them cautiously as the half-Skay continued: "You were reborn to prey on human weakness and purge them from this land."

"I am not a beast like you!" Garren thundered, turning quickly to point his sword at the half-Skay, gaze filled with rage. "I was born of *human* blood! You are nothing but filth and dust! Raised from earth and sorcery!"

The half-Skay's lips curled into a slow smile. "We cannot be defeated. You will come to understand this. The beast in you knows. It will convince you with time. Oh, the humans are filled with such folly, to have thought their experiments would aid *their* cause. Why do you think we have not stopped them? Because you will become one of us. It was meant to be. We know this." His voice rose: "You will fight with us and our victory will be attained swift and sure!"

An arrow flew out of the darkness past Garren's head and pierced the nearest approaching Skay through the throat. It jerked backward in shock and dropped with a few desperate twitches and the guttural sound of it drowning in its own blood.

At once, Garren cut down the other Skay coming at him, as the half-Skay jerked back abruptly, surprised by the disturbance.

Garren managed to distract the half-Skay from Ora's presence in the shadows behind him, but now Ora stepped forward from the darkness, standing in the center of the tunnel. She held the bow in her hands, an arrow drawn taut and aimed steadily at the half-Skay's head. "Stand aside, now," she said steadily. Garren felt pride flood his heart at her bravery, but again masked his emotions and expression.

"You are intriguing…for a human," the half-Skay purred, backing away.

Garren felt a bitter taste in his mouth at the half-Skay's admiration for Ora. Ora shot the arrow and the half-Skay twisted aside, out of the arrows path and back behind the corner of the hallway for cover. The shrieks of oncoming Skays filled the air. Garren yanked one of the corked, clay vials he had obtained from the alchemist Gan from his belt. He flung it against the wall near the corner where the half-Skay hid, backing away quickly.

The vial shattered beside a wall torch, the flames igniting its powdered contents. An explosion rocked the earthen tunnel, causing dirt to spray in all directions as Garren turned and wrapped an arm around Ora, protecting her by shielding her with his body. "Run!" Garren barked before the piercing hum of the explosion died away, pushing Ora up the main tunnel to daylight ahead. "Run, now!"

Chapter 58

Ora paused and reached out to steady herself against a nearby tree. She fought to catch her breath. "James," she called and immediately Garren stopped ahead of her and turned. She shook her head, looking down. "I…I have to stop…a moment. I cannot—I cannot do this." She fought to keep the pain from her voice, but knew he would sense it.

He stood before her suddenly and touched her chin with the side of his forefinger, lifting her face to look her in the eye. "What is it, Ora?" he insisted. "Where are you hurting?"

"I am cold," she admitted, voice falling to a whisper. "It is my feet."

Garren glanced down at her soft leather shoes and glanced at the terrain to his left. He looked back at her. "There is a hot spring just over that rise. Can you make it?" he spoke with veiled frustration, but concern for her filled his darkened gaze. They were only an hour away from the For'bane nest, and seemed to have escaped pursuit, but they were still deep in enemy territory.

Ora forced a nod and took several steps past him. Garren turned after her and swept her up into his arms. Her startled gaze flew to his, but he did not look at her, his jaw set with determination. The warm strength of his body soaked into her, and she felt herself relaxing against him despite herself.

She still could not understand why he would come to save her. Why did he insist on protecting her? A Singer. A Captain. She was nothing—an archer, without rank or circumstance—and now reduced to a weakling who could not even walk.

She had not said thank you. She did not know how.

Garren carried her effortlessly, as if she weighed no more than a feather in his arms. He took the steep terrain of the hillside without slowing, and shortly they approached smooth, moss-covered rock surrounding a pool. The air turned warmer and steam rose off the surface of the water and nearby boulders.

Garren stepped down to a smooth slab of stone that angled into the water and bent to sit Ora down at the edge. "Take off your shoes," he instructed, then moved away.

Ora undid the leather ties slowly. Her breath came easier and the tightness in her lungs eased as she breathed in the warmer air. She pushed off her shoes and stretched her toes to touch the edge of the water. She bit back a whimpering cry. The water—though only moderately warm—felt like fire against her cold skin.

She pulled her feet back and breathed deep, biting her lower lip. She looked toward Garren and stared as she saw his bare back. He had stripped to the waist, his tunic and leather armor discarded on one of the boulders near him. His skin glistened with a light sweat over grime, and she saw the play of impressive muscle across his shoulders. He turned to look at her. His tags lay against his chest, but she could not make out what was written there. She had never seen a man's naked chest before, and the sight left her strangely uncomfortable.

He approached and she had to look away. "You have to get in the water, Belle."

"No," Ora insisted. "I will be fine here." She looked at the pool with trepidation. She could not tell how deep it went and she had never learned how to swim. The stream by the village only came up to her ankles.

Garren slipped into the water, stepping down off the ledge of rock and turned to lift her into his arms. "You will become ill if you do not get warm."

Ora clutched him in surprise and her heart jumped to her throat. He held her firmly and waded deeper into the pool till the water came up to his rib cage. Ora felt her lungs constrict. Pain flared across her skin; a cry escaped her clenched teeth. The water rose over her, covering her legs and torso, rising to her shoulders, and she clung to him in terror. A tear slipped past her defenses and down her cheek.

"Relax," Garren commanded. "Lay back."

More tears stung her eyes and she turned her face helplessly into his shoulder. He stood in the middle of the pool, holding her as the cold and pain slowly dissolved from her body. Little by little, she forced herself to relax, as Garren's arms and stance never wavered.

A trembling sigh escaped her and she closed her eyes, resting her ear against his breast. She could hear his heartbeat, strong and steady. "Thank you, James," she whispered, her voice trembling with rare vulnerability.

Chapter 59

The steam of the pool rose all around them so perspiration gathered across Garren's brow and upper lip and dampened his thick, short hair. He looked down at his charge, her face so near to his as she kept her arms curled around his neck.

She blinked back another tear and met his gaze waveringly. He found it difficult to swallow. Her damp hair flowed dark gold against his arm, the water steaming the grime from her face as the color returned to her cheeks and lips.

He had kissed women before, in years past. But those had been bold and crass women who flaunted themselves before him and were drawn to his darkness, the monster. He had let their kisses and attentions entertain him, to distract him from the hatred and rage inside of him, but it only left him empty. He knew their attentions were false. They were shallow and cold hearted. So he withdrew back to the battlefield, and let the War consume him.

Many women were drafted into the King's Army, but they were not built for war. Most perished, and those strong enough to survive became hard-hearted and tough. Ora was different. She had a strength about her that had carried her through this far. Yet, she retained a sweet purity and gentleness of heart that brought an ache to Garren's chest. She was everything he had been looking for, everything his human heart secretly longed for.

His desire for her had tormented him these last weeks. He had contented himself with doing his best to protect her and watch over her. Learning she was older than he thought eased his guilt, but with all the younger, more suitable men out there—could she ever love a man over fifteen years her senior? More importantly, a man who could hardly be called a *man* at all? Age did not change the fact that he would never be worthy of her love. She still saw the darkness in him. Though he may never kill the monster inside, for her sake he would do the best that he could, whether it brought him redemption or not.

Walling in his desire to kiss her, he took a steadying breath and held her gaze. "I will always come if you need me," he promised quietly.

Chapter 60

Once all the cold and pain left her, Ora felt comfortable and even a little drowsy. Garren lifted her from the water effortlessly in his strong arms and carried her out onto the mossy rock slab at the edge of the pool where he had left his clothing.

Ora released him as he bent to set her on the rock, and a moment later he wrapped his cloak around her once again. She studiously avoided looking at his bare chest until he covered himself again. She worked her fingers through her tangled wet hair and began weaving it into a braid.

When he sat beside her, she glanced at him, their shoulders nearly touching. "I think I can walk again. How far until we reach camp?"

Garren shook his head slightly, looking at her keenly for a moment before gazing across the pool. "We are quite far from the border, and we must take care not to expose ourselves to the enemy. Let yourself rest a minute."

She nodded slightly in acquiescence, finishing her braid. She pulled his cloak more tightly around her, and pressed her lips against the inside folds, burying her nose in the warmth of the material.

She could not shake the strange connection she had felt between them before they left the pool. Another wall seperating them seemed to fall to dust, evaporating like the steam above the water.

Garren's movement drew her gaze as he attached his quiver to his back and picked up his Singers bow. "I will find us something to eat," he explained before climbing over the boulders and vanishing from her sight through the fog.

He left his waterskin within easy reach and after a moment, Ora lifted it and took a small swallow, not wanting to deplete what they had but grateful for the ability to soothe her parched throat.

Should I hate him still? she mused, disturbed. *Am I betraying the memory of my guardian and friends by forgiving Garren?*

She glanced in the direction he had disappeared.

Yet...after all Garren has done for me, all he has sacrificed, is that not enough to redeem him of his past? How can I know what this is, what he means by it all?

Can I really trust a Singer?

A stronger thought surfaced. *I am tired of hating him. If I am to be honest with myself, I grew tired of it the first day I faced the For'bane at the front lines—when I saw a real monster up close, and what war is doing to this kingdom.*

Fear clawed suddenly at her heart. *This is not just about hate anymore. It is not only forgiveness at stake. I need him now. I need him more than I ever would have imagined possible. There is no one else.*

She hid her face in the cloak. It did not matter that no one was around to see her tears. *I am alone.* And what a desolate feeling that thought brought.

She lifted her face again, resting her chin on her knees, still holding the cloak around her, and stared across the pool. Her mother taught her that Creator existed above the earth, and that He saw everything and knew everyone by name. That no one, not even a lowly villager, escaped His notice.

She believed He existed—to say there was no Creator was madness. However, to believe that He cared enough to know everyone by name seemed less certain to her.

"I miss you, mama," she whispered aloud. "You always had strength without fear. No matter how badly you were treated, you still believed in love." She took a shuddering breath. "But love abandoned me when you died. And it abandoned me again when my guardian was killed. And still again, with Carter. You taught me love is just as important as power; that without it power is ruthless and destructive. I am afraid I have nothing left to love." She glanced again toward the boulders, to be sure Garren had not returned, and rested her cheek on top of her knees. "I might have died. I am a coward, because…I wish I had."

She pressed the tears away with her fingers. "But I must continue on. I must try. I must keep fighting. And I must do it alone now. For if Creator watches us, and if you can go before Him, and ask what He sees, I want Him to tell you to be proud of me; that I am being all I can be, for your sake."

Chapter 61

Garren pressed his back against a boulder that hid him from Ora's view. He heard everything she had spoken aloud and determined she not know, his heart stirring within him at her confessions. If he had not been sure of his love for her before, he had no doubt of it now. Just as he was certain he had made a terrible mistake in bringing her to the battlefield. She did not belong here. She deserved better than this life.

He clenched his jaw as a pang shot through his head and he took a slow, deep breath. No. He could not let this happen, not now. He must get Ora to safety. He pulled out the cord holding his glass vial and studied the empty reflection of glass with a frown. He should have filled it before he came after Ora, then he might not have run out. But that meant more time for Ora to suffer alone at the hands of the enemy. He had been using more of the powder than usual lately.

He waited in stillness several moments more, till he was certain she would not speak again, then slowly eased his frame away from the boulder and masked his expression, focusing on the task ahead. Slinging his bow over his back against his quiver, he moved around the boulder and back to the edge of the pool where she waited.

"Squirrel," he announced and dropped the mangy carcass on the stone in front of her. "Think you can start a fire if I bring you some brush?"

He silently applauded her ability to so quickly regain control of her emotions and strength. Had he not overheard her, he never would have guessed her distress. She sat straight, with no trace of tears on her face.

"Is it safe to build a fire here?"

Garren glanced around them. "The steam and fog from the pool will hide it," he insisted. "Keep it small. We will extinguish it as soon as the meat is cooked. Do you have your knife?"

"It is in my kit." Ora rose cautiously and went to retrieve her kit from the moss and earth covered boulder a few feet away, near the crest of their oasis.

Garren's senses of another's presence went on high alert. He lurched forward and grabbed Ora's arm roughly to stay her. "Wait," he commanded sharply.

Ora froze, and he felt her pulse jump. His good eye narrowed, intent on the place between the boulders where he had entered moments ago.

He stepped in front of her.

Chapter 62

A figure rose before them, startling Ora. She instinctively grasped Garren's arm from behind with a soft, quick intake of air.

Garren looked over his shoulder at her in veiled surprise at her touch. She found she was unwilling to draw away from him, as it might be more awkward than just staying her hand. Her reaction showed her open trust in him in a rare, intimate moment.

"It is all right," he conferred in a low rumble. He nodded to the man in shadow, not moving away from her touch. "He is friend, not foe." He addressed the dark, shrouded figure. "Adven Grey, this is Orabelle of the Freelands."

"You have a partner in crime now?" the stranger's voice was deep and gravely. The sound of it struck a chord of fear in Ora, making her think of a wolf's throaty growl.

Like those magnificent predators, Adven Grey moved forward from the shadows and seemed only to grow in size. Not realizing it at first, Ora's fingers dug into Garren's arm until a quiet, warning hiss between his lips urged her to ease her deathlike grasp.

She released him, stepped away, and lifted her kit, pulling the strap over her head so the satchel rested against her hip. She kept a wary eye on Adven.

"I have not seen you in over two years," Garren stated simply. "I thought you died."

Adven flashed a wolfish smile. "I cannot make that many people happy. It would upset the balance of evil." His tone dripped sarcasm and he glanced at Ora. "My lady."

"Garren did not hear you coming," she spoke quietly.

Garren shifted uncomfortably and his lips thinned.

"I have a gift." Adven's smile remained firmly in place. Cocky, and yet bitter.

"Hold your tongue, Grey," Garren growled. "How is the trail? We need to get back to the Divisions."

"Well, she is not going anywhere tonight," Adven crouched by the edge of the pool. He wore black leather gloves over his hands. Without removing them, he dipped his fingers into the water, washing the dirt from his gloves. "You stirred up a hornet's nest, Captain. The For'bane are everywhere."

"What?" Ora gasped. She turned to look at Garren accusingly. He had tried to make her think they were safe, that they had time. She had been slowing him down, putting both of them in danger and he'd never said a word.

Garren's expression turned to stone. "They have not found our trail yet."

"And if they do…you are ready for a fight, I am sure," Adven said confidently. He straightened and drew his sword, laying the flat end against his shoulder comfortably. "Need an extra sword?"

"Know a good place to hide for a few hours?"

Adven nodded over his shoulder. His tone turned serious. "There is some ruins that way, not far. Can the lady walk?"

"I can walk," Ora insisted, before Garren could answer for her.

Garren moved toward her. "You need to rest," he insisted for her ears only.

Ora stared up at him. "I am a warrior," she answered steadily. "A warrior who remembers the training of a Captain who once told her that weakness on the battlefield is death."

Anger flared in Garren's eye at the reminder. "And as your commanding officer," he replied firmly, "you will obey my orders and follow my command. I know what I am doing." He turned back to Adven. "Let us go."

Ora stood still a moment. She had not meant to question his authority and wisdom, but clearly Garren took it that way.

Adven took the lead, moving forward with a dangerous and powerful grace. Ora never expected to meet a man possessing strength equal to Garren's, but something about the man brought an uneasy fear to her heart. She stayed close to Garren, determined she not slow them down.

They reached the entrance to a cave as the sun set, sending brilliant orange light slanting between the branches of the trees. Warm light highlighted two, white stone pillars flanking the entrance, overgrown with a tangle of vines, moss, and weeds. The cave rested on a rise, jutting out near an overhang of rock that looked down over a lower valley of woods.

Ora looked inside and saw the cave was somewhat shallow, more like a decaying room of a building, half-buried in the earth, the walls made of the same white stone as the pillars. The white stone slab above them tilted up to a broken, jagged peak. They could build a fire just inside and the smoke would rise through the peak.

"What is this place?" she wondered.

"Part of the ruins. What used to be the cities of the keepers, before the For'bane took it over[18]," Garren answered.

Ora looked up at the pillars and saw intricate patterns near the tops, nearly worn away from the elements and decay. "What happened to the people?"

"Most of them died. The survivors sought refuge in the other four territories." Garren took her by the arm and directed her into the room, then turned away and left without another word or glance. He returned minutes later with an armload of wood, and prepared a fire.

Ora stood to the side, watching his movements. Something about him was wrong. A subtle change came over him since he had returned with the squirrel. A tension came over him, and his brow was furrowed.

He had not sensed Adven, until the other man was nearly on top of them. She should not have so brazenly made that observation, but it was true.

"Garren?" she ventured quietly. She glanced outside where Adven stood guard in silent shadow.

Garren ignored her. He struck a piece of flint. The soft scent of smoke and fire teased her nose before the fire lit the tinder and blazed up. Expertly, he fed the flames and then straightened. He faltered.

Panic set in. Was he injured? She moved toward him without thought and reached out to touch his shoulder. "Garren?"

---

[18] See *Brief History of Asteriae and Genealogy of the Kings* at the back of the book

The muscles of his shoulders spasmed beneath her touch. Her panic turned to fear, as he pulled away from her and looked at her sharply, sensing her fear. "I am all right, Belle," he insisted, but his voice was tense.

Ora took a hasty step back.

Perspiration dotted his brow and dampened his hair. He turned away from her again and hesitantly, painstakingly, lowered himself onto one knee near the far wall, his back to her. "I will be fine," his murmured words lingered in the air between them. A moment later, he lay on his side in a weariness she had never witnessed from him. It frightened her.

She looked out to where Adven stood. After a moment of indecision, she approached him as he stood watching the scene that just unfolded.

"Grey," she greeted as he held her gaze without moving.

"You need not fear him," Adven encouraged quietly, watching her to gauge her reaction. "He is only dangerous to those he considers his enemy,".

Ora glanced back at Garren. "What is wrong with him?" she insisted. "He will not tell me."

Adven sighed. "He has the blood of the For'bane within him. It is a constant battle, a war over the body, that he must fight. Does he carry a vial around his neck?"

Surprised, Ora shook her head. "It is empty." She had seen it hanging against his bare chest while he held her in the water.

Adven's gaze grew dark. "The vial contained a powder to combat the pain in his head. Without it—."

"What pain?" She could not imagine Garren ever suffering pain. He was like a rock, solid and unmovable. "I do not understand...."

"It is a side-effect from the blood, from his change. Every Singer fights against something. That is why some go mad, because their bodies will not accept the change. For the Captain, he survived the blending, but his head—," he nodded back to Garren, "—pains him. Without the powder, it could overwhelm him."

Ora felt a strange desperation come over her. He must be all right. After all he had been through—for her. She withdrew from Adven, still wary of his presence, and returned to Garren's side.

"What is it, James?" She reverted to his first name. The name he had given up to her, though it went against every law of nobility and war to have done so. She still did not know why he relinquished that right to her. She tried to sound commanding, "Please tell me how I can help you." A pleading tinted her words; a fear.

She sat and bent her knee against the earth-crusted floor near Garren's head, hesitating as she watched his features tense with pain, shifting restlessly. He turned his head to acknowledge her nearness and she brushed her fingers cautiously, lightly over his temple.

A soft sigh passed between his lips as he lifted his head and lay it on her thigh. Taking his motion as acquiescence, Ora continued to gently stroke his forehead and temples, watching his face intently. His body slowly relaxed its rigid tension. The violent tremors running through his muscles startled her.

She carefully slid her fingers gently over the taut muscles running up each side of his neck to his head and against his temples. As she soothed the nerves and muscles with her touch, his tremors gradually eased. His shallow breath deepened and calmed. It must have been a good thirty minutes before she saw the pain leave his features.

As he calmed, her attention shifted from his pain to the feel of his hair against her fingers. The warmth of his body beneath her hands. The strength of his muscles, relaxing to her touch. Her motions slowed with some uncertainty. "You scared me, just now. But I suppose you already know that. You know everything." Ora pulled her hands back, suddenly uncomfortable with touching him. "How can I ever hope to conceal anything from you?"

Garren shifted. At last, he opened his good eye and slowly blinked, raising his gaze to meet hers above him. "I feel your emotions," he replied. "I do not know what you are thinking."

She studied his face for a moment with reserved curiosity.

He closed his eyes again. "Thank you, Belle."

His gratefulness and praise warmed her heart more than it should have. She tentatively let her hands rest on his shoulders, the heat of his body warming her fingers, and leaned her head back against the cave wall behind her. A strong weariness gripped her suddenly. She only meant to rest her eyes, but with Garren's head resting on her thigh, and the silence surrounding them, she fell asleep from exhaustion.

Chapter 63

Garren roused, not sure how much time passed since Ora's ministering hands grew still. All he knew for sure was that his headache was gone, and it was Ora's tender care of him that brought it about.

He blinked, feeling rested, and looked up at Ora as she slept, his head still cushioned against her thigh. His brow furrowed as he studied her. His perception and emotions were foggy and disconnected while the headache plagued him, but now he felt a strengthening awareness of Ora's mental condition. A disturbance in her dreams. He felt the flutter of her pulse in his spirit, the fear and stress she was under as she slept.

Slowly, so as not to startle her, he sat up so he could see her face more clearly.

He noticed Adven sitting at the cave's entrance, watching them without a word. Garren could feel his gaze though he did not pay him any attention. Adven possessed a danger that compelled him to keep away from the towns, but he was not Garren's enemy.

His concern was for Ora, whom he knew was suffering right before his eyes. Dare he touch her? Would his actions only cause her more distress? Or would his touch ease her terror and give her much needed rest?

He remembered her in the For'bane nest—deep in the dank darkness, cold and alone. If only he could have been there sooner. If only he had been at the First Division so he might have protected her as he should have.

Her features were pale with shadowed smudges under her closed eyes. He crouched near her and lightly touched her hand. It felt cold. She moaned softly in her sleep.

Her distress sharpened in his senses, an intensity that caused him to move closer to her in an effort to calm her. The race of her pulse was the same reaction as someone desperate to flee something terrifying. And it was not him. It was something darker, pulling at her through her dreams.

Garren pulled her gently into his arms, lifting her to carry her closer to the fire. She relaxed in his arms and unconsciously snuggled closer against his chest.

His breath caught at the motion and he glanced toward Adven. Adven lowered his head and turned his gaze outside the room.

Garren looked down at Ora. Her distress eased. "Sleep. All is well," he spoke very softly. He let himself kiss her brow before he settled with her near the fire, holding her until he was sure the nightmares left her.

Chapter 64

Ora slept soundly at first, before her mind grew riddled with dreams and she shifted restlessly in distress. Somewhere in the depths of her dreams, Garren appeared. He lifted her and she curled into his arms. His lips touched her brow and his kiss soothed the turmoil within her nightmares—they fled away in his presence, and she rested safely in his embrace. Peace came and the dreams left her.

Ora woke slowly, feeling weary. A few moments passed before she opened her eyes and stirred. She felt the light weight of a blanket around her and sat up, blinking against the soft light of morning and the flickering flames of the fire, freshly stirred and fueled.

She did not see Garren anywhere about. Her searching gaze encountered Adven sitting at the entrance. He watched her patiently.

Ora cleared her throat and straightened. Seeing the level of the morning sun streaming into the room alarmed her. "Why did no one wake me?" she insisted.

"You were having nightmares. The Captain held you until you calmed."

Ora caught her breath quietly, recalling the sensation of being held against Garren's solid chest. So, it had not been a dream after all. Why had he done that? It did not seem in his character, though she had witnessed glimpses of gentleness in him; like when Carter died; like when he carried her into the pool.

Adven turned away to gaze across the wood below them. "He will return soon. He went to scout ahead."

"Who are you, Grey?" Ora urged, watching his strong, intimidating silhouette against the morning sun.

"They call me the Grimm." Adven stood and brought more wood to the fire from a small stack near where he had been sitting. As the flames leapt up to receive the offering like hot, hungry tongues, he continued: "The townspeople threw fire on me and tried to burn me alive. But Garren intervened."

"Your hands...," Ora guessed softly, shocked, as she noticed he still wore his gloves.

"I feel nothing," he replied with a hint of wary defense. "I cover my hands not just to spare people the sight, but to keep from...harming myself...without realizing it."

Ora watched him turn away and walk back to the entrance, looking out at the woods below them. She braced her arm against the wall to help her stand. Her body did not ache as much now, and her feet no longer pained her. She walked slowly toward him, stopping several feet from him. She felt he would say more, yet did not feel comfortable pressing him.

He turned back to look at her over his shoulder. "I am sorry if my presence has disturbed you—it is unintentional. It is the reason I remain here, secluded and shrouded from others. It is not my desire to bring fear or cause harm."

The dreams. How did he know? She had nightmares before. She had trouble sleeping before. But this time had been different. Filled with shadows, haunting, and fear, a sensation she picked up on when Adven entered the scene.

"You are like Garren then?" Ora spoke quietly, with some uncertainty. While Garren could sense emotions, it seemed Adven could *cause* them.

Adven's smile pulled tight with gentle sarcasm. "I am cursed," he corrected.

"Why are you cursed?" Ora kept her tone calm. She did not feel so afraid of him now, just wary. And if he was not a Singer…what was he?

He looked at her steadily. "Because my mother was an acerdae."

Ora swallowed hard. She had heard of the practices of the worshippers of darkness and the evil they were steeped in, an ancient mix of old tongue and new. "You were born to an acerdae…," Ora began slowly, "but you do not call yourself one. Adven[19] means 'blessed coming'—does it not? That is not an acerdae name."

Adven's jaw tightened. "Never. I did not choose to be one of them. I saw what it made of my mother. She was a wicked woman. But I am still her offspring, and that darkness is still a part of me." She heard the bitterness in his tone.

He fought a different war, one not of the physical realm. She knew there were other realms that intersected and affected the physical one. Could she not try and help him win that war? "Before he…died," Ora began steadily, suddenly determined to help Adven if she could, "my guardian always said in every situation, and in every struggle…we always have a choice. Our greatest failure is when we tell ourselves we have not a choice at all. It is true

---

[19] Adven : from the Latin 'adventus' meaning 'arrival'

you could not decide your birth—but only you can decide your life and what path you will take."

Adven turned slowly to face her as she joined him on the rock at the entrance. He shifted his gaze beyond her shoulder, to the woodland path leading up to the room.

"She hopes to save the wretched souls of battle and hate." Garren's quiet voice brought Ora around in surprise. His words stung her heart, but as she caught his steady gaze, she saw no scorn or rebuke there. "Tell me, Belle," he continued, "do you believe mankind's salvation will turn the tide of war? Is peace to be sought instead?"

"Like you," Ora began after a moment, "I was born into war. While I may have been brought up on the other side of it, with the mirage of freedom, you know well the Freelands are not without toil and violence. Do you not wonder what it would be like to rest without fear of the For'bane, to be at peace with who and *what* you are?"

"It will never happen," Garren spoke with conviction.

Adven stirred. "There is no use arguing with him," he said. "What he says is true. In this War or the next, as long as man walks this earth, there will always be bloodshed, because there is lust and greed in the hearts of men that can only be quenched through fire and death." His dark and ominous words, spoken in his wolfish, gravelly voice sent a chill down Ora's spine.

"We should go," Garren spoke after a moment of tense silence. "We need to make the Divisions by nightfall."

Chapter 65

Walking single file down a narrow, ancient path between bramble and the side of a rocky cliff, Garren took the lead with Ora following close behind. Adven took up the rear, following at a slower, more cautious pace as he made sure no one followed them. Garren suspected his distance was also meant to relieve Ora of the distress his presence always seemed to inflict upon others.

He discreetly glanced back at her, when he knew she was distracted and would not catch his gaze. She was not as bothered by Adven as she had been the night before. Understanding the darkness chasing Adven's every step, he knew her nightmares had been triggered by the man's presence.

I will not let anyone hurt you, Belle, he promised in his heart. *Not ever again.*

His hand tightened around his Singers bow.

For two hours they made steady progress without incident. Then Garren slowed his steps as they entered an open space in the woods, a small dirt and leaf-strewn resting place.

"Belle, come here," he commanded quietly. "Keep your back to me. Do not leave my side."

"What is it?"

"Something different…."

Suddenly, there were creaking and rustling sounds in the trees. Hauntingly familiar shrieks and calls rippled through the air all around them.

Adven drew his blade and held out his left hand toward Garren, who tossed him his own sword. Adven caught it smoothly by the hilt. "The trees. Above us!" Adven called to them in warning, looking up as Garren prepped his bow.

Garren grabbed Ora's arm and yanked her forcefully to his side. She stood still, looking up and searching the thick, entwined branches forming the forest canopy high above. "Arrows," he barked in command.

Ora hastily drew her bow and fitted an arrow to the string, aiming upwards as the first of the creatures dropped to the ground all around them.

"Muels are *different*?" Ora shouted above their screams.

"No," Garren replied, drawing back on his arrow.

The earth beneath their feet gave a violent tremble and the young trees before them split and cracked as the brush flew apart.

"*That* is different!"

Chapter 66

Ora stared in mute shock. The creature stood like a Skay. It looked like a Skay—only heavier—and it stood twice as tall, making even Garren's six-foot-two frame seem dwarfed. Its arms were twice as thick, like two tree trunks. A giant gold ring hung from its flattened nose, its head covered in a scaly-armor so its eyes were veiled.

Heart thundering with adrenaline, Ora swallowed hard. "All right, then," she said, not daring to take her eyes off the creature as it raised its face and seemed to smell their scent over actually seeing them. "He is big. We have faced bigger…."

The creature let out a roar, causing the forest around them to fairly shiver in fear.

"We cannot shoot it."

"What?" Confused, Ora looked at Garren, sure she had heard wrong.

Garren's grave expression latched on to hers.

A scream to her left. Ora spun on reflex and shot her readied arrow into the throat of the nearest Muel. "What do you mean!?" she shouted back to Garren.

Garren shot a Muel on his right. "Look at its skin. It is protected. Our arrows cannot pierce it!"

Ora looked and saw what Garren meant. Her mind scrambled for another solution, as the creature took a confident step forward and let out another roar, sweeping one giant arm across its path and killing two Muels in its way. It kept its head up, and seemed unaware that it had killed its own.

Her breath caught in her throat and her eyes widened with revelation. "It cannot see! Captain, it is blind!"

Garren swerved to face her, then back to look at the giant Skay. He saw what she'd noticed. "I have to get closer!"

"What is your plan?" Adven shouted as he leapt forward and struck a Muel through the throat with his right-hand blade.

"I will distract it," Ora said bravely, looking steadily at Garren.

The Muels hesitated now and most kept their distance with the new threat of the giant blind Skay.

"No, Belle, not this time."

"Last time…," Ora began.

"This is not last time!" Garren cut her off sharply. He turned to Adven. "Grey," he commanded and lifted the hand not holding his bow. Without a word, Adven tossed him his left-hand sword and Garren caught it at the hilt.

Garren slung his bow over one shoulder, as Ora aimed her next arrow toward a slowly advancing Muel. The Muel screamed at her in frustration, half-limping in its typically awkward monkey-gait toward her.

"Stand clear," Garren ordered, and sprinted for the nearest tree. The first branch hung at least ten feet in the air. He effortlessly jumped and grasped the branch with one hand, swung himself up to balance on that branch while he straightened and reached for the next. Up he went, higher and higher, with the grace of a panther.

Ora lost sight of him, keeping her attention on the Muels around them as Adven took Garren's place, guarding her back.

"What is he doing?" Adven called to her over his shoulder.

"How should I know?" Her fingers slid against the bowstring and she prepared to skewer the nearest Muel.

All at once, the Muels scrambled and scattered. Ora lowered her bow, stunned, before the tremble of the earth brought her and Adven's attention to the giant Skay. It came toward them. Ora aimed her bow, knowing it would do no good, but otherwise defenseless.

Garren dropped out of the tree, sword drawn and pointed downwards. He landed on the giant Skay's shoulder, the blade digging through the tough, leathery hide and acting as a handhold as the creature roared in pain and anger and tried to shake him loose. It swung viciously and its massive arm caught Garren in the side, flinging him several yards back into the dirt.

"James!" Ora cried out, running to his side as the giant Skay stumbled. She fell on hands and knees over Garren's prone form and shielded him with her body as the earth trembled and dirt sprayed up around the giant Skay as it fell with a heavy thud. She stared down into Garren's face. A bruise quickly formed on the side of his head and a thin line of dirt-smeared blood trickled from his nose. He coughed and rolled his head to the side with a wince, but did not open his eyes.

Ora turned her head to see the giant Skay struggling to rise again. "It is not dead!" she shouted to Adven, still several yards away.

The next moment froze inside Ora's mind. Each second pounded against her chest. Her breath sounded loud in her ears, drowning out everything else. She looked at Garren. Knowing he was helpless terrified her. Her hand closed around a clay vial in Garren's belt, like the one he had used in the For'bane nest. How did it work, exactly?

Adven was too far away and, just like her first day on the battlefield when the Skay raced toward her, she knew she did not have time to hesitate. If she did, this time they would all die.

Garren's normal eye flickered open, disoriented, and looked at her. She yanked the vial out from his belt, holding it in her hands, and ran toward the giant Skay. Adven shouted behind her, but she did not have time to look back. She felt each slam of her leather-clad feet hitting the packed ground, the thud of her heart against her rib cage; the sharp stab of each lungful of winter's air in her already aching lungs.

She heard Adven yelling again and realized he was trying to keep the giant Skay's attention away from her. She dodged as a shadow fell across her face, and narrowly escaped the slam of the giant Skay's arm as it made a wild swipe at her.

She teetered on one leg, still in a half-run and nearly fell to the dirt. But the giant Skay seemed disoriented, torn between the scent of human blood and Adven's shouts. And perhaps more damaged by Garren's sword than it appeared.

She grabbed up Garren's blood-and-fluid-smeared blade from where it had fallen in the dirt with her free hand, struggling with its unfamiliar weight. She stood in the giant Skay's path, and raised the clay vial to throw. "Come and get me!" she shouted, adrenaline rushing through her like fire.

The giant Skay turned at her voice and roared. She threw the vial at its face and open mouth and gripped the sword with both hands to raise it. The vial broke open against the giant Skay's sharp, front tooth. Powder erupted, coating the giant Skay's face and inside its mouth. Its roar turned into a choking scream. It stumbled backward, threw its head back, and twisted it side-to-side as if to shake the powder loose. A hint of acrid, burning stench filled the air. Splatters of blood and fluid from the deep tear in its shoulder sprinkled Ora's face and arm as it writhed.

She drove forward, blade pointed out, using her whole body weight to swing the sword. She slashed the inside of its leg below the knee joint. Its leg collapsed beneath it. Ora scrambled out of the way. She rolled and fell onto her back, still holding Garren's sword tightly in one hand as the weight pulled her off balance and a spray of dirt pelted her back. Dizzy, she turned onto her back and crawled backward several feet, staring with wide-eyed surprise as the giant Skay writhed on the ground a moment, then lay still before her.

She caught sight of Adven out of the corner of her eye, near Garren. She staggered to her feet, dropping the sword, and went toward them. She fell to her knees before Garren, relieved to see his eye open. Garren wiped a smudge of blood and dirt off her brow as she leaned over him. "Show off," he muttered wearily.

The thrill and exhilaration of victory rushing through her veins, she grinned down at him.

Chapter 67

Four days after their return from the For'bane nest Garren passed by the Archers Quarter, his shadow falling across the side of the tent where Ora slept. He sensed she was awake, and found he secretly hoped she would come out to him. He had been busy with his duties ever since their return, and had not had a chance to check on her.

She relied on him. He could not fail her. No matter what it did to him, he would do everything in his power to protect her and look out for her. This particular night, he knew something was wrong. He felt her sense of desperation—or fear—though he knew not of its source. It weighed heavy on her heart like an ache.

He made his way to the campfire on the rocky hillside, where he spoke with Ora a sennight after Carter's death. His thoughts felt crowded tonight, more so than usual. He had had very little rest. He knew weariness more than many men felt. But, he was not truly a man anymore. The blood of the For'bane in his veins made him capable of handling more than a normal man ever could.

He sat on the end of the long log before the campfire, using a stick to poke at the logs and entice more heat from the glowing coals. Several moments later, Ora joined him. She sat beside him without a word, hands in her lap, watching the fire.

He sensed her fear more strongly now, and it turned his stomach. He had not sensed that kind of fear since the night he nearly killed her with her own knife. Instinct made him want to draw away from her. He fought it and remained where he sat.

"Will you tell me what happened, or do I have to guess?" he spoke. His voice sounded cold. He did not mean for it to come across that way, but he felt his muscles stiffen.

She remained silent a long moment. Her answer, spoken quietly, surprised him: "Why did you tell me your name, James?" The fear had not left her, but she fought it. He watched her hands tremble, how hard she gripped them together.

He did not answer her. She could not know his reasons.

She looked at him. "The dreams I have been having… are not only about Carter, or the War. You are in them, too." Her eyes looked haunted and it hurt him somewhere deep to look at her.

After a moment, when she did not explain, he asked: "And am I the monster in your dreams?" He searched her emotion, but emotion only revealed so much. Fear was still just fear. He did not know its source anymore than he knew what she was thinking.

Ora hesitated and looked at her hands, fingers twined together tightly. She licked her lips, a nervous motion he had never noticed before. She gazed at the dancing firelight. "Did you know when you dream, you cannot run? It is as if your legs are stuck in mud, and no matter how hard you try, you cannot escape. You know it is possible, but you cannot make it happen."

A log in the fire shifted with a pop that shot up a shower of sparks into the smoke.

"You want to know the worst thing about the dreams?" She looked at him again and he thought for sure she would start crying, but she did not. "When Carter changes…when he is not *Carter* anymore. When…I am fighting to save him, and he turns into the very monster I have been risking my life to destroy every day."

Garren breathed in slowly and silently, drawing air into his tight lungs. *Carter* was the monster in her dreams. It did not make sense. Whatever changes affected Carter after the blood transfer did not matter, he was dead and gone now. He could not hurt anyone. Yet, her fear was not just the conjuring of an idea or dream, a notion of a past. It was present—and very real.

"And you," she continued after a moment of struggle, drawing his full attention. "Sometimes you are a shadow...hovering at the edges. I cannot see your face, but I know you are there. Other times…."

Garren's jaw tightened. *There it is.* "And how can a shadow hurt you? What warrior fears a shadow?"

"I am not afraid *of* you, James," she blurted in a barely audible whisper. "I am afraid you will *leave* me."

A feeling like ice breaking filled his heart. He sat very still for a moment. Then, with a deliberate move, he cupped her cheek in the palm of his hand and looked directly into her eyes. "I *will not* leave you."

"I am afraid for you," she confessed quietly, holding his gaze. "I—I honestly did not believe you could bleed."

Garren's gaze grew troubled at her words. "I would like to say I am invincible. I know I pretend to be. But I am made of flesh and bone, it is true."

Ora stared at him for a moment longer, searching for something. Was she searching as desperately for the human element as he was? She seemed content with whatever she saw in his returning gaze, because in the next moment she lowered her head to his shoulder, and relaxed against him with a weary sigh.

Chapter 68

Ora found a table near a corner of the food tent, where she joined a few of her fellow archers for lunch. She kept an eye out for Thane, but did not expect to see him. She wanted to search him out, but since the experience with Greer, she had been hesitant to venture far from the Archers Quarter.

She also feared what she may find out if she did; that Thane had died from his weak health and illness. She could not abide facing another death so soon after losing Carter.

"The officers are meeting together," Decklan spoke, drawing her attention. "They are keeping things quiet, but I heard a rumor that they expect the King himself to visit the battlefield…."

"What? Here at the line?" Ora broke in with surprise. She shook her head. "Why should he do that?"

Decklan, sitting across from Ora, looked at her. He shrugged. "Royalty," he answered, as if that was answer enough. "They live in their castles, longs away from any real fighting. To them, it's a game…."

"Yes, coming out here to watch us all get slaughtered," inserted another archer farther down the table.

"I hear they still eat fresh meat," Stevan informed. "Imagine. Fresh cooked meat with fat and everything."

"I hear they separate the strongest horses out for their own use, because they are so fat and lazy from all that food they cannot walk anywhere, and our skinny war mounts could not carry their bulk twenty paces."

Several archers snickered at this, except Ora. She had never met a palace noble, and wondered how much of the stories could be true. "Do you really think they do not care what goes on here?" she queried.

Decklan regarded her seriously. He also did not laugh with the others, and she had always found him to be the level-headed one of the group. "If they truly cared…do you think the War would still be happening sixteen years after it began?"

"Maybe…maybe they really do not understand what is happening here," Ora ventured.

Several looked at her with disbelief in their eyes. Decklan shook his head. "Or maybe they profit much better by letting it continue." He turned back to his plate but Ora could not let the subject drop that easily.

She leaned against the table as the others focused on finishing their meager rations. "Profit? Where is the profit? Who will plant their crops or deliver the gold for their economy and jewels?"

Decklan stopped chewing a moment to stare at her. He kept his thoughts to himself and swallowed before speaking: "Where are you from again?"

Ora flushed. "I am from the Freelands."

"What is left of it," remarked someone down the table, catching her answer.

Ora looked at the archer, a narrow-shouldered boy. The tip of his ear had been shorn off by an arrow two days before and its ragged tear was turned her way, making her stomach twist. "As long as there is one Freelander our people will survive. We know how to survive."

"You live in the fields, a bunch of weakling farmers," accused the boy, challenge in his eyes.

Ora took a deep breath, her hand clenched around her wooden goblet. Decklan rose from his seat abruptly, startling Ora. He calmly walked around the table and bent near the boy's ear, tapping the wound with his forefinger. "I would be careful how you speak. We outnumber you ten to one. That arrow may not have come from a Skay."

The boy blanched, glancing around to see several pairs of eyes staring him down.

Decklan glanced over the boy's head and winked at Ora before turning and leaving the tent. Ora relaxed her tight grip and breathed easier. *I am not alone,* she reminded herself, catching supportive looks from several archers around her. It was true, there were more Freelanders fighting in the Great War than any other province, despite its shrinking borders and war-torn hillsides.

She shoved the last of the gruel from her trencher into her mouth and hurried out of the tent after Decklan. She pulled her leather jerkin closer around her against the blast of arctic winds and looked around. Instead of Decklan, her gaze fell on a small group of Council members dispersing from their tent several yards away.

Catching sight of Garren's tall, athletic form—his dark hair already salted with tiny beads of snow pelting the ground—she walked toward him. Garren turned when she neared as if he sensed her presence.

"Captain," she greeted respectfully.

"Belle," he returned. He kept his posture stiffly erect. A Captain to his soldier, despite the informal name he called her.

"Is it true?" She glanced at the tent he and the Council vacated, then met his gaze again. "Is it true the King is coming here?"

Garren took a breath, not expecting the question. He looked around the area, making sure no one observed them or listened in on their conversation. He made a slight motion with his hand toward the edge of camp. "Walk with me," he commanded quietly.

Ora fell into step beside him, disturbed. She could tell he was not happy about something. She waited, assured he would explain when he was ready.

They continued past tents and soldiers moving in all directions. Garren remained tight-lipped and silent. At one point, he took her arm to step out of the way of a passing cook's cart. "This way," he said, leading her to a side practice field, empty now, and in a quieter section of the First Division.

Ora watched him as he faced the targets at the opposite end of the field and set the notch of an arrow against the string of his Singers bow. "How is your aim?" he encouraged quietly.

"I hit the center mark two out of three."

Garren pondered her answer. "You have been practicing. Good." He drew taut on the bow, and released the arrow to the soft vibrating song of the Singer. The arrow embedded dead center of the target. He continued to face the target as he spoke again: "I cannot tell you what was discussed in Council."

Of course. She should have known. It was not her place to approach any of her commanding officers with questions of Council business. To distract herself from embarrassment, Ora drew an arrow and faced the target as she took her bow into her free hand.

"Belle." She felt his gaze, but did not look at him as she drew taut on the bow. "I did not bring you here to lecture you on the rules of warfare. I cannot confirm your question…I will not deny it either."

Ora slackened on the bow and lowered the arrow. "So… he is coming," she concluded in quiet surprise. Uncertain frustration coiled in her gut, and she tried to ignore it. She looked at Garren. "Have you ever met him?"

"The Boy King?" Garren raised a brow. She sensed a slight lilt of cynicism in his voice as he turned back to the target and drew another arrow. "No." He let the arrow fly. Center of the target, right against the first arrow. "I met the Great King, however. Before…well, when I was still human."

Ora ignored the last statement. She was convinced at last that he was not a monster. "What was he like? The Great King? I was only ten when he died, but I heard that the kingdom deeply mourned his passing."

Garren glanced to the skies. "He knew how to be a leader, and he treated his subjects with respect."

"And does not the Boy King also know how to treat his subjects?" Ora asked, still wondering if the rumors could have some truth to them. After all, the War continued worse than ever.

Garren turned to face Ora again. "There has been talk?" His tone suggested he knew there was. "What has you so disturbed?"

Now it was Ora's turn to grow silent and turn her focus on the archery targets. She lifted her bow again and drew the arrow back taut against the string. She released. The arrow grazed the edge of the target. She let out a frustrated breath. "I cannot shoot when you are staring at me."

She glanced at him when he said nothing. His gaze searched hers. Ora lowered her head as she set another arrow against the string. "It is nothing really."

"If it were nothing, you would not be upset."

"Reading my thoughts again?" she said, dryly.

Garren's jaw tightened.

"I know," Ora sighed. "You cannot read thoughts." She stared across the field. "Some of the archers were talking; insulting actually. I never realized how many people look down on the Freelands; how much they despise us. I think it has something to do with the Unity War, but that was over three Ages[20] ago…and we have sacrificed the most in this War. We have lost the most…." Her voice trailed off.

"And you blame your King for your suffering?"

Ora shot. This time the arrow landed near the middle. "As you said yourself, I do not know the King. I can only hope that he is wise and just. But I am tired of war, tired of the blood and the dirt, of the dying…."

"Belle…."

Ora drew another arrow hastily and shot again. Straight in the very center of the target. She released a breath and flexed her fingers.

She turned her head, but only held his gaze a moment. "Make that one out of three for today." She looked away again. "I will be fine."

"I need to see that, Belle. Because I need you on my side these coming days."

Her stomach knotted and quivered with uncertainty—his words sounded ominous. Ora replaced her bow at her back, over her quiver. "I am on your side," she murmured.

---

[20] Ages : an age equals the rule of a King, and spans the length of years of that rule

Garren stepped closer and gently slid his hand against her cheek and jaw and spoke with confidence, “I know you are strong.” He took a breath. “Stand proud before your adversaries, and remember that we have all won...and lost.”

Chapter 69

It had taken great effort on Garren's part to conceal his joy at seeing Ora. That she would come to him—without a wall of hate or anger standing between them, without scorn. It felt like a gift from heaven.

He let her walk away from him without expressing the tenderness he felt for her, just as he had done so many times before. It was easier to hide it when she despised him. Now he would have to fight much harder to keep his emotions under tight control.

He reminded himself she was a soldier and he was her commanding officer. Captain James Garren could not afford emotional entanglements. Captain James Garren may one day have to give an order, sending her into the enemy's waiting jaws; an order which may result in her death. He could not act partial toward her. He must treat her just as he would treat any other soldier under his command.

'I need you on my side....'

Could he be impartial when the time came? Was not his heart already more involved than it should be? Had he not already told himself he would protect her at all cost? Would he be willing to pay when it came time?

He strode to his own tent in the opposite direction from the Archers Quarter. He needed to refill the vial around his neck.

The familiar surroundings of his own quarters helped him relax. Though most days he felt a stranger to himself and to others—a soldier who had no home or direction—this small space with his own effects gave him some sense of belonging—of purpose and identity.

He loosened the ties down the front of his armor, and shed his leather jerkin, depositing it across the end of his cot. He rubbed his shoulder, injured when the Skay attacked him on the ridge. His For'bane blood helped him heal more quickly than the soldiers, but the muscle had been damaged and still bothered him after a long day wearing the stiff, heavy leather.

Chilly winter air slipped in around the edges of the drawn curtain serving as his doorway, dried the sweat between his shoulder blades and cooled the dampness of his tunic against his chest. His hand shook as he reached for his top dresser drawer which contained the white powder. He pulled his hand back and fisted it for a moment, trying to steady himself.

Unbidden, the words of the half-Skay came back to taunt him. Tension knotted his stomach, and an unfamiliar anxiety ate at his insides.

Despite his determination, despite having not given in to the half-Skay's claims, he felt unwelcome doubts assail him again. What if the half-Skay was right? There must be some truth to the claims, twisted and vile as they were. The half-Skay was not a normal Skay, because he had human attributes, but neither was he human, because he clearly looked like a Skay, and spoke for the For'bane cause.

"Do not let it be," Garren whispered, despising himself all the more. "Do not let them change me." He knew his rage and lust for violence was enhanced by For'bane blood. He had always sensed that—always known there was a war going on between his human flesh and the enemy's blood coursing through him.

His mind and heart fought to grasp hold of reason. He could still remember a time during his childhood, before he entered the Great War. Those memories, bittersweet and heartbreaking, he kept cautiously buried.

He faced these new dilemmas, once again reminded of the war within him. He fought to destroy those monsters, yet found they never seemed to die—rising anew every dawn. The memories from his childhood became the source of reason he needed.

His mother had been a praying woman of quiet, dauntless faith in Creator. He had always been amazed by her, how she never tired in her prayers. She never asked anything for herself but only for her son. He could close his eyes now and still hear her sweet voice praying over him every night as he fell asleep. 'A man of sound mind and unwavering spirit.'

A man, he mused. *Not even the first part of her prayer could be answered. I am not* even *a man.*

He sometimes wondered if Ora was stronger than he. She did not think so, he knew. But he knew she was strong enough to outshine the other soldiers around her. She had been through worse than many and still survived. She guarded her scars carefully, but still managed to turn that brokenness into beauty and courage in his eyes.

He reached for the drawer again. His hand was steady this time as he withdrew the pouch and carefully filled the vial around his neck. Before replacing the pouch, he took an extra pinch and pressed it on his tongue to dissolve there.

Ora was right. The King *was* coming. The challenge of keeping him safe while on the battlegrounds had fallen to

Garren. The officers believed he could choose a team of skilled men to protect the King's Envoy. He thought the King's coming here was foolish, but that was not his concern.

The half-Skay claimed the Singers were created for the For'bane's own purposes. But who or what had created the For'bane? It was a question no one seemed willing or able to answer.

Garren sank onto the edge of his cot and ran his fingers through his short, greasy hair, still damp from the snowfall outside. How much did the Boy King know about his father's reign? How much did he know about the War and the established leadership?

No one talked about where the For'bane came from—when they first appeared, or how they had grown so powerful so quickly. Many who might have known died in battle during the course of the War, including the Great King, the Boy King's father. And whoever might have answers had not seen fit to expose the truth.

'What are you?'

'I am the For'bane! We are the same—you and I....'

He stood abruptly and pulled on his leather armor, leaving the shoulder-ties loosened as his shoulder still ached from the confinement. He turned and stormed out of his tent.

Chapter 70

Two days passed. Ora withdrew from the line at dusk, bone-weary to walk the two longs[21] back to the First Division camp. She pulled her leftover meal from her kit, and chewed on a roll of salt-water bread. She paused alongside the deeply rutted footpath at the outer edge of camp, and sank down onto a boulder protruding from the frozen mud.

A shadow fell across her face in the light from a row of torches flickering across the line of soldiers coming and going. Decklan knocked her lightly on the shoulder. "No time to sit around. We have hard, scratchy-blanketed cots waiting for us." He grinned, the dark shadows under his eyes and strain between his brows testifying to his own weariness.

Ora managed to lift one side of her mouth into some semblance of a smile, but it did not last. Her shoulders slumped.

Decklan plopped down beside her and she shifted to make room for him on the boulder. He sighed. "You are different."

---

21 Two longs : half-mile (see footnote 4)

"I am tired," Ora admitted, passing the back of her hand across her dirt and blood-stained forehead.

"No…I do not mean that," Decklan insisted. "You are different. Ever since you came back from the For'bane…."

Ora felt bile rise in her throat and her stomach twisted. "That is not open for discussion," she warned softly. "I—I do not talk about that."

Decklan watched her closely. "You are stronger."

Ora looked at him in surprise. "I am?" she whispered, not so sure.

Decklan nodded, watching her. He spoke calmly: "You know, I defended you in the food tent the other day—" (he inclined his head toward camp) "—because, though I confess I was not born of the Freelands as you were, I believe in you. A lot of us do. I assumed you knew that."

Ora fingered the salt-water bread, too disturbed to eat any more. "I meant to thank you."

"That is not why I bring it up. If you knew why, you would not feel it necessary to thank me, and you would not apologize for not having done so." Decklan leaned forward, elbows on his knees, an intense expression on his face, as he turned his head to look at her. "We are family, Ora. We are your friends and your comrades-in-arms. I am singling you out because of that bond…. I saw you seek the Singer Captain outside the Council tent. A few of the others have noticed it too—it is no secret he went after you when you were captured by the For'bane." Ora found herself locked in his gaze. "Do not shut out the only people who truly care about you."

Ora stared at him. "Deck, whatever do you mean?" she spoke stiffly, her muscles tense with strain.

"Remember he tried to kill you."

Ora stiffened. She had not seen Garren since he stood with her on the archery field. "I am not sure who you mean…." *And I tried to kill him first….*

"Yes, you do. He went after you, and brought you back. The Captain would not do that for anyone. A Singer does not make friends with a human."

Ora pressed her lips together a moment in thought. Her instinct was to strike out at his choice of words. But, because he had been good to her, and because he did not understand Garren anymore than she had before, she must be kind in return. She could not blame him for his caution. She always focused on Carter as her best friend, but since his death and her own traumatic experiences, she could not talk to just anyone. Garren had seen her through all of it. He was the only one who had seen her fall apart and still believed in her.

"I do not mean to shut the others out, or to seem unfeeling. Perhaps the Captain was right and perhaps I am wrong. I have seen much of battle, and a lot behind the lines. It is not that I believe the Captain has changed, but I have changed in my knowledge and understanding of him, and why he does what he does. He is not evil, Deck."

"Perhaps you do not know the same Captain Garren that everyone else does," Decklan spoke darkly. Ora wished she could make him understand—make him see what she had come to see.

"No," she whispered. "Perhaps we do not know the same man." *'My name is James….'* She pulled her bread into two halves and offered him one. "If we remain divided, we will never win the War," she reminded quietly, steadily. "Whatever you choose to believe about him, he is fighting against the For'bane, and he has been faithful to continue fighting these sixteen years."

Decklan sighed and accepted her offering.

They sat quietly for several moments, watching soldiers pass by on the path, weary and bloodied from battle. A hesitant calm descended across the front lines, as both sides took a short truce to rest, regroup and re-strategize.

Ora wondered how long this one would last. She had learned this was not an unusual occurrence, as many such breaks had taken place over the course of the War, some as short as a day and others as long as a few weeks.

A break might give her some time to search for Thane, if she could procure permission to go to the Third Division. She had not been able to locate him across the expansive camp of the First Division, and had not seen him since that day in the food tent. He must have been re-stationed at his Commander's tent.

She wanted to ask Garren to find him for her, but it felt wrong to use his command and position. Decklan had a point, she still needed to remember that despite everything, Garren was her commanding officer; not her friend.

Something inside her ached with the reminder. She had begun to view him as her friend.

'I will not leave you.'

She stared at the row of flickering torches, letting the play of flames mesmerize her as she felt her thoughts wander. *How can you make such a claim? I do not want to believe you are just like any other soldier.... You must have honor, because I have seen it. You did not abandon me, even when Bron did. You stood up for me.... But why?*

"I am tired," she whispered, still staring at the torches and did not see if Decklan heard her. "I do not make an effort with friends because I do not know who will be alive come the next dawn."

"We all feel that way." Decklan slipped one arm around her as, weary and emotionally defeated, Ora leaned her head against his shoulder.

Chapter 71

"Those records were destroyed ten years ago, and any reference to them was confiscated."

Garren's jaw tightened as the scholar spoke. He asked himself why he had wasted a day's ride to be intercepted by this pale dwarf swathed in stark-grey robes. Though the man stood only four feet tall, Scholar Phillips' mere presence had become an impediment to Garren's search.

"By who's authority?" he demanded from within the shadow of his hooded cloak.

"I—I do not know. I only know no one has access to them."

"Well," Garren said dryly, "is that not convenient." He looked around the tall, stone room that made up the front section of the Brothers Cathedral, now the largest cathedral located in Greavens, since the Ancient Cathedral was destroyed in what was now For'bane territory.

"Who *would* have access to this information?" he said, turning back to the scholar.

"I have heard of a journal written by an alchemist in the Third Age, at the time of the Great King. It is rumored he assisted with some early experiments and may have been involved in the study of the For'bane when they first appeared, before the Ancient Cathedral was destroyed. The alchemists are known for keeping journals. Whether those journals were destroyed or not, I cannot clarify." Scholar Phillips crossed the stone floor with the hasty slap of his sandaled feet, hidden beneath his long robes. He mounted three stone steps where a table stood before a tall bookcase. He grabbed a large book off the end of a shelf and opened it on the table.

Garren moved forward as Scholar Phillips spoke again: "We keep meticulous reference of our books. We do not want any of them to get lost, so we keep a record of their movement, as some get shuffled from place to place."

"Would this journal be listed here?"

"Perhaps," Scholar Phillips pondered, "its location and information may be mentioned in another document."

"But you said anything about the For'bane origins would be confiscated or destroyed. Why would this journal, or any document containing its evidence, still be public?" He turned as he sensed another presence coming near.

"Who comes asking questions about our enemy?" spoke a new voice from a tall, grey-robed figure who approached from a shadowed corridor to their right. He stopped when he saw Garren. "You are a soldier," he noted.

"I am a Captain. Captain Garren."

Scholar Phillips drew back in uncertainty at the name.

Garren kept his gaze fastened on the tall scholar, who continued to meet his gaze without fear. The newcomer's fine, closely shaved hair was silver, and the finely-stretched skin and slight wrinkles testified to age. He calmly accepted the news of the Singer with a slight, gracious nod. "The Singer Captain," he said. "Your reputation proceeds you."

"What reputation is that?" Garren rumbled stiffly.

"That you have never been beaten in a fight, no matter the odds against you." The tall scholar crossed slowly to a kneeling rail and prayer table arranged with candles. "I am Brother Keelon." He lifted a piece of straw into the single lit candle at the center of the table, and used the burning straw to light one of the smaller candles. "You wish to know the history of the For'bane?" He extinguished the straw in a cast iron bowl under the table. He turned back as Garren stepped down from the platform to face Keelon. "May I ask why?"

"To understand why we have fallen, and why we continue to do so. To understand why we let their power grow so greatly."

"Scholar Philips, carry on," Brother Keelon instructed as the other scholar merely stared at them both, unsure what to do next.

"May I see your face, Captain, as Creator fashioned it?" Brother Keelon waited patiently.

After a moment's hesitation, Garren reached up and slipped the hood back off his head. "That may be difficult, Brother," he said politely. "It is not as it once was."

Brother Keelon's gaze took in the eyepatch and deep scar without scorn or rebuke. "The cost of battle is the marring of Creator's perfect design," he agreed as Garren stood stiffly under the inspection.

"Do you know anything of the For'bane origins?"

"You have been fighting them for so long," Brother Keelon reminded. "And you still do not know how to defeat them...."

"I was created to be their destruction," Garren insisted. "But I have not succeeded."

Brother Keelon pondered his answer a moment. "Hmm," he said vaguely. He turned back toward the shadowed corridor. "Come with me, Captain."

Garren glanced back at Scholar Phillips, who remained behind the table and gave the Captain a blank look. Garren turned and followed Brother Keelon.

They followed the narrow, shadowed corridor to the only room at the far end; a library. The walls were covered with bookcases, filled top to bottom with volumes. More stacks of books sat in even piles on two tables taking up most of the room. A short, arched door at the room's far end was the only space not covered with books.

"Not here. Come."

Garren noticed Brother Keelon moving around the tables toward the short door, where he turned the ornate brass handle and let the door creak inward, revealing a deep yawning darkness with a curved staircase beyond. He saw faint light below the steep stairs.

"You realize if you are trying to entrap me, I will kill you," he spoke firmly and calmly.

Brother Keelon smiled slightly, though Garren had not meant anything amusing by his warning. The silver-haired scholar ducked through the doorway and began his descent. "I have been trying to catalogue these ancient documents. Some have been here for more than a century, long forgotten and buried when the far section of the Cathedral fell," Brother Keelon said as he descended ahead of him into the room. "A few were salvaged from the Ancient Cathedral at the start of the War."

Garren stepped down the last step into a small, square room. Tables and benches in the middle of the room were covered with haphazard documents, books, and repair tools. The space was lit with oil lamps and flickering torches on opposite walls. One wall held a decaying, wooden floor-to-ceiling bookshelf. All of the books it contained looked old, some falling apart. The room smelled musty, but the floor was dry.

Brother Keelon approached the table nearest the shelves and brightened the oil lamp. "I have reserved much of our burning oils for this room. I spend as many hours as I am able trying to copy these books." He took a plain bound book off the shelf and looked at Garren. "If you want to know about the For'bane, I may be of some help to you."

Garren came closer. "What *do* you know about the For'bane?" he urged.

Brother Keelon laid the book on the table, gently opening the cover to lay flat. Garren saw several pages were falling out of the binding. "I have read much during my time here," Brother Keelon began. "I have learned many things and kept many secrets. But, only for the ear—" he tapped his ear "—that desires Truth."

Garren hesitated, searching Brother Keelon's gaze, deciding how much information to give him. He crossed to the other side of the table and spoke slowly: "The For'bane is my enemy. But I have heard…disturbing rumors. I do not like secrets."

Brother Keelon raised a brow. "For a man who does not like secrets, you seem most secretive."

"I said I do not like secrets. I did not say I do not have any."

Brother Keelon nodded. He gently turned the pages of the book, searching for something as he spoke: "Sixteen years ago the War began, but the For'bane were mentioned in texts long before that time. They first appeared in an account given by Charles Binn—."

"Charles Binn," Garren interrupted in surprise. "The alchemist? The revolutionist?"

"If you call the acerdae movement a revolution…."

"Charles Binn was an acerdae?" Garren narrowed his eyes, then shook his head slightly. "He is still spoken of today as a great philosopher. He gave lectures here, did he not? And became a close friend to the Great King…."

"Charles Binn referred to a new creature he called the Bane." Brother Keelon found what he was looking for in the book and turned it around to face Garren, tapping an image in the book.

"Bane," Garren said. "A creature of darkness." He studied the image, an ink sketch of a shadowed creature that stood on two legs, hovering just inside the hole of a earthen cavern.

Keelon continued as he turned the book back to himself and turned a few more pages. "They came from the depths of the earth, from a pit called Aker. Not long after, Binn's 'revolution' became known as akerdai. Which, as you probably have concluded, has now been reformed into the acerdae. Worshippers of darkness."

Garren took a slow breath, feeling his chest tighten with foreboding. "So the For'bane is the Bane? This creature of the earth Binn discovered?"

"Not exactly. The Bane were not creatures of destruction, not like we know our enemy today. They were afraid of daylight, which is why they lived in Aker's pit, the only place dark enough for the Bane to exist. The acerdae believe it is the place where all life originated—where time first began. We hold to the Ancient truths however, of Creator's design of all life and order, as recorded by the keepers." He withdrew a loose page carefully from the book. "Charles Binn says nothing more on the subject. He disappeared just before the War. A few years after the War began, any records pertaining to the For'bane were seized and confiscated by the leading officers at that time."

"Why would they do that?" Garren demanded.

Brother Keelon turned the page—worn and wrinkled—toward Garren and offered it to him. "I do not believe they wished anyone to know of their secrets either," he said, referring to their earlier conversation. Garren took the page as Brother Keelon explained, "This is a letter salvaged from the Ancient Cathedral.... Most of the words are worn away."

Hand-scripted words filled the page and Garren read what was legible. *'We were forewarned of the Bane. When we thought we had conquered our own weaknesses, we thought we would enhance our skills. We would become the masters of earth, and nothing would be more powerful than us. The For'bane.'*

"Is whomever penned these words implying that we somehow created the very creatures bent on destroying us?"

Brother Keelon watched Garren steadily: "You were created for a purpose, but your creation did not come from the For'bane blood. Creator never intended for man to taint what He had already perfected with something so dark."

'I am the For'bane...' the half-Skay's words returned.

Garren handed the letter back to Brother Keelon. "And if this darkness is inside of me now, is there no redemption? Will I always be the monster?" He met Brother Keelon's wise gaze.

"We are who we choose to become."

'...To be monsters or men.' Ora's words whispered through his heart, but so familiar with wearing the mask, Garren kept his thoughts veiled beneath a firm exterior.

She had already done her work on his heart, changed the way he viewed the War, and the hope that might come after. He had begun to feel again.

He straightened away from the table and lowered his head to lift the hood back into place, shadowing his face before he looked at Keelon again. "I must go then."

"There is little else I can tell you. The journal you are looking for—the last I heard, there was a collection of books an ancient keeper smuggled into the Freelands as Scholar

Phillips suggested. It may be among them, or it may just be rumor…. I trust you will find the answers you are looking for."

Chapter 72

"We are organizing a game of foot-ball," Decklan announced as he plopped down beside Ora at lunch in the food tent.

Valara sat on her other side. Ora had not seen much of the female archer since Carter was taken to become a Singer. She looked tough; toned muscles formed along her previously slender arms, her skin darkened by the sun and soot. She had cut her hair off close to her head, appearing more masculine in her leather armor and calloused hands.

Among the women serving in the Army, most had shorn off their hair, trying to make themselves appear as un-feminine as possible. Ora could not bring herself to cut off her hair, so she settled for keeping it braided. After the incident with Greer, the entire camp seemed to recognize the Captain as her protector and she had no more trouble with men.

"The skies are clear today. No snow. And it is warmer than it has been in days," Valara agreed. "You will come? Deck's getting a whole group together. This is our chance for a little fun during the reprieve. The officers will assign us to practicing fields soon to keep us from turning lazy."

Decklan reached across behind Ora to flick melting snow off Valara's shoulder. "No snow, huh?"

Valara reacted lightning fast and grabbed Decklan's hand, yanking him backward off the bench so he landed on his backside with his feet up on the bench. He stared at her in shock as she calmly resumed eating.

Ora fought hard against a laugh and bit her lower lip to contain her smile. She reached back and grabbed his arm to help pull him to his feet again.

"Remind me to always sit between you two," she chided.

"Remind me that her bite is just as bad as her bark," Decklan returned, pretending wounded pride, "…and to never marry a soldier."

"What? Too tough for you to handle?" Valara raised an eyebrow. Snickers escaped a few nearby soldiers.

Decklan grinned, including the rest of the table in his glance: "Who would ever want to snuggle with a block of ice?"

Valara took a drink of water from her wooden goblet. "Hmm...maybe when it's summer you will feel differently about a little ice," she teased back. She spun around on the bench to lean back against the table, combing her fingers through her short hair. "I say she will be docile as a sheep and pamper you day and night, and you will command her like a Captain, because that is what you will be in thirty years."

Groans. One of the soldiers across from them spoke up: "Valara, if the War lasts another thirty years—I will marry *you*."

Barks of laughter.

Valara raised her voice above the ruckus as she twisted part-way around to look at the soldier who had spoken. "I accept, gracious and noble man."

The soldier beside the speaker nudged him in the ribs. "A fine catch, that one," he teased.

"Hey," Decklan spoke as the ruckus quieted again, answering Valara's ribbing, "what is wrong with a little pampering? I am a war hero, right?"

"Oh, and how many For'bane have you killed?" someone challenged.

"I did not realize there was a scoreboard," Ora returned. "I guess if there is, it must be for those who can still *count* how many."

"Ooohh!" scattered around the table.

Decklan shook his head and chuckled. "I think if you do not join us in a round of foot-ball, you are going to have a riot on your hands."

Ora hesitated. She had hoped to see Commander Kane with a request to go to the Third Division. She had not been able to learn anything concerning Thane. She knew he was likely to refuse her, but she had to try. "All right," she said to Decklan. "*One* game." *Then I will look for Thane,* she silently promised herself.

They finished lunch quickly, feeling more like carefree children for the first time since becoming soldiers facing impending death and horror. A large group of them took off for the nearest empty training field.

Valara was right. The snow clouds held at bay for their sport, offering patchy blue skies. The group split into two teams, opposite each other on the field. It was a surprisingly large group, about thirty people per team. Valara and Ora were the only women to take part so it was agreed to split them onto opposing teams.

Ora had not had so much fun in a long time, and found herself laughing and smiling. She could almost forget her surroundings. She could almost forget she was a soldier. Even in the cold air, her hair grew damp with perspiration, the shorter strands pulled loose from her braid and curled against her face and neck. She competed with determination, focused completely on the game.

The teams were of equal strengths. When Ora drove home and scored the final victory goal, a roar erupted from her team. Decklan ran up behind her and wrapped an arm around her shoulders, nearly knocking her over in his enthusiasm. "Whoever said a woman cannot shoot?" he teased with a shout.

Ora shouted in surprise as he and another boy from her team threw her up to balance her on their shoulders. A smile lit her face as her team surrounded her.

She caught sight of Valara in front of the other team. Valara shrugged a shoulder, and hid a smile. "Nice moves, archer," she congratulated calmly.

Chapter 73

Garren stood shrouded in the shadow of a tent, quietly observing the game from a distance. His gaze remained fixed on Ora as she led her team to victory, expertly moving with speed and twisting away from the opposing team members who tried to intercept her. It did his heart good to see her smile. Her smile made him realize how much he'd missed her the last several days.

The things he had discovered on his quest concerning the For'bane in the days he was gone disturbed him. He needed to tell the Council, but a sense of caution held him back—for now. Brother Keelon's words echoed in his mind, about the officers confiscating the records; about them not wanting to expose their secrets. He needed to consider who he could trust where leadership was concerned.

Now that he had returned and seen Ora was safe and well, he was anxious to speak with her as well. She could not continue being ignorant of what he had discovered. But how could he explain it? There was more he had kept from her in order to spare her the darker truths of the For'bane and what they did to their prisoners. It was all too dark and disturbing for casual conversation.

His heart ached as he watched her. He loved her with a deep and tender passion, but he could never touch her. He could never let her be aware of how deep his regard for her went; that could be disastrous. She no longer looked at him as the monster. That alone was too precious a gift to see damaged or destroyed by his own selfish hopes.

His gaze swept the group as Ora was lifted up into the air, and the whoops and hollers drifted on the wind to his ears. What if there were traitors in their midst? Everything anyone had ever believed about the War would change with the information Garren found. He felt his muscles tense.

He turned and slipped away, moving between the tents to the Council tent. Commander Dillion met him at the entrance. "It is official," he confirmed Garren's questioning look. "It is foolish if you ask me. And dangerous."

Garren followed him into the tent as the other Council members gathered. The interior remained dim against the bright outdoors, lit with a few torches against the heavy, dark canvas walls. The Council filed in and sat.

Commander Strell rose at the far end of the table. "We have received confirmation that the King is indeed on his way," he began. "He is taking advantage of this brief reprieve. I am informed his Envoy is coming with twelve guards."

"Twelve guards? Does the King not understand the risks he takes in guarding his Envoy?" Garren insisted. "And why was I not informed of this at once, if I am to properly arrange his protection?"

The Commander's gaze glinted as he glanced at Garren. "I am sure I have informed you as soon as I knew, Captain," he said silkily, "I do not have the power to persuade the King not to come, as indeed we should all agree would be safest. If the challenge is too much for you, I am sure we can make other arrangements…."

Commander Dillion cleared his throat as Garren stared hard at Commander Strell. "When is he to arrive, Commander?"

"Less than a sennight, Captain," Commander Strell relayed firmly. "I trust you will be prepared for his arrival." Something glinted in his gaze. A question? A challenge?

Garren felt a muscle twitch in his jaw. Something dark stirred in his breast; a bitter, metallic taste rose in his mouth that he recognized as the reaction to blood lust that came from the monster within. He did not care to pretend he did not hate Commander Strell. He had never challenged a snake before, but he had no interest in charming one either.

He caught Commander Dillion's gaze as he turned on his heel to depart. Commander Dillion caught up with him several feet from the tent entrance as Garren strode out into the daylight and matched his steps.

He tipped his head in the Commander's direction but continued walking, keeping his gaze on the path before him. His voice was low, firm, and laced with veiled anger. "I will not wait seven days to meet the King. He must already be only a few days away. I depart this day, this very hour…or else the King will surely be dead before he arrives."

Commander Dillion stopped and turned to face Garren, his features carved in the light of the nearby blazing fires of the open blacksmith forges. Garren paused as well to look at the man who was as close to a friend as he had ever had. Commander Dillion spoke, "You think the King is in danger?"

"I think he takes much risk; he does not know the danger of the roads fraught with enemies he cannot see…," Garren glanced aside, back toward the Council tent, "…or what exists here."

"You think the Commander persuaded him?"

"I think the Commander takes great risk as well." Garren looked at Commander Dillion intently. He knew he could trust Commander Dillion, and he would be the first Garren would confide in regarding the truth of the For'bane when the time was right. "I think we can both acknowledge it would be of great effect if Asteriae would lose its King so soon after the loss of the one before—no matter his age or ignorance—and perhaps beneficial to some who would seek to profit from it."

"This is not a task we can risk failing," Commander Dillion urged. "As capable as you are, Captain, you should not undertake this task alone."

Garren looked out across the spread of tents toward the field where the game had been played. His deep grey eye searched the distance for a glimpse of those he'd been watching just before. "I have a troop in mind," he spoke gravely.

His previous thoughts came back to haunt him. *One day I may have to risk her life...because it is my duty. Because this is war.*

He prayed she was ready.

Chapter 74

Sitting on her cot in the archer tent after the game, Ora picked at her tunic, pulling it away from her perspiring skin for some respite. The Archers Quarter had no private place to disrobe and bathe properly, though she swiped a clean cloth beneath her clothes as best she could. As a young woman among men, she kept her tunic on despite the discomfort.

Her lungs still burned from the exertion in the cool fresh air; her cheeks were still tinged pink from the excitement of the game.

Two footmen entered suddenly, calling for attention as Commander Kane strode into their midst. All the archers turned quickly at attention. The Commander's gaze swept the group. "Archer Orabelle, you will come with me," he ordered.

Surprised, she caught Decklan's gaze briefly. He showed as much surprise as she. She quickly grabbed her leather, long-sleeved jerkin and pulled it on before slinging the strap of her kit across her shoulder.

She fell in behind her Commander as he strode out of the tent. The light had left the sky and the grey dusk was quickly gathering. The wind picked up, snapping the canvas cloth of the flag flying at the center of the yard.

A quiet step pulled her gaze from the flag. Garren stood at the other side of the yard. He wore his usual leather armor, one hand resting against the hilt of his broadsword at his hip. The straps that crossed his chest held a light-weight shield between his shoulder blades at his back. He was prepared for battle, his free hand held the reins of his great black beast, standing just beyond his shoulder.

"Captain," the Commander stated. "Here is your archer, ready for orders."

Your archer? Ora stepped forward, caught in Garren's steady grey gaze. His lips were set firmly but there was no anger in his eye.

He turned slightly aside. "Follow me." He moved to mount his horse in a fluid, easy motion and it was then she noticed another horse standing behind him. The spotted grey, a few inches shorter than Garren's mount, stomped a hoof impatiently.

Garren looked down at her. "Mount up, archer," he commanded.

Ora obeyed, wanting to ask where they were going but knowing such questions would be frowned upon. She fitted her soft leather shoe into the stirrup, gripped the front of the saddle, and swung up onto the back of the grey, quickly gathering up the reins as the mare snorted and took a ready step forward.

Garren wheeled his horse around and Ora hastened to follow his lead as they trotted from the yard. She turned her head for one last glimpse of the place she now called home. Decklan stood in the entrance of the tent, watching her leave.

She pressed down her fear of the thousand-pound animal between her legs. The mare obeyed her direction without hesitation. Keeping firm control of the reins, she followed

Garren's broad shoulders through gathering shadows and torchlight to the outer edge of the First Division.

Seven other riders waited to meet them. These guards were trained for Envoy protection. Their weapon of choice was a short sword strapped to their thighs. Most had shields between their shoulders, like Garren did—protection from a flanking enemy. Garren and Ora were the only two archers among them. The guards immediately came to attention as Garren appeared, looking to him for their orders.

Ora reined in her mare as Garren dispensed orders: "The King's Envoy arrives within a sennight. We are to meet him on the way and lead him and his party safely to camp. We will give our lives if necessary." His voice thundered with command. "We will ride hard and there will be no rest tonight. Our priority is to reach the Envoy without delay."

The group of guards formed a column, two horses wide. When Ora moved to join them, Garren reached over suddenly and gripped her mare's bridle with one hand to stay her. "You will remain at my side," he said, holding her surprised gaze, reflected in the camp torchlight behind them.

Ora stared at him a moment that felt lengthened by the intensity of his gaze, though it could not have been more than a few seconds. "Yes, Captain," she murmured.

Garren released her mare's bridle. He spoke to his beast and the horse jumped forward to join the rest of the riders, with Ora matching pace beside him.

He had not exaggerated. They rode at a canter into the night. Ora's horse seemed to know better what to do than its rider, as the mare kept pace alongside Garren's horse. The darkness outside of camp held no moonlight to light their path. Ora's fingers cramped around the reins, believing that if she fell no one would see her, and she would never find her way back to camp.

Sometime later, Garren switched his mount to fast trot; the others followed his lead. The horses kept pace without tiring—bred and trained through the centuries for power and endurance. Ora lost track of time. They stopped to rest the horses twice, only for ten minutes at a time and without a word spoken between anyone in the troop.

When, at last, they reached a shallow creek bed just before dawn, Garren whistled low, turned his horse to the side, and brought it to a standstill at the water's edge. Ora made out his outline in the grey pre-dawn light, the water reflecting what little light the sky could offer.

The guards dismounted, fanning out along the bank of the river to make room for the horses, and let loose the reins so their mounts could drink. Several snorts and soft grunts let them know their horses' thanks as they drank eagerly.

Ora's leg muscles ached and threatened to spasm after so long in the saddle without shifting, and she remained beside her mare. She slid her hand over its sturdy shoulder—rough and thick with a winter's coat of hair.

Garren approached. "You will need this." He pressed something into her hand. The touch of his warm calloused fingers brushing against hers sent strange shock waves through her skin.

She gripped what he gave her and felt canvas material and something soft and pliable inside. A strange mint-like odor assaulted her nostrils as she lifted it nearer to her face for inspection.

He did not have to explain. She had seen and smelled it before. It was the same ointment the healer applied to her back after she had been whipped, to help ease the pain and tension in her muscles.

Quickly, sensing him moving away again, she turned to look at his shadowed outline looming above her. "Do you expect trouble?" She spoke quietly, not wanting the others to overhear.

She felt rather than saw his gaze, and the intensity of his words fell over her like a cold winter's wind, spoken with deceptive softness, "I expect Hell."

"And why would the King risk his life to come here? Does he not understand what we face?"

He leaned closer, and she felt his breath on her face as he spoke with husky depth: "Perhaps he is coming so that he might understand. And we must make sure he lives to understand the truth."

"The truth?" Ora whispered.

"That we will lose."

Before she could question him any further, he turned and barked orders to continue on. Quickly, as she heard the others mounting, Ora smeared some ointment on her thighs beneath her pants, rewrapped the supply in the canvas material, and dropped it into her kit. She forced her resisting muscles to return to the saddle and take up the reins of the mare once again.

So, she contemplated as they rode. *Garren still believes the War is failing. And yet, he continues to fight and train others to do the same.* She glanced over at his silhouette in the darkness, riding beside her at the head of the column.

Did he hope the King's arrival might change something? Was the Boy King as naive as the gossip of the other soldiers claimed him to be?

Chapter 75

They stopped again to rest the horses as the sun burned golden across the sky in mid-morning. Garren was pleased to see Ora handling herself so well around her mare, knowing she feared horses and knowing the reason. She had never verbally linked the day her mother was dragged to death with her fear of horses, but she did not have to. He sensed her response was triggered by that past event.

He made her face her fears just like he would have with anyone under his Command. And because he knew she was stubborn enough to overcome them. She had live longer if she learned to face her fears now, rather than during a crucial moment in battle.

He handed the reins of his horse to the guard nearest him, Caspian, to let it graze in the narrow valley along a thickly-wooded hillside. He noted with satisfaction that the rest of the troop stood beside their horses, letting them graze.

Garren observed Ora for a moment while she stood by her mare, unaware of his scrutiny. The ointment had helped; she was not as sore as she had been at the river.

He glanced ahead to the tree-line, black shapes against the sunlight, their tangled limbs and bare branches lifted to the skies. "Take point," he ordered quietly to Caspian. He approached Ora. "Come with me a moment." He did not wait to see if she would follow, but turned, hand resting on the hilt of his sheathed sword and started up the hillside. He felt Ora hurry to catch up and spoke quietly over his shoulder. "We are close."

"Are we in danger?" She sounded calm. Her heart picked up an extra beat but then returned to a steady, certain rhythm. They had traveled in an arc behind the Divisions up toward the Highlands, before cutting across between the Fifth and Second Division, stationed near the Birchlands, and into For'bane territory, following the valleys between hills and forests toward the sunrise. Garren knew they were now nearly one-hundred longs into For'bane territory, but Ora would have no knowledge of that. There were few For'bane nests this close to the Highlands. The rocky mountain terrain that bordered the territory was more difficult for them to dig through, acting as a natural defense against invasion into the Highlands—so far.

They reached the ridge near the tree-line and Garren turned to look at her. "We are not in danger. Not here; not at present. The For'bane are following something more important than our presence."

"The Envoy," Ora breathed.

She guessed right. The Envoy was traveling too close to enemy territory, following a path through the forests that tempted For'bane attack. Garren removed his eyepatch. Ora's only reaction was to shift her gaze away from his. He could not blame her. There was a reason he kept it covered. He crouched and let his enhanced vision take over, searching the forest ahead. "I need you to protect the King. It was no accident that I was informed so late of his coming. I should have been told at once." He looked over and caught her gaze. "This troop is capable. They have experienced the battlefield enough to understand what we face in protecting the Envoy, and they are trained for this. But I want you to be careful, and be alert for anything."

This time, she held his gaze. "You do not trust the officers…do you?"

His jaw tightened, disturbed that she could read him almost as well as he read her. He was not used to that. "Few men have the strength to withstand all that the War has become," he said cryptically. "Some of us are monsters in disguise."

"What are you talking about?"

If only there was time to explain all that he now knew. His lips parted to say the words—to begin—but looking at her, he suddenly saw the girl who played in the creek by her house; the frightened child who was forced to hide whenever the soldiers came thundering into her small peaceful world. The words died in his throat.

What I mean to tell you is we are all monsters, and we will get what we deserve in the end, he confessed inwardly instead.

He replaced his eyepatch and turned back for the valley. "The horses are rested. We must keep moving."

Ora reached out and latched onto his arm before he could move away. Garren felt his muscles react and he yanked back before he might accidentally harm her, drawing in a sharp breath. "Do not touch me," he growled, sucking in air between clenched teeth.

Ora flinched and drew back, but her chin rose a notch.

Garren stepped forward quickly, voice softening: "I could hurt you. You surprised me. I was not prepared. I do not *want* to hurt you." He held her gaze intently, wanting to make her understand.

Ora took a steadying breath. "You said you might need my help. Is this what you were talking about?" Ora spoke steadily.

Garren sighed faintly. "Protect the King," he insisted. "That is all I can say for now. We need to move."

His muscles eased with relief when she moved ahead of him back down the hill to retrieve her mare. The haunting memories of his discovery refused to leave him. Watching her, how could he take this precious thing of beauty—his Belle—and stain her with the darkness he faced?

We are all monsters.

We have made this War, and it will never end.

Was there anything left worth saving?

He mounted his horse and watched Ora turn her mare to position herself at his side.

If I can save you from this fate...I will.

Chapter 76

Less than an hour later, they entered the forest, their horses at a canter. Another two hours of hard riding drove them deeper and deeper into For'bane territory. The sunlight shifted through the branches as the day turned to afternoon. Suddenly, Garren veered to the left, breaking formation. Ora could see the Envoy just ahead, coming toward them, as she hastened to follow Garren's lead. The Envoy had twelve guards, five in front and five behind, with the royal enclosed coach driven by two guards in the center. Garren's troop broke formation into a wide line of attack.

Skays. The realization hit Ora in the throat, tightening into a lump that she forced her breath around. The ring of steel as swords were drawn from scabbards rose on each side of her.

"To the left!" Garren boomed above the thunder of horses. Ora jerked her mare's head to direct it toward the sound of his voice before she even saw him.

A Skay launched itself into the air toward the mounted guards at the head of the Envoy. Garren released an arrow with the vibrating song. It screamed as the force of Garren's arrow through its heart sent it backward against a tree to hang there limp, the head of the arrow buried deep in the tree.

The Envoy guards fought before and behind, horses turning and squealing with fright. The horses were not used to this kind of assault. Neither were their riders.

'Protect the King.' Garren's words came to Ora as if spoken again. Suddenly, her mare stumbled, upsetting Ora from her seat as she reached to steady herself against the high pommel of the saddle.

A Skay barreled into her mare's side, slashing its hindquarters with a vicious swipe of the Skay's curved sharp blade. The mare screamed in pain and surprise as its legs buckled.

Ora kicked her feet free of the stirrups and leapt clear, stumbling and falling on her side as she pulled her bow free and notched an arrow.

She twisted onto her back and shot the Skay as it stood over her. It stumbled back and sank to its knees with a grunt.

Ora did not wait to see it fall, the arrow protruding from its chest. She struggled to her feet, already notching another arrow, and spun to find the next closest target.

A Skay fought one of the guards who had been unseated from his horse, and now stood with his back against the lead horse of the coach.

The Skay drove him backward with a jagged bone broadsword to the stomach. The guard crumpled back into the horses, who squealed and danced sideways, tugging at their bits as, with a terrified scream, the driver of the coach was yanked off the side of his perch by two Skays.

Ora saw Garren to her left—dismounted and on his feet —with his sword swinging in a vicious outward arch that nearly severed two Skays in half as they advanced toward him. He pierced the tip of his blade into the ground beside him as a Skay climbed to the top of the coach. He quickly fit an arrow to his bow and shot the Skay straight through the eye.

Ora ducked as a rush of air warned of an incoming blade. The attacking Skay raised his sword again only to be rammed in the side by Garren's black beast. The horse reared, long legs flailing in the air. The Skay screamed as the weight of one powerful hoof snapped its ankle and pinned it to the ground.

Ora spun away from the threat of the angry horse as the great beast bared its teeth and struck the Skay again, this time in the skull. The Skay's animal-like squeal gurgled out in death as blood pooled in its throat and rushed from its wounds.

Ora's fingers instinctively slid along the shaft of another arrow, the bow lowered at her side as she hurried for the coach.

The lead horses jumped forward and the coach lurched into motion just as Ora reached the back wheel. Holding bow and arrow in one hand, she reached with her free hand for the wooden perch at the back, just above the wheel. She grabbed hold and cried out as she was nearly dragged off her feet. Her muscles protested with the effort of holding on. Kicking her feet against the wheel, she found a brief foothold, enough to leverage herself up for a better handhold.

She lost her arrow in the effort, and tossed her bow up onto the top of the coach to use both hands to climb up the side onto the roof. Several rolls of canvas tents lashed to the top cushioned her as she pulled herself to her knees. Her searching hand found her bow once more.

The coach swayed unsteadily as the horses gained ground into a gallop. Trees flashed by on either side. Another Skay gained the top of the coach, pulling itself up from the other side just as Ora grasped her bow. They saw each other in the same moment. The coach hit a bump which nearly threw Ora over the side. She grabbed the nearest ties of rolled canvas.

The Skay must have lost its dagger during its climb to the top, because its searching hands came up empty. It squealed in anger and threw itself at Ora, pinning her down as she raised her hands to defend herself. The curved wood of her bow pressed across the Skay's throat to hold it back.

It was far stronger than she. Ora cried out as her arms trembled and nearly gave way to the Skay's crushing weight. She raised her knee and jabbed at the Skay's midsection just as the coach bounced again over the uneven trail. It upset the Skay's balance just enough for Ora to roll out from beneath it and kick out with the heel of her foot against its leg, knocking the Skay over. It squealed as it tumbled over the side, its cry cut short as it fell beneath the wheels of the coach.

The thunder of approaching horses slowly registered in Ora's ears. She forced her aching, tired muscles to move and began a cautious crawl over the rolls of canvas to the front of the coach. Her fingers tightened around handholds to keep from being tossed about as the wheels hit more ruts and tree roots on the forest floor. She flattened down abruptly, heart in her throat, as a thick, low branch swept over her.

She reached for the reins, flapping in the wind. "Whoa!" she called to the horses.

A firm command sounded behind her. The lead horses of the coach jerked to a stop, locking their knees. The two rear horses stumbled to a halt as well, nearly throwing Ora forward as the coach stopped.

For a moment, Ora could not breathe. She had not realized she was holding her breath until a pang went through her chest and she gasped.

"Ora!" Garren's sharp tone broke through the stunned fog of her mind. He had jumped from his horse and now stood with sword drawn, bow slung over his shoulder. The fight was not over. The enemy followed the coach and now poured from the surrounding woods, closing in on them.

Ora grabbed for her bow and loaded an arrow. "Captain," she called back in acknowledgement. She climbed down from the coach just as its door unlatched and began to open. She turned quickly in surprise, arrow drawn, and looked into bright blue eyes staring back at her.

"Stay in the coach!" she shouted, blood pumping with adrenaline. She felt a familiar thrill rush through her veins, replacing the fear of her first reaction to the attack.

As the Boy King hesitated on the threshold of the coach step and began to draw himself back inside, Ora saw through the coach windows another Skay approaching it from the opposite side. She drew back taut on the arrow as she twisted toward the coach. "Get back!" She barked the command, giving the King only a second to comply before she shot, the arrow zipping through the coach windows and burying itself in the throat of the Skay, just as its claw-like fingers grabbed hold of the window frame.

The King pulled back into his seat as the Skay tumbled backward to the dirt. Ora gasped in a breath and lowered her trembling arms, beginning to feel her strength ebbing. Her fight with the Skay atop the coach had taken a toll on her muscles. She caught the King's stare of surprise and relief as he looked straight at her.

She turned toward Garren, whose back was to her as he killed the last Skay in front of the coach horses. Garren turned toward her suddenly, bow drawn and arrow aimed at her. He released without hesitation.

Ora stared. She held perfectly still as she felt yet another Skay advancing behind her grunt and fall to the earth with a thud that made the earth quiver beneath Ora's leather shoes. She reached a hand up to her ear. It came away with blood from a small slice near the top where Garren's arrow grazed her flesh on the way into the Skay's heart.

Garren's jaw tightened as his gaze held hers. The trickle of blood was punishment for not watching her back. A small price compared to her life.

Chapter 77

Garren surveyed the activity and the survivors. The remaining guards gathered around the coach and their King, taking stock of the losses. Most of the horses were dead or had run off. Only five of the original twelve guards accompanying the King were still on their feet. Another was badly wounded, carried by two guards to lay in the shadow of the coach. Garren's troop suffered only one loss, which put them at seven, including Ora.

He rolled his shoulders, wishing he could relieve the tension he felt there. His muscles screamed in protest, though he knew he would recover fast enough from all the exertion. It was the incoming headache that aggravated him.

Ora had replaced her bow and gathered her arrows back in her quiver. Even from a distance, he could still see and smell the blood from her nicked ear. Several drops stained the edge of her tunic beneath the collar of her leather jerkin. She knelt by her mare—lying on its side and breathing its last—and spread her hands in a soothing motion across its shoulder in comfort.

Garren remembered how those same small hands once soothed him, the feather-light touch across his aching brow as his head throbbed with overwhelming pain. He lifted his sword, wiped the blood from the blade, and slid it back into the scabbard at his side. What he would not give to feel that soothing touch now.

Instead, he took hold of the vial hanging around his neck and shook a few flecks of powder onto his tongue. He took a slow deep breath as the powder dissolved and he felt the effects of the medication slipping over his senses to the back of his neck, relieving the familiar pressure building there.

"We need to keep moving," he said, striding over to the guards by the coach. He glanced at the surrounding woods and met the Captain of the Guard's gaze. "Our enemy will regroup and come at us again, this time in greater numbers."

He turned his gaze to the King, the boy who ascended too early to the throne after the death of his father. He was indeed young, a pair of bright blue eyes burdened with the weight of his responsibilities within a boy's smooth-skinned face, too adolescent to grow a beard yet, though nearing seventeen.

Garren bowed his head. "My King," he greeted with a low rumble of respect in his voice. "I apologize for the delay. With your permission, my men and I will escort you the remainder of the way to the First Division."

The King nodded his head. "I am most thankful for your timely arrival. What is your name?"

"I am Captain Garren, Sire."

The King turned to his Captain of the Guard, who looked at him with question. "Obey the Captain, Lenorr. He is here to take us the rest of the way."

Captain Lenorr bowed his head. "Yes, Sire." He turned and shouted orders to what remained of his guards to lift the wounded guard to the top of the coach where they could secure him.

Garren watched Captain Lenorr leave to assist one of his guards, then turned back to the King. “Sire, you should return to the safety of the coach.”

“Of course, Captain.” The King took the order calmly, gathering his cloak about him. The rings on his fingers flashed in the afternoon light filtering between the tangled tree branches high above. As he turned, the silver lines of seven eight-point stars showed on his cloak. A cluster of six small stars below a large seventh star. The crest of the Kingdom of Asteriae.

As the King disappeared back inside the coach, Garren turned and made his way to Ora, still beside her mare. He approached from behind and circled around to the mare’s head. He crouched, cupping one blood-spattered and dirt-streaked hand over its muzzle. “She is dead,” he determined quietly.

He caught a hint of anguish raise itself inside Ora. “Come,” he instructed as he rose. “You will ride with me.” His gaze moved to her ear as she also stood. “Your aim has improved. But you should pay attention to your instincts. Distractions always cost something.” His finger brushed the edge of her wound, snagging a strand of hair that had gotten stuck against the drying blood.

He felt the sting of pain his touch inflicted though she hid it from her expression well. She shrugged away from his hand, moving her head aside. She spoke stiffly in order to conceal the pain from her voice. “Should I apologize, Captain, or should I thank you?”

Garren revealed a slight smile. “You can thank me by watching your back next time. And no, if you wondered, I will not apologize for a wound that saved your life. Because I would do it again in an instant.”

Chapter 78

She could not hold the intensity of his one grey eye, as his words lingered in the air between them. She had not realized how close he stood until that moment. She found herself wondering with surprise: Would he do anything to save her? And why? He had made it perfectly clear that in war you lived or you died on your own strength and skill. And now, he spoke as if he had made it his personal mission to protect her. It left an unsettled, uncertain feeling in her stomach that she did not care to analyze.

I have fought hard to be strong in your eyes; to be strong like you demand of everyone who is a part of this War. What is it you want from me?

She found herself trapped in his gaze again before she remembered he could read her emotions. Could he guess her thoughts as if she had spoken them out loud?

She was startled when Garren turned his head and whistled. A moment later, his great black beast appeared from the woods and trotted toward its master with ears pricked. She recalled how the horse trampled the Skay. "Did you train him?"

Garren mounted and looked down at her as he took up the reins in one hand. “Since I found him as a colt.”

“The Skay that killed my mare, it might have harmed me. Your horse intervened and killed it.”

He bent down and offered his arm to her. “He hates the For’bane as much as any soldier.”

Ora lifted her hand and accepted his arm up. He hauled her up swiftly behind him and she immediately wrapped her arms around his waist. He smelled of sweat and dried blood, but the strength of his body comforted her weary muscles.

“It seems you both have saved me today,” Ora murmured into his shoulder.

Garren signaled the horse and they lurched forward as they headed for the front of the Envoy.

He twisted slightly in his seat to look over his shoulder toward her. “And you have saved the King. Well done, Belle,” he said seriously. There was admiration in his gaze and Ora felt her heart skip a beat.

They moved slowly forward, the coach creaking and bouncing over the uneven ground. Ora glanced back from time to time and decided she much preferred riding horseback to the coach. It did not look at all comfortable to ride in over this terrain, though she had seen the plush cushioned benches that made it a luxury.

The Envoy snaked its way through the forest, Garren leading the way with Ora. They came to the woods edge abruptly where the pathway split in two before them, one along the face of a cliff and the other winding through the hills.

Garren pointed his horse’s nose toward the cliffs.

A commotion rose from behind them as the Captain of the Guard maneuvered his horse out of rank to approach them. “What are you doing?”

Garren eyed him. "The path ahead is treacherous. Inform your men to steady their horses."

"That way is longer," Captain Lenorr insisted, suddenly distrustful.

"It is a longer way that may save the King and all of you —unless you wish to face what we did earlier?" he bit out firmly. "That is what lies ahead of us if we continue this path through the hills."

Captain Lenorr glanced behind them to the Envoy.

"Dismount, archer," Garren ordered without taking his gaze off of the Captain of the Guard. "We walk from here."

Ora obeyed. Her leg muscles threatened to spasm under the abrupt change of position and weight. She stood still a moment to gather her strength.

Garren nodded to Captain Lenorr. "Inform the King. He will need to walk with us while we guide the coach and horses."

Captain Lenorr's lips thinned and he twisted his mount's head around to fall back to the Envoy, relaying Garren's orders to the rest of the men, who all began to dismount. The King exited the coach to walk with the guards, who stood near him protectively.

Only when the last of the guards dismounted did Garren do the same. "Take Ohev," he commanded, handing Ora the reins, before he made his way back to the coach. "You and you," he pointed out two of his guards. "Lead the horses." Then, to his third guard, Caspian: "You will assist me with the coach. The way will be narrow. Do not let the horses spook or waver. One wrong step and we go over the side."

The men leading their mounts went first, and Ora joined them with Garren's horse. They veered off onto the trail along the rocky cliffside. Garren and Caspian remained behind, at the heads of the horses guiding the coach. They held the lead horses by their bridles.

The trail began as a path, then it fell away suddenly to Ora's left. Her heart jumped into her throat in surprise as bits of rock and dirt from her steps crumbled and fell into the empty void down to a wide rushing river a few thousand feet below.

Ora placed a quick, steadying hand against the horse's tall shoulder, more for her own benefit. The horse snorted but otherwise continued on steadily without hesitation. Its ears flickered backward then forward again when it heard Garren speaking calmly to the coach horses behind them.

She hoped Garren knew what he was doing. If they were attacked, they would all go over the cliffs. There was no room for a battle here. She breathed deep through her nose, fighting a wave of dizziness. *Do not look down,* she ordered herself silently.

They crept along at a slow but steady pace. The narrow path angled downward and then up again. About the time Ora felt her nerves could take no more and that they would never reach the end, the path widened again and trees began to spring up on their left along the cliffside, creating a welcome barrier from the steep drop-off.

The sun dipped low behind the trees ahead of them. They must have been walking along the cliffs for a couple of hours.

Just as the sun cast deep shadows over the group, a crater appeared in the side of the hill to their right, creating a small, rounded valley.

Garren appeared at Ora's side and took the reins of his horse without a word to her. He turned as Captain Lenorr approached. "We can rest here the night. Post two watchmen at each end of the path," he instructed.

Ora took her first full, deep breath since they started along the cliffs, relieved to be able to rest at last. She did not want anyone to know how exhausted she felt. She was not sure she even had the strength or the stomach to eat any provisions.

The horses were clustered at one side of the crater where they could graze. The guards gathered brush and dried wood to kindle three small cook fires to help spread out and minimize the appearance of smoke in the sky. Most of it would evaporate in the cold air before reaching the peak of the cliff wall behind them. Ora followed Garren toward the nearest fire.

"There is an extra tent," Garren informed her as she approached to stand beside him. He stared into the flames, the light casting sharp shadows across the chiseled lines of his face and glinting in his grey eye.

"I would rather see the stars tonight," Ora confessed quietly.

Garren glanced over at her but said nothing.

Ora hesitated. "Why did you want me to come? Why did you choose me?"

Garren met and held her gaze. "Because I trust you," he said steadily.

She searched his unreadable expression. "I once tried to kill you. You chose a would-be-murderer to watch your back?"

"If you had the chance again…would you take it?"

She swallowed hard. The very notion twisted the pit of her stomach and revolted her. The glimmer in his eye told her he accurately felt her answer, but she said it anyway: "No. I would never take your life."

He nodded slightly. "Then I was correct to choose the best archer to accompany me."

Best archer? She could not deny the thrill of warmth that praise brought. He considered her the best. She was far from that, and yet his confidence in her abilities was true and unapologetic.

The corner of his lips lifted slightly in a barely visible smile. She felt her face grow warm under his intuitive gaze. She wished he could not read her emotions so well.

She lifted her chin and opened her mouth to deliver a smart reply to cover her embarrassment, but his gaze shifted beyond her. He tensed and reached across the small space between them to grip her arm.

The King approached from the other side of camp, flanked by two guards. As soon as Ora saw the cause for Garren's change, he dropped his hold and stepped back from her. She felt the cold rush of night air around her again.

The King faced Ora and she quickly remembered to bow in his presence, bending at the waist as her legs were too stiff and chilled to move fast enough for the customary curtsey. From a soldier, this was enough.

His bright blue gaze flickered from her to Garren behind her shoulder. "Captain, I thank you again for your most timely arrival." He spoke with a boy's voice, yet filled with the authority he had been born to wield. Was he wiser than his young face made him appear?

"And you—archer," he looked at Ora again. Admiration lit in his blue eyes. "You have saved my life."

Ora felt staggered by his words, not expecting such praise. The King did not seem arrogant—though he held himself proudly—and his words were almost eager with a desire to compliment her.

She stood as if dumb. Her lips refused to form words. She had been too long among the filth and dirt and blood of the battlefield to know how to be a lady; to remember words of eloquence before someone dressed in the splendor of wealth and prestige. He was clean and she was still stained with the blood of the monsters they'd fought.

"We will be well guarded here for the night," Garren spoke for her, stepping forward. "If we leave by daybreak, we should arrive at the Divisions by midmorning."

"Of course," the King forced his gaze from Ora and she suddenly felt released to breathe again. He regarded the Singer Captain with only a hint of the wariness she knew Garren was used to receiving. There was more curiosity than fear in the King's countenance. "You are her commanding officer?"

Her. It took a moment of confusion for Ora to realize the King was talking about her. Her discomfort return in a rush.

Garren nodded stiffly.

"Hmm," the King murmured. "I am impressed. If all my subjects were as brave as this one," he smiled slightly at Ora, "we should have won the War long ago." He nodded to the guard on his left and walked away as suddenly as he appeared.

Chapter 79

The fires were mere embers as Garren settled himself to rest near the edge of the cliff by the narrow tree-line. He removed his eye patch and breathed deeply of the cold crisp night air. He shook a few more flecks of powder onto his tongue to dissolve, and then rolled his shoulders to help relieve the tension.

The camp grew quiet as the men went to sleep in their tents. The two posted watchmen stood further away in the shadows, one at each entrance to the walled-in valley.

A soft sound rose from the place where Ora lay, back cushioned by a smooth boulder. Ora was singing softly, watching the midnight sky. She kept her face turned away from the fires. Garren's head lifted as his gaze traced her silhouette in the faint glow of the embers.

Someone else stirred. The King's tent cracked open, the canvas stirring at the pressure of a hand drawing aside the heavy fabric.

Garren focused on the sound of Ora's voice and the words she sang. It seemed familiar, touching at long suppressed or forgotten boyhood memories. It was an old

Freelander song, sung as a lullaby to calm children who had nightmares.

The horrors of battle she had faced today must be bothering her more than she let on, now that all was quiet and at peace around them. Was this her way of coping?

Listen, listen. I tell you a tale of old,
Of ladies and lords and lovers,
Of men and their white steeds,
Slaying all of your dragons.

They come on the western wind,
Carried by the sounds,
Of songs and lullabies,
As I sing them to you now.

Look, look, they stand as your guard,
Their swords are the bright stars,
That shine from above,
The moon is a shield and its beam,
Scatters all of your shadows.

Fear not these dragons,
These demons of night,
For lords and their horses,
Are chasing them far.

Their ladies are crossing,

Softly to and fro,

Across the rushes,

All 'round your bed,

They are singing, singing, to guide you to safety.

So sleep, sleep now,

No dragons will find you…

Her voice faded away and she stopped mid-sentence and did not finish.

Garren murmured the final verse to himself:

Dream of men and their white steeds,

Slaying them all.

He watched as the King's tent fell softly closed and all became still and silent once more.

Sometime later, Garren jerked awake to the feel of Ora's presence near him. "James," she whispered, standing a few feet off. "Are you awake?"

Garren forced himself to relax. "Belle," he murmured and cleared his throat. "What has happened? It is still night."

"I cannot sleep. It is Carter." Her voice choked off and he felt her shiver and saw her hug herself. "He was chasing me. He was—he was a Skay."

Garren sat up fully. The fires were out and everything was dark around them. His enhanced vision allowed him to see her, to separate her from the deep shadows around them. "Come here," he murmured at last, unwilling to turn her away.

She hesitated, then moved to sit beside him. He slid his arm around her slowly, watching her reaction, but she turned toward him willingly and pressed herself against his side, trembling as she buried her face against his shoulder. "You are warm," she whispered and began to relax against him.

Garren became painfully aware of the soft curves of her body so close to his side. She did not smell like blood and sweat like he did. She smelled of earth and woodsmoke from the fires.

Her hand slid across his chest trustingly, settling over the steady thump of his heartbeat. "I heard you singing," he spoke quietly, trying to distract himself from the manly desires suddenly clawing at the inside of his chest and threatening to choke him of all strength and restraint.

She lifted her face to look at him. Her gaze was haunted and wounded from her dreams and, he could imagine, from the horrors of their recent battle.

"I never should have let you come here," he confessed. "I should not have made you face this…after everything you have gone through."

Ora shook her head slightly. "I would go anywhere as long as I can be with you."

There was such trust in her eyes he could not help himself. He had yearned to taste of her for longer than he cared to admit. His hand slipped to cradle the back of her head, fingers tangled in the thickness of her long hair, undone from her braid, and lowered his head toward hers.

She held perfectly still as his lips covered hers. A soft sigh rose to her lips. Garren groaned in response and pressed his advantage, deepening his kiss hungrily, trying to pull her closer into his embrace.

Cold air hit him suddenly. Garren gasped and bolted upright away from the tree.

Everything was dark. Ora was gone. In fact, she had never been there at all.

Singers do not dream.

Garren lurched to his feet, unexplained bile rising to the back of his throat. *What is wrong with me?* He pressed a hand to the back of his neck and sucked in a slow, deep breath.

He glanced across the faintly glowing fires to where Ora slept on her side, turned away from him, her head resting against the boulder. She slept; he did not sense any distress coming from her dreams…just the confusion of his own, racing through his head and heart.

There would be no more sleep for him tonight, he determined.

Chapter 80

Ora combed her fingers through her long hair, taming the night tangles as best she could and smoothing it back into a thick braid down the center of her back. She used a strip of leather cord to tie it at the end.

Attaching her bow over the quiver at her back, she turned to see the King with two of his guards watching her. His bright blue eyes unnerved her. He spoke quietly to the guard on his left and nodded in her direction, not even pretending he was not watching her.

She did not understand men or their motives when it came to women. Her only experiences had been that men viewed women as property—as a meal to satisfy their lusts and desires—then thrown aside when they were no longer pleasing enough.

She clenched her jaw and turned her gaze aside, jerking on the buckle of the quiver at her chest. She was a soldier, not some plaything. She would never let a man treat her like the soldiers had treated her mother; or as Greer had treated her. Never again. She pursed her lips and jerked on the buckle again in determined agitation and anger.

"You ready to ride?"

She turned to meet Garren's steady gaze. Her lips parted, but whatever she thought to give in answer got lost in the coldness of his expression. A chill rushed up her spine. He reminded her of the day she met him.

He looked every bit the Singer Captain. Ruthless and unemotional. The man who did not hesitate to put an arrow through a boy whose only crime was running for safety. The soldier who killed her guardian without remorse or regret. The one who sentenced her to thirty lashes that nearly took her life.

She swallowed hard and nodded slightly, taking a side-glance towards the King again to see with some relief that he had turned to retreat into the shadowed safety of the coach.

"Let us depart then." Garren turned and strode away to his great beast, dressed and waiting.

Ora stood still a moment, confused. Had she been mistaken, to think Garren was different than the cold, calculating monster her friends warned her about?

No. It could not be that. He had his reasons for the things he had done. She knew there was more to him than just the monster. How many times had he saved her life? How many times had he offered comfort and, yes, even tenderness—despite all his verbal claims to the contrary?

But what is wrong with him? Has something happened? Is he angry with me?

She shook off the uncertainties and turned her mind to the task ahead. They still needed to get the King to the First Division in one piece. Garren was relying on her to be the support he needed to get the job done. She tried to avoid the feeling of being watched. What was it about the blue of the King's eyes that affected her so? And why did those eyes have to follow her every move?

Garren's horse stopped beside her with the dancing, powerful stamp of its front legs on the frozen earth. The

Captain's grey eye stared firmly and coldly into hers. The firm line of his lips pressed together. The scar on his face seemed more pronounced in the cold mountain air, almost angry.

The horse snorted, as if equally impatient.

Garren did not say a word. But he reminded her of the first day, when his troop with their new recruits stopped in the woods and he demanded that she dismount the horse. He had not verbally threatened her, but his stare was enough to make her obey him.

He put out his arm to her and—just like that day in the woods so long ago—she obeyed him at once. She gripped his arm, feeling the powerful muscle bunch and tighten beneath her fingers, and with his assistance, pulled herself upward behind him.

Her hands settled at his hips uncertainly, gripping leather armor to stabilize herself as the horse jumped forward.

Garren reined in toward the front of the guards where Captain Lenorr waited. "We will be entering Muel territory. Watch the trees, or they will drop on you and take you down before you know what hit you."

"How much further, Captain?" Captain Lenorr inquired.

Garren looked ahead. "About twenty longs and we will be in range of archer support from the Fifth Division."

Garren kicked in his heels and Ora twisted slightly to look behind them to see the Envoy following, the coach moving within their midst.

"Notch your arrow, archer," Garren's voice rumbled, pulling her attention back to the path ahead.

Archer? What happened to calling her Belle?

She freed one hand from his belt and reached over her shoulder to grasp the first arrow her fingers encountered. As her body adjusted to the familiar movement of the horse beneath her, she released Garren completely in order to hold her bow and notch the arrow, keeping it to the side, her body shielded by Garren's broad back as she looked around his shoulder to see the trail.

The path widened out into the woods as they left the cliffs behind. The horses plodded forward at a quick but cautious walk. The wheels of the coach creaked quietly in the silence of the woods.

The men behind them remained mute, hands steady at the reins of their mounts while their heads tipped back and eyes swept the limbs above on all sides for signs of the enemy.

One of the horses snorted softly. Garren's horse lightly jerked at the reins, ears flickering backward then forward again. The tension of the Envoy was almost palpable.

Trees creaked and groaned above them with the slightest of breezes. A squirrel crept across a large tree root, searching for nuts and seeds beneath the dried leaves. They kept moving. No one said a word.

Ora's fingers began to ache, but she kept her arrow notched, her muscles tense for the first sign of trouble.

A light rapping sound caused Ora to lift her bow and sight down the arrow at a tree several yards to her left. A woodpecker. It flew away in a flash of black and red. Ora relaxed slightly. If there was animal life, the danger could not be too close.

The wheels of the coach rolled over a branch in the path, the sharp sound of timber snapping echoing in the quiet. Captain Lenorr's horse snorted and jerked his head up, pulling against the reins as the Captain of the Guard tightened his hands around them. He pressed in his heels and a moment later brought his horse alongside Garren's.

"How much further?" he said quietly, eyes on their surroundings.

“Not long now,” came Garren’s only reply.

Ora ignored the desire to stretch the kinks from her back. They had been riding for hours.

“Pick up the pace,” Garren’s voice jerked her from the tired daze she had begun to slip into. She twisted slightly on the back of the horse to watch as Captain Lenorr returned to the coach. She could not see the King within the swaying cloth shades drawn over the windows. Good. He needed to stay inside and away from the prying eyes of the forest. The coach was well fortified and no arrows could pierce the thick, dense wood. As long as he kept back from the windows, he was safe.

A guard’s shout came from the back of the Envoy. A Muel dropped from the trees and landed on a horse, dragging it and its rider to the ground. Ora saw the flash of a sword as the fallen guard stumbled to his feet to defend himself.

Shrieks filled the air, all too familiar to Ora’s ears. More Muels dropped from the trees as Garren twisted his horse’s head around to bring them to the back of the Envoy. Ora raised her bow and shot the Muel who had attacked the horse and guard.

Then Skays began to appear all around them from the forest, around trees and through thickets. They surrounded the Envoy as the guard on the ground abandoned his dead horse and raced to the back of the coach, still in motion, to hoist himself up to defend it from the roof. The shield on his back saved him from the Muel’s teeth, or he would surely be dead on the ground like his horse.

Ora heard the shouted orders of Captain Lenorr as his guards obeyed and moved in tighter formation around the coach. Captain Lenorr moved to the lead horse of the coach and grabbed hold of the harness. They could not let the horses spook and take off, not like last time.

The Skays were closing in on three sides. Soon, the path ahead would be overtaken.

"Hold on to me!" Garren shouted over his shoulder. He did not wait for her to acknowledge before digging in his heels and loosening the reins to give his horse its own head. He drew the bone knife from the sheath strapped to his forearm.

He squeezed his left leg tight against his horse's side, so it turned slightly, angling to avoid the Muel coming toward them as Garren reached out and slashed the Muel's throat in passing.

Blood sprayed his arm and Ora's as she turned her face away and gripped Garren's waist to keep from losing her balance.

With the coach on their right, Garren shouted to the guards surrounding it. "Keep going! Do not stop! We are almost in range!"

A moment later, they broke through the tree line. A shower of flaming arrows rained down toward them. Ora shut her eyes, expecting to feel the flaming points pierce her skin. Garren's great beast leapt forward, and the cut-short screams of Muels stumbling and dropping behind them made Ora gasp with relief.

Chapter 81

Several officers approached as the King stepped from the coach in the midst of the First Division. Garren stopped his horse just beyond the Envoy, and extended his arm to help Ora dismount before following suit.

He allowed a waiting footman to take the horse as Commander Strell appeared from within the midst of the other officers. He easily felt the Commander's surprise and watched as he stopped before the King and bowed. "My King. Thank the great Blue Star you have arrived safely. I hear you had trouble along the border."

"Not all of us fared unscathed," the King answered, glancing over each shoulder at what was left of his Envoy. "My men are weary. They require rest."

Garren looked at Captain Lenorr. The Captain of the Guard did not show any surprise at his King's concern for his Envoy. Garren would never expect such words to fall from the lips of a young King who lived to be served and obeyed. Someone born into such great power rarely recognized those beneath him.

"There are tents raised for you and your men," Commander Strell replied, "and footmen to attend to your needs."

The King nodded decisively, with all the airs of regality he'd been born and raised in. He glanced at Garren and Ora standing nearby and motioned towards her. "These will be rewarded. They saved my life. They showed true bravery and have made the King proud," he instructed firmly. His gaze lingered on Ora before Commander Strell hastened to speak.

"Certainly, my King. They will be rewarded."

But the King continued: "This one will join the Council sessions while I am here." He gestured toward Garren. "I would like to hear your perspective on the War, Captain."

Garren bowed his head in respect but said nothing. He could feel Commander Strell's disdain reeking like rot in his senses. No doubt the Commander expected the Singer Captain to continue on his patrols and other lone duties, while the other commanding officers met in Council with the King.

"Captain Lenorr," the King turned and the Captain of the Guard stepped forward with a bow. "You may attend to the wounded and get settled. Then I require you to join me for the Council."

"Yes, Sire."

The King raised an eyebrow at Commander Strell. "Will you lead the way, Commander?"

The Commander hastened forward. "Certainly, Your Majesty." He seemed just as surprised as Garren that the King showed concern for his soldiers.

Captain Lenorr turned and motioned his men to lift the wounded, and the Envoy followed the Commander through the camp.

A muscle flexed in Garren's jaw, and he glanced at Ora, who still stood beside him staring after the King and his Envoy. As if sensing his gaze, she looked up at him. He searched her gaze, but the mental distance he had put between them kept him from analyzing her emotions. “You may go, archer,” he dismissed her quietly but firmly.

Chapter 82

As dusk blanketed the First Division, a breeze stirred the tents, snapping canvas against wood. The smoke from a nearby campfire rose in eager tendrils to meet the air and blew in Ora's direction. She walked without hurry through camp, having just finished eating at the food tent. Most of her friends were on duty at the lines and she would not see them until later. She wanted the time of solitude anyway. Commander Kane would need her at the line in the morning.

There was only an occasional outburst of fighting at the front lines now. She worried about what that must mean; more For'bane on their way? The silence was almost as stressful as the sounds of constant battle.

The wind tugged at her long hair, pulling strands free from her braid. She paused at a campfire and stretched her hands over it for warmth.

"Ora," spoke a familiar voice from across the fire.

Ora looked up, startled. "Bron," she blurted. He looked the same as he always did. Subtle arrogance glittered in his gaze. He stepped forward into the light of the fire and tossed a stick he had been fiddling with between his hands into the blaze. Sparks shot up into the breeze, rising with the smoke before going out. "I thought you would have more sense."

"Excuse me?"

"What hold does Captain Garren have over you? Besides being your superior?" Bron motioned vaguely with one arm to encompass the other end of camp. "Do you not know better than to fall in love with a Singer?"

Ora gasped softly, stunned. Love? She would never fall in love. The thought made her cringe with a bitter taste in her mouth. She stood firmly. "I do not know what you mean," she insisted. "And where were you when I was taken captive? Who was the only one who bothered to come after me?"

"What did he say to you? Did he tell you I thought you were dead anyway? No one has ever survived capture by the For'bane."

"I survived. And, no," she continued quietly, "Captain Garren told me nothing of what you said."

Bron glanced aside with sudden discomfort. Suddenly, Ora felt sorry for him. Perhaps she should not, for the way he failed time and again to prove himself. For all the times he could have stood up for her and did not. But when she looked at him now, she realized he was more lost and confused than Garren. She pressed her lips together a moment.

"I do not need your sympathy," Bron growled in irritation, sensing her change of attitude.

Ora ignored him. So, he did not want sympathy. Well, she was not interested in giving it. "Why do you hate the Captain?"

"I do not care for anyone in power."

"But you are both the same—."

"We are *not*," he denied vehemently.

"You are both Singers," Ora insisted. "You both fight for the same cause and against the same blood. Why are all the Singers not able to work together against a common enemy? You are stronger than anyone. You could give us a fighting chance."

Bron smiled, trying to assert that casual ease he always maintained, but it fell somewhat stale this time. "We are loners. We cannot get along. It is just the way it is. And Captain Garren has gained the confidence of the Council. I will fight until my dying day, but even in death it will not change who I am. I will not have any honors. I will be treated as the beast that I am. They forget the Captain is a beast because of his status. And when that fails him…." His gaze shifted beyond Ora's shoulder. "Is that not so, Captain?"

Ora turned in surprise. Was he always so near? Was he always lingering in the shadows, hearing all that was spoken? Her heart tripped inside her, wondering how much he had heard.

Garren stepped forward, arms folded across his chest casually, gaze trained on Bron. "Take heed, Bron," he warned. "If you want to challenge me, do it to my face."

Bron turned to Ora abruptly. "Some men will always be monsters. Remember that, archer."

Ora tried to respond, but her voice stuck in her throat. Garren turned his head to meet her gaze. She saw the veiled pain there. She took a quick step in his direction but stopped when he tensed and took a step away from her, rejecting her instinct to comfort him. "Captain," she began in protest.

"You would do well not to discuss matters you do not understand with him or anyone else," Garren upbraided her stiffly, a flash of anger in his eye. He stared at Bron. "We monsters understand each other well enough."

Stung by the hostility in the air, Ora watched as Garren walked away. She felt Bron's gaze.

"You are wrong," she said firmly, looking at him again. "Your actions define you, not your status. Unlike you, the Captain does what is right and yet asks for nothing in return. He risked his life to save me. A monster would not have bothered."

Bron stared at her, speechless. Ora took a breath to calm herself. "Good night," she spoke hoarsely, emotion choking out her voice, and turning, strode away into the night before her trembling unease might betray her.

Chapter 83

Meeting with the Council some minutes after his confrontation with Bron, Garren let his gaze sweep over the faces of the other officers, as they all stood to greet the King as he entered and came to stand at the head of the table with his Captain of the Guard.

Commander Strell stood at the place to the King's left, with a self-righteous and proud tilt to his chin, though he bowed with deep flourish. Commander Jeshura and Captain Ward—just returned from the Fifth Division—stood to his left.

Commander Kane stood to the King's right, with Commanders Dillion and Baire beside him, and Garren at the far end with Captain Mason opposite the table from him.

The Commanders' and Captain Mason's footmen stood behind them against the walls of the tent. Garren was the only one present who did not have a footman. He had been offered one when he came into the position, but he refused. He did not stay in one place long enough to need an attendant. They would only fear or hate him anyway, and who needed that kind of trouble?

As the King took his seat and Captain Lenorr stood at attention behind him, the Council took their seats once more.

"My dear Commanders and Captains," the King began with a gracious and regal bow of his head toward the rest of the table. "My apologies for all the trouble my coming has stirred up. You have your hands full with this War. When I heard the Divisions had been overrun some months ago, I knew I must come and offer my support and see for myself how you are faring."

"My King," Commander Strell responded smoothly. "We are honored by your presence. Though we would not have wished you to put yourself in harm's way."

The King studied the Commander a moment. He nodded slightly. "My Captain of the Guard advised against it." Captain Lenorr's only response was a slight shifting of his feet. The King leaned forward slightly in his chair. "Ultimately, my advisors agreed that the people have been too long without the face of their King. My dear departed father—" a touch of sorrow softened his already boyish features, "—passed so suddenly and his advisors, now mine, had their hands full teaching me how to take over control of my father's kingdom. This is the first time I have found opportunity to join you, my Commanders and Captains. To speak with you and hear directly from you; your concerns, your plans, and what support I may lend to you."

Captain Mason cleared his throat, drawing attention before he spoke. "If I may," he said. "It is not for lack of capability that we remain here, still fighting and yet losing after sixteen years. Yes, the For'bane grow in number as fast as wild dogs, but where has been the focus of our efforts? Our Divisions suffer for lack of a plan and resources to see it to fulfillment."

"Where do you expect to find such resources?" Commander Baire insisted. "After sixteen years, we can hardly expect much. These lands are being stripped bare."

"Something has to change," Captain Mason continued. He raised his hands in a questioning motion. "Will we make excuses and simply continue on as we always have? I think everyone wants an answer to that question."

Garren listened in silence as the other officers spoke back and forth and filled the King in on the progression of the War and the latest battles. He watched the King's face closely. How much did he understand about the beginning of the War? About Charles Binn? About the experiments and where the For'bane truly came from? Or was he as ignorant and innocent as his young features portrayed? There was depth to him, Garren concluded, and in his gaze was wisdom and capability beyond his years.

Will it be enough? If the truth comes to light, on which side will he fall?

"Captain Garren," the King inquired, locking eyes with Garren. "Would you care to add anything? You have seen more combat I think than many here."

For the last several minutes they had been discussing the causes and effects that lost them their foothold in For'bane territory; the night they were overrun and forced to retreat—the same night Garren brought Ora and the others from Neice to Torr Guard.

Garren cleared his throat and straightened in his seat to answer: "I was coming in with a troop, having just collected some new recruits on the way…." His gaze flickered toward the footman standing behind Commander Jeshura. He recognized Thane as one of the recruits from Neice, and he did not look well, though he stood ramrod straight and at attention, as the others. "The Second Division broke first and were completely overrun; all were killed or captured. They were right on top of a nest, only they did not know it until it was too late. Once their line was taken, the rest of the Divisions merged to establish a new line and we lost six months' worth of progress. We lost all the ground that we had recovered in that time."

"This one incident—," Commander Strell began.

"*One* incident?" Garren challenged stiffly. "Sixteen years and there is only one to speak of?"

"—should not be used to determine the whole of this War. In battle, you give and you take."

"And that is giving the lives of the men and women of an entire Division in the Army? And what is it we have taken to compensate for the loss of these?"

"No loss can be measured," Commander Baire spoke, his chair creaking as he shifted his large, muscular frame, laden with steel armor and the blue sash matching those of the other Commanders. "For the greater good, death is a surety. We must believe that when the War is over, it will have been worth the sacrifices."

"We lost our foothold because we were lazy," Garren concluded.

"Come now, Captain," Commander Strell patronized, stretching his words as if bored, sending prickles of irritation down Garren's spine. "Considering you were not even there when the battle happened.... We are not all as daring and invincible as you."

"We should have kept moving forward while we had the advantage. Plugged up their nests in the valleys and driven them back at least another ten longs before setting up our defenses," Garren continued in a firm voice.

When the Commander tried once more to interrupt, the King held up a hand with calm command. "Wait, now, Commander. You have led the conversation thus far and I appreciate your wisdom. I would like to hear the Captain explain himself."

"Thank you, Sire," Garren inclined his head. "The Second Division was a perfect example of one of our greatest mistakes. Instead of pressing forward and clearing the land, they set up their defenses and waited, and it cost them their lives. They did not even know they were atop a For'bane nest. The nests are the birthplaces of the enemy; the home of hundreds, perhaps thousands, of our enemy. Let the nests be their graves as well."

"These…nests…," the King spoke after a moment of silence. "How would you propose to destroy them? If indeed they house so many, my Army will be hard pressed to overcome them."

"I have been in a nest before. I know how they tunnel and, while large and vast, there are weak points. Because it is made of earth and rocks, it can be destroyed with the same. An alchemist in Torr Guard, Gan, has developed a substance I believe can help us. With the materials and his assistance, I believe we can use this substance on a grander scale to bury the nests and kill the For'bane inside."

"This is absurd!" Commander Strell burst out. "The alchemist Gan? His experiments are unstable at best! Captain, you have never approached the Council with this before." Accusation tainted the Commander's final words.

"I was unaware of it until recently," Garren turned to the King. "Your Majesty, consider it. I have used this substance and seen that it has effect. All we need is to dedicate time, effort, and strategy for its success. We cannot continue this dangerous dancing with the enemy." His gaze glinted. "If we cannot commit to their destruction, completely and totally, instead of this…compromise…then we will be committing to our own end."

The King glanced over at Captain Lenorr. A moment of silence fell, before he rose and addressed the Council as they hastened to their feet as well. "I am interested in what this alchemist Gan has to offer. You say he is in Torr Guard? Summon him, and have him join us on the morrow. We will speak more on this subject."

Chapter 84

Haunted by Bron's words and Garren's change of behavior towards her, Ora found herself unable and unwilling to rest. She avoided the Archers Quarter and wished she knew where to find Thane. She needed someone to talk to; someone from home.

She wearied of this constant pull between monsters and men. The Singers could be one or the other and sometimes both, Garren most of all. Every time she thought she understood him, he confused her all over again. He insisted he was a monster, and then seemed desperate to prove to her that he was not. Surely Bron's words hurt him; she had seen it in his gaze. And though Singers were the only ones who could read emotions, she was almost sure she'd felt his. Perhaps it was only her own agony.

Still, the monster had not given up his name to a lowly archer. It was not the monster who held her patiently when she'd mourned Carter's death. Nor was it the monster who held her in the hot springs or promised to always be there for her. Were they just shadows of what he used to be before the change? Or could he become that man and finally overcome the monster?

She was passing near the Council tent when she heard Garren's voice coming from just inside the entrance. All else was quiet, and not moments before she had seen the other officers depart for their own quarters. She had come, not realizing till that moment she hoped to speak with Garren when he was through with his meeting.

She hesitated, keeping a safe distance away to avoid detection, and peered around the corner of another tent to watch the entrance of the Council tent. With the flap drawn back and secured to a post, she could see Garren speaking with someone inside.

He shifted slightly and Ora's gaze widened at seeing the King in conversation with him. And they were talking about *her*. She strained her ears to hear.

"Where did she come from?"

"We gleaned her with several other recruits in Neice."

Ora bristled at his choice of words. *Gleaned.* As if they were no more than wheat to be cut down and thrown into a cart.

"So, she is a Freelander?" the King sounded surprised. "Her features are quite—remarkable. I thought I saw traces of Imperial[22] blood. Who are her parents."

Ora stiffened with a flash of fear. *Imperial.* She caught and held her breath. In a moment, the memory of Garren with her in her tent as she confessed the horrible truth of her parentage returned like a blast of frigid winter wind. Would he betray her? But what was worse, he could not betray what he did not know…the worst part of the awful truth that she had been too afraid to give up.

---

[22] Imperial : another way of saying noble—specifically of men descended from the Unknown Islands, to the outlying Northern edge of the kingdom.

"Poor Freeland farmers," Garren said simply. "They are dead now."

Ora let out her breath in a soft rush of relief.

"She is near the same age as my sisters. She seems more suited for the royal court than a battlefield."

"You fancy her for service, Your Majesty?"

"Surely you will not miss a single archer, when I take her back with me. The court will adore her, I am sure. As the brave woman who defended my life, I will give her anything she asks. She will be well cared for, better than what a battlefield ever could provide, for certain."

Ora felt her heart slam against her rib cage and quickly ducked out of sight, hurrying blindly away for the Archers Quarter and the safety of her own cot.

Suddenly, a group of soldiers stepped into her path. She flinched in defensive mode, mind still wrapped around her past, before she recognized them as fellow archers. She forced a smile as they shouted greetings to her.

"Come for a drink, Ora," one urged. "Freddy has some special brew, will burn the hair off your head."

"It has been a long night." She was glad for an excuse.

One of them nudged her in the shoulder as they passed and Ora stepped aside to watch them go. As they disappeared between the tents, she saw Garren approaching. The flickering light of the torches framed his face and he caught her gaze.

Ora turned slowly to face him fully and stood still, watching his approach. Her heart pounded fast with uncertainty.

"Something is wrong," he said, searching her face.

"How very astute of you," Ora murmured. She crossed her arms defensively. "How was your counsel with the King?"

Garren stopped a few feet away. "Why does his arrival bother you so?" His gaze narrowed slightly.

"I do not like the way he looks at me—," Ora whispered and swallowed hard. Sudden confusion rose in the pit of her stomach, recalling Bron's accusation. She glanced up and searched Garren's closed expression and felt a trickle of fear return. *I do not like the way* you *look at me….*

Garren's voice remained steady. "And how does he look at you? Has no man ever noticed that you are beautiful? Do you fear admiration?"

His words stung. Did he not already know? Greer tried to take her by force; to take what was hers. Just as the soldiers took from the village women. Just as they had taken her mother. She'd only seen men use their passions to inflict hurt and power on the weak. And she had never sought any man's attention for that very reason. Because it terrified her.

"I am a soldier now," she insisted when she could find her voice, trying to sound brave, hating that a tremble distorted her words. "I do not know how to be anything else. That may mean nothing to you, because you are a man who is free to make your own way and they expect you to—."

"None of us are free, Ora," he reminded her sharply.

"I do not want to be anyone's puppet!" she shot back at him, trembling, then sucked in a short breath to compose herself again.

Garren's jaw tightened and anger flared in his visible grey eye. "Then do not be," he said darkly, staring at her. Then his lips softened, parting slightly and he looked as if he would say something else. But, he abruptly turned on his heel and disappeared into the darkness.

Chapter 85

Garren raged inwardly at the way he handled his meeting with Ora. He sensed her confusion towards him; the hint of fear. He knew it had to do with his behavior. He was turning into the monster. Always, he risked turning into the monster.

He gritted his teeth, pausing in the deep shadows not far from where he'd left Ora standing alone, knowing she would not be able to see him in the darkness.

She was terrified of men and their attraction to her. He was terrified because he was attracted to her. More than that, He had never felt anything so powerful. Even his own defenses were reeling. His dreams of her left him shaken and caught off guard. He knew he cared for her more than he should, but he had not admitted to himself just how strongly he cared.

He wanted her more than he had ever wanted any woman. It was not just a physical desire. He wanted to know her heart, her dreams. He wanted to wake up every morning with her in his arms. For her to belong to him and no one else. To listen to her speak. To share in things outside of war and bloodshed. He wanted to make her smile. He wanted to hear her laugh.

He wanted her to choose him.

He did not want to be her Captain. He wanted to be her lover for the rest of time; her confidant, her second soul[23].

She was clueless of the passions of a man—the good kind. Her fear of the King's admiration was born from the fear of being ruled by any man—from watching soldiers wield their power in immoral and cruel ways.

And yet, within her existed the best qualities for love and tenderness. The way her hands soothed his temples when he was in pain. The softness in her eyes when she sought his approval. The grace in her spirit that tried to see the best in him—and looked past his constant failings.

He wanted, more than the air he breathed, to nurture those qualities. He wanted to help her trust in what love could be, what it should be, and to show her the best of that world.

It had been so long since he dreamed….

He let his gaze trace the soft, smooth line of her jaw against the shadows and firelight, remembering what it was like those rare times he had let himself touch her face. Despite his hopes and longings, he could not offer her that life. He needed to protect her. He needed to think realistically. Though it bothered him—the idea of the King's interest in her—removing her to Asteriae palace would save her, and assure her protection from the battles ahead.

He removed himself from her presence, but her tangled emotions stayed with him, haunting him. He needed to distract himself. He needed to kill some monsters. As soon as he saw to the King's safe departure, and Ora's with him, Garren would throw himself back into this fight and back into the ever present darkness. He would forget his longings —his foolish desires. With her safe, he could begin this new

---

[23] Second Soul : soul mates

battle and root out the traitors among the Army's leaders. It would be an ugly affair, he had no doubt. He had already felt it when he spoke of the alchemist Gan during Council. Resolving to end the War and actively working to that end meant a division of new friends and enemies, of exposing what was in the hearts of the Council and beyond—who wanted the War to be won and who did not.

He returned to his tent and lit a lamp on the narrow table. He undid the buckles and straps of his leather armor, removing a piece at a time until only his tunic covered his chest, hanging loose over his leather-clad thighs.

He tossed his leather armor atop the end of his bed and paused to lift his hand and press three fingers thoughtfully between the ties of his tunic to the sweat-dotted skin of his chest, feeling the steady pounding of his heart underneath. A reminder he had not succumbed. His heart was human and beat with a human rhythm. The day that changed he determined to put a knife through it.

"Runner!" came a warning shout, jarring Garren from his brooding. It had been some time since anyone attempted an escape, considering the consequences. For him, not since that day in the woods when he shot the boy after battling with the Muels. The look in Ora's eyes as she had witnessed it would never leave him.

He grabbed his bow and a single arrow—he would only need one—and shoved the tent flap aside, rushing into the cold night air—not bothering with his armor. Tiny flakes of snow began to fall, and the ground crunched frozen and hard beneath his booted feet as he hurried toward the call. A group of curious soldiers parted quickly to let him pass, winding between tents and camp activity.

"Archers Quarter! Runner!" came the shout again.

It hit him then, a moment before he had her in his sights, running between tents with her back toward him. "Ora!" he shouted as he dropped to one knee and drew back on the bow, his fingers sliding along the string to elicit the haunting song of the Singer. People parted quickly, terrified to be in the path of his arrow.

Ora, her kit hanging over her shoulder against her hip, swung around, her steps hesitating as she stared at him with shock and disbelief in her wide golden-brown eyes.

Grief and anger clawed at his heart. *Do not make me do this,* he silently pleaded. He drew back taut on the bow and aimed for her heart, though it would be like putting it through his own to follow through with the action he was required to make. The one he had done countless times before without feeling anything.

He had been hardened and calloused towards the killing and now he felt too much.

Do not make me do this.

Suddenly, as Ora hesitated, caught in his gaze, a soldier moved quickly from a nearby tent and raised his sword high. Garren turned the arrow toward the soldier in alarm, in instinct to protect her even in her own error. But the soldier did not move to wield the blade. Instead, he brought the hilt of the sword down hard across the back of Ora's head and she crumpled, unconscious, to the ground.

Garren ran the remaining distance to her side—her form hardly more than a slight shadow on the ground. The soldier who had struck her stood over her, holding his sword at his side. Seeing Garren's swift approach and not aware of the focus of the Singer's fury, he began to speak, "She nearly escaped—."

Garren grabbed the soldier by the throat with his free hand, shoving him back against a supporting pole of the tent behind him with such force it nearly snapped the pole. Red-hot fury blinded Garren's senses as the pressure of his hand squeezed off the soldier's airway.

The soldier dropped his sword at once, and grabbed feebly at Garren's strong arm, eyes wide with surprised terror. He choked, trying without success to take a breath.

"Do not *ever* interfere with a Singer's business again! Do you hear me?!" Garren shouted in rage.

"Captain Garren!" the voice barely registered as Commander Dillion appeared at the soldier's side, facing Garren. He grabbed Garren's arm to stop him. "He was only doing his job."

Garren drew in a sharp breath and abruptly released the soldier, shoving him aside. The soldier fell to the ground and scrambled away from the angry Singer Captain on hands and knees, gasping for air.

Garren stared at the Commander a moment, fighting for control over his fury that anyone would harm the woman he loved. It did not matter that Garren's job was to shoot her as a runner, and the soldier's blow kept him from that. Inwardly, he knew he never could have released the arrow.

The Commander stepped back, recognizing Garren's need for space and wise enough to not say anything more at the moment.

Garren turned and knelt on one knee beside Ora's unconscious form. Her long hair, pulled loose from her braid lay in dark-golden waves across her face. Gently, pressing his anger aside, he slid his hand beneath the veil of hair against her cheek and revealed the already darkening bruise at her temple. With his free hand, he turned her face away from the frozen earth toward his searching gaze. Her skin was pale, her lips pink from the cold. Her mind was lost in slumber.

He picked her up in his arms, straightening to his full height, and held her close against his broad chest as he faced those around him with a stony expression.

As he turned, movement in the shadow of a tent several yards away caught his attention. Commander Strell stepped back into the shadows with a cruel, knowing smile twisting his lips. As if he had just discovered a disastrous secret. Garren did not care what anyone thought of his actions to protect Ora, so long as no one ever hurt her again.

He carried her away to a holding tent, leaving the crowd of onlookers staring after them.

Chapter 86

Ora slowly came to. She felt the scratchiness of a hard rug beneath her, as she lay on her side. *What happened?* Her head ached and her eyelids felt too heavy to lift at first. She tried to piece together her last memories.

She had been running away. She had not truly considered her foolish actions, but reacted on the impulse of her tattered emotions and wounded desperation.

In a flash of fear, she remembered Garren and the Singer's song as he prepared to shoot her.

James. Her breath froze in her chest as she heard his voice shout her name. Somehow she had known he would be her death sentence. He was good at his job, and nothing would keep him from it.

When she had swung around to find his gaze across the distance, a feeling of betrayal closed around her throat. A terrifying fear at seeing the bow drawn tight, the arrow aimed true. In the next moment she had expected to feel its cruel point rip through her body.

She had caught the fierceness of Garren's grey eye even from the distance, and her steps faltered with her morbid, anguished thoughts.

Whatever tenderness he had begun to show her no longer meant anything and would not keep her from his arrow. His fierce withdrawal from her, sudden and cold, had left her feeling alone and desolate; abandoned once more to the unfeeling realities of a war-torn kingdom.

Maybe it would be better this way, she had shamefully thought. Her last act of defiance to the War, that they could not use her and sell her at their pleasure. Everyone she loved was gone. The sweet balm of Garren's goodness also was gone, the one thing left in her life she had clung to. The one thing that kept her breathing.

How appropriate that it would be his own arrow that ended it all?

His determined gaze was the last thing she had seen as a sudden sharp pain shrouded her mind in utter darkness. No, she had not been shot. Someone must have come up behind her and struck her.

Something hard and cold circled her wrists and she could not lift her arms.

She forced her eyes open and an involuntary moan escaped her lips. She turned her head as her vision swam with blurry shades of light and dark. As her vision sharpened, she found herself staring at the canvas interior walls of a small tent.

With a wince, she lifted her head from the rug-strewn floor. She looked around the room to find it void of furniture.

Each wrist was shackled and the chains led back to a single round hook on a wooden post struck deep in the ground a few feet away from where she lay. The chains gave her several feet to move and walk but did not allow her any further freedom.

She sat up slowly. Movement caught her eye at the tent entrance. She turned to see a footman standing guard just inside, bearing full armor (as if she was that dangerous!). He watched her a moment without expression and then looked resolutely past her at the far wall. Ora wondered if she should be relieved that she was still alive or disappointed.

The tent flap lifted just as she gained her footing and tested the strength of her wrist cuffs. She stared as Garren entered, his expression masked, his features firm.

A wave of mixed emotions assaulted Ora at the sight of him. She moved toward him abruptly, her feet moving as if of their own accord, but the chains grew taut quickly, stopping her advance. For a moment she strained at the cruel bond.

Garren stood still, staring at her. She quickly turned away from him so he would not see the tears threatening to spill over her eyes. "So, you wish to hurt me?" he said cooly.

Ora shut her eyes tightly, refusing to turn back around.

"Leave us," Garren ordered the footman.

The footman departed and they were left alone, encased in silence, until a moment later when Garren's soft tone betrayed him, "Belle." He stood directly behind her, and the breath of his voice fell lightly against the back of her neck, as her hair lay in a tangled sweep across one shoulder. She shivered.

"Whatever caused this terrible fear I feel in you?" His voice rumbled.

"I was standing outside the tent. I heard the King ask for me, to take me away with him to the palace…. You did not argue with him. You did not defend me," she said coldly.

"You should know there is no arguing against the wishes of our King and what he wills," Garren reprimanded. "How could you, Belle? How could you run?"

So, he had come back to calling her Belle again. Only it was too late now. He had already rejected her and every hint of care he had ever offered her. She was the runaway archer he had almost been forced to shoot. She could not shake the mental image of his determined gaze or the aim of his arrow towards her.

"Belle—," Garren began with a sharp catch in his breath.

Ora sucked in a sharp breath and shook her head insistently. "No, Captain. Do not call me that," she managed, voice breaking as she tried to hold herself together. It was all too confusing. "I cannot bear for you to call me that." *Not now,* she silently added. *Not after the way you have been.*

"I would never have hurt you," Garren insisted with a low rumble. Ora turned and stared at him. "I could not have harmed you." Was that haunting guilt deep in his gaze?

"Do you think I do not understand what Bron meant? Do you think I do not know how to recognize the monsters? I would know better than anyone…." Her voice choked up despite her best efforts.

Garren stepped closer and lifted one hand to the back of her head, gently tangling his fingers in her hair and taking a slow deep breath, question in his eyes. Could he feel her grief, still so fresh? She knew he could.

Ora raised her face to search his gaze and explain her words: "I came to the tent to talk with you, to find you. After Bron…. That's why I was there."

"Everything he said was true," Garren spoke huskily.

"I have seen the things you have done. I have been witness to both the man and the monster, in you and in others. I know more than you give me credit for. I vowed my revenge against you, I vowed my hatred and never took it because you have changed. And so have I. I thought—I thought you…." She trailed off with the slight shake of her head.

Garren shook his head. "The choice has been made. I cannot go against it."

"So, it has been decided? I have no say in the matter?"

Garren's jaw tightened, and his gaze hardened. "After what you have done—trying to run when you knew the punishment—I would be a fool to argue, and so would you. The King will overlook your lapse in judgement, I am certain. Your aid in saving his life counts for something." He shook his head at her. "Your anger is misplaced—."

Ora shoved her hands against his chest. "I would rather die on the battlefield…."

"This is not a punishment—."

"It is to me! It is worse than a punishment. It is denying me my right to live as I was born—*free*." Her tone became pleading against her will: "You should understand! They will try to mold and shape me into something that I am not."

"Belle—."

"Is it not enough they took me away from my home and forced me into this War? Is it not enough I have forgiven them for that? I have accepted it and my life here. But there they will try to change me for their own purposes. I am not a painted doll to be dressed up and paraded around the court, as the King's *favored one*."

Garren looked at her solemnly, determined. "You will be safe. Someday, you will learn. You will learn to put aside your foolish behavior and limited understanding, and accept that there is more to this kingdom and the fate of her people than your own misguided pain, even your own fate."

"This is war, James, you know that nowhere is safe," Ora whispered as tears flooded her eyes. But even that was not true. She had felt safe in his arms. She had felt safe at his side. How could he do this to her? What right did he have to decide her fate? To batter her with cruel words? Was she being selfish to desire her own life and will?

"And if the King wills that I become his bride? Or the bride of a noble?" Ora nearly choked on the words.

Garren shook his head firmly, anger sparking in his gaze. "You are not of a noble bloodline. He will not wed you. There would be no advantage to it."

"Then I will be what? His mistress?" Ora cried in frustration. "Just as the soldiers take the village women? Do they have a right to take who they wish and is the King the same way?"

Garren grabbed her by the upper arms, his hold so tight she winced in pain as he dragged her toward him, a dangerous glint in his eye. "No," he snarled with possessive warning. "He will not touch you."

He must have sensed the pain he was causing as his anger tempered. He eased his hold. His gaze softened with veiled agony.

Ora felt her own defensive anger drain. "You cannot promise that," she whispered. She shook her head. "You do not know—."

"What? What do I not know?" he spoke stiffly, a muscle in his jaw flexing.

Ora looked away. "Nothing," she whispered with a tremble. But her hands, held together by her shackled wrists, pressed against his chest and her fingers curled around the front of his tunic in silent desperation.

His hands eased their hold to move lightly up her arms to cup her face gently between his palms. "You do not hate me," he murmured, as if reading her thoughts.

"No," Ora agreed softly and lowered her face. "But sometimes I still want to…."

He wiped a tear from the corner of her eye with the pad of his thumb. "Goodbye, Belle." His tone was gentle but hinting at command. He would not be swayed.

He stepped back and let his hands fall away resolutely. He turned away, shoulders straight and stiff.

"James!" Ora cried, standing as far as the chain allowed. She yanked at the restraints, desperate.

He hesitated.

Look at me! she silently screamed at him.

But he would not. He ducked out of the tent without another word, leaving her behind.

Everything in her wanted to collapse under the weight of his exit—not just from the tent, but from her life. It felt like a part of her died inside, like when Carter died. Only, this time, no one remained to lift her up, to hold on to her. She never imagined how devastating his removal would be to her. Garren was all she had left in this war-torn world. He *was* her world.

Chapter 87

Dawn met Garren's watchful eye, changing the horizon from grey and red to a flushed pink like the blush of hopeful innocence. Did the sun not know it would look upon a blood-bathed world full of hatred, battle, and suffering the same as the day before? Did it rise in hope of some miracle of beauty to change the ugly scars?

Bitterness rose on Garren's tongue as he silently cursed the dawn that would take his beloved away from him. The only thing of beauty that remained—and he was giving her up. He had not closed his eyes all that long night.

He had not slept since the dream of her that had shaken him so. He did not want it to come again. He did not need the torment.

He would watch the Envoy leave with the soldiers appointed to guard its safe travel back to Asteriae palace, safe in the shadow of the High Mountain—to lands guarded by a long high wall in the mountains, untouched by the terrors that lived and breathed here in the hillsides and valleys. Once gone, he expected to sever the strange ethereal connection he shared with Ora forever. The distance was greater than she had ever been from him since they met.

It was a small comfort that the Envoy would follow Garren's advice for a safer path home, skirting the dangerous parts of the For'bane territory. She should be safe.

And then, after the Envoy disappeared from his sight, he would return to Torr Guard and speak once more with Captain Mason concerning the journal he had discovered. Life would return to what it had been before Ora arrived.

If only it would not bother him so much.

He turned toward his tent, when Commander Strell stepped from between two tents and came toward him with a gleam in his eyes. "You are not going soft on me now, are you, Captain? Has the archer tamed the great beast?"

"Do not give me yet another good reason to kill you, Strell," he said coldly as he made to pass him, insulting him with a lack of title. He was in no mood for a verbal sparring with the one man he despised most in the camp.

The Commander turned as he went by. "You have continually shirked your duty where that *girl* is concerned."

Garren stopped, pulling in a sharp breath between his teeth as he felt a curl of rage rise in his stomach.

"That alone is enough to bring you before the Council. It is at the very least enough to bring her before the board.... Law commands she be put to death, an order you failed to carry out at the proper time."

Garren turned suddenly, moving to stand inches from the Commander's face, glaring at him with dangerous warning. "That *girl*," he spat, pointing a finger between the eyes of the Commander, "is one of the best archers you have in this Army. She saved the King. She has the King's heart and if I were you, I would not test that." He leaned in even closer so their noses almost touched. His lip curled in disgust for the man. "But his wrath would be nothing compared to what I would do to you."

"You dare threaten me?"

Garren's grey eye narrowed and he stepped back. "The Old King promoted me into rank. It is not in your power to take that away. And even if it were...for all your quivering efforts to be rid of me, you are nothing but a whimpering dog." His lip curled again. "You may keep on barking till you asphyxiate and choke yourself for all I care."

He turned on his heel and strode away, forcing the violence within to be restrained with the trembling of his limbs.

"We shall see," he heard the Commander mutter darkly toward his back, but this time he chose to ignore it and kept on walking. He took a slow deep breath, ashamed he'd allowed the Commander to anger him. It was because of Ora. He could insult and degrade Garren all he wanted, but when his threats included Ora, that changed everything.

He wanted to see you react like that, a voice of reason cautioned inside him, a voice he long thought dead. *You gave him exactly what he wanted. You showed him the monster.*

Garren took another deep breath. Regardless, Ora was safe now. The Commander could not harm her even if he truly wanted to. She was too far out of his reach.

And too far for Garren as well.

Having walked out of Commander Strell's sights, Garren paused to lift his face to the Heavens. *'We all have a choice,'* Ora's words whispered with sweet tenderness to his soul. *'I do not think you want to be the monster.'*

Chapter 88

Ora sat across from the King as they traveled in the safety of his coach. She heard the occasional snort of the horses and jingle of the harnesses, as the mounted guards surrounded them. The cloth coverings on all sides were drawn down to block the wind, but as the coach jostled, the material moved and admitted the occasional breath of winter air.

She wished more than anything to be one of those guards, outside of the King's presence. She knew her role as a soldier. She did not know how to act or what to say sitting inside the coach, letting everyone else face the danger of their enemy.

She kept her hands clasped together in her lap, fingers itching for the feel of a bow and arrow.

"It will be four days before we reach Asteriae," the King spoke with a congenial smile. His teeth were straight and white. She wondered if they were fake. She had heard the nobles sometimes paid for a false set of teeth and had their own removed by a surgeon. She withheld a shudder. It was not a pain she ever wanted to undergo.

"Are you excited to see my kingdom?"

Ora licked her lips, suddenly feeling like her mouth was filled with cotton. She had barely met the King's stare since they set off, twenty minutes ago. She glanced at the coverings on her right, welcoming the chill that rushed in to greet her face every time the coach hit an uneven bump in the trail. "Is it not all your kingdom? Even the road we now travel?" she asked.

The King laughed. "You are right." His blue eyes twinkled when she looked at him in surprise at his laughter. "But here there are only trees and mud and hillsides. The palace is something quite different, filled with the wealth of my father, his father, and his father before him. It is something to behold."

Ora felt emboldened and even a little irritated by his boasting. "The trees and mud and hillsides, Sire, are the only home I have ever known. I see no need to mock what I have long loved and relied on."

A tense silence fell. Ora swallowed hard, wondering with sudden trepidation if the King would get angry with her. What action or form might his anger take? She had no right to speak out against the King. She was only a common archer. He had the power to kill her with a single word, and he would not have to explain his reasons.

The King's lips parted with a soft intake of air. "I do not know why, but I like you, Orabelle of Neice," he said. "I find your honesty refreshing. Few would speak their minds before me as you have just done."

"Forgive me, Sire. I am only a poor farmer's daughter," she insisted, remembering Garren's claim of her birth. "I do not know how to hold my tongue."

"I know you have not been accustomed to a genteel life, but you can learn," the King said confidently and settled back more comfortably against the cushioned seat.

Ora's heart jerked painfully. "I am a soldier, Sire. It is the best I will ever be." She felt the pleading tug in her words, the wish to return to the battlefield—a feeling she never thought she would carry. But what was worse than leaving the battlefield was leaving when the battle was far from over, turning her back on her own people and lands to live in comfort as a stranger in a foreign place.

The King merely smiled at her slightly. He did not understand. She wanted to ask if she might ride outside with the soldiers, but this time she wisely held her silence.

She turned and shut her eyes, cheek brushing against the cushions behind her head and pretended to sleep. With every creak of the wheels, she forced herself to breathe evenly and press down the panic swelling in her chest; the fear that nothing was ever going to be the same; the fear that she would never again see her beloved Freelands.

Hours passed and she hardly moved in her seat. The King watched her often, but rarely broke the silence. He seemed to know and respect her silent need for quiet. They stopped occasionally to rest the horses and allow the King and Ora to stretch their legs. Captain Lenorr kept everyone near the coach and horses and Ora was not allowed to wander off. As night fell, they made camp. The King placed Ora in the small tent nearest to his, within the circle of the guards' protection. She ate very little and stared at the ceiling of her tent most of the night, unable to find rest, consumed with dread and worry for what lay ahead.

The second day, the King tried to draw Ora into conversation again by inquiring about her life in Neice and her time spent as an archer in the First Division. Ora answered in short, polite sentences. Eventually, all fell silent between them once more.

They arrived at the great wall protecting Asteriae and the High Mountain beyond without incident late the fourth day.

It was like nothing she had ever seen! Great stone walls guarded the fortress within, so high that Ora—unable to hide her curiosity—had to tilt her head as far back as she could to view the turrets as she peered out the coach window. There were four turrets along the front, two flanking the portcullis gateway, one to the north end, and one to the south end. She could not tell how deep the walls went or guess how large the inside might be.

"Welcome to Asteriae. Kingdom of Stars." She caught the King's amused glance as he watched her. "Do you like it?" he asked.

Ora forced herself to sit back in her seat. She glanced aside. "It is…impressive," she admitted.

"Wait until you see the inside. These are just the outer guard towers. We will pass into a courtyard where the market and commoners reside, and then there is yet another wall beyond that which surrounds my palace."

The coach swayed slightly as it crossed from the rutted dirt path to paving stones. Stones! Would the wonders not cease? Ora had only ever known the small, mud and straw cottages and muddy streets of Neice, like most of the Freeland farming villages.

She heard the clatter of horses' hooves on the stones. A shout rose up and Ora peered out the window again to watch the portcullis—the heavy iron meshed gate—being raised, cranked upward by huge chains wrapped around spoked spools on each side of the inside entrance. It took four guards—two at each spool—to raise the gate.

The coach paused a moment until it cleared the portcullis, then drove through.

Ora pulled her head back as if afraid the sharp points of the portcullis would fall on them and pierce the coach. Once they passed through unharmed, she peered out again at the faces of the townspeople. The coach guards would not allow the townspeople to get too close. They pressed in, looking at her with strange expressions. They stared unblinking at her. Ora felt a shiver race up her spine in uncertainty and turned her face aside.

"Do not be afraid," the King spoke calmly. "You are a curious sight to them."

"And why is that, Sire?" Ora spoke quietly, but her words were stiff. She self-consciously brushed her palms against the sides of her archer's pants, trying to hide her discomfort.

The King smiled as if he knew her nervousness and it amused him. "I have never traveled with a woman in my coach before. I have never brought anyone back from the outside—and they have never seen a Freelander."

"I am glad I am so amusing to them," Ora's tone sharpened with anger. Would she be treated like some exotic and strange wild beast? "Shall you set me on display in the town square?"

The King's face darkened. A note of warning in his voice turned his boyish features wiser and stronger. "Within the confines of this coach, I am not offended by your brash speech. However, I cannot be so obliging once we step from it. You must not speak against me at every turn." His features softened as Ora felt a wash of uncertain fear and guilt. "I desire your confidence in me. I believe I will earn it, in time. I can see that you are not happy with this arrangement, but I hope you will grow to be. It is best to think before you speak, and sometimes to refrain from being so bluntly honest. It is best to not always let on what you are thinking."

"Forgive me, Your Majesty," Ora said, nearly choking on the words. Though she despised her circumstances, he had been nothing but kind and understanding—far more than he should have been, considering she had taken advantage of his latitude.

The coach stopped abruptly. They had arrived.

Chapter 89

Tender shoots of new spring grass were trampled underfoot in the mud of the first of the new season's rains that fell the night before on the fields of Torr Guard. Commander Dillion paced the sidelines of the field, issuing orders and correcting a band of new recruits as they squared off in mock battle.

Despite cool breezes and clear skies, Garren could smell storms in the air. He quietly observed the recruits' progress from further away near the side of a supply tent. His trained eye recognized varying potential in each of them.

It was not through any intentional planning on his part to observe their training. He had come with the purpose of talking with the Commander about arranging a meeting with Captain Mason. Captain Mason was away from Torr Guard on a personal leave to visit his family home. Apparently his father, a veteran who had served in the War several years before injury retired him to the Freelands, was dying.

Garren stood immovable as the breeze picked up suddenly to blast against the side of the tent. The sound of canvas snapping against the tent supports drowned out the sound of Commander Dillion's instructions. He crossed his arms as the Commander took one of the recruit's training sword to demonstrate blocking with the recruit's opponent. He pointed a finger at one and then the other, each jab punctuated by some firm correction that could not be distinguished over the wind.

Presently, the Commander handed the training sword back to the recruit with a final word before leaving the field to head Garren's way. "Captain," he greeted, and wiped a sheen of cooling sweat from above his left eye with the back of his arm. "What brings you to Torr Guard at this time of the day?"

"I need to speak with you and Captain Mason at your earliest convenience," Garren replied. "When is he expected to return?"

"Three days." Commander Dillion shook his head slightly. "For a moment I dared to think you might have come for a footman."

"Why do you say that?" Garren looked at the Commander in surprise.

The Commander shrugged and began to walk toward the tower, Garren keeping pace beside him. "Commander Jeshura arrived shortly before you in search of a new footman. Apparently, his footman is ailing and no longer capable in his tasks."

Garren paused, recalling the boy from Ora's village—Thane—and how sickly he had looked at the last Council. "Indeed," he agreed out loud. "The boy was never meant for this life, to be sure. Though I hear tell the Commander is none too considerate of those who serve him. If the boy is forced to sleep outside the Commander's tent, exposed to the elements, it is of no surprise his health leaves him."

"The Commander insists it builds up their strength and endurance. A footman must be strong and endure much, for much is required of him."

Garren did not respond. They entered the tower and Commander Jeshura turned to greet them in surprise. "Why, Captain, what brings you here?"

"The same as you," Garren replied calmly. "Have you found a footman worthy of you?"

Commander Jeshura hesitated, searching Garren's words for insult. Garren casually leaned back against the wall beside the entrance and folded his arms across his chest, as if he had all the time in the world to linger.

The Commander drummed his fingers lightly atop the edge of the map table before stepping around it. "The choices are limited. All that is left to our armies are children, hardly experienced. Though, I think a few show promise."

"So, what is to become of your footman? Has the boy done something wrong?"

Commander Dillion watched the exchange curiously, but Garren ignored him.

"He is unfit for service. The healer examined him. He has weak lungs. It is doubtful he will survive the wet spring weather and he cannot travel," Commander Jeshura answered. He smiled at Garren. "I am surprised. Did I hear you say you too are looking for a footman? I thought you had no wish to take on such a—what did you call it?—a troublesome burden. Which I find amusing, indeed, considering he is meant to relieve *you* of burdens, not be one."

"Perhaps I found it unnecessary since I am perfectly capable of looking after myself. It has been too long since I had a nursemaid—I must have learned how to improvise."

Commander Dillion faced Commander Jeshura and cleared his throat. "You were asking about Lucan, earlier. He shows remarkable promise on the training field—a natural fighter, and of considerate speech and mannerisms. I am told he hails from the Mirklands."

"Mirklands? Is he the son of a Count? Few from those swamplands even know how to read," Commander Jeshura spoke with surprise, successfully distracted from what could have quickly grown into irritable verbal sparring.

Garren took a breath. What was wrong with him? Why did he want to get a rise out of everyone around him? Was he so desperate for a fight, he would encourage one from within his own circles?

"His father was a scholar, I think," Commander Dillion continued.

"Perhaps I will speak with him," Commander Jeshura concluded. "Is he on the practice field now?"

Commander Dillion stepped aside to allow Commander Jeshura to leave the tower.

Garren straightened away from the wall and stepped forward to intercept the Commanders. "You are right, Commander," he addressed Commander Jeshura, "it could be useful to have a footman to keep order. I have been staying closer to camp these last few months, but I have little time to train a new recruit. Perhaps if you no longer have need for yours, I could see if he could manage the simple tasks I require."

Commander Jeshura's eyes narrowed, as if trying to determine what angle the Captain was playing. "I will give you my footman, Captain, as a gesture of respect. If you can make something of him, then I am all for it. Though I fear you will soon have a corpse to trouble over. And I will take on a new footman who is able to travel and tend to me as duty requires." He spread his hands, palms up, with a shrug.

"I have no need for a traveling footman, so that should not be a problem," Garren concluded calmly.

"I will see Lucan at the field. When I return to the First Division, I will send the ailing boy to your tent."

Chapter 90

Upon entering the palace, the King and the Captain of the Guard moved one way through a large door to the right of the great stone entryway. Ora found herself handed off to a servant, and escorted up a spiraling staircase to the left that led to upper rooms for the royals and noble guests.

Guards stood stationed outside doorways down a wide, grey stone hallway. Large blue and silver banners hung from the walls and ceiling high above their heads. The same pattern of seven stars was embroidered on the banners: six small stars with the seventh, largest star above them. Ornate, golden sconces supported lit torches that scattered the shadows and glimmered off the fine silver threads of the banner stars.

Ora stared, knowing her wide eyes openly expressed her awe for the splendor around her. She had never been in a building so large before. The hallway was taller than the wheat barn in Neice! A blue and silver runner ran the length of the hall.

She watched the guards as she passed, hurrying to keep up with the servant's quick strides. Dressed in padded brigandine armor in a dark-blue color, they kept their gazes on the far wall and never shifted—not even a twitch.

"Here you are, miss," the servant opened a door near the end of the hall for her. He stepped aside to let her pass into a room three times—no, four times—the size of her house in the Freelands. The grey stone ceiling rose twenty feet above their heads and tall, arched windows fitted with glass panes faced north and east. A great fireplace occupied the west wall, left of the door. Blue and silver banners, much like in the hallway, hung from the south wall, where a large bed sat near a giant wardrobe.

Before the fireplace—blazing with a warm, cheery fire—sat twin, high-back chairs with a small table between them.

From across the room, a wide-shouldered woman came toward Ora. "I am Dinah," she said in a deep, pleasant voice. "I have been assigned as your maid while you are here."

Ora heard the door to the room close behind her and knew the servant had departed.

Dinah glanced her up and down and made a soft *tsking* noise as she shook her head. "My first challenge awaits. I will call for a bath—*immediately*." She paused for effect. Ora glanced down at her archer's uniform, stained with dirt. Did she smell that bad? Who had time to wash with more than a splash of cold water on the battlefield? "Then we will see about getting you into some decent clothes. You would look like a boy if it were not for that long hair." She came closer and lightly touched Ora's braid as it hung in a dilapidated state over one shoulder. "I have some fragrant oils and spices that should fix this. You have pretty hair, if it would be tended properly."

Ora watched, speechless, as Dinah bustled over to the wardrobe and unhooked the doors to swing them open. The heavy wood creaked in protest before revealing the colorful splendor of several gowns inside. Dinah kept her back to Ora as she sorted through the hanging material. Ora moved closer to the fire, letting its warmth chase away the sudden lonely and uncertain chill from her skin.

A moment later, Dinah returned and held out a gown for Ora's inspection. Ora stared. She had never seen anything so lovely. The material shimmered like flecks of silver within blue so pale it was almost white. The gown slimmed toward the waist with a stiff bodice of tiny ocean pearls and silver thread, and buckled at the hips with a wide, dark leather band. Unlike the leather of a soldier's uniform, this was soft and smooth and inlaid with precious gems to match the gown, with a pure silver buckle and clasp so polished she could surely see her own reflection if she looked close enough. She reached out in wonder to touch the fabric and see if it were as soft to the touch as it appeared.

Dinah pulled it quickly out of her reach and made a *tsking* sound again. "Bath first," she insisted.

Ora resisted the urge to respond with a meek, 'Yes, ma'am.' Beneath Dinah's stern, unrelenting gaze, she dropped her hand and allowed the maid to lead her to the far corner of the room, beyond the bed. A freestanding, wooden folding wall concealed a large wooden wash tub, already filled with steaming hot water, and a washstand held various soaps and glass bottles of fragrant oils and spices.

Self-conscious, Ora undressed and stepped into the tub. Dinah made no comment about the scars criss-crossing her back, only a hesitant pause in scrubbing. Ora bit her lower lip and refused to explain the marks, embarrassed enough to have this woman helping her bathe.

After she had been washed and scrubbed until her skin shone bright pink from the effort, Dinah assisted her out of the tub and toweled her dry. The oils Dinah used on Ora's back soothed the more sensitive skin of the scars.

Dinah helped her into the new gown. The soft material caressed Ora's clean skin. She ran her fingers across the bodice that fit her frame snuggly and accentuated her feminine curves. Even while living in the Freelands, her gowns had never been so close-fitting. It made her self-consciously aware of the shape of her body and that she was no longer a little girl but a blossoming young woman.

"I—I cannot wear this," she whispered in sudden fear and uncertainty. She was not ready to acknowledge the woman. Inside, she shrank from the notion—wanting to hold on to the girl for a little while longer—wanting to return to the comfort and familiarity of the soldier she had become and the protective layers of her archer's uniform. She looked at her maid and wondered if the cause of her confusion and fear were obvious.

Dinah took Ora's hands and gently squeezed her fingers, standing before her, and gave her an encouraging smile. "You look just as a young woman should. The gown is perfect on you, miss. The King will be pleased with the transformation when he sees you at dinner."

Dinner. Ora felt her fingers grow cold, despite Dinah's hold. Would she be forced so soon to face these strange people?

Dinah released her to gather up Ora's discarded archer's uniform piece by piece, holding it away from her body as if touching it might infect her. Ora forgot her fears for a moment, watching her, and hid a smirk. Would she faint dead away to see the muddy hillsides of the battlefield?

Dinah moved toward the door.

Suddenly, Ora sobered. "Where are you taking those?"

"I will have a servant burn them," she answered, as if Ora should have known that.

"No," Ora commanded firmly. "They will be washed and returned to me at once."

Dinah raised an eyebrow at Ora. "Very well, miss."

Ora took a steadying breath as Dinah disappeared into the corridor. That uniform was now her only link to the life she'd known for months. She looked down at herself. *I do not want to forget who and what I am,* she silently insisted. Her stomach clenched and growled from hunger and the icy butterflies returned to her chest. It must be nearing dinner time.

Sure enough, when Dinah returned a few minutes later, she announced that dinner would soon be served and Ora was expected in the Great Hall with the royal family and the palace nobility.

Before stepping into the Hall, Ora reminded herself that she represented the King's Army and all her comrades-in-arms. *I will not be an embarrassment. I will not be afraid. I faced the For'bane at the front line and beyond. I can handle this.*

Chapter 91

Three days later, Garren stood against the shadowed wall inside Torr Guard, arms folded across his chest. He studied Commander Dillion's face as the Commander stood in the center of the room, leaning over the table, reading from the book open before him.

For long moments there was complete silence. Captain Mason paced behind the Commander, rubbing two fingers back and forth across his top lip in a clear sign of restless agitation. Garren stood still with solemn patience and complete stillness. Captain Mason had no practice in hiding his impatience and frustration, nor did he care to do so.

At last, the Commander lifted his head and stepped back from the table. "If this is to be believed. If this is true—," he began quietly.

Captain Mason interrupted: "This could start a whole new war—it could be disastrous!"

Still, Garren said nothing. They had the right to vent—to be given leave for initial reactions—without explanation or judgement.

Commander Dillion pressed his lips together. He tapped the journal's open page with two fingers. Always the calm and rational one. He looked at Garren with a keen eye. "Where did you find this?"

"I visited the Brothers Cathedral in Greavans and spoke with a Brother Keelon. He directed me to the archives of the Freelands."

"Those records were destroyed."

Garren's jaw flexed. "Many were taken and destroyed. Some were lost in the chaos of the War and the For'bane's invasion into the Starlands; the desolation of the Ancient cities. This journal was among the latter—smuggled out along the trade routes."

"And it has survived."

"Indeed. It was rumored to belong to a Freeland soldier. Now we know it belonged to one of Charles Binn's closest research assistant. It was another soldier who got hold of it and smuggled it out. I doubt anyone knew what it was. It was mixed in and lost with other records and books."

Captain Mason's brow furrowed. "We are in a war that we have been steadily losing for sixteen years," he insisted. "This evidence—," he waved to the journal with the sweep of one hand, "—could betray all we have stood for, all we have stood against. It could expose something more sinister than we can control. A beast greater than we imagined—a beast from within the very heart of us."

"And who should we trust? Who should we believe?" Commander Dillion added. "If those in Command are responsible, if they are to blame for all of this, why have they hidden this from us? Years of bloodshed and death—for what? What was it all for?"

"Sixteen years is a long time to bury a secret," Captain Mason said. He met Garren's eye. "A long time to forget."

Garren held his gaze steadily. A muscle in his jaw flexed. The gravity of his words were not lost on any in the room.

The half-Skay's words haunted him once more with perfect clarity, *'We are your brothers. Your blood calls to us and we answer it .... The beast in you knows. It will convince you with time.'*

Chapter 92

The King introduced Ora to his two younger sisters at dinner that first night: fourteen-year-old Princess Jacquetta and twelve-year-old Princess Ullysa. They were sweet girls, though somewhat spoiled by blood and circumstance. They took an immediate liking to Ora, and urged her to sit with them through their daily studies and to join them for walks in the spring gardens. Princess Jacquetta preferred visiting the stables and introduced the horses as if they were part of the family. The two Princesses gave Ora little chance to mourn her old life, or think about her past and the friends she had left.

Over the next several days, Ora felt herself going through the motions and feeling as if she were detached from her body. Her mind grew numb from lack of proper sleep, as her nights continued to be riddled with strange, disconnected dreams. Her days were filled with the slow boredom of keeping company with the ladies of the court: Walking the gardens, sewing, and gossiping about people and events Ora knew nothing about; watching the ladies flirt with the men and titter amongst themselves over the eligible bachelors of the palace.

To Ora, they all seemed ridiculous, dull, and pale. Nothing like the warriors—the men of sweat and toil and blood—that she was used to being surrounded by. She imagined each one fainting if ever challenged by the tip of a blade.

At meals, she picked through her food, pushing aside any fruit, meat, or delicacies she was unfamiliar with. She had never eaten like this before and did not have the slightest inclination to start now.

It sickened her to watch the others stuff their faces with sweets and pastries, and gorge themselves on so many different meats and delicacies. Did they not care that below the mountains their soldiers were starving? Did they not care that ten men fell to swords in pools of blood every time they called for another round of wine?

She felt the King watch her from his place at the raised head of the table and tried to ignore his pointed stare. The food tasted like ash in her mouth and she felt more listless than ever.

One afternoon, when Princess Jacquetta was out riding with a guardsman—as riding seemed to be her favorite sport—Ora sat in the royal women's day room with Princess Ullysa and her friend Meanah. They sat in relative silence for a time as Ora focused on the napkin-size tapestry she had been practicing embroidery on—and making a tangled mess of—enjoying the younger girls' company and chatter. Suddenly, Princess Ullysa spoke up from her spot on one of the lounging cushions across the room.

"Sing something for us, Orabelle. My brother says you have the voice of a woodland Mera, whatever that means. But his praise is rarely bestowed and he must like what he heard to have spoken so."

Ora looked at the Princess with confusion, trying to recall when the King could possibly have heard her sing. She rarely sang and never with the intention of others hearing. Then, after a moment, she realized he must have heard her when they made camp in the cliffs, the night Garren suddenly became distant and reserved.

She pushed away the troublesome thoughts. Thinking of Garren made her feel such a lonely wash of homesickness it nearly choked out her voice as she prepared to reply.

"I know very few songs. I am nothing like Lady Aballesk." Ora had never heard anything so lovely and accomplished as the woman who had enchanted the entire hall at last evening's dinner.

"Oh, but I have long heard that the Freelanders are known for their story-songs. Songs about brave men and battles and glorious adventures," pleaded the soft, airy voice of Meanah. Her eyes looked like stars, the lightest blue within pale skin, the kind of ivory skin ladies of the court would kill for, Ora supposed. Meanah's kind and thoughtful disposition was refreshing compared to the jealous, self-serving attitudes of the court ladies.

Ora pressed her lips together a moment in uncertainty. She loved these girls. She had thought love of any kind could never exist inside her after Carter died. She could not resist their hopeful expressions. "All right," she agreed, setting her tapestry down beside her. "There was a song the people in my village used to sing in the fields while they worked."

"Yes," Meanah urged. "Do sing it for us." She plopped down on one of the large floor cushions, facing the veranda where Ora sat on the bench in the doorway.

Light from the midmorning sun streamed in behind Ora and warmed her back. She shut her eyes, seeing in her mind's eye the waves of wheat in the sun and the people standing in a row with their sickles, old men and women, and even some children—the ones not yet taken to War or too sickly to fight. She saw a boy with a clubbed foot and a hunched shoulder, struggling to hold the sickle and cut the wheat in rhythm with the others. Worn faces. Tired faces. Faces darkened by the sun and filled with pain. Faces etched with determination. The song had a rhythmic beat to swing their sickles, to cut in harmony. Ora began humming to get that same rhythm and then sang:

River. River flowing.
Red is the sun. Red is the flower.
We are covered in the red tide. The crimson tide.

White is the sun. White is the field.
Bright white is the water flowing. River flowing.
We are covered in the white tide. The wintertide.

Mountains. Mountains falling.
Black is the sun. Black are the skies.
We are covered in the black tide. The storm tide.

Blue is the sun. Blue are the waters.
Deep blue is the earth falling. Mountains falling.
We are covered in the blue tide. The final tide.

Harvest. Harvest gathering.
Gold is the valley. Gold is the dawn.
We are covered in the gold tide. The living tide.

Ora opened her eyes in the silence that stretched as her voice fell away. Meanah's gaze was fixed on Ora with unspoken question and Princess Ullysa had tears in her eyes.

"Do you miss your home?" the Princess whispered.

Ora's lips parted, but only an empty breath came out in reply. She swallowed and movement in the hall outside caught her eye. But when she looked to the doorway, she saw no one. Still gazing at the doorway, she answered the Princess: "There is no one there for me now. There is no one who would know me." It was true. It seemed like another life. She felt like a completely different person. The War changed the course of her life so completely. She did not belong there any more than she belonged here in the palace. Her memories of that village seemed so peaceful and set-apart from the world she now knew. And everyone who had gone with her was dead now—or soon would be.

Would there ever again be a place where she belonged? Someplace other than a field of blood?

"Are you going to cry?" Meanah asked innocently, her voice somehow cutting through Ora's faraway thoughts.

"No," Ora said, her response coming automatically. She blinked and cleared her throat, looking back at the two girls. '*Tears are weakness ... You must never cry,*' Garren's words came to her. "No, I am not going to cry."

Princess Jacquetta entered the room suddenly. "That was beautiful, Orabelle," she commented. "You have a beautiful voice. Far more pleasant than Lady Aballesk, if you ask me." Before Ora could react, the Princess turned to her little sister and put her hands on her hips. "You have wrinkles in your skirts, Ullysa. Stand up before Mot sees you."

Princess Ullysa's eyes widened and she bobbed to her feet like a spring. "Mot is here?" she spoke, using the genteel pet form of Mother. "She has come back?" She nearly squealed with hopeful excitement.

Princess Jacquetta cracked a smile that made her deep green eyes light up. "Mot is coming, little sister. Brother just informed me of the guard that came ahead of her to announce her arrival."

Princess Ullysa grabbed Meanah's arm and pulled the other girl to her feet. "Mot is coming! Oh, Meanah, it is wonderful is it not?" she gushed.

Ora stared with some apprehension. She had heard about the Elder Queen, the King's mother, from the two Princesses. The Queen spent most of her time on the High Mountain, where her own private palace was located. She only visited her children when weather permitted or if some great event or matter needed her wisdom. Ora's heart beat with uncertainty at the thought of meeting the Queen, so regal a woman and a great beauty according to the rumors.

Princess Jacquetta's words caught Ora's attention: "Remember your training, Ullysa. You know I am the only one allowed to bounce about in such a wild, unrefined manner." And she winked at her sister, who giggled. "Mot will not be here for another few hours. Enough time to straighten those wrinkles and fix your hair. Up now, and go see your maid." Princess Jacquetta made a *tsking* noise as she herded her sister and Meanah out of the room.

Princess Jacquetta stopped in the doorway and turned to look at Ora, who still sat in the same place on the bench. "Do not make yourself uneasy, Orabelle. Mot will love you, I have complete confidence. I will leave you to rest. Your maid will of course dress you when it is time." With a smile, she breezed out the doorway and disappeared from sight, shutting the door behind her.

Chapter 93

A full moon shed light in the deep darkness of the valley. Commanders Dillion and Baire and Captain Mason stood with Garren and Gan, the alchemist, in a circle as they spoke quietly. Several troops of soldiers flanked them, gathered several paces back, awaiting orders for battle in tense silence. Among them were three other Singers.

"My scout reports movement here…and here," spoke Commander Baire, pointing to two locations on a map Commander Dillion held open between them.

Commander Dillion nodded. "I believe our troops can approach undetected—through this valley—and take down the nest before dawn's light."

Garren glanced at Commander Baire with steel in his grey eye. "The nest is far closer than it should be. How is it no one reported this before now? There are villages eight longs from here."

Captain Mason shook his head. "They continue to appear all about the territories between the Freelands and Asteriae Palace. As you know, For'bane do not stay long in one place."

"Which makes them difficult to keep track of," Commander Baire added. "But their move is a bold one. Never before have they settled so near the borders."

Garren stared at the map. He recalled how the young Rammer had come upon him and the recruits when he was bringing Ora to Torr Guard. Yes, it had been confused. But perhaps it had not wandered as far from the enemy's position as they assumed. He looked to the alchemist. "All right, Gan. Tell us about what you have been working on."

"Since speaking before the Council, prior to the King returning to Asteriae Palace, I have been attempting to increase the effectiveness of the substance Captain Garren used to infiltrate the nest and retrieve a captive archer in their hold." The tall man, his pale robes concealed in the darkness by a dark cloak, spoke in a low, even tone that only those in the circle could hear. Gan's gaze—black in the moonlight—moved to each man to be sure he had their undivided attention as he spoke. "This is an exploding powder that I hoped to develop some time ago, so it is not entirely stable or certain for success. It *must* make contact with open flame to react, and for your own safety, it should be thrown from a distance or broken by another force apart from your body, to avoid injury." He nodded to Captain Mason.

"Here. These are what you will be carrying." Captain Mason reached into the satchel at his side and extracted a corked, rounded clay vial, like what Garren used against the half-Skay to aid his and Ora's escape.

Gan took it and held it up for the officers to see. "I have increased the amount of the powder, and I have coated the vials with a flammable pitch." He handed it back to Captain Mason. "It will take several together to cause tunnel collapse. This part of the strategy is your foray, not mine. I leave the attack plans to your capable heads."

"The For'bane nests usually have one main entrance, with between one and three back entrances, depending on the size of the nest," Garren inserted. "From what Commander Baire's scout has determined, this nest has three entrances total. One main, and two back. There is a central tunnel leading down into the belly of the nest, with other tunnels branching off of this one. We must be certain to cover all exits, and bury the enemy inside like a tomb."

Commander Baire placed his index finger on the map. "Captain Mason, if you will lead a troop to take this entrance on the far side to stop the enemy trying to escape. Captain Garren will take the second. Commander Dillion and myself are prepared to lead the assault on the main entrance."

"When the main entrance has been infiltrated," Garren concluded, "we will bury the tunnels by collapsing all three entrances to deter other For'bane from re-nesting."

"Each of your troops needs to carry these," Gan said, "and position them well."

"We will use flaming arrows to ignite them," Garren instructed. "It is the best way to avoid injury to our soldiers. Get the vials into place, take out any For'bane that may present a threat or sound an alarm. A Singer will accompany each troop to assist. Then, get clear for the archers to fire their arrows. The explosions must be simultaneous. As long as we have enough, it should shake the rocks and dirt hard enough to cause a collapse."

"I suggest at least five vials per entrance must explode to have effect," Gan said.

This is the way they should have been fighting all along. Garren's muscles bunched with anticipation. "Thank you, Gan," he praised the alchemist.

The officers disbanded to their troops. Garren silently moved to separate his troop from the others and led them to the far side of the ridge, circling to the back entrance. The other troops took positions at the front, and he heard the soft shuffle of their movement.

Garren crept through the darkness on the ridge before the back entrance of the nest, where he and his troop would attack and flank the enemy, alongside Captain Mason and his troop.

Logan—one of the soldiers from Torr Guard who had worked with Garren on previous occasions—settled in beside him. Garren said nothing and they both watched the shadows of the troops moving through the night toward the For'bane nest. They moved more quickly and Garren motioned his troop to follow. Dawn was not long in coming. If they were successful here, a new day's victory would mark the beginning of the end, and the start of something new.

Chapter 94

Ora crossed over the threshold into her room late that evening to shadows cast by a fire burning in the hearth. She dismissed Dinah, who had been waiting at her door to help her change after dinner. Still fully dressed, she paused in the solitude of her room. She reached down and pulled off her evening slippers, kicking them away from her to let her bare toes sink into the thickness of the rug before the hearth.

Her mind was in a whirl with the evening's happenings. She ate very little—as usual—though there had been a bowl of sweet green apples at her place that she enjoyed. Hers had been the only place setting with apples. She had snuck a glance down the table to the King and caught the soft twinkle in his eyes as he looked back at her knowingly.

Coming here, I thought he would be as unfeeling as the cold winds coming off the High Mountain. I did not expect such kindness from him, Ora considered as she sank down wearily into the cushions of the chair before the fire. *But he is surprisingly thoughtful. And kind.*

The Elder Queen sat on the right side of the King during dinner and Ora saw she was indeed a woman of great beauty, despite the age lines around her mouth and at the outer corners of her eyes. Her hair was streaked with grey and drawn back at the sides, perfectly smooth within a jeweled hairnet. Her eyes were green like Princess Jacquetta's, only light and vibrant like emeralds and framed by thick dark lashes. She wore customary black mourning attire for her deceased husband. The dress was woven and trimmed with fine silver thread. She greeted those at the table with a regal tilt of her head and the slightest of polite smiles on pink rose-petal colored lips. Ora noticed she only spoke to her son, leaning toward him slightly so as to address him alone and no one else sitting near her.

She wondered all through the meal what brought the Queen from the High Mountain palace. Did the King ask her here for some important matter? Had she come because she missed her children and wanted to see them? She was gracious to the King, Princess Jacquetta, and Princess Ullysa, but certainly not overly enthusiastic or affectionate toward them.

Maybe that was just the genteel way. Perhaps royals did not carry deep affection or fondness for their relations.

Ora shut her eyes and leaned her head back against the chair headrest, suddenly too weary to rise and undress. Perhaps she should not have been so hasty sending Dinah away and let the maid assist her. Still, she did not think she would ever get used to having someone wait on her.

She feared she would grow soft living in such comfort and luxury. Her body ached in different ways now than on the battlefield. Her feet hurt when pinched in the heeled slippers. Her fingers hurt from spending too much time knitting and sewing. Her shoulders grew stiff sitting in one position for too long.

She missed the feel of the bow in her hands, the protective comfort of the weight of the quiver between her shoulder blades.

Unbidden, the words of the song she had sung that afternoon to the Princess Ulyssa and her companion Meanah came back to her, softly haunting her memory.

An overwhelming ache of homesickness returned, threatening to choke her, and she bit back a lonely sob. *I am not going to cry.* There was no use wishing for the past, for the time of her childhood—those moments of relative peace. How she missed Carter! The only light of goodness in this dark and evil world.

I am only tired. I always feel more emotional after a long day. Trying to uphold the standards and social etiquette of palace life sometimes seemed more draining than twelve hours stationed at the front lines. Her exhaustion claimed her before she knew it, and before she could gather the strength to stand and undress herself for bed.

In her dreams, the song drifted toward her from the darkness, a little girl's voice singing, strangely familiar. Sunlight, warm and golden, pierced the darkness and Ora found herself standing in a field of wheat ready for harvest with her village in the distance. Home.

The harvesters were before her, cutting down the wheat with the rhythmic sweep of their sickles. They were humming along to the song. Faces old and grave. Then she saw the girl that was singing. It was her mother. Though she had never seen any portraits of her mother as a girl—such were far too costly for poor farmers to consign—somehow she knew it was her mother. Her eyes were the same liquid gold that Ora had inherited. Her angelic smile lit her face as she sang, walking ahead of the harvesters, her small hands running over the swaying heads of grain.

SWISH! SWISH! rose the sound of the sickles.

I am home! Ora rejoiced. She ran forward to greet her mother.

But her mother stopped walking and became quite still, as if her feet were fastened to the earth.

Mountains. Mountains falling.

Black is the sun. Black are the skies.

We are covered in the black tide. The storm tide.

Thunder rumbled through the earth. The sun—warm and inviting moments before—vanished suddenly, replaced by dark storm clouds and flashes of lightning.

Ora looked to the sky in surprise, and at once collided with the line of harvesters, as she had been rushing toward her mother. Confused, Ora searched their faces as they stood suddenly in front of her mother, their sickles barring Ora's way like a fence between her and the village.

That was when she saw the blood on their faces. That was when her mother stopped singing and seemed to transform before her eyes into an adult, into the woman Ora had known. Blood stained her chest and her eyes dimmed.

"No! Mama!" Ora cried, trying to push through the line of harvesters. But they only looked at her with harsh faces, as if they did not know her or care. They would not let her pass. A fork of lightning ripped through the sky and struck her mother through the chest. Ora's lips parted in a scream that stuck in her throat, threatening to choke her.

The harvesters and her mother disappeared into the flash of light, and the field darkened to night as rain fell from the sky. The wheat beat down low to the ground in the onslaught that soaked Ora, turning her skin cold as ice, as she stood trembling. The village stood dark and abandoned in the distance, the houses blackened, crumbling shells of wood and pitch.

Out of the dusky light, a shape emerged, coming toward her from the village. Ora stuffed a hand against her lips to keep from crying with fear. She could not turn away and run. She had to see who came toward her.

"Belle." Garren's shape materialized from the darkness and stopped ahead of her.

With a cry of relief and trembling from the cold, Ora's feet grew unstuck and she ran for his arms. She was only a few feet from him, however, when the hum of the song returned and she stopped still. She saw Carter standing behind Garren, singing, his blond hair plastered to his forehead in the rain and his blue eyes bright in the shadows:

Blue is the sun. Blue are the waters.

Deep blue is the earth falling. Mountains falling....

"Do not make me do this, Belle." Garren's emotionless voice brought her gaze back to him. Her eyes widened and her breath caught in her throat. He held a bow, arrow drawn tight, aimed at her heart. His gaze gleamed with intention. His eyepatch could not disguise the glowing of his abnormal yellow eye.

"Captain, please. James, I need you," Ora burst with agony. Tears filled her eyes as she pled with him.

"Do not make me do this, Belle." He repeated the words without a change in expression.

"Carter?"

Carter continued to sing:

We are covered in the blue tide. The final tide.

Lightning flickered on the horizon behind them.

"James. Please."

Garren released the arrow.

She felt the arrow strike, felt the pain pierce her body. She grabbed for the shaft as she stumbled. She looked up at Garren as he stood suddenly above her. "I love you," she whispered with betrayal and pleading, tears dripping down her cheeks.

"I told you tears are weakness."

Ora awoke screaming. Her arms flailed in search of a weapon, for something tangible to grasp hold of. She knocked over the glass and pitcher sitting on the stand beside her chair, and both crashed loudly to the stone floor.

As she tried to rise, sobbing and disoriented, she tripped on the hem of her dress and fell, palms out to catch her fall, only to slice her palm open on a shard of glass. She remained in a crumpled heap on the floor in front of her chair, the dwindling ashes in the fireplace offering no warmth.

The door to her room was thrown open, but Ora could not stop crying. The pain in her heart was still sharp, as if the arrow in her dreams had truly pierced her there. She held her injured hand to her chest, unaware of the blood smudging the bodice of her cream-colored dinner gown.

She was startled to suddenly find the room filled with concerned faces. Two guards flanked the doorway, looking on from the threshold, while she noticed Princess Jacquetta and Princess Ullysa. She started when the King knelt in front of her suddenly, ordering the guards to fetch fresh water and wraps in a voice sharper than she had ever heard him use. He had never been near her chambers before. She met his blue gaze—gentle and full of concern—as he bent on one knee in front of her. He tugged her forward into his arms and held her, gently rubbing her back.

Overcome with a feeling of loss and confusion, Ora cried her heartbreak into his shoulder.

Chapter 95

Her agony hit him in a rush, nearly knocking the air from Garren's lungs as it slammed into his chest. He gasped, already winded and breathless from constant battle. All night they had been combining their efforts—Singer and common soldier alike—to flush out and eliminate the nest of For'bane before they could prove a threat to the nearby villages of the Freelands.

He turned toward the unknown distance where she was; the endless woods and hills and valleys separating them. It was too far to even see the palace on the horizon, and yet he felt her emotion and presence as if she were breathing in the space beside him.

Belle.

He turned suddenly to find himself inches away from a yellow-eyed Skay. The creature's eyes widened and it grunted in surprise and pain. Garren shoved it away, pulling his blade from its gut as it crumpled to the ground amidst the blanket of fallen For'bane all around him.

'You have left me,' Ora's emotion accused him. *'You have abandoned me to this empty darkness and I cannot find my way out.'*

Garren breathed sharply between clenched teeth. *No, Belle—***dodiy**[24]*—I have not abandoned you!*

A familiar, bitter scent of fear touched his nerves. She believed he had accepted the monster in him and turned away from the man she had come to trust.

It nearly killed him to realize that. He dropped to one knee with sudden weakness, burying the tip of his blade in the blood-soaked and body-torn earth. Leaning upon the hilt, he turned his face to the sky as a shaft of dawn's sunlight broke through the grey clouds and smoke. As the light fell across his head, he opened his chapped lips and released an angry cry to the sky.

---

24 Dodiy : Ancient Tongue meaning "my beloved"

Chapter 96

The King stood aside as a healer cleansed and wrapped Ora's hand. He looked on silently, standing near the open door of her chambers. Ora felt his gaze but refused to look at him. She knew the shoulder of his tunic was splotchy and wet from her tears, yet he had not complained once nor urged her to contain her emotion. She did not explain her tears or the nightmare.

Princess Jacquetta wrapped a blanket around her shoulders without a word, and—after catching her brother's gaze—dismissed herself and her younger sister with a soft smile of encouragement to Ora.

Princess Ullysa protested, wanting to know what was wrong, but her sister shushed her and steered her out of the room as the healer arrived. Only the healer and the King stood in the room with her as the glow of dawn framed the windows of her chambers.

"Give her something for the pain," the King instructed quietly.

At last, Ora looked at him. His blue eyes were shadowed, but at her look, he quirked a hint of a smile, as if to encourage her that all would be well and not to be distressed or embarrassed.

The healer gave her a small draught—and as she took it, she could not help thinking that the greatest pain was the one that was lodged in her heart. And no amount of draught would take that away. While the King had offered her comfort, his arms did not feel the same as Garren's arms.

Her gaze flickered away to the bandaging around her hand, and she picked at a loose thread near her thumb absentmindedly as the healer rose and prepared to leave. He paused at the door to wait as the King spoke, addressing Ora: "Would you join me in the Great Library? Once you have gathered your strength and your maid has attended you?"

Ora nodded. "Yes, Your Majesty," she managed.

The King nodded, then departed with the healer.

Presently, Dinah arrived. "Let me help you, my lady," she urged and unfastened the ties at the back of Ora's dinner gown. She held it open as Ora stepped out of it, balancing herself with an arm against the back of the chair. "Well, your undergarments do not seem to be damaged," Dinah noted, rubbing a hand over the drops of dried blood on the dinner gown. "Stand here and I will get you a new gown."

Ora clutched the top of the chemise at her chest. She stared into the freshly stoked fire. "Have you ever been in love?"

Dinah pulled a new gown from the wardrobe and turned to retrace her steps to Ora. "Why do you ask, miss? Has someone caught your eye—or has someone taken a fancy to you?"

Ora bit her lower lip. "I see the women here…I see how they behave around the men, and it confuses me. They like to draw attention to themselves and show off their bodies to draw the men's attention. They seem to like when a man touches them. They seem to like making men jealous of them by turning their attentions to other men, and then back again." She looked at Dinah. "Is this what love is? I have always been afraid to let a man touch me. I would never dream of letting anyone come near me. To have a man show interest in me…." She felt a shiver race along the fine hairs of her arms.

Dinah lowered the new gown to the floor. "Step in, miss," she encouraged. Ora obeyed and Dinah drew it up over her shoulders and began fastening it down the back. The maid sighed softly. "I would not call that love, miss. I would call what they do games. I have always believed that love is something precious—costly—and not a cheap trinket to be purchased, sold, or traded. Love is a sacrifice of one's own wishes and desires to seek the better of another. A man's touch, a man's kiss, is like the joining of two souls—something powerful enough to reach into a secret place in a woman's heart. It should not be unlocked by any man, only to a man worthy of it."

"And who is a worthy man?" Ora urged curiously. Garren's face impressed itself upon her mind, only adding to her confusion. "How do you know him, if he comes?"

Dinah turned Ora to face her, straightening and smoothing Ora's hair with skillful fingers. She paused to meet Ora's gaze. "Love as it should be is nothing to fear. I would rely on Creator's definition, as quoted from the Book of the Name[25]." With a soft reverence, each word spoken with Ancient Tongue lilt, and an almost sing-song cadence, she quoted: "**Come and discover, all that Love has done. It has brought us back. It has turned darkness away and rekindled the Light. See this Love? It guards on**

---

[25] Book of the Name : one of the Three Books of the Chronicles of Asteriae

the left, and on the right. It stands afore and ahind[26]. It will always be in confidence, through unquenchable fires and the breaking of bones and bleeding of wounds. Wait, be true, and it will find you. It cannot give up, it cannot falter; it will not wound, nor steal, nor kill. It is never-dying and stands without fear."

A tremble passed through Ora's limbs. She inched nearer to the fire, believing a chill in the room was affecting her. "I thought I loved someone once. But he died. I feel so much older now, though it has only been a few months, and those feelings seem so distant and faded. Now, I am not really certain what it was I felt. Or if it is meant to be more than a feeling, then perhaps I only wanted to hold on to something that was already gone or never truly was."

Dinah stepped back to look at her work. "Perfect. All you need is a smile to offset those pale cheeks." She nodded once. "I would not concern yourself with the noblewomen, miss. I think you wiser than they may ever be. You will know love when you find it. The War has claimed many lives, yet do not despair, there are still plenty of good men left in the kingdom. Now, the King is waiting for you and I must not delay you any longer with my prattling."

Ora withheld a sigh.

When she arrived at the Great Library, the King waited for her and approached to greet her. He lifted her hand to his lips for a light kiss across her fingers before releasing her. "I am sorry you were in such distress earlier," he spoke sincerely. "I do not like to see you hurting. I would not wish it for all the world."

Ora stared at him a moment. The words he spoke and the way the light hit his blue eyes as it streamed in the tall narrow windows—he could have been Carter. If Carter had

---

[26] Ahind: behind

been older. If he had not been a poor village boy. If he had not been killed by the experiments.

The King looked at her strangely, with question.

"You reminded me of someone just now," Ora confessed in a whisper. "Someone I…lost in the War." A tinge of bitter regret touched her final words.

He startled her by placing a finger beneath her chin to lift her face. Her skin felt a warm shock at the gentle comfort of his touch and she caught her breath, suddenly wary as she obeyed his silent command to meet his gaze. He dropped his hand with a slight smile of apology tipping up one corner of his mouth. "My dear lady," he said, serious again. "I feel for your loss, for all that the War has put you through."

Ora took a step back. "Mere sympathy will not save us from slaughter, Your Majesty. Words hold little weight to the Freelanders. We are tired of words." They were alone, which somehow emboldened her to speak her heart. "While you enjoy comfort and prosperity, your people are dying by the day. I thought you came to the Freelands, to the First Division, because you desired to have your eyes opened to the truth. But since then, what has been done to change anything? Will you let my friend's death be for nothing?"

The King studied her with a reserved expression, his thoughts well veiled while he listened to her. "Come with me," he said abruptly, though not unkindly. He never raised his voice and was rarely sharp or harsh, no matter to whom he was speaking. He offered her the crook of his arm. She knew it would be a cruel insult to refuse, so she slipped her fingers into the bend of his elbow and allowed him to escort her across the room to a side door.

A glance about the room showed they had entered a war room—one of several in the palace used for meetings, council sessions, and strategies. Three walls were covered with bookshelves, the fourth with tall windows, and a lone, eight-candled chandelier hung from the ceiling over a large, square wooden table in the center of the room.

The King led her to the table where a map was nailed to the surface. Ora looked at it in amazement. She had never seen a map of their lands before. Her eyes drank in the inked lines that marked territories and shaped the coasts of the seas. The distance between the Highlands and the Freelands seemed so vast, even on parchment.

The King kept silent for a few minutes, letting her look everything over. "Do you see the coastline, here? The inlet is called Trader's Cove. It is home to the finest sea vessels of the region and brings in everything from silks and silver to food and supplies. Foreign trade with the islands to the West makes up seventy percent of our goods."

She followed his hand as his fingers traced out the cove on the map west of Asteriae Palace. "And this trade is instigated by the IV Seatraders Guild."

The King glanced at her with surprised approval. "Not all. But the IV Seatraders Guild is the largest, and accounts for a great deal of our goods."

"And they are leased by the Counts of the region."

"How do you know all of this? I confess I still have trouble wrapping my mind around the politics."

Ora felt her face heat. "I—uh. I cannot help but overhear Princess Ullysa's lessons each day. I must occupy my mind somehow, if all I am to do is sit and mend and stitch tapestries."

The King smiled. "No need to be defensive. I think I would go mad too, sitting around all day sewing. Especially for one used to a soldier's life."

Ora felt her lungs—suddenly tight—ease with his words.

The King sighed. "Trade is a complex thing. It is want and demand. If we are in short supply of silk, there is a rise in prices and suddenly silk is a rare commodity that cannot be bought for a decent gold coin. While—say—wool is in overabundance and it is the middle of Summer. It is the same with weapons and tack. The War has stripped our supplies and a purse of gold could hardly purchase a single, worthy blade."

He turned to look at her as she continued to stare at the map. "People in the position to do so will always seek to make a profit off war. It might be an ugly, detestable thing, but that is the way commerce works. Even as King, I cannot control or prevent that."

"But, it is wrong," Ora blurted. "What good will it do to stand by and watch while we are dying? It is perverted and unjust!"

The King bowed his head to her. "How would *you* seek to resolve this?"

Ora caught her breath and looked at him quickly to see if he was mocking her. To see if he was simply indulging her need to vent. But he seemed in earnest as he looked at her, waiting for her answer, though he doubtless believed she would have no more of an answer than anyone else.

She looked at the map, thinking over what she had learned from Ullysa's lessons and what the King was explaining to her now. "Seek other means," she murmured. She looked at the King. "You are King. You can empower and employ whom you wish. If it is true that, given the chance, they will exploit you to satisfy their own greed, then why do you stand aside and let them? Surely another merchant guild—even a small one—would risk the wrath of a giant like the Seatraders if given the opportunity to expand its trade. Would it not? Or at the very least, the competition for goods might bring them down from their lofty places."

"How do you know such a game would work?"

"It is not a game. Though, I suppose some might see it that way. It is what we Freelanders call Free Trade. If you find a price you cannot afford, you seek another seller who can offer a better one."

Holding her gaze, he smiled slightly, and a look of admiration came to his eyes so clearly it made Ora want to squirm with discomfort beneath the weight of it. "And perhaps you make a wise and valid point. Perhaps the Seatraders are a little bloated in their purses for their own good. No one has ever dared to speak that way about them."

As if sensing her discomfort, he turned and withdrew, striding confidently to the high-arched and narrow windows to look out at the mountains. He spoke with his back to her: "I have sent a bird to the officers stationed at the line with an invitation for two of them to attend a ball I am hosting a sennight from this day." He turned from the windows and searched her face. "Captain Garren. He was your commanding officer at the time we met in the woods, was he not?"

Ora felt her heart lodge in her throat. *James.*

"I do not expect he will come. He seems to come and go as he pleases, with all his efforts in the War. Something of a lone wolf, though this was my first personal encounter with him. How long he has served, yet he keeps to himself. He puzzles me. But he is a Singer, and my advisors tell me the Singers are not to be understood…."

Ora hardly heard him, lost in her own thoughts. *He will come.* She did not know how she was sure he would, but she was. Perhaps it was only her desperate need to see him. And perhaps she was equally as terrified to see him come. Would he want to see her?

"It is these issues that I wish to discuss with the officers. To see if we can bring the War to an end."

"Do you have some reason to think that after sixteen years, the enemy will suddenly give up and surrender?" She meant to sound skeptical and she would not apologize for it.

The King studied her thoughtfully. "Do you really think that I do not care about the War? That I benefit from its continuance? That I sit here in the palace, ignorant and helpless in this tide of darkness?"

Ora caught her breath, unable to turn her gaze from his. Is that what she thought? Had she unknowingly accepted the criticisms of her friends on the battlefield, that the royals and the nobles were all greedy and self-serving?

The King did not match that description at all, though Ora could point out a number of nobles who did. Was he simply caught in the crossfire, trying to find a solution?

"I think—," Ora began slowly, "I think I have been unfair to you, and perhaps you are a better King than I gave you credit for." Ora lowered her gaze. "I am sorry if I misjudged you."

"Everyone gives judgement based on what they know," The King answered quietly. "I have advisors all around me, telling me what the War is and how it should go. But none of them have lived it. You have. If I would seek counsel from people like you, perhaps I would be a wiser King." He sighed. "I hope for your sake, Captain Garren is among the officers in attendance."

Surprised, Ora raised her gaze again to stare at him.

"I hope seeing a familiar face will ease your distress. And the Captain seems to hold your every confidence."

Chapter 97

Weary, as dawn fell across a body-strewn battlefield, Garren gazed across the valley and let the morning breeze cool sweat from his brow, as the fringe of his short dark hair stuck to his forehead. He gripped his bow at his side and rubbed his free hand across his mouth, feeling the bristles forming across his jaw and above his upper lip.

"Another nest destroyed," spoke Commander Dillion as he picked his way to Garren's side and followed Garren's gaze across the landscape to the distant mountains.

Garren felt his friend's unspoken question and quickly turned his gaze away from the mountains to stoop and pluck an arrow from the For'bane body at his feet. He would not let the Commander realize his distress or question him concerning Ora. "We should take whatever supplies we can find and move on from here." He paused to search for his footman, Thane. The boy was helping gather weapons and arrows from the fallen bodies a short distance away. Even with better meals and a sheltered place to sleep each night, the boy was still entirely too frail.

"You should rest. You have been up nearly forty-eight hours straight," Commander Dillion commented.

"I am fine," Garren bit out. He stepped over a body and yanked out another arrow, collecting the bloody arrows in one hand, after slinging his bow over his shoulder. There were other footmen sweeping the field with swords to slay any For'bane that still lived among the fallen.

He felt the Commander's skepticism ripple through his senses. He ignored him and continued to search the field. The last thing he needed was sleep. He had not slept since Ora left. Whenever he tried, he was assaulted by dreams. Sometimes dreams of Ora, but mostly dreams filled with violence and anger; dreams in which Garren fought a constant battle that left him wearied and irritable when he woke. The headaches came more often—more severely than before—and he had increased his intake of the powder to keep the pain at bay.

He yearned more than ever for Ora's gentle touch to soothe his distress. He yearned for her confidence in him, that he would never succumb to the monster inside. Because right now, his faith was wavering. Especially after today. If Ora gave up on him—he would have nothing.

"You should see the healer," Commander Dillion's words brought Garren out of his self-destructive thoughts.

"I am uninjured," Garren said, plucking up another arrow.

"I was not referring to your physical state, Captain," the Commander said dryly. "I can see you have been affected by the archer's departure. If you did not wish her to go, why did you agree to it?"

"What would you have me do? The King wished it." Garren jammed the handful of retrieved arrows into a leather satchel he slung over his shoulder. He turned to look at the Commander at last. "Should I stand against the desire of my King? Besides, she is better off away from this place."

The Commander nodded slightly. "Still, how long since you checked in with a healer?"

"They do not know what to do with me. They do not understand the blood of the For'bane. I am the same as I have always been. Nothing has changed, Commander." Garren looked at Commander Dillion steadily. "All they ever give me is the powder. It is all they have ever had to aid me." He glanced across to the mountains again with a quiet sigh. "I weary of the War, is all."

"As do we all...," the Commander murmured in agreement. "If we are to address the Council concerning the experiments, it should be done soon."

"I hope to at the next session."

"And the King?"

"He listens to the advisors, and until we can determine who has his ear, I would prefer to consider our options and tread carefully."

Commander Dillion took a breath as if to speak, but was interrupted by a shout from somewhere behind them.

Both men turned to see a footman on horseback picking his way toward them around the bodies. He stopped the horse beside the Commander, who patted the bay's sweat-dotted neck and looked up at the footman. "What is it?"

"Commander. Captain," the footman greeted. "You have been asked to return to the First Division. A bird has arrived from the King."

Chapter 98

The next seven days were filled with activity. The palace kitchens baked and cooked night and day, wafting delicious aromas of pastries, cakes, fruit tarts, sweet breads, and more through the halls. Ora felt caught in a whirlwind storm of dresses and jewelry. The Princesses were fitted for new gowns, and mountains of fabric were paraded through the living chambers by a line of servants.

Ora stood to the side, wishing she could melt into the walls. This display of frivolous wealth reminded her of what the King told her about trade and commerce, and the greed of wealthy Counts and nobles who controlled the tide for their own power and gain. There were plenty of material and luxury goods to be found, for a price. Somehow the needs of the War, the safety and survival of the soldiers on the battlefield…those were not to be found. Would anyone be so greedy as to stand aside and watch thousands die just to control trade? And how far did it spread? From the traders, to the Counts, nobles, sailors…. Could the officers also be making a profit on the losing War? The thought turned her stomach.

Garren would not have anything to do with something so sickening, would he? She felt a wash of guilt that the thought even formed in her head. She had always believed him different than the others. He was a man who had risen to his station without the benefit of wealth. A man whose desire to end the For'bane and determination to the point of self-recklessness spoke for him. She had seen the haunting in his eyes—for all he had suffered trying to end the War. She had seen his sacrifices—the evidence marked his face and the scars ran deep into his heart.

Thoughts of him brought back an overwhelming ache and remembrance of the dream—creating a nervous mix of fear and longing—to possibly see him again and wonder how he would react to the sight of her. How different she would look to him in a ball gown instead of her dirt-crusted uniform. To see him again would surely wipe away all vestiges of the nightmare.

With that hope to steady her, she stood patiently while the dressmakers and her maid worked tirelessly to fashion her a gown day after day.

Without a mirror to see the progression, she could only look down at herself as yards of fabric were draped, pinned and tucked about her. Even her slippers were being created with an ivory cream satin, and a deep gold ribbon to match her gown.

At last, the head dressmaker instructed her to look in the mirror. Ora stared at her full length reflection with wide eyes at the finished gown.

The ballgown was deep golden yellow, like harvest-ready wheat, shimmering with golden flecks whenever she moved. It reminded her of the fields of wheat at her home in the Freelands, in the glow of sunlight on a fine autumn day, like in the song she had sung for Princess Ullysa and her friend Meanah. A field promising a golden harvest.

The color enhanced the soft sun-kissed skin of her face, arms and bared shoulders. A sash of golden-cream crossed over her breasts and wrapped around over her arms to the back, serving as off-the-shoulder sleeves. And the flecks of gold in the gown falling to her ankles brought out the gold in her hair and eyes.

She was told the King ordered the color especially for her gown. How did he know this shade would be perfect for her?

While she was staring in the mirror's reflection, trying to overcome her surprise at the transformation, the doors burst open to admit Princess Ullysa. The young Princess flew across the room to the open windows, her skirts billowing out behind her. "The first of the guests are arriving!" she burst with child-like glee.

"Do not speak so loudly, Ullysa," Princess Jacquetta scolded calmly, following her sister into the room and to the windows. "They will hear you…." She sent Ora a smile of greeting.

"Nonsense," Princess Ullysa insisted. "It is much too far. They cannot even see us up here." As if to prove it, the young Princess leaned head and shoulders out the window to peer down at the procession far below making their way to the front gates of the inner courtyard.

Princess Jacquetta followed her sister's example. "Anyone interesting yet?"

"Boring nobles," Princess Ullysa reported as Ora, unable to contain her own curiosity, moved to join them. "Ooh! And that pompous Count from the last time—what was his name? Who stepped on your foot and nearly broke your toes?"

"Where?" Princess Jacquetta urged.

Her sister pointed down toward the front of the procession. Ora could make out their forms even from the great distance. The one in question was large and rotund, with a balding fringe of grey hair circling his head. He rode with a contingent of look-alike guards around him, the front guard carrying a blue banner with the Count's crest emblazoned upon it. Ora could not make it out.

"I thought he would be dead by now," Princess Jacquetta said with a resigned hint of frustration.

"He is determined to catch your eye. How many times has he approached our brother to ask for your hand?"

"Never you mind. Just let the King continue to refuse him. I want never to suffer his presence."

"You will most likely have to endure it tonight at the ball," Princess Ullysa reminded her sister with a teasing smile.

Ora scanned the others in the procession. Her heart leapt with traitorous confusion almost before her gaze picked him out of the crowd.

Garren.... James.

Even from the great distance, there was no mistaking him. He rode in the midst of the procession on his great black beast.

He had come. Just as she had known—hoped and dreaded—he would.

No sooner did her eyes find him, when he drew back on the reins and looked up toward her window. Her heart jumped to her throat and she caught her breath. He could not possibly see her from this height, with all the many towers and walls and windows that there were. And yet, she still felt his gaze seeking her out, as if he felt her eyes on him. Or could he feel the frantic uncertainty of her heart reaching out to his?

'I can feel your emotions, remember?' his words returned to her, whispering to her: *'I have grown accustomed to ignoring it, but with you—with you I cannot.'*

His strange emotional connection to her had been a cause of discomfort before. Now, somehow, the thought he might still carry that connection made her feel less alone. Perhaps his sending her away had not completely severed that.

Would he want to see her? Or would he ignore her?

A moment later, Garren resumed his forward movement along with the procession and she lost sight of him—uncertain questions tangling around her heart—as he passed beneath the walls surrounding the palace.

Ora drew back from the windows while the Princesses remained, unaware of Ora's sudden distress or of her retreat.

Ora placed a hand against her breast—she could feel the thunder of her heartbeat through the material of her gown. *What is wrong with me?* she wondered.

Several hours later, as evening fell, she was still asking herself that same question as she followed the Princesses into the grand ballroom. Her gaze searched the crowds for Captain Garren.

Chapter 99

Rich golden light filled the ballroom, radiating from twenty giant, polished-brass chandeliers hung high in the vaulted ceiling. The crowds were thick with palace guards and servants moving back and forth, Counts and nobles, journeymen and Masters, huntsmen and tradesmen, Commanders and Captains. Of the officers present, Garren and Commander Jeshura were the only ones active in the War.

He silently observed the retired Commanders and Captains, notable by the insignia and color of their dress jackets. Though having served longer than the other active officers at fifteen years, Garren had no plans to retire into a life of luxury and ease. Where would he go to find peace while the War was still being fought over his homeland—with the war waging in his own blood? He was still young enough to remain active, at nearly thirty-three.

Most of those retired officers showed their age, with faded hair of silver or white and lines deepening their faces. Some carried the visible marks of war—a missing arm; scars on their faces; a noticeable limp—which said more than any badge or ribbon sewn to their uniforms. They had given a part of themselves for Asteriae.

Still, others used their wealth to rise above the rest and keep out of harm's way. They also wore insignias and ribbons on their uniforms, but to Garren it meant far less. They were the observers standing behind the lines, watching from their safe towers; they retired amidst the shower of fame their title had given them. Their honor did not extend past the threads that bound the ribbons to their clothing.

"This will be us in a few years," Commander Jeshura spoke as he stepped away from the refreshment table to join Garren at the sidelines of the great room. The Commander held a crystal goblet of new wine and swirled the deep golden liquid distractedly as he took in the room, especially the women in brightly colored gowns mingling among the crowd.

Garren kept his gaze on the room even as he responded with quiet disinterest to the Commander. "If High Collar[27] is what you aspire to."

Commander Jeshura laughed. "I take it you do not. Maybe you have been on the battlefield too long, Captain, and you do not know how to enjoy the comforts and finery that High Collar offers to men like us." He eyed Garren with thinly veiled amusement. "Have a drink, Captain. Enjoy it while it is here."

Garren refused to reveal his disgust. "It is not to my taste," he said instead. He knew the Commander was not just referencing the juice, but the company. Men of rank could enjoy the attention of any woman present, be they married or single, with very little effort. Garren had no interest in their company. Only one held his heart. Only one knew him and accepted him for who he was, not what insignia was sewn to his jacket.

---

[27] High Collar : a term applied to the luxury class life, because of the high collar on the dress jacket uniforms those in rank wear in society.

Though his gaze searched the room for her, she had yet to make an appearance. Amidst so much commotion in the crowded room, his heightened senses could not find her either.

He had felt her earlier. Had it been hesitation that touched his senses? Hope mixed with fear? He could not know until he saw her. He told himself he only needed to see that she was well and whole. That would be enough. He did not need her acceptance, he did not even need for her to see him. If he could only catch a glimpse of her, then he would know and be satisfied.

"Commander Jeshura! Captain Garren, is it?"

Garren jerked his attention away from the doorway across the ballroom to the rotund man shuffling toward them, his drink splashing out of his too-filled goblet and his face red from exertion. Garren recognized him as Count Rugent, who had led the procession to the palace and spoken in the King's Council hours ago. A tall young man in a steel-grey dress jacket with a braided leather cord attached to his breast pocket lapel followed at the Count's elbow.

The Count stopped before them and placed a beefy hand over his chest as if to help him catch his breath. "I am Count Rugent." He angled slightly toward the room. "I am most impressed with your progress in the War. This explosive powder that your alchemist developed—what was his name, again?"

"Gan," Garren inserted quietly, watching the Count with secret caution.

"That is the man," the Count tossed back the contents of his glass into his mouth and swallowed, the action followed by a quiet burp. "Truly a brilliant man, if something so simple could aid you in the War effort."

"Yes. It is a shame you did not discover his brilliance long ago," Commander Jeshura eyed the Count, apparently as unimpressed as Garren with the red-faced man. "Its development would surely be the envy of the farthest lands."

Careful, Garren silently cautioned the Commander, sensing his attempt to goad the Count. Count Rugent held a great deal of power over the shipping industry, as a holder of sixty percent of the Guild that provided trade. He came as its representative, filled with smooth words for his King about his struggle to provide for the War effort and all the difficulties of the sea and the many, unending costs of keeping the ships and sailors in order. He hinted at the greed of the Four Islands and her people, but, after searching the Count's emotions and not liking the darkness he felt there, Garren believed Count Rugent only meant to deflect blame and suspicion from himself.

Count Rugent's interest in Gan's powder had nothing to do with destroying the For'bane.

The Count's jaw ticked with irritation, but instead of responding to Commander Jeshura's comment he motioned to the man in steel-grey uniform. "This is Master[28] Jariel Easton, of the IV Seatraders Guild." Even as he introduced the man standing silently beside him, the Count's gaze slid past the group to observe Princess Jacquetta, standing on the dais beside the Elder Queen.

Garren did not miss the greedy lust that lit the Count's eyes as he beheld her. His dislike for the gluttonous man deepened further still. Yet, he kept his expression firmly neutral as he focused on the younger man whose introduction had just been so half-heartedly made.

"What is it like to be so far inland?" Garren questioned. "I am told you men of the sea cannot abide the earth beneath your feet."

---

28 Master : the rank of a sea captain, who leases the command of a ship under the ownership and authority of a Count

"I admit it," Master Easton spoke with a grin. "I have just returned from three months in wintertide, some of the roughest seas of the season. Keeps a man at his wits, or out of them in some cases. Yet, I know my way through the ice caps with more confidence than this sea of people."

Garren nodded briefly in understanding. He felt that way about the battlefield. He would rather be back at the front lines, surrounded by the familiar. There was far less pretense. Still, he could not give up the opportunity to see his Belle.

She is not yours, came the inward nagging that sparked a twinge of possessive irritation. *And you made sure of that by sending her away with the King.*

The intense emotion he had felt from her on the battlefield just days ago clung to his heart like a damp fog, souring his mood though he tried to ignore it.

The first notes of the orchestra on a raised platform at the far end of the room drew his attention. He was glad for the distraction as the Master, Count, and Commander also turned to observe the musicians.

As was customary for palace balls, the musicians wore elaborately painted masks to disguise their faces. Once, the head musician had worn a complete headdress in the shape of an elephant, those giants from the Arid North. Few Asteriaens had ever seen one, and the depiction of one had created quite a stir.

The King had chosen a very small orchestra for this ball. Three background musicians remained seated, and wore masks painted half black and half silver. The head musician was a woman in a many-layered gown of pale green and blue that shimmered like water whenever she moved. She wore an aqua-green mask that covered her upper face, but left her lips showing, as she stood at the front of the platform with a violin. Her first few lingering notes were a call for the King to start the first dance.

That was when Garren felt her presence. He turned his head to find her and stared. He felt his lips part as if to say her name, but nothing came out. She would not have heard him anyway, there were too many people between where he stood and where she was. She had not seen him.

Pain pierced his head with such intensity that he turned abruptly away from the men standing with him, and moved quickly to a shadowed pillar apart from the other guests. *Not now. Creator, help me.* He took a deep breath, willing the pain to abate. A moment later it did.

He searched Ora out once more. She was beautiful. She looked like the warm sunrise over the Freelands in her golden-yellow gown. Her skin glowed with warmth and health. Her hair was bound in golden waves atop her head, accentuating the graceful curve of her slim neck.

An acute pain pulsed in his chest. He had known her beauty even in the blood and filth of the battlefield, and to see it so unblemished, enhanced, and put on display took his breath away.

He did not want anyone else to see what he had seen. How could any man love her as he would love her, if only given the chance?

As he watched her, the King stopped in front of her and offered her his hand with a quiet word that Garren could not decipher through the commotion of the room.

The King had chosen her, a commoner, from a room full of eligible and appropriate women to partner with him in a first dance.

It felt like the day he watched the Envoy take her away from him. It felt like he had lost her all over again.

Chapter 100

She had hardly entered the room when the King approached her. She had not had a chance to look about the room. The violinist carried the music for the opening dance, as the King led Ora into the middle of the room and the crowds cleared the floor to stand along the sidelines. His hand was warm beneath hers as he kept his arm steady and straight. He guided her to stand before the violinist and angled to face her, standing at arm's length.

With only a few dancing lessons for experience, Ora faced the King with nervous uncertainty. Though standing an arm's length apart, she still felt too close. She felt every eye was watching her; scrutinizing her from head to toe. Was Garren among them? The thought of his deep grey gaze following her made her tremble. She must not think of him.

The first steps were the easiest: Move toward her partner —the King—turn, and then retreat without touching. Then, she stood still while the King moved forward, then back.

She kept her gaze on his, which held her own with both encouragement and soft amusement.

He stood still while she moved toward him and back, listening to the cues of the music.

Then, they both moved forward to touch for the first time. The King raised his hands between them and she lifted hers to meet, palm to palm, lightly touching. "You are doing well," he said quietly, for her ears alone.

"I hardly know what I am doing," Ora confessed.

They moved in a circle opposite each other, keeping their palms together.

"These dances are mostly the same, with slight variations to match the theme of the music. All you need are the basic steps and a knowledge of music. You seem to come by that quite naturally."

They circled once more, then she followed his cue as they each stepped back again. He moved in one direction around her and raised one hand as he came full circle to stand by her shoulder. She raised her hand to meet his, palm to palm, and they turned once more in equal motion.

Other couples were joining them.

The King flashed his boyish grin at her. "Relax. Enjoy yourself," he whispered. His gaze circled her face as he stepped closer to her. His hand settled lightly at her waist to guide her sideways then turn her in another circle.

Ora felt herself relax slightly and felt a small smile lift her lips. His blue eyes danced with approval.

That was when she saw him, standing against the far wall opposite her near the shadow of one of the giant pillars. No sooner did she catch his direct grey eye watching her, when the dance separated her from the King once more and she turned to move in a wide loop. She forced her mind to the movement so she would not collide with the other dancers, while her heart suddenly began thundering in her chest with wild abandon. *What is wrong with me?* She fought for breath, feeling dizzy.

Suddenly, the King was in front of her again. Their hands touched as he guided her into a gentle spin, then brought her back in front of him as the music quickened their rhythm slightly. But her gaze could no longer focus on him, as she immediately sought for that shadowed pillar almost without conscious thought.

"Your Captain seems intent on you," the King's voice broke through her concentration and she startled a little as she looked into his soft blue gaze. Had he seen Garren watching them dance? "Do you suppose he recognizes you?"

"I am not so different. I am the same." At least, she hoped she was. She did not want this life to change her.

"You hardly look the soldier tonight," the King insisted, not understanding. "May I be the first to compliment you?"

"Th—thank you," Ora managed. Her throat suddenly went dry. She nearly missed a step, and flushed as the King reached out to intercept her error and correct her. The motion was so fluid, she doubted anyone else noticed her near mistake.

The dance was ending. The violin played a final, sweeping note that lingered in the air. The dancers separated. The men bowed and the women gave a low, graceful curtsey.

"I will surrender you to another partner. But promise me another dance before the night is over."

She hardly had the chance to open her mouth and respond before he stepped away. She raised herself from her curtsey and caught her breath. Garren's form approaching filled her vision as he came to stand before her.

He wore dark breeches and a dark-blue dress jacket with a high, stiff collar, trimmed in gold braiding. When he stood before her, she saw three insignias and a number of ribbons sewn to the dark cloth. His face was freshly shaven, accentuating the firm angular line of his jaw. His dark hair was washed and combed. His dark leather eyepatch covered his discolored eye, but the intensity of his grey eye held her attention.

Her lips formed his name, but nothing came out. She stood, feeling very much exposed with her bare shoulders and arms and her bound hair.

The music for the next dance began.

"Will you dance with me?" his voice rumbled through her senses.

"Yes, Captain," Ora whispered, finding her voice at last. She stood still as he stepped forward, holding her gaze, and placed a hand lightly at her waist. She told herself to breathe as he guided her back into line amidst the other dancers.

The warmth of his hand soaked through the silk material of her gown to her skin. A moment later his hand left her side as he stepped back to face her for the start of the dance.

Chapter 101

Having her in his arms was like holding a piece of heaven. It could not last—it would not remain with him for more than a fleeting moment—and yet it was what he had longed for all evening. He could not bear to watch her in the arms of the King, smiling into his face, her hands and her steps moving with trust and certainty under his guidance.

This dance was longer than the first—a simple introduction to the evening—its melody more haunting and intimate; with slower motion and grace. It brought her closer to him, and as he turned her in the circle of his arms and their hands came together, he felt her uncertainty and the way her heart rushed erratically whenever he came near her and whenever he touched her. She was no longer smiling, and she hardly looked at him.

When the dance brought them together again and his hand took hold of hers, his fingers inadvertently tightened around hers. Her gaze lifted to his in startled surprise. "Are you still angry with me?" he asked, his voice more gruff than he intended.

She searched his gaze. "I am here, and the War goes on without me. I am far away from everything I know and everything I have ever loved." There was no hostility in her words, and yet he sensed her pain. She looked away again and he felt her tremble. He wanted suddenly to take her into his arms and still her fears, but the dance took them away from each other again.

He clenched his jaw and a muscle flexed in his cheek. Ora turned to face him again. "How is your head?" she questioned suddenly, watching him.

"I have not been as well without your ministering hands," he confessed with blunt honesty and forced a slight smile. "You have a gift, I think."

"I am sorry," she murmured when they came close again. He felt the intoxicating wash of her tenderness, and wondered how she could still be concerned over him after everything he had put her through. And what of the sense of pain, fear, and betrayal he had felt from her on the battlefield? Where was that now? Somewhere tangled inside the flutter of nerves he felt coming from her now? Somewhere between the frantic beats of her heart he desired only to soothe?

"You once asked for my forgiveness," she spoke.

He lifted her hand, entwined with his, above their heads and turned her in a twirl, then drew her back toward him, closer than was necessary for the steps of the dance. But she did not pull away.

She tilted her chin, lifting her face to hold his gaze. "Now, it is my turn to beg you of yours."

He frowned. "Whatever for?"

"You are my commanding officer. I began to expect your friendship over your duty, and that was wrong of me. I have tested and tried you." They moved in a close circle around each other, only a few inches separating them. She continued to hold his gaze. "It was wrong of me to run. I—I was hurt, but that was no excuse. I reacted like a child instead a soldier."

Suddenly, her gaze shifted beyond him to the others standing along the sidelines. He felt she was unconsciously avoiding looking at him any longer with the pretense of sweeping the room. But then her steps faltered and her features turned pale, a sharp intake of air passed between her slightly-parted lips. Fear like ice pulsed through her veins, the emotion hitting Garren square in the chest.

Garren stopped still, forcing Ora to stop as well while the other dancers continued on about them. He stared at her, frustration growing in his chest. He lifted his head and gazed about the room. "Come with me," he said stiffly, lowering her hand from its upward dance position. He did not let go of her hand, however. He threaded his fingers between hers and pulled her from the dance floor with their hands held close to his side. The dance was coming to its conclusion as he took her through a side door leading into the darkened back halls which led to the unused south wing of the palace.

The music fell to an abrupt silence as the heavy doors shut behind them. The halls seemed cold and blue in contrast to the warm golden light of the ballroom. But after the dancing, the soft breeze coming from the open arched windows to their left was refreshing and inviting.

Garren released her. She seemed not to notice for a moment, as she took a few steps forward and looked out the windows at the brilliant starry skies above. He watched her, remaining by the door. "You can speak honestly with me. You must know I care little for pretense and false mannerisms. It is me. The same Captain who fought alongside you numerous times in battle." His tone firm and gritty, he gazed at her back and saw her wrap her arms around herself with a slight shiver.

"This is a very different battleground, Captain," she said quietly at last, keeping her back to him.

Garren's jaw tightened. "So, that is how it is?"

His question caused her to turn and look at him.

"You cannot speak my name?"

She stared at him. "You are all I have left in the world. And here you are, a freeman, a soldier, my captor. And I would talk to you as if we are equals? As if I should have some claim to you? And that terrifies me. You are my commanding officer and I am nothing but a servant." He noticed her hands tremble slightly.

"You are *not* my captive. I would free you if I could, were it within my power. I would have done so long ago. I do not own you and never required nor wanted your service. I know that our first encounter and my part in your recruitment will always stand between us—will always remind you of what the monster is capable of—I cannot help that. There is nothing I can do to change that." His words were thick and tight with emotion. "But surely you must know—*surely*—by now, that I have only ever tried to redeem all the tragedy and pain I have brought on your heart. To lessen it, even when I cannot prevent it." He searched her gaze a moment and shook his head with anguish. "And I know. I felt your spirit cry out to mine. You despise me now. Hate me, perhaps."

Ora let out a sudden desperate cry and stepped toward him. A feeling of deep agony not his own came over him filled with Ora's tenderness. He nearly staggered beneath the weight of it. "No!" she cried. "That would never be!"

She looked at him with such pleading and anguish. Garren stepped closer and caught her face against the palm of one hand with sudden passion. "You do not hate me?" He was not sure he could or should believe it.

Her hand lifted to cover his, her cold fingers against his. “I do not hate you,” she whispered, but the fear lingered in her eyes still.

He frowned, sensing her distress. His free hand moved to her arm to keep her from drawing away from him again. “What is it?”

Chapter 102

Ora knew she would never escape his questions. His gently tightening grip on her arm said it all. He would not let her go until she told him the truth. She felt ill, her mind still swimming with the revelation of what she had seen in the ballroom. Of *who* she had seen. A haunting nightmare she thought long dead, now arisen with a vengeance. A final, horrible truth she had wanted so desperately to forget.

As a barely-restrained fear gripped the pit of her stomach, he sensed her anxiety and drew closer to her, slipping his hand from her cheek to brush his fingers against the nape of her bare neck. A deep, unknown storm brewed in his grey eye and she reached up, hesitated, then slowly removed his eyepatch. She needed to see his face unhidden —to see him as he was. To see the scars that marred his skin before she revealed the scars that marred her heart.

He stood still without reaction, but held her gaze with a searching intensity.

"It is not fair," she whispered. "I cannot know what you are thinking. You never tell me what you are feeling, and yet you demand answers from me?"

Her heart still stung from his behavior. From the way he had withdrawn from her. From the hurt he had caused by sending her away. Could he not understand that? And yet, he had never betrayed her confidence. If only the truth was not so awful.

She pulled away from him, shrugging away from his hands and turned slightly aside as she glanced away. "That night of your counsel with the King: I heard the King say I looked like I was of Imperial blood.... And I heard you say I was the daughter of poor farmers." She paced away from him toward the great pillars, watching the soft sweep of sheer curtains billowing in the light mountain breeze. "You know my past, but still you did not betray me. You did not reveal that I am a bastard daughter of a soldier." She glanced over her shoulder at him and caught his gaze for only a moment. "There is more I have not told you," she whispered, looking away again. She clenched her hands together in front of her, bowing her head to study his eyepatch still held between her fingers.

Garren remained still, standing where she had left him.

"The man who assaulted my mother, when the War began. I...know who he is. I—I have seen him," she whispered. She swallowed hard and pressed her lips together.

Garren approached. She felt the soft brush of air stirring with his movement though she did not turn to face him, afraid she would never get the words out if she did. "What do you mean, Belle?" he urged with a deep rumble.

Ora shut her eyes. "My mother spoke of him. She feared he may return one day to destroy us. The man who is my father by blood," she whispered.

Garren gripped her shoulders suddenly and forced her to face him, pulling her toward him. "You *know*?" he half-growled as a single tear forced its way out and down her cheek. He searched her gaze, ignoring her tear. "You know who your father is. Is he in the Divisions? Is he here?" he demanded harshly, anger brewing deep.

Ora flinched.

Garren fought for breath. She could feel the violence churning through him, pulsing through his muscles. "Why did you not tell me?"

"I was afraid," Ora managed. "I was afraid of what you would think of me. I was afraid of what that would mean—."

"Why? Who is he?" he commanded firmly.

"I was afraid," Ora forced out, heart slamming against her ribcage as the confession spilled forth in a quiet voice for only Garren's ears. "Because he is not just a common soldier. He is a Commander, a man of power and influence. I did not know—I did not know he was even still alive until I saw him, only moments ago. Until I caught sight of him while we were dancing." Tears spilled down her cheeks and her fingers curled around the front of his uniform, keeping him close. "And…I saw the scar on his chin."

"Commander Jeshura," he rumbled, his words laced with anger and realization.

Ora shook her head insistently. "I am in no danger from him, no more than I am from the For'bane. He—does not know me. He does not—recognize me. Please, James…."

"No," Garren contemplated, searching her face. "Because he has a hold on you that even the For'bane cannot boast. A terrible fear…I can *feel* it." His hold gentled and he pulled her closer.

Ora pressed her hands against his chest, not to push away from him, but to feel his strength and find her own through it. "Because I am not what you think I am. I am not what any of them believe," she whispered. "I only tried to forget. And then Greer…. And you saved me…."

“I would never betray you, Belle,” he murmured with a look of agony. “I only ever meant to keep you safe. I sent you away to keep you safe. Whatever else you must think of me, I would do anything to save you.” He pressed his forehead against hers, as if he could make her feel the truth of his words as he felt them.

Suddenly he drew in a sharp breath and lifted his head to stare at her, and she knew he understood.

Imperial.

She *was* of noble blood.

“So you see now,” she managed in a whisper choked with emotion. “I—I am more than a child of war. I am a *product*,” she nearly spat the word and her voice nearly failed her. “More than anyone knows….”

She pulled away from him, leaving his eyepatch in his hands. Turning with shame and agony, she fled down the passageway into the shadows. She left him standing there, staring after her, but she could not look back at him. She did not want to see his expression as he realized that in his effort to save her, he had cast her among the wolves.

Chapter 103

After a few minutes, Garren moved slowly in the direction Ora fled. The agony she felt tangled with his own. But where she held fear, he held anger for the injustice of what had been forced upon her: Anger toward Commander Jeshura, for harming her mother and subjecting her to secrets and humiliation. Anger toward himself, for trying to protect her and only causing her more pain in the end.

Her life was not his to control. He had not given her the chance to explain herself before, and how he wished he had done so! It had not made sense before, that she would try to run away—her greatest fear of admiration from the King, and of being taken away from the Freeland life. Now, there was no mystery behind it all.

He tucked the eyepatch into his uniform breast pocket. There was no one else in these empty darkened hallways. He let his enhanced vision guide him through the corridors until he saw the heat of her body. He felt the strengthening of her tattered emotions build the closer he got to her. She stood around the corner of one of the half-circle balconies overlooking the mountains and cliffs below. She stood against the wall, leaning back as if to gain strength from the cold stone.

He did not turn to acknowledge her as he quietly stepped through the open doorway and passed her, flanked by filmy white curtains with gold embroidered edging fluttering softly in the high-mountain breeze. He stepped to the balcony railing and spread his hands upon the stone surface on each side of him, bracing his arms as he stared out into the red-tinged night sky where the distant battlegrounds lay. In that moment, it meant little to him compared to the battleground right here, between himself and the woman he loved.

As if she read *his* thoughts for a change, she spoke softly from her place against the wall behind him, "The sky never changes. I watch it every day. But it is always a blood sky."

Garren lowered his head slightly, otherwise he remained motionless. His gaze swept the tops of the trees below the castle, rising and rolling away in the hills and mountains and caverns hidden beneath. "I am not sure anyone would remember what it looked like before the War," he spoke with a quiet rumble in his voice.

When she said nothing—when he felt quiet desperation take hold of her—he turned to face her, searching her gaze.

She held his gaze, hers glimmering in the starlight with unshed tears. "I am sorry I ran from you. That was terrible of me," she whispered. "After all you have done for me."

Garren stepped toward her. "I do not want to cause you pain. Belle, I do not know if there is a way to make this right." He reached her and stopped, standing close in front of her. Ora held his gaze without fear. In fact, it seemed she grew steadier the nearer he came.

"Why did you come here?" she whispered with quiet desperation, searching his gaze. "Not even the King expected you to come all this way. You were under no obligation. If you had business about the War, then why are you standing here with me? Why do I feel as if you were searching me out in the ballroom?"

"I needed to see you," Garren found himself confessing. "I needed you—to understand."

"Understand what?"

His heart cried out: *That I cannot live without you.* Instead of speaking, he glanced away and cleared his throat, trying to regain control over his desperate emotions.

"If—if they find out I am Imperial...," Ora began quietly.

Quickly, he looked at her. "They will not," he said firmly, wanting to soothe her distress and his own at the mention of her dilemma.

"I have been trying for so long to measure up; I have been trying for so long to prove to you that I am strong." She paused, and her last words were spoken in a resigned whisper: "But I am not. It is all a farce. I will never be as strong as you."

Garren brushed his thumb across her cheek, relishing the satin feel of her skin. "No," he murmured. "You are strong in the best way, and you are weak in every way that is beautiful. You should not want to be like me. That would be a cruel fate, and I would despise it and myself if it ever came to that."

Ora lightly touched his fingers, still lingering against her cheek. "And so you sent me away from you...even after your promise to never leave me," she whispered with an ache in her voice.

He sighed as he caught her gaze again and bowed his head slightly. "I am just a monster, clumsy in my attempts to keep you safe. To keep you away from me...."

A tear trickled down Ora's cheek, melting against his fingers.

"Do not give up on me. I do not have the strength, without some measure of faith on your part," he confessed with sudden passion, searching her gaze and studying her tears as they fell.

"Truly?" Ora whispered. "The only Singer who attained the rank of Captain—who can fight a band of Skays alone without growing weary—doubts his own strength?"

"You exaggerate my capabilities," Garren insisted. He glanced aside a moment. "But, no, this is different. If I die on the field of war, I do not care—there is no consequence in that. No one to bother with the aftermath of my exit from this world. But in life, when it is my own soul at stake?"

Ora removed her fingers from his hand to lightly trace the scar on his face, starting just below his discolored eye down his cheek. She lingered at his jawline. "You are not a monster, James." Her gaze pleaded with him. "You are all I have. Please do not give up. I could not lose you. I *cannot* lose you." She searched his returning gaze. "I love you." Her confession came soft like the petals of a spring violet against his skin; pure, lovely, and innocent.

He caught his breath and slipped his hand around to the back of her head and moved closer in yearning desperation, until their breath mingled in the same space. She did not pull away. He moved against her, capturing her mouth beneath his.

It had been a long time since he had kissed a woman, but he had not forgotten. This was different than anything he had ever experienced. She fit perfectly in his arms, like she belonged there, and her lips were softly yielding and tentative against his. He felt the leap and race of her pulse tangle with his own as he pressed her back against the wall and lifted his hands to cradle her head.

"You do not know how long I have wanted to touch you. To hold you," he whispered huskily, his voice nearly strangled in the onslaught of his longing, his lips near to hers.

His heart thrilled as she lifted her chin slightly to invite another kiss and he met her lips once more, tasting the faint hint of honey water, lingering like a man drowning and she was his oxygen. He freed one hand to slip his arm behind her, encircling her waist to pull her closer. His kiss deepened with long restrained passion. As she trembled, he softened his advances—fitting her protectively in his embrace, defying anyone else's claim to her—and gentled his kiss with aching tenderness.

Chapter 104

She could not breathe. Ora's pulse jumped to her throat to lodge there. Never had she believed such explosive feelings could exist within herself. She had truly believed for so long that men were cruel, cold tyrants. But Garren slowly and patiently changed that—despite his initial appearance.

Never had she believed she would give her heart to anyone. When she spoke of her love for him, up until that moment she had not known what it really meant: What passion was. What a man's desire could feel like.

The strength of his body against hers surrounded her. The heat of his kiss drove away the chill of the night. Her confession came from an innocent, nearly child-like naivety—drawn from the depths of the forgotten revelation of her dream. His response was fully man.

Is this what Dinah meant when she spoke of a man's passions? She remembered the woman's words now with new understanding—that a shared kiss was more than just a physical motion, but the sharing of two souls. She had felt a connection, something more powerful than she had ever felt toward Garren before.

A touch of confusion wormed its way through the pit of her stomach. Uncertainty. A tentativeness.

Garren leaned his forehead against hers a moment to steady them both, her eyes still closed. Then, he lifted his head, one hand still cradling her cheek and his other arm locked around her waist. Ora dared to look at him. What would his gaze reveal? In the pale moonlight, his good eye looked more blue than grey.

"Are you afraid of me?" he murmured, brushing his thumb beneath her eye to catch her tear, his face still near hers with a look of tender agony deep in his eyes.

She pressed a hand against the scarred side of his face. "No," she whispered with a breathless tremble. She hid her face against his shoulder and took a deep breath as he secured both arms around her, cradling her close. *'It is never-dying and stands without fear,'* Dinah's words regarding love echoed in her head. And, perhaps at last, Ora saw the truth in it. These were the arms she had longed for, even when waking from her nightmare, because she knew the truth would dispel the horrid fear of the dream. Garren was not the monster, but her protector, friend, and confidant. The only man her heart dared to love, though it took her until a moment ago to finally realize it.

"It is all right," he murmured against her ear. She felt as if his strength absorbed her trembling as he held her tight and shielded her against the wall. She believed that nothing could ever hurt her while in his embrace.

He felt her uncertainty, her hesitation, and her wonderment. Did he understand? Words failed her now when before they had poured forth without restraint. He had awakened her. She was breathless with a swirl of emotions.

She heard the thunder of his heartbeat matching the thrill of her own. His touch—his kisses—spoke of a powerful desire he had kept buried. Why? If he wanted her, why in all the Freelands had he sent her away from him? Why had he never told her how he felt?

Suddenly, he pulled away from her and took several strides back, leaving her leaning against the wall, staring at him in surprise as he dipped his head a moment to pull his eyepatch back on. He stood in the doorway of the balcony. He looked at her, his expression closed, his features suddenly masked.

Something in his expression kept her from speaking aloud, and a moment later she knew why. The doors at the end of the hall, toward the ballroom, opened and she heard the sound of men's boots approaching on the stone floor.

"Captain," a voice greeted Garren, unaware Ora stood just around the corner against the balcony wall. "We apologize for the intrusion. You are needed back in the First Division."

"What is it?" Garren demanded coldly. Ora had nearly forgotten that tone after his gentle rumble while speaking to her. She felt a shiver rush down her spine, despite the heat from his lips still lingering upon her skin. He had not looked her way since the men entered.

Ora held still, sure they had not noticed her. She did not want to need to explain why she was alone in a darkened hallway with the Captain, still trying to steady her breath.

"Commander Strell requests your presence," the guard answered firmly. "You are needed in Council. New evidence regarding the War. You are to speak before them."

Garren strode forward without a word and the guards filed out ahead of him. Ora turned the corner, letting the wall hold her up, and stared into the hallway at his broad back, her lips parted with a soft intake of air. Garren paused at the end of the hall, hand on the door as he prepared to close it behind him. He turned his head, caught and held her gaze for a moment. Then, he disappeared through the doorway. The sound of the door shutting firmly echoed in her chest.

For a moment, she remained where she stood, stunned by his sudden departure, and imagined she could still feel the warmth of his presence lingering in the air before her. He had said nothing to her, not even goodbye.

She peeled herself away from the wall, its existence cold and grey and formidable now. Her fortress. Her prison.

She could not breathe.

Chapter 105

Garren left Asteriae and the woman he loved behind him, knowing he would never return to her. He had been wrong, betraying himself to her in that way when his only hope remained that she stay alive and safe. If they discovered her noble bloodline, there would be nothing to keep her from being married, either to another noble or to the King himself, if he wished it.

Why did that thought still send daggers through his heart? He had known all along, even when he sent her here, that she would never belong to him. That he could never claim her. *She does not belong to you,* he reminded himself firmly, coldly. *You are a soldier. You have a duty. That is all.*

He had felt the thrilling ache of her heartbeat and the sweet yearning in her emotions; all too much for him to resist. He did not want to resist. One taste of her was hardly enough to compensate for the passioned yearning he had kept hidden for too long.

She had not been expecting that, he could tell. He had taken her innocent confession of love to a whole new level with the manly desire of his response. He had felt it in the softness of her surrender. She had never kissed a man. He had responded too quickly and too eagerly without stopping to think about that. He had reacted out of his own selfish fantasies.

Even after a few days of steady travel, he still could not shake his guilt, nor the look on her face just before he shut the door between them.

It was late afternoon with heavy laden grey skies promising a cold spring rain when he and Commander Jeshura arrived in the First Division with little incident. He and the Commander were ushered at once to the Council Tent while a couple of stable boys took their horses to tend them.

"How went your advisory with the King?" Commander Dillion questioned in greeting the men as they entered.

"He is encouraging the tradesmen and guilds to be more forthcoming and cooperative with supplies," Commander Jeshura answered, "and he is arranging transportation for more of the elements and supplies Gan needs with his advisors and palace alchemists. What has happened that we need meet so suddenly?"

Garren saw the others were already gathered—Captain Mason, Commander Strell, and Commander Baire.

Commander Baire nodded toward Garren when he caught his eye. "I am glad you have returned, Captain. Commander Dillion was telling me you have discovered some information about the great Charles Binn, and concerning the For'bane. I have just returned from the fourth and sixth Divisions to the south and am very interested to know what you have to say."

Commander Strell spoke in a bored voice, sitting back in his chair at the head of the table with a strange contented gleam in his eye that Garren did not miss: "Do tell us."

"I would not consider him the 'great' Charles Binn... quite the contrary," Garren said and moved to stand at his chair. The others took their seats and looked to Garren to explain himself. Wondering if this was why they had been called to return so suddenly from Asteriae Palace, he began warily, "Yes, it concerns Charles Binn and the origins of the For'bane."

"Did he discover them, then?"

"He *created* them. The For'bane are the creation of human and Bane. An attempt to enhance and evolve men's genesis—with disastrous consequences."

Commander Baire frowned. "What are you implying?"

"The monsters we battle are the same monsters he created, though perhaps grown worse the longer we allow them to control our lands. Charles Binn was once considered a great alchemist and philosopher during the Third Age. He was a dear friend and advisor to our Old King. He made no secret of his discovery of the creature called Bane. He wrote letters and records of his research—which was later discovered to involve Akerdai. He described these creatures in detail and pursued knowledge and understanding of them. Then, suddenly, shortly before the War began, he disappeared along with his research. A few years later, the enemy emerged, their leaders calling themselves 'For'bane.' No one knew where they came from or why. No one knew why they were so committed to our destruction. They seemed like something out of children's nightmares. Beasts large and powerful, with the physical elements of humans; and yet animal-like, and violent, blood-lusting creatures." Garren observed the reactions of those standing before him.

Commander Strell asked, "And how do you come to know these things when, as you have said, anything regarding Binn's research and the Bane were destroyed?"

Garren tasted the bitterness of the Commmander's disdain. He stared at him firmly, not to be discredited so easily by the man's twisted reasoning. "First of all," he rumbled cooly, "I said the records disappeared, not that they were destroyed. Most of Binn's research was destroyed, but the important truth is not all of the evidence regarding his research has been lost. I was led to an important discovery of a journal through the Brothers Cathedral in Greavans. They confirmed some of the research was smuggled into the Freelands. I found the journal, which recorded detailed information on this subject, at a small library in Shelt."

"Shelt? Nothing comes out of Shelt but liars, thieves, and witchery."

Garren felt his muscles tense along his shoulders, tightening between his shoulder blades at the censure in Commander Strell's tone. He remembered all too clearly the last time he ha ridden through Shelt some years before—similar to other poor, uneducated Freeland villages—when the villagers lashed Adven Grey to a pole at the center of town and set him on fire, because they feared what they could not understand. No one knew how to fight against the source of the darkness they feared, only inflict pain and punishment upon its victims. Men of power and greed preyed on men and women of those uneducated towns, taunted them with fears and misinformation, then blamed them for the resulting bloodshed, fear, and panic. Evil preyed on innocence—it had been his fear for Ora if he had let her stay here, because they might try to destroy her.

"Shelt is a poor hamlet, ravaged by the War and looted ten times over. But that aside, it was at one time a thriving mainway of trade and knowledge. The library was burned to the ground near the beginning of the War, but most do not know that it was the only Freeland library with an underground vault." Garren's steel-grey eye glittered as he sensed Commander Strell's veiled surprise—and a touch of fear?

"Which," Garren continued, "was safely sealed when the library collapsed on top of it, effectively protecting everything within it from the looters."

Commander Dillion rubbed a hand against his chin, rough with the stubble of a night's growth of beard. A motion of fatigue and of too many sleepless nights. Still, he cleared his throat and spoke, leaning forward in his seat to rest one arm upon the table. "I have seen this journal—writings of Charles Binn's assistant, confirming and detailing the experiments."

Commander Baire also leaned forward. "And where is this journal?"

"It is in…safe keeping," Garren said cryptically.

"So we are expected to take your word for it, that whatever you say should be accepted as truth?" Commander Strell raised an eyebrow.

"I will present the evidence when required of me," Garren growled. "I was not prepared to speak of it so suddenly. This is a warning that we have long ignored. This is the work of an evil, long present upon this kingdom that we have failed to stand against. What our alchemists have been attempting—what *you* have been supporting—is the same disastrous and vile experiments that brought Binn to his downfall. We are creating monsters once more, using the same methods that brought forth our enemy. We need to end this. Are we not repeating our past sins by ignoring the evidence? Are we not once more creating monsters—as Binn did—in hopes of evolving our genesis to match theirs?"

Commander Jeshura shifted in his seat. "This is all well and fascinating, Captain, and certainly intriguing. But I fail to see what this has to do with this Council being called together. Or why we should be called away from the King's ball after a single day of feasting. What are we doing here?" He spread his hands in an upward motion of irritation and challenge, looking around the table, as he leaned back in the corner of his chair in the typically arrogant, casual way of many Commanders of privilege.

Commander Strell, waiting for a chance to bite, stood from his chair to command the attention of the rest. "*I* have called you together to determine whether or not Captain Garren is fully capable of continuing his duties in the manner the Council demands. And after his words to you all, I think you can hardly doubt the truth of his incapabilities. If we are to believe his words, unless he would like to reevaluate his concerns?" The gleam in the Commander's eyes grew with his sudden confidence. Garren realized with sickening clarity why the Commander let him speak in the first place. He was caught. By claiming the evil that was taking place, he was condemning himself as the monsters they must destroy. If he pressed the issue, he would only be encouraging them to question his abilities as a leader among them.

"This is preposterous!" Captain Mason snorted, speaking out for the first time. He motioned to Garren. "We all know Captain Garren is the most capable man here. Even with the experiments, he was changed many years ago and has never once turned on us. Whatever are you getting at?"

"The War is the very reason I bring this to your attention," Commander Strell insisted. "And Captain Garren has compromised the integrity of our system."

"We are not a democracy, Commander," Commander Jeshura piped up with thinly veiled impatience. "And this is not a government. If you have issue to raise against the Captain, I suggest you send a bird to the King."

Garren felt some surprise at Commander Jeshura's defense of him. If he had not already hated him so much for his responsibility in Ora's traumatic upbringing, he might have appreciated this sound judgement from the Commander.

"I have just cause and evidence, well enough to bring him before the Council," Commander Strell defended. "As a collective, we are required by the laws of the King in time of war to protect our interests. As that collective, we may condemn any officer, should he fail to uphold that law."

"Proceed, Commander," Commander Dillion urged in a firm, though weary voice. "We have no need for fancy words. Get to the point."

A look of childish irritation crossed Commander Strell's face, and his lips pulled thin against what Garren was sure would have been an equally childish outburst. "In time of war, mistakes and compromises can have disastrous consequences. He has continually shirked his duties—"

"What duties?" Captain Mason scoffed.

"I have a list, if you will permit me," Commander Strell said and unrolled a parchment from the table in front of him and held it up. "One: At the time of the insubordination of one particular archer, resulting in the injury of the soldier Greer, Captain Garren issued the due sentence of thirty lashes—though a demand for death was given—and then rescinded that order after only fifteen—."

"She would have died," Garren blurted. "And death was *not* the sentence."

"—were given," Commander Strell continued as if Garren had not interrupted. "Two: At a second incident—with the same archer as it turns out—Captain Garren stabbed and killed the soldier Greer…."

"He attacked her!"

Captain Mason stood, lifting a hand as if to encourage peace. "The Captain is correct. Greer's death, while unfortunate in its circumstances, was entirely warranted."

"Without so much as a trial?"

"This is war, Commander," Commander Dillion reminded. "Trial or no, Greer was caught in the act of assaulting the woman."

"I am afraid the good Captain," Commander Strell mocked, looking at Garren, "has let his power go to his head. He thinks—as it seems some of you commend him for—that he can go around the rules and laws. We are rational, thinking men. *We* are not beasts to kill whomever we raise issue with. To kill Greer was a violent reaction that could have easily been prevented." He jabbed a finger at Garren. "You could have stopped and subdued him *without* killing him."

"Carry on, Commander." Commander Jeshura waved an arm as if to dispel a pesky fly.

"Three: This same archer tried to run. All runners are to be shot to the death by Singers in charge of the Division's borders, Captain Garren among them. Instead of killing her, he assaulted another soldier in order to protect her, showing his violent tendencies toward our own. He was only prevented from harming this soldier by Commander Dillion's fortunate arrival upon the scene." He rolled up the parchment. "The blood of the For'bane can be a dangerous and toxic mix in a human, as we have seen. I, for one, have never believed promoting a Singer to the rank of Captain was a wise move. The Singers have a purpose to serve, but not in Council leadership. Now, based on these instances, I am more sure than ever. Now, he stands before us with claims that we are creating monsters in our attempts to save Asteriae?" He took on a look of offense and disgust. "I say *he* is the monster."

"I think my record for the last fifteen years serving in the Great War speaks for itself," Garren began tightly.

"Are you having trouble sleeping, Captain?" Commander Strell interrupted smugly.

Garren stared at the Commander with a hard look in his eye. Commander Strell could not possibly know of Garren's restlessness, or the dreams that had come to him.

"I fail to see how the Captain's sleep cycle is relevant," Captain Mason insisted.

"Or anyone's business," Garren added coldly, still staring at the Commander.

"Your physical and emotional health *is* this Council's business," Commander Strell spoke pointedly. "I received a report from one of our healers who has the Captain in his care. The Captain is experiencing abnormal sleeping patterns. And we all know anything abnormal in a Singer is a serious thing."

Garren bit back a growl. How had he come upon that information? The Commander was using everything he could find to try and tear apart Garren's integrity and character, by implying his For'bane blood was making him unstable and unpredictable.

"You cannot be saying you think he will go—" Captain Mason began, but was also interrupted.

"There was another instance in which the Captain abandoned his post after erratic behavior toward another Singer to travel deep into enemy territory to rescue—yes, again this same archer—from one of their nests."

Garren worked hard to keep his anger at bay. His jaw began to ache as he clenched his teeth. He caught Commander Dillion's gaze and the slight shake of the Commander's head warned him not to give Commander Strell anything that might prove his point.

"I hate to concede that the Commander has a point," Commander Jeshura said gravely with a sigh. "As a Captain, you are responsible to this camp and this Council. You entered dangerous enemy territory alone and without consulting or revealing your intentions to anyone. What if you had been captured? Whether the girl survived or not was not your responsibility, and was not worth the risk to the War, nor your place in it."

"What do you say, Commanders? Captain?" Commander Strell nodded toward Captain Mason to include him. "Weighing the evidence, I think it is our duty to take a vote. We cannot ignore our duty to the Divisions and to the War. As the Captain expressed at the beginning of this counsel, experiments have a way of *failing. I am* not saying these For'bane are some strange human monsters, goodness, that seems highly unlikely—."

"Because then your precious war would be found out?" Garren narrowed his eyes, his temper fighting to get the best of him. "And you who profit from a grave experimental error all these long years would be put up as mockeries for public shame?"

"*—highly unlikely*," Commander Strell insisted. "But Singers, on the other hand, have always been unstable and susceptible to fault—something we are working with the alchemists to correct, I assure you."

A moment of silence descended.

"I stand with the Captain," Captain Mason said with a nod toward Garren. "His record of fifteen years serving our cause cannot be unraveled by a few questionable incidents. And I see no evidence that strongly supports the claim that he is in any way incapable of continuing his duties as Captain in this Council. As far as the journal is concerned, Captain Garren is hardly condemning himself to seek out the truth of the For'bane origins. I believe we should take great care in how we proceed where the experiments are concerned."

Commander Baire pressed his lips together grimly in thought and then nodded in agreement with Captain Mason.

Two votes for Garren, and two against—since Commander Jeshura sided with Commander Strell.

"I was made aware of his intentions with regard to the archer's capture," Commander Dillion spoke after he had risen from his seat. "But I did caution him against it." He looked at Garren now and slowly shook his head in apology. "We cannot let personal feelings get in the way of our duty. I am afraid I must vote against you, Captain Garren, with my deepest regret. This is a matter that should be investigated fully, along with the idea presented in regards to the journal —"

"That swings the vote then," Commander Strell interrupted Commander Dillion with barely concealed eagerness. He stood abruptly, as if afraid someone might decide to change their vote at the last minute. "You are relieved of your duties as of this moment, Captain, and will be reduced to common soldier status while we take you into custody for pending investigation and trial." He motioned to the footmen guarding just inside the tent entrance.

"Is this really necessary?" Captain Mason spoke up as the footmen moved to position themselves behind Garren as he rose to his feet, expression stony.

"I agree," Commander Dillion insisted. "Captain Garren is not a criminal and is not a threat to this Council. Can we not dispense with such overbearing formalities?"

"*Garren*," Commander Strell stressed the lack of title, "is subject to the rules of this Council, the same as any of us. He will not be permitted to leave the First Division and will be confined under guard in a holding tent. The vote has been given and the decision is made." He motioned again and the footmen took Garren's arms.

He felt their wary fear of him, and they kept their free hands on the hilts of their swords, ready to defend themselves at a moment's notice. His muscles reacted to their grip by tensing for a fight, but he took a calming breath through his nose and let them walk him from the tent without protest.

Chapter 106

When Ora retired to her room past midnight, the ballroom was still filled with guests mingling, eating, and dancing. She could not have borne the evening much longer after Garren's abrupt departure. She fought to keep her chaotic thoughts and emotions from showing on her face.

The King had approached her through the crowds when she reappeared in the ballroom after Garren left and his intuitive blue eyes glanced her over with concern. "You are tired," he said kindly and graciously dismissed her to escape the crowds and return to her chambers to sleep.

However, upon entering her room, her gaze fell on a square package sitting in her chair before the blazing fireplace.

Dinah rose from the window seat. "That was delivered by a servant a few minutes ago." She watched Ora with a question in her eyes.

"Who sent it?"

"He would not say, only that a man at the stables paid him to bring it to you. One of the guests."

Ora stepped over to the chair to find the package was a cloak wrapped into a square and tied with a cord of leather.

Ora lifted it into her hands. Garren's cloak, she knew instinctively. The same cloak he had wrapped her in at the pool after rescuing her from the For'bane nest. But it was heavier than she expected. There was something hard that the cloak was wrapped around, concealing it.

"You may go," she said quietly to Dinah.

"You do not plan to sleep in that gown, do you?" Dinah insisted with surprise, hesitating. The last time she had dismissed her maid before getting undressed, the gown had been stained with blood when she woke from a nightmare and cut herself.

She turned her back to Dinah. "You may unlace me. I can undress from there on my own."

Dinah blew out a sigh from between her lips and obeyed. She plucked the laces loose, and Ora took her first full breath all evening as her corset eased its death-like grip on her ribcage. She did not turn as she heard Dinah quietly retreat and close the door, leaving Ora alone.

Ora peeled the gown away, let it drop to the ground, and stepped out of it, leaving only her lightly-laced knee-length chemise to cover her. She untied the cloak and let the object from within slip out onto the chair. It was a book, slim, with an aging leather cover and a creased binding. Ora shook out Garren's cloak and wrapped it around her. She sank to the floor in the warm glow of the fireplace and settled the book in her lap.

Why would Garren give her a book? And why hide it inside his cloak? He had said nothing about it when they were together. She felt certain he had entrusted it to her for safe keeping. For secrets.

Ora rubbed her fingers over the material of the cloak. Its warmth enveloped her with Garren's masculine scent. Her heart jerked with the reminder of the strong heat of his body and the feel of his kisses on her skin.

She took a deep breath and opened the cover of the book. Her fingers trailed down the page, across the ink handwriting. She read—page after page—late into the night. The further she read, the colder she felt. Even the warmth of Garren's cloak did little to comfort her.

> I am haunted by that moment when it turned on us, thirsty for our blood. It seemed to writhe before us and something within it—some dark evil—was let loose. Its eyes. Dear Creator! The eyes haunt me. They burn into my mind every time I close my eyes. They burn in the darkness of each night, a reminder and a warning of what hell we have unleashed upon our families and friends.
>
> I am so ashamed of my part in this. Creator may never forgive me.
>
> It killed the man standing next to me. I cannot begin to describe the horrific sight. I will not. My hand shakes penning these words and I will not be able to continue if I go into detail. I can still hear his surprised screams. The screams seemed to go on forever. It was human, but it was also inhuman. It took from us what it wished. Its darkness consumed what was meant for our genesis, our image.
>
> An accident. Charles called it a mistake. He said it would not happen again.

> It would *not* happen again. Because the King, upon discovering Charles's failure and the deaths of his three other assistants in the process, ordered it to end. He ordered the research burned. But Charles is still out there somewhere. I sense it like some deep evil lurking, waiting to rise more terrible than before. And I think he succeeded at something. He succeeded in creating monsters with a thirst to consume us. Our ashes are like food to them. Our bones become weapons in their hands.

Nausea twisted in Ora's stomach, threatening to erupt. She remembered with horrified understanding her time in captivity—deep in the For'bane nest. She remembered Garren's reluctance and refusal to explain what became of those taken prisoner and why they never returned; what they had done to the boy who had died that night. She remembered the bone blade that Garren carried, and the other bone fashioned weapons he had stolen from the For'bane.

> I must write these words because someone must know our sins before the end comes. Let these words reveal the truth and may we find some forgiveness for our condemned souls.

'I am just a monster,' Garren's anguished voice rolled back through her senses.

No, she mourned, realizing now the direction of his thoughts. The sense of hopelessness, of defeat. *No, James. This is not your fault. Do not give up. You are more the man than you will ever be the beast. I would never have fallen in a love with a monster. I have lived among too many of those, and I know what they look like. And I* love *you.*

As the first rays of dawn crept over the horizon to spill across the rug-strewn stone floor, Ora shut the book and gripped it between both hands. She rose to stand, the fire now dwindled to glowing coals.

Her jaw tightened with determination.

Chapter 107

The boy sat on the edge of his cot in the corner of Garren's tent while the healer placed his ear against the boy's bare back, just above his lungs. Thane's breath remained shallow even when the healer instructed him to take a deep breath. The boy coughed and stared miserably at the woven rug on the floor of the tent in front of him.

Garren stood just inside the entrance, jaw tight, while the guards assigned to him remained several paces behind him, standing outside the tent opening. "Do not keep your opinions to yourself," he spoke roughly. "We both know you know nothing of holding your tongue."

The healer glanced at Garren nervously. He cleared his throat and stood to face the Singer. Garren felt the uncertain flutter of the thin man's heart. The healer was wise to feel fear in Garren's presence, after divulging Garren's condition to the Council, without discussing it with Garren first.

"Put your tunic back on," the healer stalled, looking at Thane with an awkward pat on the boy's bony shoulder.

Thane slowly obeyed. Not even the warm Spring breeze gusting briefly through the open tent entrance seemed to revive his tired, sunken eyes and drooping posture. Garren did not need to hear the healer's diagnosis to see that his footman was growing worse.

The healer eyed the two guards with Garren, skeptical of their ability to hinder Garren if he wanted to do harm. "The sickness is deep in his lungs. I have seen it before. All the soot and ash on the field. He has spent too long sleeping outside on the ground, breathing it in."

"He sleeps in my tent now," Garren informed him.

The healer shook his head. "It is all well and good for him to have what accommodations he can, and yet it cannot undo what damage has already been done."

"And so what exactly is your prognosis?" Garren's tone was sharp.

The healer's gaze slid toward Thane as the boy curled up on his side with his back to the room to fall asleep once more. He looked at Garren. "Find yourself a new footman. One able enough to dig a grave."

"That is not a solution," Garren growled.

"It is the only one you are going to receive." The healer took a step back, but his words and gaze remained firm and direct.

"Get out." Garren nodded his head briefly toward the entrance. His gaze moved toward the boy, ignoring the healer as the thin man made a hasty retreat.

Garren remained where he stood for some minutes, watching Thane's ribcage rise and fall with each labored breath and listening to the boy's failing heartbeat. His final act of goodness, and he had acted too late.

He rubbed a hand over his jaw, bristled with the new growth of a beard. He had not shaved since returning from the palace. The light beard helped conceal one end of the scar on his face.

One of the guards behind him cleared his throat. "Sir."

Garren's jaw flexed with frustration. How long could he practice restraint? Did they not know better than to entrap a wild animal in a cage? And yet, that was exactly what Commander Strell determined to prove: That James Garren was a dangerous animal who should be struck down. He would have a trial, where all the Council would gather to discuss any and all evidence brought against Garren. Soon he would know where everyone stood. He dare not give them more reason to distrust him now.

He turned stiffly and led the way back to the holding tent where he had spent most of the last four days under guard. While he entered, his guards stayed outside, flanking the entrance. With a cot serving as his only furniture, Garren sat on its edge and pulled at the cord holding the glass vial of powder to shake out several flecks onto his tongue. He shut his eyes and swung his legs up onto the cot, lying down. He breathed slow and deep, waiting for the pain to dull.

Suddenly, his eyes opened with a start. "No," he muttered. He rose abruptly to his feet and faced the tent entrance, holding stiffly erect. Several moments later, the tent flap lifted and his guards appeared. Ora stood between them, wrapped in his great cloak that swamped her small frame. His gaze took in her face, from the slightly parted lips to the wide eyes that silently questioned why the Commanders would place him under guard.

"Leave us," he ordered the guards. They hesitated a moment, then withdrew again.

"What have you done?" He took a step towards Ora, glancing her over. Sudden uncertainty seized him. "Where is the journal?"

"I gave it to the King." She hastened to continue even as he opened his mouth to upbraid her actions. "Because he deserves to know if he is ever to lead the people without falling into the same mistakes that have been made in the past. He has a keen mind, if only given the opportunity to know and act on the truth."

Garren stared at her, hard. He fought the desire to lash out at her. Perhaps she was right. But could he trust her judgement? He had trusted her enough to give her the journal to safeguard, because he knew it would be dangerous to let Commander Strell get his hands on it.

"I told him about Carter's death," she continued when he said nothing, "and what I witnessed; how it effected me. He is King, and he must see the truth for what it is, not as his advisors paint it for him. He must choose to lead us toward healing and redemption, or seal our destruction."

"What else did you say to him?"

"If the For'bane blood is to dominate us, we will no longer be a people of free will and sound mind. We will no longer be true Asteriaens, but a kingdom of depraved slaves."

Garren's eyes narrowed. "And how did the King respond?"

Ora hesitated. "He…let me leave. I came with the supply carts sent from the palace alchemists."

"Do you trust your King?" he said in a low voice. He remembered all too clearly the vision of her dancing with the King at the ball with such ease, and how comfortable and relaxed she had become in the King's arms. If she had spoken of Carter and her loss, then she must have some confidence in him to open up her heart to him.

She searched his gaze. "Are you asking as my Captain… or as my friend?"

"Both."

"I believe his heart is good. I believe he desires to see this land free of darkness." As she held his gaze, her emotions turned to a soft yearning. "I saw something in him that I recognized in you—a desire for peace."

"And…does he know the truth of your blood?"

"No," she whispered. "No one knows that but you. I have no wish to be claimed by their kind. I am and will always be a Freelander."

Garren came toward her. His hand lifted to brush her shoulder and she took his silent invitation and moved against him. "There is dissension in the ranks, and sides are being chosen," he warned, giving in to the desire to embrace her. "This War is about to turn ugly."

Chapter 108

Ora pressed her face against the front of his shoulder, grateful beyond words when his arms came around to hold her and pull her closer. "Then I am glad I came when I did, to stand by your side when you need me," she answered his warning.

"Why did you come here, Belle?" his voice was husky and deep against her hair. "Whatever possessed you to travel across For'bane territory to come back here when I gave you up to protect you from this place? If I still had my rank it would be well within my right to punish you."

Surprisingly, Ora felt a smile tug at her lips. "You would not do so," she said with soft confidence.

"You do try my patience, darling," Garren growled gruffly.

Her heart warmed at the term of endearment, as it seemed to slip out without intention. He made no move to separate her from him. Her hands slipped slowly and tentatively up his chest to rest snuggly between them. "I am a Freelander. I will go where it pleases me. And it pleases me to stay with you," she whispered, voice thick with emotion. She lifted her face to gaze up at him with agonized pleading in her eyes. "If only you would let me stay with you. If only I could fix this mess you are in, because—do not lie to me—I know it is my fault you are here. Because of what you have done for me."

"Commander Dillion should learn to speak less," Garren said with frustration. Only Commander Dillion knew of Garren's love and loyalty for Ora. "How much do you know, exactly?"

"I know you should not have gone against your own order to give me thirty lashes. I know you did not shoot me when I tried to run. I know you defied the rules and went against the Council's opinion to rescue me from the For'bane nest—"

Garren silenced her with a hungry, searching kiss. Her mouth parted, softly yielding to his demands. His kiss gentled as her eyes closed, and his lips brushed hers once more with longing before he lifted his head to look at her upturned face. He moved one hand from her back to brush his thumb along her jawline. "I will ask you again, why did you come here?"

Heat raced across Ora's skin where his thumb moved as she stared at him. "Because you need me," she whispered truthfully.

He drew away, distancing himself from her and half-turning away from her to take a steadying breath.

Ora continued to watch him, brow furrowed. "Because you think the monster in you is winning."

"And was it selfish of me to want to spare you that?" he bit out with thinly-veiled frustration.

Ora continued: "I came to tell you that you are wrong." She paused to touch her lips where the heat of his kiss still lingered. It was her turn to take a slow breath to steady herself before continuing, even while Garren kept his face averted. "There is a reason I told you about the Commander and what he did to my mother. It was not only your insistence that I tell you. I have kept the truth silent for a decade and a half. I kept the fullness of that truth—the truth of my past—from you at first and I only confessed it to you because I know I can trust you. Because I believe in the goodness inside of you. I do not mean to mock you with it—I know you are trying to protect me. I tell you because I need you as I have never felt the need for anyone before. I want to know that you can still look at me in the same way even with all my scars revealed—despite all the ugliness of my past and my creation—that you can still speak softly to me and call me your Belle. No one has ever called me that but you. Because, when I look at you, I know you have scars and you wear them on the outside, and you know that everyone can see them and either accept you or reject you. I am afraid to show the world my scars because they have always been hidden and guarded. I do not know if my friends would forsake me and my enemies accept me; if all things will turn upside-down. You are my one and only constant. I do not want anything to destroy that. Because the fullness of our essence is not bound to the circumstances of our past, or even to the kind of blood flowing through us. Mine, tainted with the cruelty of a violent, abusive Imperial. And yours… tainted with For'bane."

"There is a difference. You are of noble blood, and I am a monster," his voice was husky and raw. He glanced at her. "What happens if my blood makes the choice for me? What happens if I become just like them; without my own mind? Would I turn and destroy you? Could I stop myself from causing harm to the one thing I cannot bear to see destroyed?"

"I will not believe that will ever happen. I believe a man only becomes a monster when he truly decides that is his only destiny. Only if you stop fighting does the monster win. Creator made a division between man and beast for a reason.

My mother taught me it is His breath inside us that makes it so, because He breathed life into the beginning, and spread the stars. You only lose that breath if you choose to forsake it."

His voice quieted as he studied her, "And that is what you believe?"

"There is a lot of wrong that has been done. And a lot must happen to make it right again," Ora concluded just as quietly. "If we belong to Creator, can He not forgive us if we ask?"

Garren turned toward her and stepped closer once more. He traced her jaw with his thumb again while his gaze searched hers. "I wish it were so simple," he murmured with a hint of longing. "If only I could believe so purely as you do."

Ora hesitated, hand lifted toward his, before lightly brushing her fingers against his, holding his gaze. Garren gently clasped them, bringing her hand to his chest. He drew his hand free from hers and flattened her palm, pressing it against the place where his heartbeat could be felt. The heartbeat that belonged to a man.

She noted, not for the first time, how large and capable his hands were compared to the smallness of hers, and raised her gaze to his again. "I would trust you before I would trust any of the other officers in the War. I would look to your guidance and direction before theirs, because I have learned to trust you. And you have let me down because you are human, but I have watched you time and again turn around and protect me and look out for me…and value me. You have a strength beyond the physical, a strength of integrity and goodness I have found lacking in others. *That* tells me you are more the man than you will ever be the monster."

A look of anguish and long-harbored inner pain stole across Garren's features.

"Sir," one of the guards spoke from outside, interrupting their private moment.

Commander Strell's voice responded sharply as he approached the guards, his shadow falling over the wall of the tent. "I am here to speak with the prisoner."

Garren removed Ora's hand from his chest and stepped past her just before the tent flap lifted.

Chapter 109

Garren stood in the entrance of his holding tent, the guards on each side. He faced Commander Strell while Ora stood behind him, just inside the tent.

The Commander caught sight of her and sneered. "*That* girl," he said with the point of one finger, "is not to be here."

"She is not under your command, Commander," Garren said flatly. "Neither is she your concern. I am still free to move about the camp and free to hold company with whomever I wish."

Commander Strell's jaw tightened and a calculating look came to his eyes as he continued to look at Ora. Garren stepped to the side slightly, breaking the Commander's line of vision. "Did you want something, Commander?"

"I was just informed about your footman. What a shame." There was no mistaking the coldness in the Commander's tone.

Garren resisted the urge to throw a punch and bloody those smirking lips which had just divulged information he had no right to speak. He felt Ora's surprise.

"Footman?" she spoke suddenly, stepping around Garren to stand beside him and look at the Commander with question. "Captain Garren has no footman to attend him."

Garren stiffened. The Commander's gaze flickered toward him. "He does now. He took on Commander Jeshura's footman. A strange act of mercy, considering the boy's condition."

Garren's shoulder muscles tensed. He expected and felt Ora's sudden fear and anguish. "Condition?" she barely whispered. "Why? What is happening to him?"

Garren stepped forward before the Commander could do further damage. He had wanted to be the one to break the news—as gently as possible—that the last of the recruits from Ora's home village was dying.

"Oh, I forgot!" Commander Strell burst suddenly with poorly-acted surprise. "He is a boy from your village. He came with you when you were recruited."

"Where is he?" Ora's voice trembled, but her words lashed out at the Commander with anger. Garren knew she was not fooled by the Commander's false concern.

"Your Captain's tent. Though it will not be his for much longer, once the trial is concluded."

Ora brushed past him, clutching her cloak—Garren's cloak—about herself against the evening's chill and hurried away in search of Garren's tent.

Feeling the Commander's triumphant satisfaction, Garren sent him a hard, cold look before moving past him to follow Ora. He knew the best way to wound Garren was through Ora's pain.

"Do not forget, Garren," the Commander said to his back. "You cannot save her this time. You will *never* save her."

Garren stopped cold and spun on his heel to demand to know the Commander's meaning, but Commander Strell walked away into the dusk.

Garren slowed when he neared his tent and watched Ora slip inside. She did not need him to hold her hand. She was strong. Her past life was a private matter, her friendships and her vow to protect them—he felt it. He had felt it from the beginning. That fiercely protective instinct.

He had been that way once, fifteen years ago. He remembered well the day he realized he was the only one alive of those recruited with him. The empty sense of loss—and failure.

For several moments, he stood outside while she comforted Thane and spoke softly to him, and mourned in her heart. He hesitated, then quietly swept the tent flap aside and stepped inside. Ora, sitting on the edge of the cot where Thane lay sleeping, lifted her head to look at him.

Would she blame him? Ultimately, this was his doing. It all led back to that fateful day when he had torn her away from her home; when he had taken all of them away to be thrust into a battle that would take their lives.

She stood slowly and faced him fully. "Will he die?" she whispered.

He looked at her for a long moment. He could not say the words. He could not be the one to deliver the final blow. He cleared his throat. "The ash and smoke have infected his lungs…."

Ora shook her head. "I confess I always wanted to do something heroic in my life…but every time I try to be brave —" her voice broke with a deep and heartfelt anguish, "—someone dies." Her eyes filled with tears. She took a trembling breath, trying to keep her wits about her. "You tried to save him. You have been kind to him. How can I ever thank you?"

Garren moved toward her. "Come here," he rumbled and folded her into his arms. She responded to his offer for comfort by hiding her face against his chest. Her hands curled against his tunic between the open leather armor.

Ora closed her eyes as a tear dripped from her eye to melt unseen into his tunic. After so long in terrifying new surroundings, of being uprooted from the familiar and dropped amongst a group full of strangers, of loss and nightmares and fears—it felt good to be held.

"Listen to me," Garren spoke, lifting his hands from her back to cup her face between his palms. He gently forced her to look at him. "That day in the forest when you faced that giant Skay. You saved my life. So you see, not everyone dies."

Tears leaked out of the corners of her eyes and slipped down to splash against his hands, sliding between his fingers. She shut her eyes tightly against their betraying presence and pressed her lips together. Her hands came up to touch his own in gratitude.

Garren pressed his lips to her brow.

"And what will happen to you now? Why does Commander Strell hate you so? What is happening with this trial? Will I lose you just the same?"

He tipped up her chin and patiently wiped away her tears. He stood before her now not as the Singer, the Captain, the soldier. He stood before her as the man, as James Garren. He desperately wanted to be the man, and renounce the monster. "I am fighting for your Freelands, and I will continue to do so as long as necessary. Even if they choose not to see, that is the truth. When light approaches, darkness is frenzied. That is what is happening now. I do not believe the Commander ever intended to see the War come to an end. At least not the way I would see it end."

"I thought you did not believe our lands would ever know peace," Ora reminded him doubtfully. "You said as much that day at the cave."

"Perhaps I did not want to hope. But you have given me that hope. You have given me a purpose again, and reminded me of the beauty that is at stake, the beauty that will be lost if we give up."

Ora searched his gaze and gently traced the scar down his cheek to the corner of his lips. She hesitated and settled her hand against his chest. "Why did you give me your name that day? That day when they killed Carter.... Why did you tell me your name?"

His jaw tightened and a faint look of exasperation crossed his face as he glanced aside. "You know why—."

"No, Garren, I do not. I cannot read emotions like you can."

Her fingertips brushed against warm skin between the ties of his tunic at his chest and collided with the chain of his identification tags. He loosened his arms from around her to let her lift the tags so they were visible. He watched her silently as her fingers traced the engravings of the words:

DARKEST BEFORE DAWN.

"Do you believe that?" She searched his gaze.

His fingers brushed the side of her neck as he moved one arm from around her to pull out the chain carrying her own tags. He held her gaze with curiosity and when she did not pull away, lifted the tags to read. His voice rumbled quietly, "Strength forged by fire."

"...makes even the weaker among us unbreakable. My—my mother taught me that, and she lived it every day of her life. She lived it up to the moment they—"

Garren covered her lips with two fingers, gently stopping her as her voice choked up with emotion. "I used to," he said, "believe it."

"What happened?"

"Everyone I knew died and the War did not end. So, I believe in darkness…but I do not know if there will be a dawn."

"But you are still fighting." There was a question in her eyes. "You are still trying." She softly pushed open the side of his tunic to reveal his chest beside where his tags rested and pressed her lips there.

His breath caught sharply at her touch. He caught her face gently between his hands and raised it toward his. For a moment her heart tripped in uncertainty, as he watched her knowingly and slid his hands behind her head, fingers tangled in her hair.

"Because I have finally found something worth fighting for," he confessed with raw honesty. "*That* is why I gave you my name."

"Because?" She needed him to say the words.

A look of pain clouded his expression. It was not easy for him to say it out loud. He took a breath and moved his face closer to hers, holding her gaze. "Because I love you," he murmured huskily.

Chapter 110

A warm shiver raced through her at the sound of his voice saying those words. Had they come from anyone else, she would have been terrified. And perhaps, some time ago hearing it from him would have terrified her, too. But not now. His love was something real, tangible, and proven. He did not use his power to dominate her. He used that power to protect her, even at the risk of losing her forever.

His good eye narrowed slightly. "You are not going to leave…are you?" he realized.

Ora shook her head. "Not a chance," she managed and, hesitating a moment, wrapped her arms around his neck. An expression of emotional pain crossed his face and deepened in his gaze, as if her touch pained him, and yet it was a pain of longing and desperation. A touch most precious to him and undeserved. His hands slid from her hair down her back and she felt the pressure and strength of his arms surround her as he clasped her closer.

"You are a brave little fool," he murmured near her ear with rugged, husky tenderness. "And I must leave you now. Another session of my trial begins, and you must remain safe." He drew back to look down at her. "Stay in my tent. I will find you when it is over." His gaze smoldered as he held her gaze—smoldered with passion and promise that no longer needed to be hidden. "If I command you to stay in my tent, will you obey me?" he rumbled.

"You said yourself…you are not a Captain. You cannot command me."

"As your lover?"

He spoke the words so directly. She felt heat rise to her cheeks. Clearing her throat nervously, she glanced at Thane to be assured he still slept soundly.

Garren stepped closer and caught her chin in his hand, bringing her attention back to him. A slight smile lifted one side of his lips. "I do not speak to give you shame or fear, darling." His smile faded into seriousness and his gaze searched hers. "I am not your father. I am not the soldiers who take what they wish through power or persuasion. I will not take what is not mine." As if to prove it, he stepped back away from her. "Will you let me protect you?"

"I will stay here," she agreed softly.

He backed toward the entrance, watching her a moment longer. Her mouth went dry. She knew he could feel the butterflies in her stomach. Her feelings toward him were so different from what she had felt for Carter. Her attachment to Carter had been like a girl's attachment to a boy, but Garren was completely man—strong, assured, and mature. She knew nothing of the intimacy between a man and woman, except what his kisses hinted at. Would they have a future together?

Garren glanced at Thane, then turned and withdrew. As a soft cool breeze blew in with his departure, Ora took a deep, steadying breath. *Now that I have found you,* she said in her heart, still staring at the place he had been standing a moment ago, *now that my heart is bound to yours, everything is different.*

She turned to Thane and sat beside him on the edge of the cot. A cot. Garren gave his footman a cot. Her heart warmed as she smoothed her fingers gently over the blanket that kept Thane warm. Had they come so far? She had once thought him a cold-hearted monster of violence and war. Why had it taken her so long to see his goodness—each little act of kindness and care he had demonstrated time and time again. She had been too angry and afraid to recognize it.

Now, she refused to give up on him. He had fought faithfully for fifteen years. He had not retired to a life of luxury and ease, even after the struggle of having the For'bane blood mixed into his own and all its side-effects. His reward? A trial with the Council, where his title, his rank, and all his achievements might be ripped away from him.

She brushed a fan of uneven hair from Thane's temple. How many times could a heart break and still have the ability to feel pain? "I am sorry I was not here to take better care of you. I am sorry I could not get you home," she whispered. "Must you die on me now? You are all that is left that reminds me of home. Of carefree days. Of childhood…." She faded as Thane sighed in his sleep, and the ragged sound of his breathing interrupted her.

She lay down beside him and wrapped her arms around his frail frame. Softly, she hummed the Harvester's Song with her head resting beside his, and as she felt him relax and his breath come easier, she fell asleep.

Chapter 111

In the Council tent, Garren stood near the entrance apart from the table where the other officers sat, debating and questioning Garren and each other as they had been doing for the past four days.

He thought of Ora. *Brave little fool.* If only the world had as much faith in him as she did. If they dismissed him, how would he protect her? She had chosen the soldier's life in order to return to him. Because he had his part in shaping and molding her into a fighter—a warrior. He could not let her down by losing the Council's belief in his abilities. He would never stop fighting as long as the For'bane walked the earth. The War came first and his desires for a future with Ora would have to come second to that, or there would be no future to look forward to.

And then, could he cleave to her as man to bride with the chaos still warring within him? When he could not claim true human blood?

He focused on Faulkner, the alchemist who entered two hours into the session to report on his studies of Garren's condition. The alchemist's tall, lean frame clothed in clean, simple white tunic and pants with a blue sash around his waist stood out amidst the armored, muscular soldiers sitting around the table. "I have examined the latest blood sample taken from the Captain." Faulkner's gaze swept the Council before he turned his attention to Garren. "Something is indeed changing—quite remarkably changing."

"What does that mean? In simple terms for men of war?" Commander Baire said.

"I am saying, his blood is in a battle. His headaches, the increase in pain and discomfort…are evidence of that battle. I am saying, the Captain's blood is winning."

Garren gripped his hands into fists in front of him. "I am winning?" he growled, hardly daring to believe it.

"I will need to continue to take samples and study the response of each sample to be sure, but yes. It appears you are rejecting the For'bane blood and your own blood is slowly purging it from your body." He nodded. "You can continue to take the powder for your headaches—as much as you need to help you manage them. No normal man could handle that much pain, but indeed the increase in your headaches is your own genesis fighting off the For'bane's."

Commander Jeshura leaned sideways in his seat to speak into Commander Baire's ear. The Commander nodded in response, watching Garren.

Commander Strell cleared his throat to gain attention. "Even if this is true, it does not change the fact that Garren has become unstable and therefore, unreliable."

"I think you have said enough, Commander," Commander Baire interrupted and rose to stand before the table. "I think we have put the Captain through enough, and I for one wish to apologize for that. Nothing that has been presented before this Council has come even close to questioning his loyalty or my faith in that. And I hope that has been as obvious to everyone else. Captain Garren's patience with these proceedings being just one exemplary example."

Murmurings swept around the table.

"He has been vital to the progress being made in destroying the For'bane nests. I, for one, would be more than happy to serve at his side once again," Captain Mason agreed.

Garren caught the Captain's steady gaze and gave a slight nod of thanks. His mind fought to grasp what Faulkner said. For too long, he had believed the monster in him was winning. To think he might have been wrong, that he might one day truly be free.... His heart thundered in his chest at the hope.

The vote was made. Everyone except Commander Strell stood in support of him and immediately, his title was reinstated along with his duties and his freedoms to continue them.

Some minutes later, the Council cleared the tent. The footmen with Garren undid his wrist irons and also departed, their duty complete. Garren rubbed his wrists, then the back of his neck with a deep, steadying breath. He glanced to the tent entrance to see Commander Dillion standing just inside, watching him.

"Congratulations, Captain," the Commander said with a smile quirking up one side of his mouth.

"The War is far from over," Garren reminded him. Commander Dillion stepped over to him and he continued quietly so no one outside would overhear. "Commander Strell will not take this loss well. There will be repercussions."

"Everyone in the Council opposed him," Commander Dillion agreed. "For whatever reason, he really has taken a dislike to you. Though I think it may be more than that. I think we need to keep a close eye on him."

Garren moved to leave the tent and the Commander fell in step beside him. The cool night air greeted them and

Garren paused, surveying the way the moonlight fell across the tents near them.

"I have a request to make. From one friend to another." He looked at the Commander steadily. He had never called anyone friend before. He had never admitted the need or the want for one. "I want to send Thane, my footman, home to the Freelands. Grant him leave. If he is to die, let it be in a place he can know peace."

"You would do this for your archer, would you?" the Commander stated knowingly.

"Life is too short to give up on goodness. He will die, I know that. And yet, perhaps miracles can still be found if we look hard enough."

"Take care, Captain," the Commander mused with a small smile. "You are in grave danger of becoming an optimist."

Chapter 112

Ora awoke abruptly to arms pulling at her forcefully. Pulling her away from Thane. Fingers pressed into her arms until they bruised. In a flash, she returned to that moment when Greer assaulted her. That helpless feeling. The terror.

She opened her mouth to scream, as her sleep-filled eyes caught a glimpse of the interior of Garren's tent, shadowed by the failing light of the single candle that had burned on the table while she had slept. Before she could utter any outward sound, a fist slammed into the side of her head and darkness crashed over her mind.

When she awoke, she found herself strapped into a chair at a reclining position. The same kind of chair the alchemists had bound Carter to for experimenting on him. She tried to lift her hands, but leather straps tightened around her wrists, restraining her. She gasped for air, feeling panic set in. She yanked at the restraints again, but they would not release her.

She looked around her. She was alone. She could not make out any light outside the tent walls of the small enclosure around her. A single candle burned on a narrow, tall table beside the chair, the only light in the darkness. It must still be night. She had not been unconscious for long.

The silence was ominous. She must be away from camp. But how far? And why?

She looked about her for a weapon, but there was nothing and she could not even sit up. She looked down at her restraints, remembering:

Carter. Singers. The For'bane blood.

James, I need you! her heart cried. She twisted her wrists, trying to wriggle free from the leather straps. The right strap seemed a little looser. Grasping ahold of that hope—no matter how desperate—renewed her determination, even as her wrists burned raw from the effort.

"Now, there. You are awake. Good."

Startled, she looked to the tent entrance. Commander Strell framed the doorway, a dark look in his eyes.

"What are you doing to me?" Ora gasped. "Let me go!" She fisted her hands. The Commander approached and she saw a corked, narrow, clay vial in one hand. She jerked to the side when he stopped near her, watching him warily. "Wh—what is that?"

"I have not fought so hard to build my kingdom on the blood and dirt of this desolate land for nothing!" Commander Strell snarled near her ear. "I have come too far to watch you and that Singer Captain usurp my place and undo everything I have achieved."

"*Your* kingdom? I believe the King of Asteriae would have something to say about your treasonous words."

"The King who rules without a crown—who has never sat upon the Throne of Stars? That *boy*. What does he know?" the Commander laughed in disgust. "He will do what his advisors tell him. He is a puppet, just as he should be. He is no threat to anyone."

"And so, you build a kingdom for what? When you have gained—whatever it is you seek—there will be no one left to bend their knee to you and pay you homage," Ora insisted. "We will all be dead."

"Yes. *You* will." The Commander's tone altered suddenly to a deep, calm confidence. He paused, his gaze growing distant in some private thought. Her gaze fell to his hand as he twisted his Commander's silver band around and around on his thumb absentmindedly.

She remembered the journal, and something Charles Binn professed with frightening clarity as she stared with wide eyes at the Commander. "Because the age of beasts will begin," she whispered in horror.

"Men like Garren will soon pass away. He was a mistake. A failed experiment that will not happen again. He thinks he is so noble. Fighting the demons while warring his own monsters," the Commander mocked. "He would fall on his own sword if he thought the monster in him would win. And maybe it will. The Council might finally see how dangerous he is to their War, if he lost the one thing that keeps him human. All this time, he has been fighting to save you, when it is he that needs saving. Beauty holds so much power. In darkness, it is a flickering light of hope. And if you extinguish it, eventually the darkness wins."

"*You* are mad!" Ora spat. "He will never let you succeed. No matter what happens to me." She yanked at the restraints.

"I beg to differ. You sparked that light in him. If you become the monster, that spark will die. Go ahead and scream. No one can hear you. We are too far from camp. No one knows where you are." He yanked out the cork on the vial with a wicked gleam in his eye. A savage greed twisted his features. With his free hand, he pried her mouth open, fingers pressing on each side of her cheeks.

Ora shut her eyes tightly, trying to turn aside and close her jaw.

Commander Strell's shout of pain brought her gaze to his with wide-eyed shock. A bloodied arrow head protruded out the front of his shoulder, and he gaped down at it in surprise. The vial fell from his fingers and dropped against Ora's shoulder to roll off the chair and shatter on the hard-packed ground. The deep-gold fluid leaked out quickly to soak into the earth.

Garren stood in the entrance, swiftly fitting another arrow against his Singers bow. His gaze burned with a dangerous rage as he aimed at the Commander. "I told you if you ever tried to hurt her again, I would kill you."

The Commander stumbled back away from him, reaching blood-stained hands for the sword at his side.

Garren shot the second arrow, straight through the center of the Commander's skull.

Ora averted her face with a strangled cry.

Garren dropped his bow and was beside her in an instant. He pulled the bone dagger from his arm sheath to cut away her restraints. He cupped her cheek in his palm, eyes nearly wild with fear as he searched her gaze. She shook her head slightly, all she could manage as she tried to catch her breath and calm her racing heart. *It is me. I am still me.* She gripped his shoulders and when the tension left him in a forceful breath of relief, she wrapped her arms around him and clutched him.

He pulled her tightly into his arms, his heart thundering against hers in equal rhythm. "James," she gasped softly, finally finding her voice. "James." She shut her eyes against a flood of relieved tears and trembled, clamping her lips together in an effort to steady herself. A broken sob of relief tore from her throat. "You came for me."

"I will always come for you. I will always hear you," he spoke with raw agony, voice rough with emotion. "And I prayed as I have not prayed in a very long time."

Four soldiers burst into the tent, followed by Commander Baire. They grasped Garren's arms and banded them behind his back, hauling him backward with all their combined strength, upsetting his quiver of arrows so that several fell to the ground.

"Stop!" Ora cried out in anger. When two other soldiers entered and flanked the door with drawn swords, Ora instinctively grabbed Garren's bow and grabbed an arrow up from the ground near her.

Surprised by the action, the soldiers raised their swords and took a step forward in defense, but Ora held the arrow against the string, bow drawn taut, fear and determination mixing dangerously within her.

"Belle," Garren warned. His arms strained against the soldiers grips, but he did not move.

Ora stared down the soldiers, eyes wide with warning, lips pressed tightly together, and nostrils flared. "Let him go!" she ordered Commander Baire.

"I cannot do that. He is dangerous."

Tears dropped down Ora's cheeks. Tears for Garren. Yet her eyes remained angry and unyielding.

The tent flaps parted and the King entered. Ora's heart jumped but she kept a tight hold on the bow, her gaze switching between the King and the soldiers. Commander Dillion entered behind him.

With a calm grace, the Boy King took in the surroundings and the tense situation. Then, he pointed his feet toward Ora and spoke. "My dear lady."

Ora's lips parted in shock.

The King glanced at Garren's bindings and Ora bolstered her courage to respond. "You will not harm him. He has done nothing wrong."

Commander Dillion stepped over to Commander Strell's fallen body and he knelt down to examine it, but Ora ignored him.

"It appears," the King answered dryly, "that this man killed one of my Commanders." He stared Garren down. "Captain?"

Garren's gaze dropped with the respect owed the leader of the kingdom, though his soldier's posture did not bend to him. "It is true that I killed him. And I would do it again."

Ora clenched her teeth in irritation. Garren failed miserably at diplomacy; his words and his short, blunt honesty would get him killed. "Your Highness," she interrupted, aiming the arrow at the footman nearest Garren with a warning look of mistrust. "He saved my life. Your Commander worked against you; he was in league with the For'bane, *your enemy*. Captain Garren has only ever served you as a faithful servant. He would see the War ended, as would I."

"Lower your bow, archer," Commander Dillion demanded. He stood up suddenly, holding Commander Strell's silver band in one hand.

Ora tightened her grip, turning her fingers and knuckles white with strain. Her gaze turned to Garren with desperation, then back to the King. If she surrendered, they both would die.

The King faced her squarely and stepped in between her and the footmen, bringing a gasp of shock and horror from those gathered. "Sire!" "Your Majesty!"

Ora trembled, eyes wide, and abruptly lowered the bow, easing the tension off the arrow.

The King nodded slightly. "I have learned the importance of trusting in my advisors," he began, bringing an ache of hopelessness to Ora's chest. He took a step closer.

"And you, Orabelle of Neice. You have spoken truly, and have been a voice impossible to ignore."

Ora stared at him in surprise.

The King drew forth the journal from his royal cloak and held it up. "My father made a mistake." He ran a finger over the edge of the closed journal, then looked at Ora. "He trusted the wrong people. If we wish to survive as conquerers over beasts, we must turn back to Creator and stand against this darkness without wavering. We must renounce this poisoned blood. It is time to end the Great War and heal our land, as you said."

"Your Majesty," Commander Dillion handed the band to the King. "If you will permit me. You will find an inscription on the inside. It is the same inscription we found on the band of a traitor while interrogating him at Torr Guard."

The King studied the band. "This language is a For'bane dialect. I have seen it before."

"Then comes the age of beasts," Garren spoke with slight surprise.

The King glanced over his shoulder at Garren. "So it reads, you are correct." He turned back to face Ora as he issued a firm command. "Release Captain Garren. He is *not* our enemy."

Tears filled Ora's eyes once more and she blinked them back.

The soldiers released him and backed away respectfully. The King turned to Garren and bowed his head with the sweep of one arm. A King bowing to a Singer. "Captain Garren, I place the War into your hands. I trust through your wisdom and skill, that one day our skies will be clear again and our children will be free."

Stunned, Ora watched as the King made a dismissive gesture and exited the tent, the others falling in behind him.

Commander Dillion filed out last and paused to grip Garren's arm in an offer of friendship and trust. "Shall we kill some beasts?" he said as a smile flashed from the corner of his mouth.

Garren solemnly gripped the Commander's arm then watched him depart, leaving him and Ora alone. He looked at Ora, still standing in the same place.

She dropped the Singers bow, a soft song gone mute as it hit the earth at her feet, and went to him. He caught her face in his hands, pressing her tears away with his thumbs, and kissed her hungrily, drawing her against him.

After several moments of bliss, she tugged back to catch her breath and tenderly traced her fingers down his scar to the corner of his lips and met his gaze. "Promise you will never send me away from you again."

Garren leaned his forehead against hers with one hand pressed against the small of her back, keeping her close. "When have you ever listened to me, anyway?" he spoke softly and chuckled when he sensed her surprise at his humor. She had never heard him tease before.

She gazed at him as he grew serious again, and his fingers brushed across her parted lips. "Help me, Belle," he murmured. "Help me end this fight—the one that is within me and the one against the For'bane. I cannot do it without you. I cannot do it alone."

She pressed her lips against his softly and after a moment of restraint, he responded. This time he drew back, carefully in control of his own desire for her.

"Then, we will be free?" she asked him. She felt something stir inside of her for the first time in a long time. Hope. She felt no need to stamp it out. This time, it felt real.

"We shall be free," Garren said with confidence. "And we shall be together."

Remember the Ancient Way. Who folded the mountains and parted the seas? Who divided the beasts from the ancient ones? Who set guard around the Light-Bringers[29] and taught them songs to live by? Remember His Name.

Remember the forgotten songs, the words written in the Light, approached and spoken only by the Name, and touched to the lips of the ancient ones.

It is not yet too late, to turn again and remember the Ancient Way, the path of a never-dying King. Let His ancient ones return, and let their many wounds be healed. Let the land that is torn and divided, let the light break forth into darkness, and overcome it. To the Name, let the ancient keepers return, and their many wounds will be healed.

—Chronicles of Asteriae (Book of the Prophecy)

---

29 Light-Bringers : there is debate among the Asteriaens as to the meaning of this word. Some believe this means angels, some stars, and still others believe they are one in the same.

Through tragic circumstances, a prince becomes King at a young age. While a war-torn kingdom begins to heal, a new battle begins—a battle for the King's heart.

Haunted by the pain of his own losses, familiar with deception, and reluctant to love—yet he is drawn to give his heart to the girl he can never have.

Because the truth may destroy their tender bond forever.

Chasing Cinders

Crown of Stars, book 2

A Brief History of Asteriae and Genealogy of the Kings:

In a time before the first King received his crown and sat upon the throne of the kingdom of Asteriae, there were two races of people who fought to unify the land (in what we now call the Unity War) and organized the wilds into the five territories. There were the Mirklands, the forested swamplands where the descendants of hunters and thieves lived; the Freelands, those descendants of farmers and peacekeepers who denied involvement in the Unity War; the Starlands, the land rich in forests, valleys, and rivers where the ancient keepers and historians built their cities for the First-and-Second Ages, before the For'bane; Birchlands, where come the descendants of soldiers and warriors, and from where our first King was brought out from; and the Highlands, the mountain territories where Asteriae and the cities of nobles and High Collar were established, all sheltered beneath the High Mountain that separates the five territories from the land of the Arid North.

After the Unity War failed, and the peoples of the Arid North retreated and the five territories were established for those that remained, the construction of the palace of Asteriae was begun and materials and workers were recorded as follows: 70,000 men conscribed[30] to cut white stone from the mountains; 50,000 men conscribed to fell white-oak and red-cedar trees from the Birchlands. 5,000 horses were

---

[30] modern 'conscripted' from Latin 'conscribere' meaning 'enroll'

used to bring the materials to the place where Asteriae would be built, with 2,300 architects to oversee the labor and construction, another 900 glasscutters for the windows, and 700 weavers for the wall tapestries and floor runners. The palace took 3 years to complete.

The First Age was ruled by King Alard Aldrin—whose father was an ancient keeper—from the time of his crowning at fifty-one years of age at the completion of the palace, until the time of his death. The years of his crown numbered thirty-six. He fathered two sons—the first, Baerhloew, and the second, Alberic. Baerhloew fought in the Unity War and was killed in battle, without fathering children. Alberic, the younger, was crowned at the time of King Aldrin's death.

The Second Age was ruled by King Aldrin Alberic from the time of his crowning at thirty-four years, until the time of his death. The years of his crown numbered forty. He fathered five sons—the first, Aldrich, the second, Baerhloew the Young, the third, Ansel, the fourth, Diondre, and the fifth, Gere—and one daughter, Josette, who was taken of a Master of the sea to unify the Four Islands in treaty of trade with Asteriae.

The Third Age was ruled by King Alberic Aldrich from the time of his crowning at forty-three years of age, until the time of his death. The years of his crown numbered seventeen years. He fathered one son—Alaric—and two daughters, Jaquetta and Ullysa.

At the time of the Third Age began the Great War against the For'bane. The Fourth Age was ruled by King Aldrich Alaric from the time of his assent to the throne at eleven years of age. At the beginning of the Fourth Age, the rule of King Alaric, the Great War was in its tenth year.

Other Books by Elizabeth D. Marie

Web of Time:

Awaiting the Dawn (#1)
As Night Descends (#2)
When Shadows Gather (#3)
Then Comes Daybreak (#4)

Captain Thorne of the SS Daring:

A Daring Christmas (#1.5)
The Daring (#1)
The Fortune (#2)

The Haak Brothers Trilogy:

The James Haak Legacy (#1)
The Haak Family Reunion (#2)
The Haak Promise (#3)

Journeys of the Heart

Contact:

www.elizabethdmarie.blogspot.com
elizabethdmarie@gmail.com

www.facebook.com/elizabethdmarie
www.twitter.com/ElizabethDMarie

Made in the USA
Coppell, TX
30 November 2021